CAGED KITTEN

All the Queen's Men, #2

RHEA WATSON

Paperback ISBN: 978-1-989261-07-1

Cover Art: Melony @ Paradise Cover Design

CONTENTS

Content Warning vii
Caged Kitten ix

1. Katja 1
2. Katja 13
3. Elijah 24
4. Rafe 39
5. Katja 50
6. Elijah 63
7. Rafe 70
8. Katja 77
9. Katja 97
10. Katja 120
11. Fintan 134
12. Rafe 142
13. Katja 156
14. Fintan 179
15. Katja 199
16. Rafe 215
17. Elijah 235
18. Fintan 244
19. Katja 258
20. Rafe 273
21. Elijah 285
22. Katja 296
23. Fintan 305
24. Katja 317
25. Elijah 330
26. Rafe 338
27. Katja 347
28. Elijah 359
29. Katja 369
30. Fintan 382

31. Katja 391
32. Katja 406
Epilogue: Katja 423

Bonus Content: Katja 445
Acknowledgments 459
About the Author 461

Dedicated to all the pretties who fell in love with my reaper girl and hellhound harem. You made this happen, and I'm humbled, touched, and thrilled to carry on writing why-choose romances for years to come.

CONTENT WARNING

Please note that *Caged Kitten* includes content that may not be suitable for all readers. In this full-length standalone novel, you'll find a Why Choose romance, graphic violence, (mentions of) abuse, and detailed steamy, steamy steam. Please know your own limits and discontinue reading should something take you beyond your comfort zone.

CAGED KITTEN

ALL THE QUEEN'S MEN, #2
Rhea Watson

I don't belong here. Seriously. I don't.

For as long as I can remember, supernatural clans took care of their own bad apples. Shifters, fae, vampires, elves, witches—we handled our crap quietly, efficiently, and within the confines of our community's law.

Until now, apparently.

How else am I supposed to explain doing inventory in my café one minute, then waking up the next in a processing cell, cuffed and shackled to a chair, wearing a collar that mutes my magic?

I've never gotten so much as a parking ticket before. I'm a witch without a coven, but I play by the rules. I don't start beef with other supers. Me and my familiar—we don't make waves. We like cozy, rainy Sunday afternoons and the smell of freshly baked bread.

So, whatever they've got on me, it's nonsense.

I know, I know. That's what everyone in Xargi Penitentiary says. Innocent. Innocent. *Innocent*.

Only the creatures around me aren't always so innocent, and even inside these four walls, trapped by wards and warlocks and wolves, my past is determined to damn me.

Until I find a non-magical way out of this, my wits are all I've got.

Well, my wits… and the gruff dragon shifter who looks at me like I'm treasure he's desperate to hoard. The gorgeous fae who delights in the fact that I'm not impressed with him. Oh, and the brooding vampire who could tempt me into darkness with his smile.

But I'm not here to make friends or fall in love.

I don't belong in Xargi Penitentiary, and if it's the last thing I ever do, I'm getting out.

Or… I just might die trying.

❧ I ❧

KATJA

"Are you sure you don't want me to stick around?"

I glanced up from the sea of tabbed spreadsheets scattered across my desk, a night of mind-numbing inventory ahead, and found Annalise loitering in my office doorway. Already bundled up for a chilly Seattle night, checkered cap hiding a head of golden curls and a thin pair of gloves poking out of her jean jacket pockets, she really was the best manager I'd ever had. In the five years of running Café Crowley, where it was Halloween every day and you could peruse weathered tomes from the stacks while slurping down artfully crafted hipster lattes, none of the senior staff ever volunteered to do inventory with me.

I mean, I always sent them home, rebuffed their offers, even told them up front that they would never suffer through an inventory overnighter. It was practically a job perk. I *liked* doing inventory alone, really immersing myself in what I had on hand, how my business was running, how the Fox coven's legacy persevered inside these four walls. As the last of my matrilineal line, the only Fox witch left, I'd opened this place with the intention of crafting something that would *endure*.

Brick and mortar, here to stay, the campy, vampy, gothic aesthetic appealed to humans and the secret supernatural world alike.

"No, no, really, it's fine. I'm good," I insisted. My chair offered a shrill creak as I leaned back in it, adding its two cents to the conversation, and we both grinned. The staff room had gotten a pricey face-lift recently: new chairs, a vintage oak table, and a pristine three-seater sofa with dizzying mandala patterns that the baristas liked to Instagram on during their breaks. It had cost a small fortune to redo that little room, but my people—all human, all awesome—were totally worth it. I, meanwhile, had an office chair straight out of the seventies, all the padding flat and the lumbar support nonexistent. My metal filing cabinets had seen better days, any semblance of interior décor dead at the door, and the only real piece of modern tech in here was my laptop.

But hey, whatever. Magic went a long way behind closed doors. I could be comfortable just about anywhere so long as the well inside me never ran dry.

"I don't think I've ever worked with someone who actually enjoys whole stock inventory before," Annalise remarked, her car keys dangling from her fingers. Even if every part of her read as ready to go, here she was, still pushing to be my little inventory elf.

I wish I'd found her years ago. Having someone I could delegate to, who I could trust unconditionally with my café baby, was huge. And with Annalise, the work actually got done. No more days or nights spent glued to the security monitors for me, willing my staff of human employees to just do what I told them. No more relying on my familiar Tully to sit on top of the safe to ensure *all* the money from the day got deposited. Annalise was the relief I never realized I'd needed until the end of her first week; back then, she had taken so much stress off my shoulders that I'd broken down crying, right here in my office, and all because something had finally gone right.

"I find it relaxing," I told her with a shrug. Who would have thought the girl who absolutely despised arithmetic growing up found solace in numbers—but it wasn't just that. Doing inventory myself, combing over every shelf, rooting through every cupboard, fed the paranoid beast inside me, and best of all, I did it alone. After long days surrounded by people, mostly human with the odd neighborhood witch or local shifter dropping by, I needed the downtime to de-stress—to relish the fact that I'd made it through another day, week, month, *year* without him finding me.

Annalise's dirty-blonde brows shot up, her incredulous smile making me only a smidge self-conscious.

"You're crazy, Kat."

I chuckled right along with her, because that was the normal thing to do, all the while ignoring the stab of loss in my chest. It had dulled over the years but still flared in moments like these, when someone inadvertently reminded me of those long gone. Few people called me Kat these days—it was just far too close to kitten.

You're crazy, kitten. I heard my dad's voice often in the five years since I'd lost him, after I held his hand through that gruesome death rattle. It wasn't real, and I knew that; unlike the odd spirit that made my beloved café its October haunt, Dad never dropped by.

Not that I blamed him.

Who would want to leave the beyond to come back *here*, of all places?

Still, a quick *hello, kitten,* just once, whispered in my ear or spelled out in office supplies across my desk, would be nice.

More than nice.

I missed him.

I missed all of them.

"Go," I ordered with a nod in the general direction of the employee back exit. At this hour, only my car and hers occupied the gravel lot, and it was just getting darker. "Have a good night—and say hello to Charlie for me."

My manager and my shift supervisor had been dating for almost a year and living together for the last six months. While Annalise was a statuesque blonde who modeled on the side, mostly for her social media fan base, Charlie was this short, squat, pink-haired punk who added a bit of authenticity to the off-beat vibe at Café Crowley. Weirdly enough, they totally fit.

And while it had been so sweet to watch from the sidelines as they fell in love, they were a poignant reminder that, as a workaholic, *my* love life had been dead for years—just like my coven, just like my brothers, my mom, my dad. *De*pressing.

Maybe that was why I looked forward to inventory nights so much. Tough to think about all the bullshit when you had to count every single thing on the premises at least three times for accuracy.

"Will do." Annalise waved as she slid around my office doorway, vanishing into the night moments later when the heavy metal back door clunked shut down the hall. Picturing it clearly in my mind's eye, every detail, I floated my hand right to left like I was sliding the dead bolt.

"*Stricta cincinno,*" I murmured. Spell cast, the door's various locks snapped into place, officially sealing me in for the night. With the last of my staff gone, I piled the stacks of spreadsheets I'd been working on since this afternoon in a single mountain, and my chair let out another high-pitched squeal when I stood. I shut off the office lights in passing, swiping at the switch next to the door. Plunged into darkness, the back-of-house corridor stood long and quiet to my left, and the only thing keeping it from being a total blackout was the parking lot's lamplight streaming through the back-door window. Some feared the dark, the silence; I found comfort in it, in the promise that at least here, I was safe.

Shouldering through the Staff Only door and crossing the threshold into front of house, I surveyed my Halloween-drenched kingdom with a sigh. As always, Annalise had killed it on all the closing procedures. Everything was locked up, floors swept, chairs on tables. To my left sat the café portion of Café Crowley, and what had once been stainless steel, top-of-the-line appliances when I'd bought them were now glamored to match the rest of the Victorian-gothic vibe we had going on around here. Black, white, and grey made up most of the counters, the chalkboards with kitschy drinks, the pastry display cases. Hanging bats and spiderwebs and pumpkins at the condiments station gave the place a pop of color, witches' brooms and pointy hats and vampire fangs dripping red on our walls, our ceiling, the guest bathroom doors. It was over the top. Some supers even found it offensive, but humans gobbled up a year-round Halloween—and I had the numbers to prove it.

Year five of operating and Café Crowley had given back eight times the inheritance I invested into it at the start as sole owner. I didn't want or need an outside opinion, and I owed that to my family, to the small bit of wealth my dad had accumulated that was supposed to eventually be split between three kids. In the end, it just went to one.

And kooky as it might be, I enjoyed the look of Café Crowley. I enjoyed the drama of a gothic coffee shop and library here in the heart of Seattle. Most places were going rustic and light these days, overflowing with succulents and sparseness. We had plants too—never mind that many in the hanging pots could kill a human in five minutes flat if ingested, or that I harvested and dried all of them for potion-work. Café Crowley gave the customers what they wanted: a fun atmosphere, delicious coffee, and pastries shaped like ghouls and goblins and cats. While I lacked a partner, I had a working relationship with an independent bakery around the corner who delivered fresh Halloween-inspired muffins, cupcakes, tiered cake slices, cookies, brownies—the works. Every morning, this place smelled like a veritable witchy Heaven, and I *lived* for that first deep breath of cocoa beans, sugar, and freshly baked bread.

But that was only half the appeal of this place. To my right, the seating area was spotless, all the old armchairs vacuumed, the board games put away, the fire in the working hearth extinguished. Beyond that, my eight stacks of sprawling bookshelves were orderly and dustless, full of manuscripts the Fox coven had collected over the centuries. Not only did I lack the room in my one-bedroom apartment, but *someone* ought to read them these days because I definitely didn't have the time. Books were meant to be devoured again and again until they disintegrated between your fingers, and here, all the works that had been bequeathed to me—the non-magical ones, anyway—were lovingly tended to 365 days a year.

The place looked great, everything cleaned and put away. All the prep done for tomorrow. Cash counted, logged, and deposited in the safe. The one element that *might* be considered out of place in a café—not for Café Crowley, mind you—was the cat hammock suction-cupped to one of the huge storefront windows. It dipped under Tully's generous weight, my familiar a magical beast in his own right, though I told any human who asked that he was a black Maine Coon to account for his size. Grinning, I set my spreadsheets on the counter next to the cash till, then sauntered over and tickled the underside of the silky soft hammock. His puffy black tail swished, dangling over the side, and after a quick stretch, he peered back, slow-blinking a set of blazing blue eyes down at me.

Witches and warlocks had the same eyes as their familiars. It made things difficult when you needed to deny that you even *had* a familiar, some fuzzy creature to bolster your magic, to tap into your more intense emotions—sometimes even to calm them, to wash them all away in your darkest moments. Dad had found Tully as a kitten, tossed in a back alley garbage bin when he was only a week or two old.

"As soon as I saw those eyes, I knew he was yours, kitten," he'd said, handing me this little bundle when I was thirteen. Some witches didn't stumble upon their familiars until way later in life; I counted myself lucky every single day that Tully had been with me for sixteen long years, and thanks to the fact that a familiar linked into its witch's lifeline as soon as they bonded, my fat, fluffy, lazy boy would be with me until the end.

"Did you have a wonderful day?" I cooed, up on my tiptoes to stroke him on his stately green hammock situated strategically beneath a heating vent. He stretched again, huge paws flexing, and offered another slow-blink. Of course he'd had a wonderful day. Tully was a Café Crowley staple. He had a cat's dream life: after snoozing in the sun for hours, he'd wander from patron to patron for cuddles and pets and ear scratches. Most of the staff even snuck him treats when they thought I wasn't looking.

Spoiled little shit.

"Well, you keep on enjoying yourself," I told him, lowering down onto my feet again, then cocking an eyebrow. "Unless you want to count cups for me?"

Eyes closed, he offered one last long, loud purr, then rolled over and curled up, tucking every limb into the hammock, even that huge tail. Seconds later, his purrs evened out—dead to the world, totally asleep.

"Yeah, thought not," I muttered, shaking my head with a smirk. After double-checking the locked front door, peering out into the quiet downtown side street that had begrudgingly accepted our gothic weirdness over the last few years, I figured tonight would be a long, uneventful night of counting and recounting and recounting again, until—

Thump.

The hairs on the back of my neck shot up, adrenaline spiking. Still as stone, I stood listening, waiting for another sound—met only by the usual symphony of the building settling for the night, the wooden groans and soft clicks and the odd water dribble nothing out of the ordinary. Not purposeful. That *thump* had intent.

Shooting a quick glance at Tully, I found my familiar had rolled back over, bright blues scanning the café same as me, his tail over the hammock's side and swishing with interest again. Although half the lights were off, everything looked pretty standard as I did a quick sweep of the tables along the windows, the clump of armchairs, the dead fireplace, the bookshelves.

At no point was I about to call out a *Hello?* like I was some idiot in a horror movie. Nibbling my lower lip, I padded toward the stacks, mindful of my heels on the hardwood. My palms prickled with charged energy, magic thrumming through my veins, surging, ready for any kind of nonsense.

Three stacks over, I spotted a book on the floor. *Herbs and their Uses: A Guide to Practical Hedge Magick.* A bit on the nose, but there was zero harm in humans reading about non-magical plants that, when brewed properly, could dull a headache or soften period cramps. Loitering at the end of the two bookshelves, I stared at the tome for a moment, daring it to move, daring *someone* to move it, and then sighed when it just sat there.

"Henrietta, *please* don't be back." Shoulders slumped, I marched in and swiped the book off the ground. Adrenaline was a great tool, but when it faded, it sapped all your energy right along with it. Suddenly my eyes felt tired, the weight of the day dragging on me as I carefully slid the book back into its place on the second-highest shelf.

Strange that it had fallen.

Henrietta was our last ethereal visitor, a mischievous ghost who liked to rifle through my office and burn the few breads we made in-house. I'd hoped she would have been reaped by now—or taken out by whatever celestial being dealt with rogue spirits. Apparently, I needed to re-check my crystals; if they had lost their charge, she might have found a way back inside the premises.

Just as I smoothed a hand over a few of the spines, checking for dust, Tully yowled.

A high-pitched, terrified *howl* that I felt in my bones, our heightened emotions twined together as witch and familiar. I gasped, pushing away from the books and racing down the stacks.

Only to find his hammock empty on the other side of the café, one of the suction cups torn from the window.

"What the *hell*?" I hissed, adrenaline back with a fury. It made me shake, heightened my senses. Somewhere deeper in the back, a door slammed shut, and I nearly jumped out of my skin at the *wham* echoing through the building. "Tully?"

Footsteps skittered through the stacks, boots clomping down one of the back aisles. I whipped around and shoved my fear deep, deep inside. No time for panic. No time for paranoia. Tully could handle himself; hopefully, he'd beelined to a high vantage point at the first sign of trouble. Sure. *Whatever you need to tell yourself to not spiral, Katja.*

Hurriedly, I reached into the ether. No vibrations of another rogue spirit—just the hum of a supernatural being. If I had to guess… Warlock, based on the familiarity.

Damn it. I'd never been in a serious duel before. Never fought with other supers, never been forced to defend myself unless I was sparring with my dad or my brothers. Besides that, I preferred to do any serious casting with my wand; although I'd been cultivating my magic for the last twenty-nine years, it had a tendency to do whatever it wanted without something to channel it. My hands were unstable when casting, sad as it was for an adult witch to admit, and I'd always wondered if I'd be less of a mess if I had the backing of a coven. At least more senior witches and warlocks could have helped train me after Dad finally passed on. Instead, I stagnated, needing a wand for anything beyond the basics just to keep things neat and tidy and *not* accidentally set on fire.

But my wand was in my office, tucked securely in my desk. Rowan wood, griffin feather core, eight inches—described by the wandmaker as, quote, *elegant*.

Right now, I'd go with *untested*.

Two more books crashed to the ground, distinct, falling like thunder. The crack of their spines set my teeth on edge, and I hesitated, scanning the stacks for the best approach to this—to a very *real* person in here, screwing with me.

"This is Lloyd Guthrie's doing." Dad's raspy voice rattled deep in the darker parts of my mind, a memory of him on his deathbed flashing yet again tonight. His withered body, his bulbous knuckles, his wispy grey hair littering the pillow—ravaged by disease. My mom had died giving birth to me. My brothers died, one right after the other, in freak accidents that had some in our community dubbing the Fox coven cursed. All his life, Dad had been capital-*O* obsessed with a warlock mobster in New York City named Lloyd Guthrie.

Supposedly, that guy had it out for our family... In Dad's mind, anyway.

Before he died, I'd thought it was just paranoia, that he was looking for *someone* to blame for all the tragedy in our family. But he had been so sincere when he whispered it to me, using his final breaths to warn me—to make me swear I wouldn't take any extraordinary risks, would never draw too much attention to myself.

"If you ever see him, hear from him, sense anything out of the ordinary..." He'd struggled to say that much in a single go, fighting, clinging to my hand with both of his, with papery skin and frail fingers. *"Kitten, don't hesitate... You just run."*

In that moment, I'd experienced real terror. I had believed him, just that once, because he had sounded *so* passionate. So desperate. And looking into my brother's accidents, they *were* suspect. No one could explain Dad's sudden and violent illness that ripped him away from me long before I was ready to say goodbye.

For five years, I had Lloyd Guthrie on the brain—all because of my dad. Never seen the mobster. Never heard of the warlock in social circles. Never experienced anything unusual...

Until tonight.

It couldn't be.

Lloyd Guthrie was like the Fox coven boogeyman... He wasn't *real*. And if he was, why would I even matter to him? Successful as the business was these days, personally I was inconsequential. A simple witch with simple dreams.

And a missing familiar.

More footsteps tromped down the stacks.

Run, kitten.

Tossing my head side to side, I cracked my neck. This wasn't my dad's worst nightmare. If anything, this was a warlock trying to rob a supernatural-run business when it looked like it was closed. Nothing more, nothing less.

My hands buzzed with offensive magic, an immobilizing hex on the tip of my tongue as I stalked back into the bookshelves. I let my heels click, wanting to draw him to me, wanting him to think my black stilettos and my flouncy skirt meant I couldn't *fight*. That my lipstick wasn't war paint. Let him underestimate me, this little witch charging headlong into the darkness.

Let him think I hadn't done this before.

I mean.

I hadn't.

But I had a lexicon of spells in my head—and I'd sparred with friendlies at the academy. So. Bring it.

Halfway down an aisle, I stopped, listening, waiting. My blood ran cold when a figure drifted down the aisle beside mine, footsteps slow and steady, a black shadow ghosting along in the corner of my eye. A soft exhale behind me had my palms burning. I licked my lips. *Now or never*.

I whipped around and fired. "*Debilito*!"

Red electricity crackled from my fingertips, fast and furious as it hurtled for my opponent. A tall silhouette dressed all in black loomed at the end of the aisle, and while he raised his hands, one clutching a thick, rigid wand, I caught him off guard. My hex illuminated the entire café, painted it red, highlighted the widening whites of his eyes and struck him square in his huge chest. Sent him flying back. Seconds later, he crashed into a table and some chairs, and victory twisted in my belly.

"*Nescius*," a masculine voice rumbled, voice soft as velvet —and his spell strong as steel. I only managed to pivot halfway around before a blue bolt slammed into my temple, and I was unconscious before I even hit the ground.

2

KATJA

Everything hurt when I came to. Head, especially where that spell had landed. Neck, stiff and achy like I'd pulled something on the left side. Shoulders, like I'd ping-ponged between two brick walls for hours. My ribs, as if they'd become best friends with a steel-toed boot. My wrists—on *fire*.

"T-Tully?" His name came out all thick and croaky, throat like sandpaper and dry beyond belief, as if I'd been sleeping with my mouth open for a week straight. I swallowed with some difficulty and winced through the sharp twinge. It didn't matter when I finally pried my heavy eyelids open, because whatever space I suddenly found myself in was pitch-black anyway. Seated on something hard, I shuffled side to side, metal creaking beneath me—and snapped tight around my wrists. I flexed my fingers in and out, and a hard jerk got me nowhere; I was cuffed to the chair, the restraints attached at the wrists and ankles.

Had I been… kidnapped?

Finding one's footing in the darkness sucked, senses somehow both on overdrive *and* painfully muted. Couldn't see. No sound. No movement in the shadows. From the smell of it, I was far from Café Crowley, and when I reached out to him through our bond, Tully was nowhere to be found.

My eyes stung with a rush of tears. We had never spent a day apart. My familiar slept in my bed, stood guard outside the shower every morning, and ate breakfast on my lap while we watched the morning news, ruminating together about the depressing state of affairs in the human world. He came with me to work, snoozed around the café all day, and then sauntered after me on the walk home. Tully was my *world*—and I'd done nothing when I'd heard him yowl. I'd left him to fend for himself.

Guilt struck, hard and vicious and *deep*, like a knife to the gut twisting when his fat fluffy face flashed in my mind's eye. Mercifully, I couldn't feel any intense emotion through our connection. He wasn't suffering, wherever he was, but he also wasn't with me. And the fact that I couldn't feel *anything* from him at all only made the guilt worse. What if he was hurt? What if those bastards had killed him?

What if—

Obnoxious light erupted above me, painting the small space in a white glow that made me flinch and squint. Sniffling, I pushed Tully deep inside, hoping that no news was good news for my familiar—that he had found a safe place to hide from whoever had kidnapped me and stuffed me inside a teeny box of a room. As I blinked back tears, I took in my surroundings: tiled walls on either side, grimy cement floor, a metal table in front of me and an iron chair beneath. Iron had a specific *look* to supers, a faint shimmer. While it had no effect on witches or warlocks, this would have been a death trap for a fae.

"*Recludo,*" I whispered, bracing for the telltale clicks of the shackles unlocking, then the satisfying *thud* when they fell to the ground. Nothing. I blinked, peering down behind me, my arms locked straight, my wrists raw and red. Thin cuffs snared me tight, and my spell had done nothing to change that. Frowning, I cleared my dry throat and tried again. "*Resigno*." Nothing. And again. "*Resero*." And again. "*Apertum*… Fucking *fuck*."

While I felt the familiar hum of magic in my palms, the buzz that coursed through my veins before bursting from my fingertips, nothing happened. Some witches had performance anxiety, unable to cast if their emotions weren't right, but that had never been the case with me. Even in my darkest hour, mourning the fact that I was all alone in the world, I had been able to spit everything under the sun successfully. Sloppily, sure, but that was just par for the course without a wand. Every spell, glamor, and hex in my arsenal—it came to me, whether I was broken or not.

Today—tonight?—shouldn't have been any different.

Yikes. No windows, not even on the huge, intimidating metal door dead ahead. Not a great predictor of my chances when I couldn't answer where *or* when.

Willing myself to relax with a deep breath, I unlocked my jaw and forced my shoulders down. The tightness remained, despite my best efforts, and the crick in my neck *hurt* when I rolled my head side to side, trying to work it out.

It was then I felt it—featherlight and barely there against my skin. Like a pair of lips whispering across my throat, so different from the shackles around my wrists and ankles, whatever it was evaded me when I peered down, high enough on my neck to hide under my chin. Cursing softly, I glanced over my shoulder…

And saw myself staring back.

In a mirror.

My heart plummeted. Was that a… two-way mirror? Were people *watching* me? Fighting to keep my breath even, to not spiral out, I gave my rumpled appearance a quick once-over.

Although my flaming red hair was no longer neatly knotted on top of my head, frazzled instead with loose wisps spilling everywhere, I wasn't beat up. No bruises or marks. No split lip. Everything hurt, but there was no indication that someone had taken a baseball bat to me in my sleep. Although, my shirt had been torn, one shoulder exposed, and then twin slashes cut over my waist. Same with my leggings, ripped up the middle like they were a cheap pair of split tights.

Heat flared in my cheeks. Sure, I was still covered from head to toe, my shirt long-sleeved and my leggings opaque, but someone had stolen my skirt. Ripped it clean off if the soreness around my waist was any indication.

Took that but left the four-inch heels. Sure. Why not?

A thick leather collar snaked around my neck, its girth suggesting it ought to be heavy and very *present*. Instead, I barely felt it.

Seriously though.

What had happened to me?

Fear made my chest tight, and after another quick scan, the room had an unnerving sense of familiarity to it.

An interrogation room.

Oh *gods*, it really *did* look like an interrogation room, something straight out of one of those human cop shows. The table, the chair, the cuffs, the mirror... None of it good.

Shitshitshitshitshitshit. Panicked, I struggled against my restraints, a string of spells flying from my lips as I fought for freedom. In the end, the cuffs just bit harder, sharper, my wrists brutalized, the skin on the verge of splitting open. No way was I going to bleed in here. Blood had *such* potency in our world, used for both light and dark magic, and I wouldn't spill any unless I had to.

Maybe...

No, I couldn't cast. Couldn't reach the ground to draw a

blood-magic portal even if I tried. And if I succeeded, I clearly had no juice to fuel it.

Craning my head back once more, I squinted at the mirror, eyes narrowed on the collar's reflection. Although it was obviously leather, with no end and no beginning, just a perfectly fitted circle, there was more to it. Runes. Sigils carved into the black, unrecognizable—but I'd been out of the academy for a while. Magical runework had never been my strong suit; I much preferred earthbound magic. But these definitely weren't for decoration. They had purpose. Marks that most likely stopped my magic like a cork in a bottle. Made me pliant. Made me *weak*.

What was a witch without her magic?

Practically *human*.

I flailed again, battling my restraints as a high-pitched whine stretched through my skull from one ear to the other, growing louder by the second—

Until the door opened.

And then everything inside went quiet, save for the hammering of my heart.

A towering blonde in a navy pinstriped pantsuit strolled in, clipboard in hand and a pair of reading glasses propped up on her head. Peering down at the documents, her heavily masacara'd eyes narrowed briefly as the door swung shut behind her, nothing but a dimly lit stone corridor on the other side.

"What the hell is—"

"Katja Fox?" she interjected, gaze snapping to mine. Ice blue—severe, like the rest of her appearance, from the too-tight high ponytail down to the svelte white heels with their ridiculously pointy toes. If she kicked me with those things, would I bleed? Because it looked like she had a pair of knives strapped to the front of her feet.

She arched a prompting eyebrow when I just gawked at

her, and I cleared my throat, the brief surge of bravado vanishing.

"Uh, yes, but—"

"I'm Gabriella Smith," she stated, tugging out a stool from under the table with her foot, then dropping her clipboard with its enormous stack of paper onto the stretch of polished metal between us. It landed with a crash, making me jump again, and I frowned as she settled down across from me, bringing with her a strong whiff of menthol and smoked salmon. Gabriella *Smith*. That was a fake name if I'd ever heard one. When I tried to steal a glance at the information on the top sheet, she placed her forearm across it and waited until I looked her in the eye again. "I'm the intake supervisor at Xargi Penitentiary."

My blood ran cold. "P-penitentiary?"

"Yes."

"But I'm a witch—"

"We're aware," Gabriella remarked, and with a curt snap, a silver ballpoint pen materialized between her fingers. Even her stationery was sleek and cold. She hastily scribbled something in the corner of that first page, distracted. "This is a supernatural penitentiary."

"Those *exist*?"

Supernatural prisons weren't a *thing*. Sure, a few academies specialized in reforming delinquent supernatural youths, but that was hardly the same thing as a lock 'em up and throw away the key *prison*. Individual communities within the grander supernatural sphere adhered to their own laws; witches had a different set of rules than vampires, and they had their own courts, judges, and councils to deal with lawbreakers. For the most part, supers also followed the human rule of law—if only to keep off their radar. There were always troublemakers, of course, but dealing with them fell to their own kind.

Vampire gone on a killing rampage? They had a freakin' monarchy to dictate law and punishment. For witches, our coven leaders were the first line of defense, and then it went higher and higher all the way to the tippy-top High Council, with representatives from each continent who met up in Rome for lawmaking and trying of the most serious crimes.

The status quo didn't seem to faze Gabriella. She sniffed, scanning her clipboard, and then glanced up. "Hmm? Yes, they exist. You're sitting in one, Miss Fox."

She spoke perfect English with a faint, barely discernable Russian accent—maybe even Ukrainian, similar to my elderly neighbors back home. Beyond that, she addressed me like I was the biggest idiot on the planet, and if my hands weren't strapped down, I could have just *slapped* her.

Not that I would. Hardly my style. But, you know, extraordinary circumstances called for extraordinary action.

I... I could hit a bitch if necessary.

And Gabriella had such a slappable face.

"But..." I licked my lips, opting to use my words instead. "But I—"

"You have been convicted of selling illegal love potions to humans from your café in Seattle, Washington, in the United States of—"

"What?"

"America," Gabriella continued flatly, fixing me with a narrowed look from across the table. "You are therefore sentenced to a five-year stay in this penitentiary."

"I-I... I *never*..." What absolute utter horse*shit*. I never brewed anywhere but my home kitchen, and even if I was growing some of my potion stock at the café, selling it to humans, unsuspecting humans at that, was worthy of a wand-snapping in the witch community. Never. *Never*. Humans had no idea we existed beyond the faint prickle of awareness they experienced around a supernatural entity, like some part of their reptilian brain realized they were standing next to a much stronger predator. Only a family member or lover could usher a human into our world, *maybe* a friend under extenuating circumstances, and even then, everything was so hush-hush.

I had *never* involved humans in magic. Never ever, ever, *ever*. I didn't even brew anything for the few local witches I knew; they had their own covens to shop from, anyway.

"I'm afraid—"

"When was my trial?" I demanded, voice cracking, palms doused in a cold sweat. Gabriella flipped through what looked like a hundred sheets of paper wedged into her clipboard, seeming bored with my outrage already. "I want a lawyer..." I wriggled uselessly against my restraints, the metal on metal grating what was left of my frayed nerves. "And I *want* my familiar."

Gabriella stared me down with a sigh, eyebrows creeping up her wrinkle-free forehead. *Are you done?* She didn't say the words out loud, but her expression screamed them at me. When I sucked in my cheeks, biting hard, she nudged her clipboard aside and tapped the end of her pen against her chin.

"I'm afraid, Miss Fox, that you are not in a position to make demands. Evidence of your crime has been presented to the Xargi Penitentiary sentencing council, and you've been found guilty."

"*When*? What evidence?" Trumped-up nonsense, *that* was what evidence—because it had never happened. Gabriella merely pursed her lips back at me, my questions pinging off her icy exterior, her perfectly smooth and flawless face. She then glanced pointedly down at my body.

"Do you have anything on you? Drugs? Weapons?"

"Excuse me?" Dumbfounded, I too looked down at my clothing, at a torn shirt that clung to my figure and ripped black stockings without pockets. Short in stature when I wasn't strapped into my heels, I didn't exactly possess the cleavage to hide anything in either. "I… No?"

"Right." Gabriella pointed her pen at my throat. "That collar around your neck stunts your power as a witch. You will be unable to practice magic on these grounds." She sounded bored again, like she had said this exact speech a thousand times before. *That* didn't bode well for me. "I'll take your fingerprints now and a drop of your blood to register you. After a cavity search, you will be issued your uniform. If you attempt to remove the collar, there are consequences."

Her lips quirked at the last statement, and I swore something sick sparkled in her eyes. The hairs on the back of my neck shot up, goose bumps prickling down my body as my belly looped.

"What kind of… consequences?"

Her eyebrows arched like I was a moron again. "Consequences I *promise* you don't want to experience. The last one who tried to test the collar is no longer with us, unfortunately."

"This isn't right." I gripped the chair legs just to ground myself, breath coming harder and faster, Gabriella's ice swimming through my veins. "It's a lie. I… I don't belong here."

"That's what everyone says," she muttered with a dismissive wave. My right cuff suddenly fell off and clattered to the floor, and she snapped at me. "Give me your hand, Miss Fox."

Numb with panic, I did as I was told. I let her fingerprint me, let her draw a droplet of blood to dribble on one of her many papers. The pitchy whine was back between my ears with a vengeance. Before, when my family had died one right after the other, shock gave me focus. I was able to block out the inconsequential and deal with the important issues. I had been *strong*—even if I did splinter apart behind closed doors. Here, I… I couldn't do anything. Couldn't access my magic, my *birthright* as a witch, as the last of the Fox coven. Couldn't feel Tully. Couldn't move any of my limbs unless the aloof witch processing me removed my shackles.

I never made waves. Outside of the café, I steered clear of most people—supernatural and human. No big social gatherings. No sporting events. Just me and Tully and work. That had been my life for five long years, Dad's paranoia about Lloyd Guthrie dusting off on me.

They thought I was a criminal.

The only link to the criminal underworld I *maybe* had was…

Lloyd Guthrie. New York mobster. Head of his crime family.

And that was all I even knew about him—all I'd been able to dig up five years ago when, in my grief, I had given some credence to Dad's warning. Just rumors and tabloid articles and the odd mention on supernatural gossip websites.

Did this have anything to do with him? Had they finally caught the bastard? Would he be my cellmate? Was my family name somehow linked to his organization?

Gods. I closed my eyes tight when the room spun and blurred, holding back tears as best I could, refusing to let the witch across the table see even *one* spill down my cheek. No. This had nothing to do with Lloyd. I'd never seen or heard from him. Never felt someone lurking in the shadows or breathing down my neck. I distanced myself from the world as a precaution, not because I saw any real reason to do so, but because maybe, just maybe, I felt like I owed it to Dad to be overly cautious, if only to honor a rambling deathbed wish.

And now…

Now Dad's fears came screeching into focus, bright and shiny and *there*, and my gut churned harder in response.

"I'm going to be sick," I mumbled, clutching at my stomach with my one free hand, thumb still bleeding from the prick of her pen.

"On your feet, inmate," Gabriella ordered as if she hadn't even heard me—or, more likely, didn't care. Another lazy flick of her hand had the rest of my restraints falling away, a whoosh of cold magic slithering across my body, but I just sat there. If I got up, it was over: I'd surrendered to the process. And… if I got up, I had serious doubts I'd *stay* up. Gabriella sneered down her nose at me, wrenching her jacket sleeves up to her elbows. In a flash, a pair of white gloves molded to her hands, and she shot me a cutting smile.

"Stand up against the wall, inmate… It's time to strip, squat, and cough."

3

ELIJAH

"Done."

Oh, for fuck's sake. With twelve cards still in hand, I looked up and across the table, only to find my vampire counterpart was, in fact, finished.

"All right, new game," I grumbled, tossing my leftover cards next to our twin piles, his substantially neater and taller than mine. "This is the last time I play Speed against a fucking vampire."

"I told you," Rafe mused. He grinned as he gathered the scattered deck into a single pile, organizing them for a reshuffle, so accustomed to winning that it made me want to clock him right in that stupidly square jaw all the ladies swooned over. "I think you're a masochist, old friend."

"And I think it's cheating to use vamp speed—"

"*Hardly.*"

My eyes narrowed. While he was wearing one of the prison's charmed collars around his neck, same as me, vampires were a little different in their abilities. From what I could tell, the sigils diminished a vampire's speed, but most of the warlock guards at Xargi Penitentiary were still required to use magic to tame the fanged inmates. That and the sun, which streamed through the windows for most of the day, even in this godforsaken territory—wherever the fuck we were. Rafe and I had spent the last six months guessing, ever since they'd hauled us in here together, nicked from my property just outside the cozy English village that had been my home for the last decade.

Although the sun could be the death of my friend here, the one supernatural being who, in my opinion, wasn't a jumped-up asshole hell-bent on ascending the ranks of his clan or coven or pack or *whatever,* that great glowing orb was also a giveaway as to where we were in the world. Somewhere north, close to the poles. *Xargi* had an eastern European twang to it, possibly Russian, *maybe* Mongolian. When we'd first arrived, there had been about an hour of sunlight each day, and the vampires inside this hellhole practically ran the show. Now, six months later, we had a good nine to ten hours of sunlight a day, which, for the most part, kept vampires in their blackout cells.

Northern Russia, perhaps.

Siberia was also a possibility.

No confirmation from the guards whenever I floated the options. Not a professional amongst them—just former criminals given a pinch of power over the rest of us. It was like Christmas came early for these fucks every goddamn day.

As Rafe shuffled the deck, mulling over a few other games we could play for the thousandth time, my inner dragon snored softly inside, constrained and confined for six long months. At this point, I was *desperate* to let him out, to stretch our wings and take to the skies. It was an itch I couldn't scratch with this collar in place, the runes designed to prevent shifting of any kind. Me, I understood. A dragon could destroy every brick of this place ten times over, our fire the hottest in any realm. But there were plenty lesser shifters in other cellblocks—Willow, a rabbit shifter in Cellblock B for instance, posed zero threat, but she couldn't stretch her legs either, couldn't shift and zoom around.

Torture.

Absolute *torture* for a shifter to be cut off from their inner beast.

But that was the point of this place: torture. Why, I still had no clue. Most of us were innocent... Rafe insisted that was just the way of the world, and some days I almost believed him. After all, he had four long centuries on top of my two. Six hundred years on this planet, living amongst humans and supers alike, was bound to make anyone jaded.

"Gin rummy?" Rafe floated, scrubbing at his cheek stubble with a sigh. I crossed my arms and cracked my neck.

"Again?"

The vampire's thick black brows shot up. "Sorry, what else are we doing? Too good for gin these days?"

I flipped him the V. "Calm down, you tit, we can play gin."

Even though the Irish vamp could sometimes be *the* moodiest asshole on the planet, I loved him like a brother. Neither of us played the supernatural politics game, preferring the simplicity of human society to our own. He'd stumbled into my English hamlet eight years ago, and as the only two supers in town, we had eventually found each other —it was inevitable. Unlike every other supernatural bastard I'd ever come across, from dragons like me all the way down to uppity elves, he just wanted to exist. No games. No power struggles. He wrote for dozens of publications in Britain and Ireland under various pen names and just wanted a space to work. I offered him the caretaker's cottage on my property, and Rafe paid for its upkeep.

In his human life, the man who looked like a modern-day supermodel, from the chiseled jaw to the startling sea-glass-blue eyes, was a poet. A deckhand working odd jobs in an old-world Dublin, sure, but a poet too. A lackluster predator today, Rafe used to order blood deliveries discreetly and quietly to my property. No feeding on the humans in the village, despite what his charges at Xargi read.

Over the years, we'd grown fond of each other—which, when it came to our current predicament, had been my undoing. The bounty hunters had come for *him*; vampires were just so easy to pin false charges on. Then, imagine their luck upon discovering the village jeweler was also a dragon shifter. Two birds, one stone—they hauled us both out here on bullshit.

Fucking silver cuffs and knockout hexes. Seriously. Nowhere near a fair fight.

By some stroke of luck, we'd ended up in the same cellblock after the vampire in Rafe's original unit refused to share with one of her own kind. Psychotic bitch, that one.

Laughter erupted to my immediate left as Rafe dealt our hands, and as he rolled his eyes, I spared our fellow inmates a cursory glance. Cellblock C was almost full, eight of us occupying the ten available cells. Although I hadn't seen any other cellblocks, I assumed they all looked the same: a huge circular room, the walls and floors made of fossil-grey stone. In its center were nondescript metal tables and stools—all bolted to the dusty ground, of course, so we didn't use them to beat each other to bloody pulps. Some mornings, guards brought in board games and card decks, and every Thursday the library cart arrived with new books. Assigned work duty spread most of us throughout the prison grounds six days a week, which left the block mostly empty for nine hours or so each day. Individual cells made up the perimeter of the space, all the doors open during the day and locked tight each night.

Deimos tended to grab the center table first thing. It was a power move, classic of most supers: take the biggest table, the *best* real estate, and fill it with his cronies—make himself look like top dog of this block. The pasty tattooed demon had been pinched collecting human souls from crossroad deals well before their allotted deadlines in Chicago, and while most of us were innocent, I had no doubt the fucker was *not*. Demons never were.

Elbows on the table, Deimos in his black jumpsuit reveled in the laughter of his underlings, who were guffawing like he had just said the funniest shit in the world. Clockwise from him, there was warlock Avery in purple, maenad Constance in grey, and rat shifter Blake in navy blue, which was identical to mine. We were classified by our type, all shifters in blue, demons in black, vampires in red. Helped the guards keep clumps of like supers apart in prison common areas.

King Deimos had also recently collected the two other Cellblock C shifters: Faustus and Helen—some kind of bird shifters, but they were too meek to share the exact type with me. While they kept to themselves at first, they had eventually flocked to Deimos, swept up by his pretty words and fleeting kindness, by whatever demonic seductions left unmuted by his collar. I had no clue what the prison gangs did in here, but I assumed it was the usual: contraband smuggling, drug trades, fight rings, paid assassinations—all the leaders competing to be Xargi's one true alpha.

Pathetic.

Alongside a few of his closest allies, Deimos had arrived after Rafe and me, and when he'd tried to float his *let's unite* nonsense on us, I'd broken two of his teeth. Since then, there had been a very clear divide in Cellblock C, and that was the way we liked it. I had a six-year sentence, Rafe a twelve, and we intended to ride it out with as little drama as possible.

A siren erupted suddenly, blaring out of the speaker next to the bright white light that never dimmed in the conical ceiling. The block door burst open, and in charged guards in black uniforms, wands drawn. Months ago, the sight made my heart race. Now, it was standard fucking procedure; we all knew the drill.

"At your cell doors, inmates!" Blemmins, head guard for cellblocks A through D, barked at us, sparks erupting from the end of his wand. A fitting display, given he practically jizzed his pants anytime he got to order anyone around. Rafe tossed the cards on our little two-seater table with a scowl, and the siren continued to shriek as the rest of us rose and shuffled for our cells.

While there were several different alarms at Xargi, this one signaled the arrival of a new inmate on the block. As I leaned back against the wall between my cell door and Helen's, the little bird shifter all squirrely and cowering against the noise, Rafe caught my eye from the opposite side of the circle. Although we were close, we couldn't communicate telepathically like shifters within the same clan. But even without a glimpse inside his head, I knew what he was thinking; the twist of his mouth, the furrow of his brow, the hardness of his gaze—all a dead giveaway.

Here we fucking go again.

I offered him a one-shouldered shrug when the siren finally died down, my ears ringing and my inner dragon snarling softly. He hated everything in here, and if he had the chance to show himself, he would turn the prison and all its sadistic guards to ash.

Save the warden for last though. Guthrie deserved as much.

With our usual trio of guards situated around the room, the superfluous blocks of warlock muscle patrolled the cellblock slowly, looking us up and down, keeping us in line. Enforcers, this bunch, there to maintain peace if any fighting broke out beyond what the assigned security could handle.

The main door buzzed, locks unbolting again, and then

swung open to reveal two warlocks from processing. They dragged in a purple-jumpsuited inmate between them, a redhaired witch that I couldn't quite see properly—

But her scent struck hard, whizzing across the room and slamming into me like a fucking nuke. Briar rose and candle smoke and the air right before a cataclysmic storm…

Knees seconds from buckling, I clutched at the doorframe behind me. No one had ever knocked me off-balance just by their scent before, and yet this—I'd never smelled anything so strong, so fierce, so damn intoxicating that it took every bit of restraint I had to not launch across the room and tear her away from the fuckers death-gripping her arms. Bury my face in the coppery-red inferno blazing down her back. Drag my tongue up the delicate column of her throat.

What the fuck is wrong with me?

My inner dragon roared to life after months of forced docility and quiet. He bellowed so thunderously that my teeth chattered, and I gritted them hard, hoping no one had noticed. Even Rafe was distracted by the new arrival, tracking her with his calculating aquamarines as the guards marched her over to the vacant cell beside his. A surge of possessive need ripped through me, and I gulped down a deep breath, ignoring Helen's meek but curious sidelong glance.

Holy fuck.

Was that *witch* my…

My…

My fated mate?

Like any shifter, I'd heard the stories. We all went through life dreaming about the day we stumbled upon our fated mate, the one soul designed by fate exclusively for us and we for them. Once, it was only acceptable to fate with another shifter, but the times had changed. Given my preference for humans, I had always thought I'd align with one of them. Some gorgeous mortal woman who I would love and cherish and protect for all her short life, then carry on for the rest of my very long one with a piece of my heart missing.

But a *witch*?

No. That couldn't be right.

Only… The signs were there. Her scent smacked me upside the head like a lead pipe, stronger than all the smells ripening in this pit. Prisons were a fucking cornucopia of odors and energies, yet without even making eye contact, hers was the most potent. And most pleasant. And most alluring.

And…

And it made me forget, just for a few glorious seconds, that I was trapped in this hellhole.

My inner dragon responded to her immediately, scratching at my chest, bellowing to high heaven, *desperate* to get out and scent her for himself. To throw her on his back and whisk her away somewhere remote and luxurious. To hoard. The stereotype had merit: we dragons loved to hoard, and I'd satiated that need for decades working as a jeweler, surrounded by gold and gems and diamonds…

But she shone brighter than any pretty stone—and I'd barely glimpsed her face yet, nothing beyond an elegant profile and a flash of bright blue eyes.

Protectiveness lanced through me when one of the processing guards shoved her into the open cell next to Rafe's. A snarl hummed in my chest, and I pressed my lips together, clenched my jaw, fighting to contain the beast within. I couldn't shift. The collar wouldn't allow me—but that didn't stop my inner dragon from trying. His anxiety spiked when she disappeared, a flood of adrenaline threatening to make me *move*, to break formation and risk the wrath of the warlock fucks who patrolled the cellblock.

Calm down, you shit.

Across the circular room, Rafe studied me with a deep

frown, arms crossed, eyes slightly narrowed. If he'd noticed my agitation, others had too. A warlock named Thompson, one of the cellblock's permanent guards, glanced my way, and without meaning to, I locked eyes with him. The man was built like a mountain, tall and fierce, the figure of a warrior—but I still surpassed him. Big as he was, I was bigger.

But he had a wand on his hip.

Usually I let the alpha bullshit go—eyes on the ground, look away first, allow the fuckery of this place to roll off my back. No point in making waves.

But the witch did something to me.

Made me want to *fight*.

My inner dragon bristled, dusting off months of slumber and *roaring*. My vision sharpened. My nostrils flared. My heart thundered. Instinct kicked in, dragon's blood scorching through my veins, a lifetime of experience in my bones. Bloodlust and war drums and the smoke of fire-bathed cities—

Thompson squared off with me, his eyes hard, daring me to make a move.

Shifters were a combination of man and beast, and contrary to what the rest of the supernatural world thought, *we* were in control of which side ruled us. In here, it was best to let the man call the shots, even if I *wanted* to sprint across the cellblock, clotheslining Thompson in the neck with my arm on the way, then rip into the witch's cell and massacre the others, keep her all to myself...

I looked down first. Bowed my head, seething, waiting, brimming with the wild energy before a shift. Useless. I'd have to walk it off when I got the chance. Faustus and Helen twitched and fidgeted by their cell doors, sensing my predicament, and I shot them each a glare. *Don't say a fucking word.*

The birds yielded to me—the only real alpha in here, no matter what Deimos thought.

Once the guards got the newest inmate of Cellblock C situated, they bailed. Left her to fend for herself. The added muscle vanished through the main door, and eventually we were down to the standard three assholes. Well, two assholes and Thompson, who, for all his posturing, occasionally seemed interested in doing his job. The other two fuckers let Deimos do what he pleased and put bets on inmates during fights.

As soon as we were given the all clear to move freely again, I charged straight for her, following her scent—such a strange scent, at that. Floral with the briar rose, yet that candle smoke was so *alluring* to a dragon. An unpredictable woman, perhaps, in the way her scent had me picturing a dark shoreline with choppy waters, the air tense, on the verge of a tempest. Had to see her. Had to meet her. Know her. *Smell* her—

"What are you doing?" Rafe intercepted me just before I reached her cell. Inside, I could hear her settling on the prison-issued bed, those cruel springs groaning beneath her. The vampire refused to let me ignore him, however, even when I tried to barrel by; he snagged my arm, grasp tight as steel, and yanked me toward his cell.

"Elijah," he growled, low enough for only a shifter to hear, "what the hell is wrong with you?"

"She… I…" I blinked hard, then shook my head. All the stories said we lost ourselves the first time we scented our mate—lost ourselves to the beast, driven by pure, uncut animal *need*. Risky, that. Dangerous for a creature who needed restraint and self-control to survive in this world.

"You look a mess," Rafe muttered. The collar also muted a vampire's unparalleled strength, their ability to snap bone with the slightest touch, but he was still strong. A worthy match for a dragon shifter—certainly. He held firm, forcing me to focus on his green-blue stare, intense in a way only Rafe could pull off without triggering my fight instinct. "Come on... Before the brat sees you like this."

The brat. Yeah. Right. Couldn't let Deimos spot a crack.

While the rest of our block meandered over to the center table, Deimos leading the way, Rafe marched me to the two-seater on the outer rim. Positioned in front of warlock Avery's cell, he sat me down—and I just went, like I was in some fucking trance, all from a little witch's scent.

Fated mates was serious business—and a weakness of epic proportions, especially in here.

Rafe left for a moment to fetch our deck of cards, and as soon as he settled across from me, he resumed dealing in silence, like we were actually going to play gin. I humored him because I felt like I had to, going through the motions, throwing down cards and picking new ones up, reorganizing my hand, all the while staring at her open cell door. Located on the southeastern side of the block, sunlight beamed into it for the better part of the afternoon, which meant she could see how depressing our holes were while also feeling what little warmth Xargi Penitentiary had to offer on her skin.

A blessing and a curse, the sun.

Nearly an hour later, supper on the horizon, she finally padded out of her cell—and I lost it. Again. Even seated, I struggled for control, my inner dragon snarling and huffing and clomping about inside, desperate to get at her, this diminutive witch with hair like copper flames. Long and wavy, it rolled down her back for the most part, the staticky pieces on top like a messy bird's nest. Somehow, she made her purple jumpsuit look *good*; it clung to her curves, to the swell of her breasts and the roll of her hips. Perfection. Sheer, untainted *perfection*. While the point of her chin and the high sharpness of her cheekbones suggested a heart-shaped face, her cheeks had a nice roundness that this gutter would trim off in a matter of days.

I mean, the food here was mediocre at its best and literal gruel at its worst. Most lost their appetite the first few weeks. Goodbye, adorable chubby cheeks. Hello, severe lines and sharp angles.

Her eyes were such a startling shade of blue, bright and electric as they danced around the cellblock. She lingered in the door, hands clutching at either side, timid and hesitant to join any of us—

And then there was Deimos, right on cue, gliding to her side like he fancied himself her savior.

I tossed my cards on the table, ignoring Rafe's curt exhale and glaring openly at the pair. Vision tinged red, blood pounded between my ears, every sense heightened when the demon swept *my* witch under his wing.

"There, there, sweetheart," he murmured, gently guiding her out of the cell. "I know this must be *terribly* overwhelming for you."

Fucker. He had the faintest of English accents most of the time, but he really hammed it up, from Cornish to Received Pronunciation, all posh and proper, when he seduced a newbie into his ranks.

Jaw clenched, hands in fists, I tracked the pair as they drifted toward the middle table, her mouth moving like she was actually giving that shit the time of day. I tensed, about to stand, when Rafe shot me a look—and then kicked me hard in the shin.

"Elijah, don't," he remarked when I turned my fury on him.

"Don't what?"

"Don't pick up strays," the vampire said with a sigh, as if my behavior was just so *tedious*. "We don't need any extra—"

"She's not a stray."

My friend faltered at my tone, at the way my glare burned hot as blue fire. I *never* turned my ire on him, but if he called her a stray one more time, he'd see what everyone else assumed about my kind: Rafe would experience a dragon unhinged.

"Elijah, I didn't mean—"

But I was already gone, shooting up and beelining for Deimos—who still had his fucking arm around my mate. Rafe stayed at the table, perhaps waiting to see the situation unfold from a distance; while we both ascribed to the don't-make-waves philosophy, we were willing to draw arms for each other.

True to form, maenad Constance was there in a heartbeat to block my path as her gang leader worked his magic on the new arrival. Amazonian in size, olive-skinned and pink-haired, the woman was straight-up batty. Deimos had promised Rafe and me a blowjob each if we joined his crew, like her mouth on our dicks was a perk that came with letting him order us around. Back then we'd refused, but not everyone could go six months with nothing but their hand to get off with. Her charms had worked on Avery and Blake, at the very least.

Statuesque as she was, I shouldered around her, physically stronger than some psychotic worshipper of an old Greek god, and marched right up to Deimos's usual table. He'd already sat the witch down on one of the stools, and he leaned over her, whispering in her ear with a wicked smile—

"Deimos," I barked, fighting with my inner dragon for control. *He* wanted to flay Deimos alive, and normally I did too—but I wasn't about to spend a month in solitary now that my fated mate slept fifty feet away from me. "None of your games. Leave her be."

The demon straightened, his grin cruel and his hand

lingering on her shoulder. "Oh, now you want to say something? Where's this fire been all along, dragon?"

"Miss, don't involve yourself in his bullshit," I said, locking eyes fleetingly with the witch. She licked her full lips, the flick of her tongue a fucking tease, and before I could get another word out, Deimos scoffed.

"Her name's *Katja,*" he sneered, purring her name in a way that made my blood boil. "She told me—practically handed it over."

Darkness glimmered in his black gaze, malice burning bright, and, as if realizing her mistake, my fated blushed crimson. Names had such power in supernatural communities, fae most of all, but demons could work twisted wonders with them too. Mercifully, our collars would put a stop to that. Deimos was just another asshole in here, though I couldn't imagine Katja relished the fact that he knew her name—that he crooned it like he already owned it.

"Right." She planted her hands on the table and stood. "I'm out."

What a *voice*. Sweet and clear but *strong*. It lulled my inner dragon, quieting his rage over Deimos, and I watched her helplessly as she strode back to her cell and left us all in her dust. At the door, she glanced over her shoulder, eyes catching mine again. My cock twitched with interest when her cheeks darkened, but in a flash, she was gone.

Her scent lingered in the air, and I resisted the urge to suck down a lungful—especially with Deimos grinning at me like that, toothily, the gap between his fake front teeth purposeful. I mean, those were the two I'd knocked out months ago, and he must have requested medical to recreate it when he got the new pair. I cocked my head to the side, refusing to let him get to me, and then glanced pointedly at his mouth.

"You sure you wanna show me those teeth, boy?"

His smile died in an instant. Good. Fucker.

"I'll be watching you," I growled—and then caught *my* mistake a second later. Deimos smirked, his expression oozing a casual cruelty that made my inner dragon seethe.

"Oh, please *do* watch me," the demon insisted, grabbing at his dick for good measure. "You can watch me *take* her, dragon."

A steely grip snapped around my bicep when I lurched forward, animal instinct on hyperdrive. Rafe wrenched me back just as one of the asshole guards sighed and pushed off the wall, like doing his job was such a fucking chore. The end of his wand glowed when he drew it, but the fight was over before it began, Rafe and I back at our table and Deimos chortling at his.

"You fucked that up," the vampire muttered, fixing me with a narrowed look as he reshuffled our deck. I gritted my teeth and said nothing, my inner dragon unleashing a hellfire that scorched up my windpipe and burned straight to the tip of my tongue.

He was right, of course. By overreacting, I'd encouraged Deimos to go for Katja—I'd stoked his interest in her.

But that didn't matter. If he tried anything, I would rip him into bite-sized pieces and feed him to the wolves that patrolled the prison grounds.

We were all in here together. I could watch her day and night. Even if my fated *was* a witch and not the fragile human I had always envisioned, I wouldn't let anything happen to her.

That was a promise.

Dragons kept their promises.

And if Deimos didn't back the fuck off, he was going to learn that the hard way.

4
RAFE

What a day.

Ordinarily that phrase never crossed my mind—*what a day*—because I slept all day, like any regular vampire. But in this hellhole, the bastards in charge were trying to change my base programming, turning the few of us in red jumpsuits diurnal rather than nocturnal. Up all day, locked in all night. At first, I hadn't been able to sleep a wink come nightfall, body alert after a day of hiding in the shadows, determined to avoid every sunbeam possible throughout the penitentiary. Elijah assisted with that, of course, using his massive shifter body to shield me if I couldn't scamper into a corner fast enough.

Contrary to popular belief, vampires did, in fact, need sleep. Not much, but if blood was in short supply or we hadn't fed in a few weeks, our bodies started to shut down. After all, fueling such a powerful machine came at a cost, and sometimes sleep was the only way to top up the battery. The first few months in prison had been a never-ending nightmare while I'd adjusted to the new sleep schedule—and never mind the new *feeding* regime. Vampires were allotted five tablespoons of blood a day. No choice in the type. Always served cold. Utterly ridiculous.

Just another tactic to control us. The collars around our necks were designed to cull magical ability. Specific runes stopped shifters from shifting, ensured gargoyles didn't turn to stone come sunrise, and kept that one phoenix in Cellblock A from bursting into flame and regenerating. But vampires weren't magical beings. We were organic—blood and bone and teeth, we were *animals,* much like humans. The collar around my neck dulled my strength to a degree, and I couldn't zip around at lightning speed anymore, but otherwise I was a fully intact being—more so than any other inmate in here.

They couldn't fully control me with this ridiculous strip of leather, no matter how many runes they carved into it.

Probably why there were so few red jumpsuits roaming the halls.

But that meant the twats running this facility relied on other means of control—cue the sleep and blood deprivation. Fortunately, by month six, halfway through year one of twelve, I'd figured out how to doze off once the sun dipped below the horizon. By keeping to myself, by sticking with Elijah, the least confrontational super I'd ever met despite his alpha status, I kept my energy reserves in check. At this point, I was practically in hibernation mode. Twelve years was just a blip to an immortal, but if I wanted to *survive,* if I wanted to walk out of here one day a fully formed man and not a shuffling corpse, then I had to lie low and conserve.

And sleep.

Sleep as often as I could, for as long as I could.

A task made *infinitely* more difficult tonight—because my new neighbor wouldn't stop crying. The witch was on hour two at this point after the guards had bolted us in our cells at curfew, and I was surprised she had any tears left to shed.

Her breath suddenly hitched, and my eyebrows shot up in the snippet of silence that followed, but I sighed curtly at the sound of her hand clapping to her mouth, followed by muffled sobs that, to my sensitive hearing, especially when I had nothing better to concentrate on, weren't really all that muffled.

For God's sake.

Lying flat on my back on the slip of paper the prison dared label a *bed*, I recrossed my ankles and picked at nonexistent cuticles. With the blackout window covering removed, starlight filtered into my private cell, no more than a six-by-twelve rectangle with a single bed, a wooden table to hold any supplies the guards hadn't swiped yet, and a toilet by its most basic definition in the corner. Not much to look at in here, the walls, floor, and ceiling constructed of dusty stones—it would have made *me* sob uncontrollably too, I suppose, if I hadn't slept in something worse below deck during my human years.

Through the two-foot-thick wall separating us, the witch's breath came faster suddenly, descending into panic, perhaps even hyperventilation. I scrubbed my face with a groan, both hands fluffing, then smoothing my coarse black scruff.

This was supposed to be a dragon's fated mate? *Her*?

I rolled my eyes when she sniffed, long and deep, sucking back two full nostrils of snot.

Yeah, she was beautiful, all petite and porcelain and freckled, her hair like fire and her eyes like sapphires. *That* fit the mental image of a dragon's mate, what with their penchant for all things shiny. Back in Britain, Elijah's countryside manor dripped with wealth courtesy of his innate urge to hoard treasures, and witch Katja was pretty enough to warrant a place on his wall.

Yet from what I'd seen today, both in the cellblock and the

dining hall, she was also quiet and standoffish, distant and dour. And now she was *sobbing*, probably on the verge of passing out if she didn't get her breathing under control.

Honestly. Her? Fated to Elijah?

I just couldn't see it.

But he was one hundred percent certain—and he should know. Shifters just felt... so... *deeply*. I couldn't imagine existing with so much swirling around inside me, all this feeling—both human and animal—and never mind that literal other creature, not metaphorical in the slightest, always desperate to get out. Even during my moodiest stint as a starving human poet, I had never gone *that* deep. What a nightmare.

But Elijah was a nightmare I had put up with for eight years—my first and only *real* friend in six centuries. When he'd told me over supper that he and this Katja woman were fated, I'd believed him because I owed him that much, but my *God* did it piss me off, because now I would have to babysit him. His reaction anytime they were in the same space, anytime he could *see* or smell her, was totally unacceptable in our current environment. If he acted out, a guard would notice.

And they'd have a grand old time making him pay for it.

Sadistic cunts.

For six long months, he and I had flown under the radar. We didn't get involved with other inmates. We let bad shit happen because it wasn't our *job* to stop it. Trapped inside a highly warded prison, with warlock guards strutting about flashing their wands—compensation for the smallest cocks on the planet, probably—every two seconds, wearing collars that kept Elijah from shifting into the magnificent and downright *brutal* dragon he could be—we were fucked. No sense in making a bad situation worse by involving ourselves in drama.

Katja brought drama.

A lot of it.

Because Elijah couldn't keep his shit together, and after eight years of living in a cottage on his property, writing and thriving and living my best life with a *friend,* I gave a damn about him. Unfortunately.

So, even if I didn't think this mewling witch deserved to be the fated mate of one of the most decent shifters I knew, the only one who didn't play the political games, Elijah believed it. He had connected with her in an instant—and it was biological, something he couldn't help, couldn't avoid even if he tried. So. Fine. If *fate* had selected her for him, for my best friend, my shifter brother, then perhaps I owed it to him to make her shut up.

Er. I mean. *Calm* her down.

And then maybe, just maybe, I could get an hour or two of sleep tonight to replenish my wasting body.

Shrouded in darkness and speckles of unfettered starlight, I finally—begrudgingly—rolled off my bed. The springs creaked and groaned, and my bare feet touched down on cool stone as soon as I was upright.

I waited a moment, listening, not needing to strain—

Still crying.

Damn it.

Scratching at the back of my neck, I stood, then dropped to my knees and crawled to the little mousehole that stretched between my cell and hers. The place was full of cracks and holes, vermin alive and well—just another means to torture innocent supers, all so the warden could show off the *first* supernatural prison in the world.

Not that we needed one, but obviously someone was in the mood to make money. Prick.

Humans had been doing it for decades—for-profit prisons—so why not us? Why not punish a community that already had to hide in the shadows, a community full of its own regimented laws, a community at war with itself half the time anyway?

No one had asked for this.

And surely no one but those lining their pockets *wanted* this.

"Hey?" I called through the little hole, settling on my side and peering through the black, my night vision as spectacular as my hearing. Not that there was much of a view: just more dusty brownish-grey stonework, then what appeared to be one of the metal legs of her bed shoved up against the far wall.

At the sound of my voice, the witch fell silent save for a little sniffle, and I raised my eyebrows, waiting for a response.

Nothing.

Fair enough.

I didn't really talk to anyone but Elijah and I'd been here six months. But I couldn't just leave it at that; scaring her wasn't the goal, and I most certainly was *not* like the majority of the *actual* criminals in here.

"Katja, right?"

"I-I'm sorry," she murmured, voice carrying through even though she was positioned somewhere out of sight, somewhere deeper in her cell. Probably next to the window, the small taste of freedom and normalcy this place allowed any of us. "Could you hear me?"

"Well, yes." *Obviously*. She wasn't exactly being quiet over there. Unfortunately, my sardonic tone set off another bout of crying, and I shook my head, rolled my eyes, and flopped onto my back. Elijah was accustomed to my snark, my bouts of melancholy, my dry wit, but it could be a touch off-putting to strangers.

"It's fine," I remarked, threading my hands together on

top of my chest. "Everyone cries the first night. I mean, the innocent ones, anyway." Really, the thought of Deimos or Constance wailing inside their cells was laughable. "The other bastards probably expected to be in something like this at some point."

Bare feet tiptoed across the stone tiles, and I listened to her hands grazing the wall between us, followed by shuffling along the base until she stumbled onto the little mouse highway. I glanced to the side, the nothingness on the other end suddenly filled with a sapphire-blue eye searching me out.

"Hello," I whispered when our gazes met fleetingly, hers disappearing just as fast as it appeared.

"Hi," she offered in return. After a little more scuffling on her end, all I saw was that brilliant red hair in front of the hole, suggesting she had adopted a similar position on the floor. Katja cleared her throat, her voice thick and hoarse as she said, "Everyone says they're innocent though."

"Again, *yes*." I pressed my lips together and swallowed the sarcasm down. "But you can hardly believe them, can you? They're all practiced liars, even the guards. And watch yourself with Deimos."

Elijah had gone *way* too far with the demon earlier today, catching his eye with that display, encouraging the little shit to take a special interest in him and Katja. From here on out, Deimos and his cronies would be paying extra-close attention to the pair whenever they interacted, and I dreaded having to involve myself in another tedious spat.

Especially over a woman.

How sinfully cliché.

Mind you—it wasn't really about Katja. Deimos had sensed Elijah's alpha qualities from the beginning, and that made the demon want to fuck with him. Simple, typical, *stupid* supernatural dynamics—all alive and well in Xargi Penitentiary.

She let out a watery laugh. "Yeah, like I'd cozy up to a demon. I'm not that desperate."

"Good to hear." At least she had a brain in that pretty head. A tense quiet settled over us—tense only because there was never an *easy* quiet in a place like this. If someone in our cellblock wasn't making a ruckus just for kicks, usually Constance, occasionally that rat shifter Blake, then someone, somewhere, was screaming, and it carried through the vents like thunder come nightfall.

"I'm sorry I kept you up," Katja said suddenly, sounding a little sheepish. I shrugged, even if she couldn't see it.

"It's fine. I'm used to it."

"The collar doesn't kill your hearing, huh?"

I picked at the leather, more habit than anything, careful not to trigger its failsafe curse—the kind that went off if you were stupid enough to try and remove the thing. "Not as much as I'd like."

"I'm sorry—"

"Stop saying that." Her breath hitched, and I rubbed the knot between my eyebrows with a sigh. "No, I just mean... It's fine. I understand, anyway."

"I'm a bit... overwhelmed, I guess," she admitted softly. Just as I was about to tell her that was completely understandable, that this place was a steaming pile of hot garbage that ought to be burned to the ground with all the guards and that fucking warden still inside, she burst out crying again. *Again*. Sobbing, probably beneath both hands, she sounded like she was trying her best to keep it in as much as possible.

For my sake?

Christ.

Her breath hitched, and something strangled and *deeply*

sad shuddered from what I remembered to be a pair of rather full lips. Strange detail to recall in the heat of the moment, but I was desperately starved in here. Starved for blood and sane women. I mean, all the ones in here were beautiful; supernatural men *and* women were usually attractive. Predatory advantage to be lovely.

But *Jesus*, she was still going.

Fuuuuuuuuuuuuuuuck.

I despised a wailing woman.

And not because the sounds grated on me, or that all the emotion irked me—I wasn't a heartless bastard, no matter the stigma surrounding vampires—I just never knew what to say. As a man who prided himself for his *words*, my vast vocabulary shriveled up to single syllables in the face of a crying woman—especially one I was determined to make stop.

So, without thinking, I launched into one of my originals. A poem from two centuries back, one that had beguiled crowds at pubs and sailors in bunks. I'd written it about the Wild Atlantic Way, the stretch of cruel, breathtaking coastline that ran the full length of my darling Éire. It was a land I knew well, savage in its splendor where the sea met the land, home to selkies and merfolk. Passages to fae realms dotted the shoreline, which turned the Atlantic bitter. The poem came out of nowhere, a limerick I hadn't thought of in centuries, yet it flowed seamlessly from my lips now, lines about the sea and the storm, the calm and the tempest, the beauty and the terror.

And when I finished, my voice soft as it always was for poetry, Katja had fallen silent. Briefly, we experienced a quiet unknown to me during my stint in prison so far—and it was magnificent. Surrounded by stone and starlight, we both lay there on either side of the mousehole, my words slowly fading into the ether—

My eyes snapped open.

What—the *fuck* did I just do? Panic-recited poetry to make a woman stop crying?

Aghast, I licked my lips, mouth suddenly too dry. "I just thought—"

"That was beautiful," she whispered through the hole, full lips right there—like she had murmured her praise into my ear. Heat flared in my chest, but as I lay there on my back, stiff and still, I was suddenly acutely aware it was no longer embarrassment that ripened inside me.

But something else entirely.

Something—strange.

Unwelcome, especially in a place like this. I'd already decided months ago that no one could affect me. No one could move me to pity. No friends. No flirtations. No *nothing*. Just me and Elijah and our survival.

Then along came a witch, fated to my best friend, her voice like silk, like the gentlest mist of the first spring rain, and I—

"Thank you," I gritted out, only because I should. No one had admired my poetry in decades, my current work erring toward a blend of tabloid journalism and hard-hitting news, depending on the publication and the pen name. Occasionally I put out the odd fiction—one psychosexual thriller had recently been optioned for a TV series. "I, er, used to be a poet… in another life."

"I run a café in Seattle," she told me, her voice thick and tired—exhausted, really, every word laced with a weariness I knew well, the sort that settled into your bones. I felt it here with the lack of blood, the isolation, the injustice of being *ripped* from my life and brutalized by warlocks in uniforms. She cleared her throat, and I blinked the flash of rage away. A quick peek through the hole showed she had rolled onto her side, one beautiful blue eye gazing at me again. "I don't have any pretty words to describe it though."

I too lolled onto my side, my cheek to the dusty stone, same as her.

"It's nice to meet you, Katja."

A tear careened down her pale flesh and plopped onto the floor. "It's nice to meet you too…"

We stared at one another for a beat, that blue orb suddenly dancing about, and I bit back a grin.

"Rafe."

"It's nice to meet you…" She shuffled closer. "Rafe."

Excitement fluttered about in my chest at the sound of my name on her tongue. *Abort. Abort!*

"Good night, Katja."

She blinked back at me. "Good night, Rafe."

Another unsettling tingle, my dead heart skipping a beat despite the fact it had been rotting in my chest for nearly five and a half long centuries.

Katja rolled away first, and I quickly did the same, returning to my creaky bed and flopping onto the mattress with a sigh I didn't need—never needed, but always felt satisfying to do, some semblance of humanity clinging to me even now. Hands folded on my chest, I stared up at the ceiling, at the thin beam of moonlight slashing in from the window. Odd how the giddy flutter had vanished, replaced instead by a warped feeling of pride, of *accomplishment*, that I had settled this crying woman.

The crying witch.

Katja.

And even after she fell asleep, her breaths long and even, occasionally hitched, I struggled to close my eyes, finding it even harder to doze off now in the prison's familiar nighttime hush than I had when she wept by my side.

And frankly—that pissed me right off.

5
KATJA

I'd never been this exhausted before. Not when my brothers died. Not after Dad passed. Not in the first year of running a business full-time at the age of twenty-four all by my freakin' self. At least then Tully had been by my side, fueling me, replenishing me, supporting me with cuddles and purrs and *strength*.

None of that in here.

And it was only the second day.

The *first* meal of the second day at that.

I'd been inside Xargi Penitentiary for a good, what, maybe twenty hours, and it already felt like twenty years.

The trio of cellblock guards who'd put us to bed were gone when the alarm tolled this morning. After a quick pee in the world's scummiest toilet, the little sink above it spewing perpetually freezing water, I'd joined the rest of the inmates in a rainbow of jumpsuit colors at our place outside the cells—right next to the door, standing in the wall between our hole and our neighbor's. Vampire Rafe glanced my way as soon as he shuffled out into the shadows, sunlight beaming from every cell but his, only I refused to meet his eye. Last night had been one of the worst of my life—and it had been utterly humiliating that he heard me bawling like a homesick schoolgirl during her first year at the academy.

I just… couldn't face him. Needed some time to, I don't know, find my dignity again.

And then let go of the fantasy that a peppy host with a camera crew was about to materialize out of nowhere with a microphone that he'd shove in my face after telling me this was all a big joke, a new supernatural prank show that someone had nominated me for…

Because…

Because that was just pathetic. Life seldom worked that way, and as they marched Cellblock C out in a single-file line, wands drawn, I accepted that this was *real*.

But I couldn't accept that I was stuck here. I *wouldn't* accept it. I was an innocent witch wrongfully detained, and if it was the last thing I ever did, I would breathe free air again.

While we had sunlight in our cells, the interior corridors of the penitentiary were illuminated by long fluorescent bulbs that flickered and tinged at random. It appeared vampires weren't permitted their usual schedule—sleep all day, up all night—which explained why the prison cafeteria was underground. Down a few winding stone corridors from our cellblock, one guard at the front, one at the back, the other stalking the line with a steely eye, a cruel smirk, and a wand as black as his uniform, we took a hard left into a stairwell.

And went down, down, *down*, three levels deep before filing into the huge circular cafeteria. With a max of ten inmates per cellblock—judging by the number of cells in ours, anyway—the entire inmate population ate together, called to grab our food by wedding-buffet rules, which meant one at a time, starting with Cellblock A. Last night at dinner, I had counted thirteen cellblocks total: A through M. Roughly a hundred and thirty inmates in one place, thirty-plus guards patrolling the area.

I'd expected chaos.

And compared to the unnerving quiet of the cellblock, it *was*, but at least it was organized chaos. As soon as we filled our trays with whatever the kitchen crew had prepared, the hair-netted supers behind the counter wearing jumpsuits like me, we had the freedom to sit wherever we wanted.

Last night at dinner, I'd sat alone. That had felt safest.

This morning, with my plastic serving tray and a breakfast of greyish scrambled eggs, a tiny carton of orange juice, and a slightly burnt English muffin awaiting me, I wasn't quite as lucky. Not an empty spot in sight, dozens and dozens of round metal tables with stools bolted to the ground situated across the center of the cafeteria. Guards patrolled the perimeter, chatting, laughing, wands always in hand.

I missed my wand.

Missed what it could do to the bastards who had first shoved me into my cell, to the bitch in processing who literally made me strip naked, right down to my bobby pins, then squat in front of her and cough.

Like I'd somehow shoved contraband into my pussy *before* whoever kidnapped me from Seattle knocked me unconscious. Honestly. *The* most degrading experience of my life: who knew how many others had been watching through the two-way mirror.

I bit the insides of my cheeks, trying not to think about it, to get lost in the events of the recent past—because I'd lose it. Again. And I couldn't lose it in here. Rafe had been sweet in his own way, but for all I knew, everyone else was a hardened criminal, and they ate weakness for breakfast, not expired eggs.

Most of my cellblock had already found their tables, that handsy demon and his posse occupying one near the middle, then Rafe and his gorgeous—albeit intense—shifter friend choosing one near the outskirts by the tray return counter. While it might have been helpful, I wasn't here to make friends. In the end, prisoners were out for themselves, and Rafe might have laid on the charm to shut me up last night, but I refused to trust *anyone*.

Especially the shifter who wouldn't stop staring at me. Elijah. A shiver cut down my spine the second our eyes clashed across the sea of tables. When he looked at me, it was like he was looking straight *through* me, right down to the marrow, and I didn't like that. Not one bit. Not when he made me weak-kneed and vulnerable with nothing but a glance.

Since there wasn't a chance in hell I'd throw my hat in with the demon who'd licked my ear twice while purring into it yesterday, I beelined away from my cellblock and scanned the countless other faces, searching for the most unassuming of the bunch. Eventually, I settled on another loner: a woman in a dark blue jumpsuit like Elijah—shifter, then, if we were all divided by our most basic identity. Smaller than me, probably a little shorter too, she sat poking at her eggs with a scowl, her hair a peppery brown, and when I wandered closer, I noted one of her eyes had clouded over.

A crippled shifter… Rare. Their genetics healed just about any wound, but as I gnawed at my lower lip, debating whether or not to join her, I also wondered if the collars muted healing abilities too. Had someone done that to her in here? Fear mottled in my belly—made my already unappetizing breakfast seem so beyond gross I gagged. Good morning, anxiety puke. Like I needed to make *that* kind of scene in front of everyone and totally obliterate my prison rep.

Okay, Katja, make a move. Supers at the surrounding tables were already starting to glance my way—strangers who looked infinitely more terrifying than the shifter. So, choice made.

"Hey." I stopped at one of the metal stools across from her, my empty belly somersaulting when she peered up. "Can I sit here?"

Her one good eye gave me a quick once-over, and she nodded, her features delicate and angular. Beautiful. Easily mistaken for a fae or elf maiden if it weren't for the jumpsuit.

"Sure," she said, her accent suggesting bounty hunters had scooped her up from Australia. As she nodded at the spot in front of me, I sat in a hurry, and the shifter grabbed her own slightly burnt English muffin, slowly picking a little piece off. "And pro tip—don't *ask* anyone for anything in here. Just take it."

Yikes. Another prison faux pas. How on earth was I going to survive this? "Oh. Right."

"It's just..." She popped the sliver of bread into her mouth, chewing daintily with a grimace. "Some of the creeps in this place will take your manners and run with them, you know? Asking makes you weak."

My stomach gurgled, looping and churning, desperate for sustenance. "Noted."

We ate in silence for a little while. No one had offered me a utensil, but I noticed the shifter had a spoon.

"You can buy them in commissary," she said tersely when she caught me staring. "No buying privileges until after your first month. They made you give bank details, right?" My nod had her rolling her eyes, the clear one a warm dark brown. "You can only have a max of twenty dollars in your account at a time so nobody cleans out the shop, but you can expect they're already charging you rent for your stay in paradise."

Fantastic. In five years, I'd probably walk out of here with nothing—especially if someone seized Café Crowley in my absence. Hopefully—*please*—Annalise would start a search for me as soon as she realized I wasn't there. Because if I hadn't opened the café, she had to know I was either kidnapped or dead.

"First day here?" the shifter asked as I glowered at my disgusting eggs, which, after a taste test, proved to be overcooked, a little dry, and… well, exactly how I imagined greyish eggs would taste: downright terrible.

"Pretty much, yeah," I muttered, moving on to the orange juice carton. It might have been lukewarm to the touch, but after peeling the plastic lid and taking the tiniest sip, it at least tasted like fresh oranges, albeit almost *too* tangy for my liking.

"Innocent?"

I glanced across the round table at her, eyebrows shooting up. "Uh, yeah. You?"

"Figured. You've got the look." She popped another miniscule piece in her mouth, delicate and deliberate in the way she ate this crap. "They said I trafficked kids." Her eyes watered, and she busied herself with her muffin, sniffling. "Because apparently the only reason for a rabbit shifter to have so many kids in their home is because I, I dunno, trafficked them in." She looked up helplessly, her lower lip trembling, and it was then I noted the faint rings around her eyes. Not sleeping all that well in here either. Another sniffle prompted her to swipe the back of her hand under her nose, and she shrugged. "I just… We have a lot of kids."

Rabbit shifter with a whole gaggle of kids? Yeah, that checked out. Many shifters reflected their animal counterparts in their everyday lives, and rabbits were said to have a boatload of offspring. Rabbit *shifters*, meanwhile, were rumored to have harems, usually consisting of a single female and multiple males. As I did a quick sweep of the pretty shifter across from me, I wondered just how many husbands she had waiting for her on the outside—and just how many kids was *a lot*. She didn't look much older than me, and at twenty-nine, I was still in the "thank the gods I'm not pregnant" phase. Thank *you,* magically brewed birth control. The stuff lasted a whole year when done correctly, and despite my abysmal love life, I still had needs—needs that I scratched every few months to mediocre results.

No babies yet.

But the shifter across from me looked like it *killed* her not to have her babies by her side. Her whole face had fallen, and she picked miserably at her muffin in silence. My heart almost broke for her, but I swallowed hard and steeled myself. After all, this was *prison*. Innocent as she looked, nice as she sounded, this rabbit shifter could be a psychopath. Maybe that was why no one was sitting with her.

"I… I'm sorry," I said at last. While I wasn't about to accept *everything* that came out of her mouth, she'd have to be an A-list actress to pull off the pain in her eyes right now. Well. Eye. "That's so awful—to be a mom accused of that." Her slight nod and a much louder sniffle tugged at my heartstrings, and I cleared my throat, pushing through. "They said I… sold love potions to humans."

She snorted, blinking back what looked like a sudden rush of tears. "Oh. Wow. That's embarrassing. Don't go around telling people that if you want any sort of reputation in here."

"I'm sure I can jazz it up," I mused, a barely there grin stretching across my lips for the first time since I'd arrived as she chuckled. "I'm Katja."

"Willow," she offered with a bob of her head. I still wasn't sure about the policies on physical contact in here, but I figured neither of us wanted to attract a guard's attention by shaking hands. Willow stabbed her spoon at her eggs, her little half-smile faltering before she went back to picking at her English muffin. "I wish they had, like, a speck of green on here."

"I bet it'd be wilted."

We swapped smirks again; nothing bonded two complete strangers like complaining about the same horrible thing. As the breakfast chatter rose, all the cellblocks fed and seated, we finished the rest of our meal in silence. At one point, it seemed like a super in a grey jumpsuit was about to make a move and claim a stool at our table, but when we both glanced his way, he scuttled off and eventually ate standing up near one of the guards. Willow rolled her eyes as she ripped open her orange juice carton, watching him with a scowl.

"*That* will get you punched. Don't hesitate. He should know better."

"Speaking of, uhm, knowing..." I pushed my tray to the side, officially *done* with the scrambled eggs and their grey tinge. If you picked off the burnt bits, the plain muffin wasn't half bad, and even though I still tasted the metallic tang with every swig of juice, at least the sugar would give me a boost for an hour or two. "You can totally say no, but... do you know anything about the supers in my cellblock?"

"They opened your block just after mine came close to capacity, so I know a bit." Chin propped up on her fist, Willow pushed her untouched eggs around her plate with a sigh. "Anyone in particular?"

My mind flashed immediately to Elijah and Rafe. Two men with ridiculously sculpted bodies, obvious from the way their jumpsuits stretched across strong chests and taut arms and thick thighs. Elijah was broader than his vampire counterpart, the sunrise to Rafe's sunset with a head full of sandy-gold waves that probably curled when they were long enough. Tanned skin. Caramel eyes. Worn hands, like he really *worked* with them outside of this place.

All that from a fleeting introduction yesterday. I had a feeling he stuck with me because not only was he handsome, but that huge shifter was like sunshine. Warm and *alive*, a little reminder that there was a big wide world out there. Rafe, meanwhile, had the whole gorgeous, brooding vampire thing going for him. Sharp jawline. Intense eyes. Black hair, brows, and stubble. Pale, but not in a sickly way. Like moonlight. The sun and the moon—Elijah and Rafe.

I blinked a few times when I realized Willow had been staring at me for… well, however long I'd been daydreaming about a pair of inmates—possible *criminals*. Yeesh. Not a good look on my part.

"Uh, no, no one in particular," I babbled, cheeks hot and chest tight under Willow's scrutiny. "All of them, I guess. I'm just not really sure what I'm in for…"

She studied me a few beats longer, the weight of her clouded eye pinned squarely on me more unnerving than I cared to admit. However, after a blink, it seemed like I'd passed the test, and she nodded. "Right, okay."

I bit the insides of my cheeks, belly looping. Had she just spotted a weakness? A chink in my armor? Something told me I'd need to keep my physical attraction for Elijah and Rafe—and maybe my connection to *anyone* in here, including Willow—under wraps. No sense in giving any of the real criminals something to manipulate, and besides, I wasn't here for *connection*. It was pathetic to get swept up in a pair of muscly male bodies and breathtakingly gruff good looks anyway, because just about every super out there was hot. It gave us an edge over humanity—and I ought to be used to it by now. There were attractive guys aplenty in my community; Elijah and Rafe were just two other smoke shows in a sea of smoke shows.

Time to let them go. *Now*.

"Cellblock C is pretty quiet from what I hear," Willow remarked, back to pushing her eggs around. "Deimos, that demon, apparently collected souls too early on the deals he made... It's a crime in Hell too, so I bet he's happier to be here than down there again. He smuggles cigarettes in through one of the guards, both the magic and human kind, and rumor has it he's trying to get into harder stuff."

Perfect—just what we needed. High shifters and supers, snorting wolfsbane and hotboxing the already stuffy cellblocks. Although Willow merely glanced his way, I turned fully around to scope out Deimos. Surrounded by his Cellblock C posse, he appeared to be engaged in a salacious conversation with some dark-haired beauty I'd never seen before—vampire, given her jumpsuit, her straight black hair thick and glossy as it spilled over her shoulder. She leaned over him, murmuring in his ear, and the second his black gaze started to slip my way, I gave him my back.

"And the vampire he's talking to?"

Willow scoffed. "She's queen bee of my cellblock—Anne."

"Ah."

"She thinks she's *the* Anne Boleyn—and the one they executed was a fraud."

Well. My eyebrows shot up. That was... unexpected. Willow smirked and nodded.

"Yeah, total psycho. Steer clear if you can."

I risked a more subtle peek over my shoulder and found both Deimos and Anne staring back. Anne's red mouth stretched into a predatory smile, like a great white scenting a drop of blood in the ocean, and Deimos blew me a kiss. I shuddered, hating to turn my back on the heavily tattooed demon, scenes of torture and gore inked along his arms and all the way up his neck, but I refused to make eye contact for longer than necessary.

"I don't know why she's got everyone under her thumb," Willow carried on. She'd dropped her voice and leaned in closer, as if worried our conversation had carried, but she didn't *sound* all that concerned about being overheard. I mean, she certainly looked calmer than I felt, my insides a jumbled mess, but maybe that kind of confidence would come with time. The rabbit shifter shrugged. "But all I know is that she screws one of our guards regularly and has an actual mattress in her cell, not just the cot cover we all have, so there's that."

"Right." No surprise sex was a currency in a co-ed prison. "And the..." *Elijah and Rafe.* I downed the rest of my juice, then set the empty carton on my tray. "And the rest of my block?"

"The maenad in the grey is also nuts... Terrible temper," Willow told me. "Gets put in solitary all the time for her tantrums. The shifters who trail after Deimos like puppies seem like nonstarters. Just a bunch of followers, you know? That warlock in your block tried to feel me up during work duty a few months back and I broke his nose, so naturally they put *me* in solitary."

Fire sparked in my gut, infuriated *for* her. "*What?*"

"Prison politics blow, girl... Get used to it." Done with her breakfast, she also nudged her tray aside, most of the food untouched. "Your other two aren't bad—the dragon and the vampire. Elijah's an alpha. We can all feel it, but he keeps to himself, which I guess isn't surprising."

I forced an air of nonchalance, even when my heart soared at the thought of finally getting some details on him. "Why not?"

"Dragons usually aren't that big on clans or packs or anything. Pretty territorial, too, from what I've heard through the shifter grapevine."

"Oh, yeah, duh." I scratched at the back of my neck, hoping to detract from the warmth blossoming in my cheeks. What the *hell*, body? *Get it together*. "I should have guessed as much."

"His vampire friend was in our cellblock for like an hour

when he first arrived, then Queen Anne pitched a fit—wouldn't share her space with another vampire." Gazing over my shoulder, Willow's eyes tracked someone on the go, slowly drifting toward the side of the huge, noisy dining hall. "I don't know much about him either, to be honest. Those two are pretty quiet. Stay out of the shit. Don't leer. Seem decent... Probably both innocent too. You'll start to notice the difference the more you get to know the, uh, players in this game."

"What even *is* this place?" I muttered, more to myself than anything, but Willow's heightened hearing must have kicked in, because she snorted and leaned back with a shake of her head.

"If you ever figure it out, feel free to share, because *I've* never heard of a prison for supers, and this place runs like they took a page out of some TV drama, you know?"

At least I wasn't the only one totally thrown by the idea of not only a supernatural prison, but a prison that held all kinds of shifters and supernatural beings in one place. I might not have blinked twice if all the American covens got together and decided to open an institute to deal with the really shitty witches out there, but this? This was unorthodox—and, frankly, unheard of.

And the fact that innocent people like me—and Willow, potentially—were just thrown in here to rot, clueless and afraid, made me want to explode.

Only I couldn't.

Because for the first time in my life, I had no magic. A whole arsenal of spells locked in my brain, from the good to the bad to the you-*never*-use-this, and I was just... stuck.

Tears burned my eyes, but I blinked them back and looked up, focusing on the fake lighting, on the aggressive fluorescent glow, so I could *stop* thinking about anything else—just for a few minutes.

At least there were potential allies in my corner. If Willow was telling the truth, then maybe I could count on Elijah and Rafe for something more than being cellblock eye candy. Silver lining, I suppose.

That, and I now had a cafeteria buddy if Willow wasn't a secret sociopath just searching for ways to manipulate me.

Unfortunately, as the alarms tolled and guards started barking for their cellblocks to get up and ship out, I was hit with a change of heart, indecision chipping away at me. No allies. No friends. They were all liabilities in here, right? Nor could I take anything *anyone* said at face value. As I joined the line for Cellblock C at the door we entered from, loitering behind maenad Constance and her bright pink hair as she heckled one of the cafeteria guards, I absorbed everything Willow had told me with a grain of salt. I'd judge Rafe and Elijah for myself, and if they *were* good guys, then great. Two less jerks to worry about in the place where I had to sleep.

I just preferred to escape this hellhole by myself—if only to ensure I didn't owe anyone a damn thing.

Because in Xargi Penitentiary, I had a feeling any deal struck came with a price you could never, ever pay.

6

ELIJAH

Shockingly, showering was one of the few activities in this shithole that made you feel normal—like a free man, not a caged animal.

But only if you faced the wall, crouching slightly under the tepid spray, and kept your back to the warlock fucks loitering a few feet away.

And only *if* you didn't pay too much attention to the gunk between the grout, the stalls in need of a serious deep clean.

Oh, and never mind that you were wearing ridiculous flimsy shoes that you bought in commissary, and that if you dared step onto the brown tile *without* them, you'd probably catch a foot fungus unlike any the world had ever seen.

Still. It was peaceful, in a way. Quiet. We were permitted to use the Cellblock C shower room every other day. The ordeal started two hours before breakfast: woken by a shrill alarm, inmates were required to stand in front of their cell doors, bleary-eyed and half-asleep, while two of our three permanent guards led inmates in pairs out for a brisk shower. If you didn't have soap, couldn't afford it, someone had stolen it from your cell—too fucking bad. Just stand under the terrible water pressure and soak it all in for five minutes.

Katja wouldn't have soap yet. Only halfway through her first week in the scummiest place on Earth, she had no buying privileges. No funds in her account—whatever the penitentiary wasn't siphoning from her already, anyway—and no access to the prison shop. Fortunately, she smelled fucking fantastic no matter what. Dirty. Clean. A little sweaty... Her body odor was intoxicating as hell, always rousing my inner dragon and getting him all riled up with just a whiff. Four days on and you'd think we would have adjusted to her presence, especially with Rafe digging his claws into my arm anytime I fixated on my mate, but nope. Seeing her now was like seeing her for the first time—*every* time.

A feeling I loved *and* loathed. No one had ever had this much power over me before, such sway. Not a human, not a super, and *never* another shifter. I'd spent centuries learning to control the beast within. My inner dragon and I—we operated on the same page, always. His moods were my moods and vice versa. We thought as one, rarely quarreled, and navigated this world as a team.

But around her, he was a beast and I was just a man, driven by lust and need and a desire to protect and *hoard* unlike anything I had ever experienced. Hoarding came with the dragon territory, and I usually exhausted that urge through my jewelry business. In Xargi, one of my workplace assignments was the smithy, forced to forge weapons and trinkets in front of a fire for hours. In the last six months, that had been enough.

No longer.

After all, I wasn't allowed to *keep* anything I made, wasn't permitted to squirrel it away in an underground safe like I did back home. Now that my fated mate had entered the scene, it was chaos. Unbridled, unfettered, absolute *chaos*.

And it had only been four fucking days.

I'd lose it by seven.

"Greystone—move your ass."

I hopped to, nudging off the wall between my cell and Helen's, headed for guard Cooper with a scowl. The fucker liked to flick lit matches at any poor bastard within range when he smoked in here, and it took everything in my power to not ram the pack of cigarettes he always carried down his throat. Beyond that, he was a sleezy warlock, one of many who had taken up Constance's offer for head, which meant there was always the chance he had allied himself with Deimos.

Phillips, the other guard escorting inmates to the showers this morning, was still gone with his female charge, and as I headed for the main door and an awaiting Cooper, who looked bored out of his skull, a quick perusal of those left waiting showed a distinct lack of Katja.

My inner dragon rumbled at the thought of her naked and wet, close enough to *touch*.

Simmer down, you fuck. There's a wall between us.

So, not quite close enough to touch, unfortunately. One of the few places not crafted entirely of dusty stone blocks, each cellblock had their own shower area. Much like a gym or a school, the tiled room had a metal showerhead jutting out from the wall—just the one. No partitions for privacy. No curtains. Just a stretch of space with a lone faucet bathed in artificial light. A tiled wall separated the women's side from the men's, and while I had never peeked around the divider, I assumed their side was the same as ours: sparse and grimy.

Towel in one hand and a thinning plastic bag hanging from my fingers in the other, I followed Cooper out of the cellblock and walked the familiar path down the hall. Ten paces, turn right. Four paces. Door. Not a thrilling venture, but any chance to stretch your legs was one you had to seize. The plastic bag swung into my knee when I stilled behind Cooper, who was in the process of stabbing his wand into the keyhole—which I assumed had been enchanted to only open the doors for guards.

Or inmates who paid the guards for favors.

I'd picked up a few new soap bars from the shop last week, and the gentleman in me insisted I should have given one to Katja. Unfortunately, I tended to lose my shit around her, which meant I, like her, had kept my distance. We hadn't even had a proper conversation yet because I was such a fucking mess, but as the door swung open and humidity wafted into the corridor, I wondered if she felt as I did.

As a non-shifter, could she sense our bond? *Feel* that fate had entwined us together?

Did it frustrate her as well, the lack of self-control?

Rafe had told me she still wept each night, only quieter now, as if not wanting to disturb her neighbors.

That gutted me.

Absolutely *destroyed* me—that I couldn't be there for my mate, that she was suffering in what was practically the same room and I had to stay in my cage and do nothing about it.

"You know the drill, Greystone."

"Fuck off, Cooper," I muttered, breezing by him through the door. The divider wall greeted me a few paces in, women's area to the left, men's to the right, and I veered right, dumping my shit on the floor and undoing the top few buttons of my jumpsuit. Whoever had been in here before me left a mess, water everywhere, and without a hook to hang my towel, it was probably already wet—useless.

From day one, I'd never had a problem stripping in front of anyone. Let them look. I had nothing to hide under my prison-issued attire save for a tattoo across my back—a pair of scaly wings reminiscent of my own that stretched from top to bottom, coiled, ready for flight. Intricate and highly detailed, it had cost me a small fortune from the mage who did it. After all, permanently inking anything into a shifter's skin, flesh that healed itself in a heartbeat, was a difficult task that required a skilled practitioner to get right.

Otherwise all that expensive ink would leech out of your pores before you even peeled the bandages off.

Beyond that, my cock seemed to have no appeal for any of our wannabe alpha guards. Cooper had already forgotten me before I'd even stepped under the showerhead, my shoes paper-thin at this point. He loitered at the end of the dividing wall, leaning against the corner and peering around it. Teeth gritted, I glowered at the back of his head as I wrenched on the shower, blasted immediately with a chilly, underwhelming spray.

Seconds later, Cooper and Phillips—the latter hidden on the other side of the wall—erupted in fits of echoey laughter.

"Always nice to have a new pair of tits in this place," Cooper mused, his voice carrying. Fire ignited in my chest, a fucking inferno engulfing me from head to toe in an instant. *A new pair of tits* obviously referred to Katja. She—

They—

My inner dragon roared, his fury like a nuclear explosion, and I planted a hand on the tiled wall, a surface I vowed never to touch if I could help it, just to keep from losing my balance.

"Baby, I know you don't have soap, but you should try to clean *everything*," Phillips sneered from the other side of the divider, his nasally intonation a fucking assault—and fuel to the fire. "You need help reaching your ass?" I pushed off the wall, my vision tunneled and the edges flaring red when that piece of shit laughed again. "How about the kitty cat between your legs? Looks like you keep it groomed..."

Furious, I shifted into pure predator mode, stalking toward the fuckers in absolute silence. As soon as I was within reach, I grabbed a fistful of Cooper's blond hair and slammed his head into the corner of the divider. Blood spurted across the tile, and I tossed the guard's unconscious body aside, peeling around the wall in a flash and knocking Phillips's wand away as soon as he ripped it from his belt. Snarling, I drove an open hand to his chest, and the blow sent him stumbling back and sputtering for air.

Sure enough, there she was—my mate, *mine*—cowering beneath the showerhead. Soaked and trembling, her arms folded up to cover her chest, her back to what had seconds ago been a pair of leering guards.

This wasn't how I imagined my first time seeing her naked. In my head, there had been passion and flame and *privacy*. Not this. Never this. Never the look on her face, the fear in her eyes as she peered over her shoulder.

"Greystone, calm down," Phillips barked, hopping to his feet—nimble for a warlock who so obviously enhanced those muscles with magic. All flash, no fucking substance. I closed in on him, fuming, my inner dragon turning my insides to magma at the injustice of it all—at the very idea of two strange males ogling *our* mate. The guard's hands sparked, magic crackling in the humid air, but I just shouldered him up against the tiled wall, pools of water sloshing at our feet. His eyes widened. "Back down, inmate!"

"Have you no fucking *respect*?" I roared, the question so beyond rhetorical it was laughable. At the second shimmer of magic in the warlock's fingertips, I locked onto his throat with one hand and squeezed tight. His cheeks darkened as he slapped at my forearm, eyes like saucers.

"I-inmate," he choked, and I hoisted him off the ground so that his fucking militant boots dangled.

"If you *look* at her like that again, if you *speak* to her like that again..." I growled, my inner dragon snapping and bellowing inside so loud that I was lost to the rest of the world, unable to hear a damn thing beyond the gnashing of razor-sharp teeth and the thunder of my pounding heart. I ducked closer to Phillips, to his purpling face, his bulging eyes, his gasping mouth so that the message really hit home—so that he didn't miss a word. "I swear, James Bartholomew Phillips, I'll rip out your fucking tongue and feed it to the wolves. Then I'll come for your *eyes*, you pathetic creature, you insidious *worm*!"

More beast than man, I was lost. Done for. *Gone*. Blind with rage, I snapped my other hand around his throat, determined to throttle the life out of him, to really make him *suffer*...

"Elijah?"

Until she said my name.

Then the world came screaming back into focus. Shaking, I looked over my shoulder, needing to lock eyes with my mate, to gaze into the startling blue and find some semblance of clarity—

Something clocked me upside the head, sharp and stinging of offensive magic. I tumbled back in what felt like slow motion, unable to focus, seeing triple of Phillips as he doubled over and sucked down air at my feet, a hand to his bruised throat. As shadows replaced the red shrouding my vision, the vague, nonsensical shouts of men trickled into the scene, followed swiftly by countless boots on tile, all of it muffled...

And then finally—all of it gone.

7
RAFE

After our first week inside Xargi Penitentiary, Elijah and I made a number of rules to ensure our survival, though they all had a central theme.

Don't get thrown into solitary. Don't look at a guard funny so that they put you in solitary. Don't pick fights with other inmates. Don't slack on work duty—Elijah, not me—and don't give any bastard out there an excuse to lock you in the hole.

Because that was what solitary was: a hole. A pit in the ground, quite literally, two floors beneath the cafeteria. From what I'd heard, each hole was twelve feet deep, all twenty of them, with barred tops where guards would drop slop through for your once-a-day feeding.

Having spent the last four days in solitary, the dragon shifter *moron* across the table from me could confirm all of that was true. The holes dug into the earth. The bugs. The manhole coverings. The food that dripped down the dirt walls. The guards patrolling, stomping over your cell. One had even pissed into Elijah's pit on the third night—Phillips, of course, just to even things out. The guard Elijah had nearly throttled to death had been reassigned to a new cellblock in the wake of my friend's bathroom heroics; *everyone* knew the story within an hour of it happening, gossip carrying like wildfire through this place. Naturally, the warlock had to reassert his dominance, and now patrolling Cellblock E, he had apparently been *the* biggest gobshite out there.

Inmate beatings.

Unlawful use of magic to subdue supers who, as far as I could tell when I saw it, were just going about their business.

A lot of barking and shouting, throwing his weight around like he had a cock the size of the Empire State Building. Downright ridiculous, but hardly surprising: all the guards were petty. At least Cooper had been unconscious for most of Elijah's ranting, which meant he was still in our cellblock, totally unaware of the specifics of what happened.

Yet he bore the scar on his forehead from where Elijah had slammed it into a corner like a badge of honor. Like he had fought in an actual *war* when shifters in here had been fighting amongst themselves, against other packs or clans, for centuries.

"So, I assume that garbage doesn't seem too bad now by comparison," I mused, thrusting my chin toward Elijah's dinner tray with a smirk. Stringy green beans. Overcooked steak strips. Watery mashed potatoes. A pathetic effort, sure, but a step above licking blended sludge off a dirt wall—definitely. The dragon shot me a look, his heavy eyes the one giveaway that said he had spent the last four days suffering.

It didn't surprise me one bit that he'd been beaten every night of his stay in solitary; he had attacked *two* guards, and the goons who patrolled this place took quite the offense to that. My friend might have been physically stronger than just about anyone in here, but he was no match for eight wands and the sixteen fists and steel-toed boots that went with them. Not with the collar on, anyway. Let him shift and *then* attack—that was a fight I'd pay to watch. Rumor had it magic bounced clean off dragon scales, just like everything else.

Dark golden hair thick and noticeably greasy, Elijah stabbed his spork into his mash, then scooped a giant heaping into his mouth before the watery potatoes spilled over the sides. He'd only been back in the block an hour, spending most of it resting in his cell before we had been lined up for dinner. Not a bruise in sight. No split lips or eyebrows. No broken nose. No fingernails missing.

All of that would have healed in an instant for him, same as me.

Vampires and shifters really were the ideal targets of torture. We could suffer a *lot*, endure the unspeakable, heal up over the course of an hour or two, and then the sadist holding the whip could get right back to it.

But what didn't heal was the soul. I'd always assumed mine had gone as soon as my maker turned me, but I saw the stain of four long days and nights in solitary in Elijah's tawny gaze, in the sluggish way he moved. That would cling to him, possibly well into his afterlife. We hadn't touched on it, but I *assumed* any future heroics were out of the question after this little stint, even for the witch who was supposed to be his fated mate.

Speaking of which…

My eyebrows shot up when I spotted a familiar mop of red hair weaving through the cafeteria crowd toward us. Lovely as ever, Katja strode about a half inch taller than when she'd arrived courtesy of the standard-issue shoes that had magically appeared in her cell yesterday. They had cost me a fortune from the shop, but I just couldn't stand to see her shuffling about barefoot anymore.

Strange that she might approach Elijah and me; she usually spent her meals with the scarred rabbit shifter from Cellblock B, pointedly avoiding anyone from our block. Not that I could blame her… Everyone else was a sociopath. Still, I wasn't all that bad, and I'd spent four days alone without Elijah. While I might have soothed her that first night, Katja and I weren't exactly on casual conversation terms. If she wasn't forced to interact with anyone during mealtimes, the witch was hiding away in her cell. She hadn't been assigned a work duty yet either, which meant when everyone else was whisked off for their shifts, it was just her and me and whoever had the day off left in the block. Bit awkward, both of us knowing the other was there, *literally* right next door, and not doing a damn thing about it.

Shockingly, tonight she strode right up to our table, white-knuckling her plastic tray, shoulders back and chin lifted. Elijah straightened as soon as he caught her scent, nostrils flared, though he scoped the dining hall with less intensity now than when she'd first arrived.

Katja stopped at our table, practically right on top of it, loitering by the vacant stools, me and Elijah seated opposite each other. She cast me a fleeting glance, her cheeks pink, before focusing solely on Elijah. His inner dragon must have *loved* that. The man, however, just stared back, exhausted but alive.

Rolling the empty glass blood vial between my hands, I waited for *something* to happen. Anything. What I got was a whole load of staring, the pair locked in each other's gazes like the rest of this shithole had disappeared. My eyebrows shot up. *Fuck* me, fated mates had to be draining. I'd never been happier to be a vampire than right this second. You would never catch a vampire going all googly-eyed over a mate. *Never*.

Still, she had the loveliest mouth—supple lips that were a lush rouge-pink, always slightly downturned and sultry, fetching even without a speck of makeup. Her lower lip suddenly quivered, snagging *my* attention with more ease than I cared to admit, and then she cleared her throat, rolling her shoulders back.

"I didn't ask you to protect me," Katja remarked, calm and firm, oddly self-assured for someone who still cried herself to sleep after lights-out. Elijah set his spork aside and smoothed his hands down his thighs beneath the table, wiping them clean, then gave her a one-shouldered shrug.

"You didn't have to."

The pair descended into silence again, just staring at each other, unflinching and unblinking and Jesus *Christ* how dreadfully dull. I ought to feel like the world's biggest third wheel, but I didn't. In fact, despite my usual aversion to most social situations, especially when supernatural dynamics came into play, I felt oddly at home. Like this was where I was supposed to be, watching the two of them sort out their nonsense, communicating without saying a word—waiting for it to be over.

Strange.

Strange that the ease I felt with whatever the hell *this* was didn't bother me. Smirking, I tapped the glass tube on the table, the red smear pooling in the bottom all that was left of my paltry supper.

"So, you going to sit anytime soon?" I gestured to one of the many empty metal stools around our table. "Or just continue to stare? I'm fine either way, but—"

Katja turned on her heel and left without a word. I snorted, watching her go, wondering if she could feel my gaze burning holes into her back—into the barely there sway of her ass beneath her slouchy purple jumpsuit.

"Elijah—"

"Shut up, Rafe."

My teasing grin faltered. I hadn't planned on giving him too much shit for what he'd done in the showers. Firstly, he couldn't help himself. Defending his mate was a shifter's prime objective, hardcoded into his DNA. Secondly, solitary had done a spectacular job of chewing him up and spitting him out already. I just... I wanted to poke fun at what had just happened like *he* always poked fun at me, but it seemed the tides had turned. Back to stabbing at his watery mash, Elijah had soured, and now *I* was the one waiting for *his* mood to lift.

Bizarre, being on the other side of our usual dynamic.

"Just... shut up," he muttered, spearing a hand through his greasy locks, in desperate need of a wash—we had both been politely ignoring the solitary stank since he'd come back. The dragon then sighed, his shoulders unusually rounded. "I know what I did, and I'd do it again." His weary eyes snapped to mine, a hint of fire shimmering like copper in his irises. "I don't really have a choice anymore."

And that might get you killed, old friend. I instantly softened, no longer in the mood to poke and prod. Instead, I set my blood vial aside, saving that little droplet until the very last moment before we had to go back to the block.

"I know," I told him quietly. "I've got your back, Elijah... I've got *both* your backs."

Our eyes locked, and he needn't say a damn thing for me to know he was grateful for my support. After all, if Elijah ran to Katja's defense every time someone heckled her in here, he'd spend the rest of his sentence in solitary. I, on the other hand, could smoothly interject as needed without causing a dramatic scene. He needed me—they both did.

My eyebrows crept up the longer we locked eyes. Honestly, shifters were so much effort sometimes. Unfettered eye contact was a sign of trust within the pack and a dangerous challenge to outsiders, but I'd had about enough with the subtle body language in lieu of actual conversation for the evening.

"So, we gonna kiss now, or—"

Elijah flicked a bit of potato at me, chuckling, and then went back to his food. I, meanwhile, wiped the smear of mash from my jumpsuit with a scowl, hating to have the smell linger longer than necessary. Out of the corner of my eye, as I scratched potato out of the fibers, a flash of red caught my attention again. Katja had found her little rabbit friend, and she sat with her back to us as the shifter chatted away.

I didn't ask you to protect me.

I rather liked that—her setting the tone for their relationship, putting her foot down on Elijah's over-the-top alpha protectiveness. Perhaps I'd misjudged her. Perhaps this gorgeous witch had a backbone after all…

And at the end of the day, maybe she wouldn't need either of us to survive this place.

Only time would tell.

8

KATJA

"Fox?"

I was off like a shot, leaping from my cot and sprinting all three strides to my open cell door. At noon on a weekday—not that it really seemed to matter, weekday or weekend—the block was quiet, almost everyone but Rafe and me dispersed around the grounds for their assigned prison jobs. I mean, that bird shifter Helen also had the day off from kitchen duty, but we hadn't exchanged one word since I woke up in this hellhole—that wasn't about to change anytime soon.

Out of habit, I glanced toward the vampire's dark cell beside mine as soon as I stepped outside; I couldn't even begin to fathom what torture each day was for him in here, sunlight crashing through all the other cells and spilling across the common area. Vampires literally burned to a crisp in sunshine, and his only protection during the daytime hours was the same dank cell we all despised.

And he was stuck in there, hiding.

Waiting for sunset—waiting for Elijah to come back so someone would help him through the shadows.

Nearly two weeks into my miserable forced stay in what I

assumed was the world's first supernatural prison, I had decided to let him be during the day. Yeah, it was kind of awkward, both of us acutely aware of each other on opposite sides of the same wall, but vampires were nocturnal by nature. If he needed to sleep—because they sure weren't feeding vamps enough to sustain themselves—then I didn't want to keep him up with small talk or nervous babbling.

Today was no different. He'd been in his cell since the others left for work, silent in the pitch-black cavern, and I'd been in mine, sitting in the sunshine, picking at my nails, trying to read one of the books I'd nabbed from the library cart but completely and utterly unable to focus on the words. You know. Just business as usual until two hours before dinner when the rest of the block returned.

Only now there was Thompson, calling my name.

"You ready for something different?" he asked, the one guard in that scary black uniform who wasn't a complete asshole. Sure, he was guilty of joining in on the snide conversations if the other guards were around. I had seen him take an inmate's food away for mouthing off, then dump the food on the ground seconds later and make the shifter in question lick it up. So, *yes*, he had the capacity to be a dick, but in my limited experience, he sucked the least of the six guards on Cellblock C's rotation. Tall, square-jawed, freckled, olive-skinned—a good-looking warlock with a wedding ring tan who had the decency to turn his back on me in the shower.

And that made him kind of okay in my books.

"What do you mean?" I asked, mindful to keep my tone subdued—docile. Don't make waves. Don't draw attention to yourself. *Survive*. Three rules that I was still trying to live by, because as far as I could tell, there was no escape from Xargi.

Especially with this collar on.

"You've got a work assignment," he told me, the edges of

his mouth quirking when my eyes widened. "Warden opened an in-house bakery a few months back, and it's finally staffed. You want to roll out dough for a few hours?"

"Oh, gods, *yes*." I started toward him, then immediately planted my feet when his hand twitched for the wand on his belt. Six inches, white-washed cedar—curved handle with ornate carvings on the grip. Ugh. I missed my wand so much.

I missed Tully more.

Did Thompson have a familiar?

I'd been desperate to ask, desperate to *try* to form a connection with the warlocks running this place, but nothing about their demeanor screamed friendly. Not the black uniform or the steel-toed boots or the grim expressions—and definitely not the way they indiscriminately tormented inmates. In here, it didn't matter that we were both from the same supernatural community. I was lesser because I was, supposedly, a criminal, and Thompson would reach for his wand every time I made the mistake of moving too fast—of forgetting myself.

"Sorry," I muttered, hands twined behind my back, palms sweaty. "Sorry, I... Yes, I'd love to knead dough."

Anything was better than here, than a cellblock with a demon who looked at me like he wanted to hurt me. Hell, he'd probably enjoy it. Elijah had cemented Deimos's interest in me that first day by making a scene, and the demon hadn't let me forget it. Always watching, always smirking, always making lewd gestures to his crotch and seductive—by his definition only—flicks of his tongue in my direction...

Ugh.

"You'll make ten cents an hour," Thompson remarked as we drifted toward the cellblock door, and I brightened at the thought.

"Does that mean my commissary account is open?"

"You think you can buy anything with today's whopping forty cents?"

"I mean, no, but—"

"Yeah," he said, throwing a grin over his shoulder as he unbolted the door and motioned for me to walk through, "your account is officially active. Congrats, Fox."

"Thanks." I ducked my chin and peered up at him through my lashes in passing. While I wasn't about to let any guard touch me, some seemed to get off on the submissive female thing—and I could at least play the part a little if it meant they wouldn't see me as a threat.

As soon as Thompson sealed the door tight behind us with a fastening charm, I followed him down familiar corridors, surrounded by cinder blocks and artificial light, until finally we ventured into hallways I'd never seen before. This place was a maze; built like an old stone fort, you'd think it would be straightforward, but nope. It was all winding and weaving and up and down, dead silence except for the odd scream or cackle from behind another magically sealed door.

We ended up one floor underground, and I smelled the bread long before we reached the bakery, fresh and crisp, a hint of normalcy as I still struggled to find my sea legs fourteen days after I had woken up in the interrogation room. No lawyer had come calling. I'd never had a trial. I was just —here.

But if I could spend the day in a bakery, kneading and baking and blending dry ingredients like I was back home over my own cauldron making my own potions, that might help a little.

Help my mental health, anyway.

Fleetingly.

Thompson motioned me through an open doorway with a toss of his head, and once inside, I found myself in a much more cramped workspace than I'd anticipated. What hit me first was the heat, six old-school ovens burning to my left. Sweat gathered at the nape of my neck, made worse by the fact that I hadn't had anything to tie my hair back with in almost two weeks. What I wouldn't do for a hair elastic and a pair of underwear; maybe commissary had something utilitarian I could spring for once I had enough money.

Illuminated by more dull artificial lighting and the tiniest of slits open to the outside world, the bakery was hot and claustrophobic, the ceiling low. Haphazardly built, almost like a badger burrow, the familiar stonework didn't extend to the dirt ceiling, from which thin roots hung, reaching for us. Huge metal towers on wheels cloistered together dead ahead, square with slots to fit baking trays into. Every table in sight —wood, for the first time, not metal—had a dusting of flour over its top.

Small and tight and dusty and earthly and *hot* as balls…

But comforting. In a way, it reminded me of the back of the café on a summer's day.

My eyes prickled with tears I refused to let fall; I had shed enough sorrow in this place already and I wasn't even through the first month yet.

"Greystone." Thompson's bark made me flinch, and I all but wilted beside him when a familiar face emerged from behind the ovens. Elijah Greystone, towering dragon shifter —overprotective hottie who made me feel… things.

His rugged face glistened with sweat, which he wiped dry on his sleeve, and his yellowing apron had seen better days, splashed with flour and whatever made those damp, dark smears.

"New recruit," Thompson announced, nudging me deeper into the bakery with a stabby finger between my shoulder blades. "Show her the ropes."

"The ropes I learned this morning?" Elijah growled back,

his arms folded, biceps deliciously prominent, the dragon very obviously *not* looking at me, refusing to meet my eye. We hadn't spoken since our encounter in the cafeteria last week; I wasn't proud of my behavior, not after what he had probably been through in solitary, but it had happened. No taking it back.

"Yeah, you should be a goddamn bread master by now." Thompson took a sharper tone with the shifter than he ever did me, scowling, his hand resting loose over his wand. No surprise there: Elijah had been on every guard's shit-list since that day in the shower.

All because of me.

Because of what he did for me.

Pummeling those pervs—it had been satisfying and terrifying and totally unnecessary.

And I'd been going out of my way to avoid him since. Anytime we were around each other, something *happened*. Gross men acted like gross men. Elijah would react. Inmates would stare—and *someone* would take an interest in me, probably just to rile him up.

That couldn't become our *thing*.

I refused to be on anyone else's radar because of a dragon shifter who lacked self-control.

A dragon shifter who, whenever he did lock eyes with me, made me taste… fire.

Not that I'd ever tasted fire before, but heat burned in my chest, scorched up my throat. Distinct, the scent of campfire smoke tickling my nostrils, reminiscent of days spent at our old family cottage, the nostalgia both comforting and heartbreaking. Still, it coaxed me to be brave, to spit those flames at every pushy jerk who made eyes at me and watch while they burned.

Especially when it sparked between my thighs, insistent

and brilliant and *strong*. Almost impossible to ignore and getting worse with every encounter.

I'd never met a dragon shifter before, but they couldn't *all* make me feel like a walking inferno.

Right?

Either way, I wasn't thrilled about the fact that anyone at Xargi could physically influence me, and, in no mood to spend the day with him, I quickly scanned the space for another jumpsuit.

Only to come up empty. Nobody here but us and Thompson—then another guard seated next to the door, on his phone, wand on his lap. I'd never seen him before, but he waved distractedly when Thompson nodded on the way out, and seconds later, it was just me and Elijah and this baby-faced warlock swiping through that supernatural dating app feed...

What was it again?

Oh. Right. *Cinder*.

Fantastic.

Better than spending the day in my cell, I guess, but that wasn't exactly a high threshold to beat.

For all my tough-girl inner monologues, standing in front of Elijah now made me feel awkward and small. I only made it up to his shoulders, and when he sighed, I got the distinct feeling he wasn't thrilled about having me in here either.

"Come on..." He breezed by, bringing with him the scent of brimstone and raw, untamed masculinity. My belly looped and my pussy pulsed with interest. Not good. Not good at all. The dragon cast me a sidelong glance as he passed, headed away from the ovens and toward a cluster of flour-dusted tables. "We have a million rolls to prep."

Swallowing thickly, I padded after him, my shoes silent to me but probably swishing along like cannon fire to a shifter. I wasn't sure where the nondescript white slip-ons had come from, but one evening they were just *there,* waiting for me at the end of my bed. Although a touch too big, anything was better than navigating the prison barefoot, and days later, with my roughened feet practically singing, I still had no clue who to thank for the gift.

Which bothered me.

Because—now I was in someone's debt.

And I hoped to all that was good in this world that it wasn't Deimos.

Elijah stopped at one of the larger prep tables, a mountain of dough piled high in front of him, along with a stack of metal baking trays. He grabbed the top one and set it down slightly off to the left of him, and I positioned myself around the table's corner, cheeks hot, unsure where to look.

I'd seen gorgeous men in the supernatural world for years, but Elijah exceeded them tenfold. This shifter *had* to be Apollo—he was everything the legends promised, a golden god, youthful and handsome and dripping with vitality.

"So, you just roll them out to about yea big," he told me, snatching a clump from Dough Mountain and rolling it between his palms. Fifteen seconds later, he had a perfectly round little sphere roughly the size of a golf ball, made even smaller by the sheer heft of his hand. "Twenty to a tray. Full trays go in the pantry over there." He pointed to a metal door embedded in the wall, shrouded in shadow. "They'll proof overnight, then tomorrow we bake them." His chocolate-brown gaze slid my way, and he arched a golden brow. "Questions?"

I shook my head, not trusting myself to talk around him yet—not with my every cell utterly drawn to him.

Not when he set me on fire with nothing at all.

Definitely getting worse. Worse every day, and I feared the more I fought it, the worse it would get.

Would I spontaneously combust? Was he doing this *to* me, even with that leather band around his neck?

Was I cursed?

Would I—

"I swear I'm not stalking you," Elijah muttered, placing his ball on the baking tray between us before going for the doughy mountain again. "I didn't know you'd be assigned here."

Obviously he knew I'd been avoiding him; I hadn't exactly been subtle. With a quick glance his way, I went for the massive pile myself, ripping off a substantial enough chunk of soft, sticky dough to make a few balls before needing to go back for more.

"This is Rafe's detail anyway," he carried on as he set his second perfect sphere on the tray, "but vamps can't work during the day because no one fucking accommodates for them here now that the weather's turned, so someone else has to pick up the slack..." His jaw gritted, muscles briefly dancing. "Otherwise the vampire gets punished. So, I... I... Normally I'm in the metal shop."

Guilt's icy cold fingers plucked at my heartstrings, and I swallowed thickly, unsure *why* I felt like this—because I shouldn't. It shouldn't matter that I'd been purposefully and obviously distancing myself from a dragon who, from what I'd seen, was a good guy. It shouldn't *matter* that we shared some weird connection, that he set me on fire just by standing close. I didn't owe him anything. I didn't owe him my feelings. Elijah Greystone was a stranger. Fact.

So... Why the guilt?

I shook my head, more at myself than anything, and peeled off a hunk of dough from my little pile. Maybe I felt shitty because I'd misjudged him; who else would voluntarily take on another work assignment in *prison*? It was sweet that he stood in Rafe's place—kind, really.

And apparently, he was better at making dough balls than me.

So not the typical alpha shifter we all heard about.

"I'm sorry," I murmured, peeling the plucky, tacky dough from my fingers and dipping them into the little bowl of flour. A good coating should stop things from sticking—I knew that much, at least.

"What?"

"For how I reacted to you," I told him, distracted enough by the dough, by trying to match the bit in my hands to his so that the buns would all be uniform, that I didn't completely notice what had just fallen off the tip of my tongue. "In the..." When I finally did, my mouth dried up, and suddenly the dough between my palms looked more like a flattened penny than a ball. Great. A quick peek his way showed that I'd caught his attention, and I cleared my throat, the fire in my belly exploding across my cheeks. "That day in the shower was mortifying and scary and I just—"

"It's okay," Elijah said gruffly, adding a third *and* fourth ball to the tray, miles ahead of me already. "I get it."

"No." I pursed my lips, some of that curious fire sharpening to frustration. "I don't think you do."

Elijah's hands stilled, and out of the corner of my eye, I noticed him frowning. Yeah, hadn't expected *that*, huh? While I so appreciated him standing up for me in front of Cooper and Phillips, it just wasn't that simple. I glanced over my shoulder and found the guard studying us, the glare from his phone giving off an unattractive underlighting that made it look like he had a serious double chin. Clamping down on the inside of my cheek, I hurriedly formed a dough ball, nowhere near as neat and smooth as Elijah's, and plopped it on the tray just to look busy.

"You made people *look* at me," I insisted under my breath, knowing that despite the ever-present grumble of the ovens across the room, the spark and hiss of their flames, Elijah could hear every last word. "Deimos, the guards... I'm a woman in a co-ed prison. I'm a witch surrounded by criminals and strangers, and I don't have my magic or my wand or my familiar." My throat tightened, breath catching, just the thought of Tully—where he was, what had happened to him, was he still *mine*—throwing me for a loop. But I steeled myself, getting better at shaking off the panic every day I was stuck in here; show no weakness, not even to Elijah. Just another one of the new rules I had to live by. "Look, I want to fly under the radar. I don't belong here, and I just want to find a way out, and you drawing attention to—"

Elijah's snort cut me off, and I found him grinning at me with dead eyes.

"Find a way out?" he said, eyebrows shooting up, hands rolling dough like they were on autopilot. "Good luck with that. Have you seen the ward?"

My cheeks warmed again, and I dropped my second dough ball a little too hard onto the tray between us. Before I could fix its flattened bottom, Elijah scooped it up and rerolled it for me.

"Through the windows, yes," I told him. The faintest rainbow shimmer stretching over this place, from the horizon to the sky and over, was a given. I'd expected wards from the second they shoved me into a cell, but as a spellcaster myself, someone who had produced a ward or two in her lifetime, I figured that was just one step to work around to freedom.

But...

Wards *were* impenetrable, and only the caster could break them. Yes, there were certain spells to weaken them, specific sigils designed by the caster that could temporarily open and close a ward like a key, and I'd heard of some witches who could dismantle them like hackers breaching computer security systems…

But I wasn't one of those witches.

So, the grin that didn't quite reach Elijah's eyes, while a touch patronizing, was warranted.

"Well, even if you somehow get outside, past the wolves and the guards with wands, you're not breaking through that ward," Elijah remarked. My heart skipped a beat, the pair of us riding an unnervingly similar train of thought. He dipped his hands in the flour bowl, then clapped them to remove the excess dust. "I heard the warden himself cast it… He's the only one who can break it, and supers here say he's incorruptible. He can't be bought—either that or the price is way, *way* too high."

Fantastic. Not that I had anything to barter with—Café Crowley did well, but I wasn't rolling in disposable millions by any means—nor had I considered making a deal with the kingpin of this hellhole, but hearing that… It was another option gone. Zip. Out of the question before I'd even really considered it. Stewing in that new and unsurprising knowledge, I fell into a dough-rolling rhythm in silence. If I focused on making my little balls as perfect as the ones Elijah so effortlessly crafted, I wouldn't wander down my mind's more depressing paths. Unfortunately, the penitentiary brought that out in you—all this time alone, locked in your cell, sequestered away from guards and other inmates, there wasn't much else to do but *think*.

Well… and work. If I was destined to be here six days a week in the sweltering heat, the dim lighting, standing beneath dead, dangling roots and next to a dragon shifter who made me *feel*, then the bakery might just be the best distraction around.

"I'm sorry, Katja."

Every inch of me lit up at the sound of my name coming

from *his* mouth, laced in a gravelly growl that made my heart sing. *Katja.* So personal. So forward. So mouthwateringly familiar. I braced myself, grabbing another chunk of dough from the mountain and hoping he couldn't see me blush.

Why did he affect me like this?

Hot guys had said my name before. It didn't matter then, and it shouldn't now—but it did. If my body reacted this way, annoyingly consistent around some gorgeous dragon clocking in at, what, six seven, maybe six eight, so tall and broad and *powerful* and—

And…

Damn it. What was the point of that thought again?

A shiver sliced through me when he glanced my way, his eyes so warm and comforting.

Remorseful, too, something I so rarely saw in supers or shifters. Snooty bunch, our kind. We almost always thought we were right, no matter the reality of the situation, and don't even get me *started* on the hierarchy. Each community thought they sat at the top, then the rest were ranked accordingly.

And not always favorably either.

"I'm sorry for drawing attention to you," he added after a beat. The hairs on the back of my neck stood on end, and I glared down at my hands when they trembled, fingers fumbling with their current dough ball. Elijah exhaled sharply and wiped a bit of flour off his cheek with his shoulder. "I know I did it… I knew it in the moment. I didn't mean to, but I just… I can't help it."

"What's that supposed to mean?"

"I think you already know."

My hands stilled, squishing my perfect ball flat again. Frankly, I *didn't* know what any of it meant—didn't understand why his mere presence influenced me. Hated the fact that he had a hold on me, so effortless in the way his body made mine react...

In the way his body almost... *controlled* mine.

Nope. Do not like.

I shook my head. "No, but—"

"Even if you don't know what it means," Elijah rumbled, "you feel it."

He faced me, still planted in place around the corner of the table, and my knees threatened to buckle under the full weight of his stare. All this time, I'd thought it was just *me* feeling like my insides were on fire; I hadn't put too much thought into wondering if the sensation was mutual. But when he reached over and nudged my hands open, touching me so briefly with his finger that it *hurt,* I saw it.

Fire.

Dragons were all fire and brimstone and ash and smoke—but I saw the flames in his eyes. Maybe this prison was driving me insane, something in the air slowly poisoning my mind, but as he plucked my warped dough ball and retreated, I *swore* an inferno danced in his gaze, turning warm dark chocolate to molten gold.

But then he blinked and looked down, focused on rolling my sad doughball between his palms until it was perfect again. Goose bumps covered me from top to bottom, and I let out a shaky breath—loving and hating every second of this interaction.

"Just know... I feel it too," Elijah murmured, pointedly avoiding my stare now that I gave it to him, my eyes wide and open for the first time in days.

"I don't understand it."

"Me neither." He pushed the tray aside and grabbed a new one, somehow having rolled out the twenty required balls despite my paltry offerings. The full tray scraped across the table, dragging flour and chips of hardened dough with it, while the new one clattered like an assault. He paused suddenly, hands gripping the edge of the table, his mouth set in a thin, harsh line. "I didn't expect a..." Slowly, his eyes lifted to mine, and he shook his head, the tightness around his mouth and in his shoulders fading. "Never mind. We can talk it over someday. Just know I'm going to look out for you in the meantime."

Amidst all the excitement, the firestorm raging inside, my lingering self-preservation protested to that. My belly somersaulted in an unpleasant way, a sick feeling cutting through everything else to the point it made me light-headed. Ahhh yes. Hello, crushing anxiety—you pesky bitch.

"I don't think—"

"And it's not because I want something," Elijah said, waving me off with a floury hand, "or I have expectations from you... I can't help it. If I don't do something, I'll explode."

"Right." I waited for him to chuckle or grin, but he seemed a little too serious for my liking. Arching an eyebrow, I rolled out my first ball for the new tray. "Figuratively."

"Yes." Finally, a glimmer of humor—in his lighter tone, in the way the corner of his mouth kicked up. "Sure." Elijah tossed his head side to side, cracking his neck, then rolled his shoulders back. Given our height differences, he had to hunch a little just to work at the same table. "Look, I'll try not to make it so fucking obvious in the future, I swear."

I set my ball on the tray. "I hear shifters are men of their word."

"When a dragon makes a vow, he'll keep it to the end of days."

And there it was again: super-serious Elijah. I didn't need or want someone making a blood pact or a binding vow for me—I just needed him to not shine a spotlight on me every time another inmate tried to ruffle my feathers. Not that I doubted his ability to protect someone if he set his mind to it. In fact, the rough tone he took, the sudden shift in his voice, was actually kind of intimidating. Add in the height and the muscle and the grit of his jaw and I wouldn't want to cross paths with him in a dark alley, wand or not.

"Well, thank you," I managed, not wanting to sound ungrateful when he sounded so sincere, "for what you did. I'm really sorry it got you put in solitary—"

"I did that to myself." Elijah shrugged, as if unfazed by a place that Willow had told me was a waking nightmare... if the rumors were to be believed, anyway. "But if you want to help me out, hang with me and Rafe." He scratched at his neck when I frowned at him, smearing dough and flour across his tanned skin. When my eyes dipped to the stain, he brushed it off with the back of his hand. "Then you look like you're part of the crew, and it isn't suspicious for crews to look out for each other in here. Nobody's forming packs or covens these days. No shifter cliques or demon gangs... It won't raise eyebrows for a witch to spend her time with a dragon and a vampire."

Of course, I understood the logic: safety in numbers and all that. I just wasn't interested in becoming part of a *crew*. If you had people, someone might try to use them against you.

But I couldn't say that—couldn't spit in the face of such a genuine offer. So I licked my lips and pretended my current dough ball was *the* most fascinating unbaked pastry I'd ever seen.

"You sure Rafe wants that—me worming into your duo?"

Elijah stilled again. "Has he given you reason to think otherwise?"

"I..." Not even a little. Rafe recited *poetry* that first night to make me stop crying. He didn't strike me as a bad guy—maybe a bit melancholy, gorgeous features always set in a judgy frown—but he and Elijah were a pair. No telling if he wanted to become a trio with a witch who might ruin that. "Er, no, not really—"

"Then there's your answer," the dragon said, sounding very much like that was that, *decided,* and back to work we both went. We filled up the second tray faster than the first, and after loading both in the pantry, we were on to the third, that mountain of dough seeming untouched—like we'd be at this for hours.

Days, even.

Elijah was good with his hands. Meticulous, careful, skilled, his fingers weathered but his work immaculate. I liked that: an alpha shifter who wasn't too macho to prep dough, who paid attention to details and did the work himself. While I hadn't met many alphas in my twenty-nine years, as I understood it, most had beta underlings to do the menial stuff for them.

"So," he started, his voice clear and booming in what had been a pensive silence for the better part of the last half hour, "what did you do, Katja Fox?"

I smirked, picking off the bits of sticky dough from between my fingers. "Isn't that a taboo question in prison, Elijah Greystone?"

Not that I had any real-world experience to back that up—just what I'd gathered from TV, honestly.

Elijah chuckled again, the whispery rasps echoing between my thighs. "Only if you did it."

"Fair." I pushed my hair over my shoulders with the backs of my hands, the bakery's heat sweltering, sweat dribbling down my neck, my back, my ass. "Apparently I sold love potions to humans."

Love potions were iffy in the witch community anyway, but it was absolutely forbidden to brew them for humans who had no idea what kind of forces they were playing with. Even the odd human ushered into the secret supernatural world knew better than to tangle with love—because the results you dreamed of were never a guarantee.

Elijah pressed a hand to his chest with a mock gasp. "My word, Miss Fox, *love* potions… How utterly *scandalous*."

"Very," I said with a roll of my eyes. "And you?"

"Don't you know that's a rude question to ask in a place like this?"

My heart plummeted. If it was only taboo to ask if the prisoner *actually* committed the crime… Had I read him wrong? Had he tricked me into believing—

"Only joking," Elijah said with a soft chuckle. He wiggled his brows at me as I scowled, then ducked out of the way when I flicked flour at him.

"*Not* funny."

"Right, right, noted." He fell straight back into his work, grabbing at Dough Mountain with both hands. "I ran the village jeweler's shop… Buying and selling pieces sort of satiates my hoarding instinct."

A dragon working in gold and diamonds? Yeah, that sounded about right.

"So, *naturally*, I've been dubbed a jewel thief," Elijah remarked dryly, tossing two perfectly round balls onto the tray. "Supposedly I swiped some huge ruby from a Russian coven… I dunno, usual nonsense." His voice dropped as he added, "Like I can't find a fucking ruby without stealing it."

I studied him for a moment, wondering how he talked about this without breaking—how he could make light of the injustice.

"How do you do it?" I pressed my lips shut tight; the question had just slipped out. Asking what an inmate had done to send them to Xargi Penitentiary may not have been rude, especially if they were guilty, but asking how they survived in here, the implication that this place didn't weigh on them as heavily as it did me, felt wrong.

"Hmm?"

But I went with it anyway. "How do you just… accept this? I want to… to… *scream* at the top of my lungs. I want to freak out and hide in a dark corner, and I want to cry and curse and hit someone as hard as I can. I want to *fight* and…" My lips wobbled, and I paused for a calming breath, emotion threatening to bubble up and boil over if I didn't. "And I feel like I can't do any of those things. You always imagine what you'd do in this situation when you have to fight and be brave, and then it happens… and I feel like a coward."

I had always thought that when faced with the worst possible circumstances, I would go down swinging—that I would be this badass heroine who took no prisoners, who knocked a guard out and stole his wand, who crept through the shadows and struck like a viper.

Xargi had shone a spotlight on reality: I wasn't a badass. I was barely a heroine. I was just a witch without her magic who cried a lot—who hadn't the courage to tell two pervy guards to screw off that day Elijah had stepped in.

Not only did I feel like a coward, but most of the time, I just felt pathetic. After the loss of my brothers, then my dad, mourning all their deaths and coming out the other side a somewhat normal, relatively stable adult, I thought I could handle anything life had to throw at me.

But…

"You're not a coward, Katja."

I closed my eyes and sucked down another deep breath. A little voice sneered that I didn't *need* his pity, but nothing about Elijah said pity.

And I couldn't explain why.

Couldn't understand why.

Again.

"I don't accept it—*this*," Elijah said roughly, smooshing the dough between his palms, then ripping it into two even pieces. "But that doesn't change anything. I can't... I can't even... They've taken away one half of me with this fucking collar. I hate it. My inner dragon hates it. I hate *them*, but I can't fight magic with might. No matter what the stories say, it doesn't work that way."

"So, you're just going to take it?" I winced: that could have been worded better. Rather than looking offended or wounded, Elijah grinned wryly down at the tray, nudging some of the dough balls farther apart.

"You got any other ideas?"

"No," I said miserably—honestly. I had approximately zero clue how to get out of this place. Sure, it wasn't the stuff of nightmares or how humans envisioned Hell, but the guards ran a tight ship and these collars limited funny business. I wasn't a player in the great political game; I had no interest in joining any of the gangs smuggling contraband and battling for power amongst trapped supers.

I was nothing here.

I *had* nothing here.

"Well, I intend to survive this shithole, no matter what it throws at me," Elijah insisted, and our eyes locked as he said, "if that means anything."

Fighting with the lump in my throat, a sudden rush of *feeling* throwing me for a loop, I nodded.

"Yeah," I croaked. Somehow, his sentiment bolstered me—gave me courage in the darkness. "It does."

With that, we got back to work, rolling dough balls in the bakery's brutal heat. Strangely unified, this dragon and I, we stood together at that table for hours and hours, until I couldn't stand anymore, my feet aching, my knees crackly, my lower back begging for relief...

But my spirit just a little stronger.

9

KATJA

"Okay, I'll deal the next hand..."

"You sure about that?"

I shot Rafe a narrowed look as I gathered the deck to me, smoothing cards across the table and organizing them into a neat pile. We had just finished our thousandth round of gin rummy, and frankly I would have killed to be back in the bakery. But work shifts only lasted so long—and stuck in the cellblock, the library cart's arrival still a few days away, there really wasn't a hell of a lot to do.

Unless you were in Deimos's posse.

Then there were games and groveling and shifting power dynamics to wade through, every day a new adventure in demonic mayhem. Fortunately, I had shifted my stance on being a part of a crew roughly a month ago.

Thirty days back to be precise.

Forty *long* ones since I'd woken up in the interrogation room, missing my skirt and my wand, terrified.

I was still terrified, but at least I had two less reasons to be afraid lately.

"Hey, we can't *all* have a vampire's dexterity," I sneered

when Rafe smirked. Across the table, Elijah watched the interaction with his chin on his fist, elbow planted on the table and a grin toying across his handsome mouth. One month after our first bakery shift together and I *still* blushed if we made extended eye contact, but no more than if Rafe and I accidentally knocked feet under the table or brushed hands on the way back to our cells.

Naturally, it was different with Rafe: he was just hot as hell. Gorgeous. Scrumptious. Beyond mouthwatering. I had a crush. Hard not to with a guy who looked like a brooding model capable of getting his hands dirty *and* reciting sonnets.

The connection wasn't visceral with my neighbor—just physical. And probably one-sided. In all the time we spent together as a threesome, Rafe catered to Elijah and me, always volunteering to step back if we were in a situation that only allowed for a pair instead of a trio.

Not that he needed to often... Besides the occasional lingering glances across the cellblock during random spot checks, Elijah and I had done a great job ignoring the fact that we felt *something*—something unnatural but familiar, unwelcome but honest—in each other's presence. He still set my body on fire. I'd never been so hot in all my life, wishing I could sleep naked at night but terrified of a guard bursting in for one stupid reason or another. It happened more times than I liked, and it was always over nothing. Hauled out of bed, we had all been forced to stand at the door for the better part of an hour while a few guards ripped our cells to pieces.

Somehow Deimos always came out of those instances smelling like roses despite being Xargi's king of contraband, his empire slowly expanding to the smaller cellblocks. He'd even offered me a place by his side—with the implication that I would be equal to Constance, which meant offering new recruits blowjobs. Flattering. My response back then was a straight-as-an-arrow middle finger, and paired with a glowering dragon shifter and his vampire bestie as backup, Deimos had gone after easier targets in the last few weeks, only occasionally tossing lewd gestures my way if the guys weren't around.

So, yeah. This was my life now. Almost every second of the day controlled by warlock guards. Two meals that seldom met standard nutritional requirements. Three to six shifts a week in the bakery, sometimes alone, sometimes with hours spent alongside Elijah, prepping dough and proofing it and baking buns so fresh and golden—buns that never made it to the inmate cafeteria. Where they disappeared to was anyone's guess. We had caught the bakery guard munching on one once, so maybe the staff quarters, but we bakery drones made enough in a day to feed a small army, worked to the bone and exhausted come the late afternoon.

Well, *I* was exhausted. Elijah had shifter resilience to fall back on, which meant he usually picked up the slack by hour nine, neither of us allowed a break at any point. Unfortunately, sometimes I had to handle the workload alone if Elijah was scheduled in the metal shop.

Those days sucked especially hard.

"You know, if you held the deck like so—"

"Piss off, Rafe," I warned in a singsong voice, fluttering my lashes at him. "I know how to shuffle a deck of cards."

The vampire's black brows shot up, the corners of his mouth twitching. "*That* remains to be seen."

I sucked in and then let out a dramatic Darth Vader-esque breath, then dropped my voice to its lowest octave. "I find your lack of faith *disturbing*."

The vampire rolled his aquamarine gaze. "Have you always been the world's biggest dork, or is it a recent development?"

"Always and forever," I remarked with a slight lift of my chin. Out of the corner of my eye, I caught Elijah's features shifting from wry amusement to outright affection. My belly looped and tightened, secretly *thrilled* with the way he watched me, but I did my best to ignore him; if I looked his way, even fleetingly, he would school his features like it had never happened.

Just as I started to deal the next hand, an alarm screamed bloody murder from the center of the cellblock's conical ceiling. Almost instantaneously, the resident afternoon guards who liked to loiter all day and do absolutely *nothing* to combat Deimos's douchebaggery hopped to like they were some elite militant squad. In rushed six additional guards, the scene painfully familiar, and I tossed the deck down with a huff.

The dramatics could only mean one thing: new prisoner incoming.

"On your feet, inmates," one of the guards bellowed—a new warlock who I'd seen around the halls, stalking to and fro like he was lording over the scum of the supernatural world's underbelly. Bald head, steely stare, a mouth that never smiled; the guy was a little much, even for Xargi. Wand at the ready, he leveled it at all nine of us, jerking from one inmate to the next. "At your posts!"

"Small dick complex, in the flesh," Rafe mused, to which Elijah snorted. While our dragon companion meandered to the left, Rafe and I hurried right, headed to our neighboring cells together. Whether he was aware of it or not, the vampire always positioned himself between me and the other inmates, his hand hovering over my lower back. After weeks of the behavior, I still wasn't sure why he did it—or who he did it for.

Elijah? The two were close, obvious friends who had each other's backs. Elijah and I had some weird innate connection that, while neither of us had explored, had probably been shared with Rafe at some point.

Or did he do it for *me*? Was it purposeful or just instinctual for a man born almost six centuries ago to protect a defenseless woman?

And if it was the latter, should I be insulted?

I still couldn't get a good read on him despite our bedtime chats on the nights when neither of us could nod off. We would lie together on the floor, whispering through the grimy, dusty, filthy little mousehole that connected our cells, talking about nothing important—and nothing to do with our old lives. Elijah and I had discussed the past here and there, but with Rafe, the conversation erred toward safe subjects.

Maybe he, like me, found talk of the outside world, of our lives *before*, depressing.

Elijah had a knack for drawing it out of me without either of us realizing, the conversation fluid and deep. With Rafe, sometimes I was *too* aware, and if I could help it, I steered clear of conversation topics that would bum us both out.

Just like the day I'd first been ushered into Cellblock C, as soon as the guards had us standing beside our cells, the main door flew open, and in waltzed two processing guards dragging a new inmate between them. The alarms finally died down with his arrival, and I stood up on my toes to get a good look at him, even as my legs protested, my feet swollen and my lower back miserable after today's bakery shift.

But…

My *gods*, this guy was worth the pain.

I had never been so instantly in lust with someone before. Dressed in green, Cellblock C's newest arrival had a willowy figure, all lean limbs and elegant fingers. A dancer's body—graceful but strong. Where Elijah was bulk and muscle and *man*, this one was subtle strength, his arms taut and corded with a physicality that had me drooling like I'd never seen a gorgeous man before—like I wasn't already surrounded by them in this prison, day in and day out. Tanned skin, as if he spent all his time lolling around a yacht in the Mediterranean. Crowned by a crop of lush, thick, artfully tousled cinnamon-brown hair, the new inmate's bright green gaze flitted around the cellblock, bouncing from one super to another before pausing on Rafe, then sliding over and lingering on me.

His stare might not have set me on fire, but it certainly made my knees weak.

A sculpted jaw. Cheekbones that could cut diamonds. *Just* the right amount of scruff.

This guy was what wet dreams were made of—excluding all the bruises. The busted lip. The black eye. A dribble of dried blood under each nostril. While I recalled being manhandled during processing, I had let it happen, too shell-shocked to fight. Apparently not everyone put up with it. Apparently *some* of us had a backbone.

Gorgeous *and* brave. Nice.

As the processing guards steered McHottie toward the last empty cell in the block, one situated between Helen and Constance, I glanced Rafe's way and found him glowering at the new arrival. A soft clearing of my throat had his eyes darting to me, and I quickly mouthed, "Green jumpsuit?"

He shrugged one shoulder and mouthed back, "Dryad, elf, or fae."

Although the guards had already hauled him into his cell, no doubt giving him the same depressing tour they had offered me that first day, I didn't recall seeing any insanely pointed elf ears. Dryads were beyond rare—an endangered species at this point.

Fae, then.

Interesting.

While I had never personally met any of the fair folk before, those that traveled into our world through portals from the Otherworld, I had heard the stories. Arrogant, dangerous, suave, seductive, fae society operated outside the laws of humans and supernaturals alike. They had their own culture, their own codes, and considered themselves *way* above the rest of us. Not that I could blame them: fae possessed the innate magic of a witch, the speed of a vampire, and the durability of a shifter. They were the total supernatural package. Immortal, their courts stretched back a full millennium at least, their social mores deeply rooted in traditional monarchies. Many supernaturals considered mankind to be their lesser, but to fae, humans were no better than domesticated pets.

Man, I bet his collar was just *covered* in symbols—far more than any of ours. So much raw ability to suppress…

How in the world had they managed to catch him?

We all stood in front of our cells twiddling our thumbs for a good twenty minutes before the militant welcoming committee finally left. After Thompson gave us permission to move again, Deimos's underlings rushed to the huge table in the middle of the cellblock, claiming it before we could—like we had *ever* tried to take it from them in the first place. I, meanwhile, studied the shadowy open doorway to the fae's cell, intrigued.

"Nap before dinner?"

"Huh?" I pushed off the wall, my entire body protesting each step away from my cell—from the cot that, for once, was calling my name. We had another hour before the forced march down to the cafeteria, and from the heaviness around my eyes, the effort it took just to shuffle around the cellblock, Rafe's suggestion sounded like heaven. But nope. Not happening. Not when there was something exciting going on here for once—and I was *finally* no longer the new kid on the block. "Uh, no. I'm fine."

We ambled back to our usual table closer to Elijah's cell—and now this new fae—all the while ignoring the smug looks tossed our way by Deimos's posse. Seriously. Their table was just a table. Constance flicked her brows up at me when I accidentally caught her gaze, and I rolled my eyes—*hard*. Not that my blasé reactions mattered. They didn't care that we didn't care. It was the same crap, different day with these supers.

Only it wasn't the same day. Not anymore.

Even as Elijah joined us at the small round table, I couldn't tear my eyes from the fae's door. Something about him... Maybe it was just the thrill of seeing a primordial supernatural creature, one I'd never thought to meet. Seattle wasn't exactly crawling with fae—

"What is it?" Elijah growled, hands planted on the table, leaning over it and so utterly fixated on me that fire exploded through my veins. I pushed my hair over one shoulder to cool the back of my neck, skin suddenly scorching.

"It's nothing."

The dragon glanced toward our new cellmate's doorway with a frown, then back to me, that frown deepening, brows knit with confusion. Rafe dropped onto his usual stool with a pointed sigh.

"She thinks he's attractive," the vampire mused, gathering the abandoned card deck between his graceful fingers and shuffling it how he saw fit. My cheeks burned brighter when Elijah looked to me for confirmation, but I glared squarely at Rafe, pissed.

"*Rafe*." The vampire's bright gaze innocently darted to mine, his hands still expertly working the deck. I bit the insides of my cheeks, allowing him a moment to realize how he'd screwed up, but when he said nothing and Elijah continued to burn a hole in the side of my head, I crossed my arms tightly and bit out, "It's rude to listen to my heartbeat."

He scoffed. "Well, it's rather *loud*."

Slowly, Elijah eased onto his stool, and when I finally

risked a look, I found him watching Rafe shuffle, his jaw clenched, the muscles rippling. *Damn.* It shouldn't upset me that the news bothered him, but it did—the stupid connection between us meant I actually cared what this gorgeous, possessive dragon shifter thought. How he felt. Why he felt it.

From the expression on Rafe's face, he was either playing dumb or he genuinely didn't realize he'd poked the wasp's nest with a sharp stick. A quick glance between us slowed his skilled fingers, and he tapped the card deck on the table, rolling his eyes again at my *What the hell, man?* scowl.

"I mean, he *is* rather handsome," the vampire added as he set the perfectly uniform deck in the center of the table. "Did you see those cheekbones? They could cut glass."

Okay, now he was just being a dick. Rafe smirked at me, daring me to argue or deny, and I responded with a swift and solid punch to the arm.

Which, unfortunately, was like punching marble. Pain bloomed on impact, unfurling from my knuckles up my forearm, and I reared back with a hiss.

"Oww," I whined, knowing full well that I deserved it. "*Shit.*"

Despite the grit of his jaw, Elijah still reached out for me—as if on instinct, driven to comfort, to soothe away the pain. He did it all the time, reacting without realizing, but like always, he stopped just shy of touching me. Scowling, the dragon withdrew his hand and stuck both under the table in a sullen silence.

"Serves you right," Rafe told me. "Honestly, beating on a defenseless vampire…"

This time, Elijah kicked him under the table, both of them wincing at the *thwack*. Seconds later, they were both grinning, and I finally settled on my stool, shaking my head and smiling. While I still didn't understand my relationship with these two, neither individually nor as a trio, I found comfort in their company and their friendship, and despite the weird tension between Elijah and me, the confusion over what Rafe and I even *were* on the relationship scale, sitting down with them at this table, at the one in the cafeteria, in my cell beside Rafe each night and at the workstation in the bakery with Elijah each day felt good.

It felt like home.

Fleetingly.

Until something in this hellhole reminded me that I was in prison, like the leather strap around my neck or my pathetic shower shoes, or Deimos and his crew fighting for a stupid table…

Then, you know, it was business as usual: feeling helpless in a system designed to break you down, to make you feel lower than dirt, like you really *were* a criminal.

Never mind that most of us were innocent.

The fae emerged from the shadows of his cell faster than I had that first day, loitering in the doorway and scrutinizing the cellblock with impossibly green eyes. In turn, I watched him over my shoulder, from his sculpted face to his perfect posture to his large, elegant hands rubbing bloody, raw wrists. What was he: innocent or guilty? Criminal or bystander?

Impossible to tell at first glance.

While he hadn't so much as peeked my way, I felt someone else watching me intently. Elijah's caramel gaze drilled into my forehead, and I let out a sharp exhale, beyond annoyed with this particular side of him. Even if it wasn't intentional, he had no right to be all huffy. So, rolling my shoulders back, I looked him dead in the eye—a challenge in the shifter community—and cocked my head to the side, daring him to say what his eyes *screamed*, what the clench of his jaw so obviously implied.

Jealousy.

Possessiveness.

Elijah stared back, his expression softening somewhat, but not once did he blink. Neither of us flinched. Neither backed down. He conceded slightly, but this dragon shifter was an alpha through and through: he bowed to no one, not even me. Unfortunately for him, spending all this time in his company, in Rafe's, meant I'd also found a slight backbone—and I wasn't about to fold either.

"Guys…" Rafe flicked cards around the table, dealing out the first hand of a new game. "You know I fucking hate it when you do this—"

"It's nothing," Elijah rumbled.

"We're fine," I insisted, mouth dry. Both of us had ended up talking over the other, which made Rafe shake his head and shoot us one of his famous *Oh my* fucking *god, you two* looks that always made me feel like we were being ridiculous. And maybe we were, but I'd never been in this situation with anyone before.

Never been in this situation—period. Never responded so strongly to a shifter, my body igniting with a look. Never floundered around a handsome vampire, unsure where we stood: acquaintances or friends or cellmates who flirted every now and again to distract from the doldrums of their current situation?

And then add a third hottie who I couldn't stop looking at, couldn't help but drool over, and I was basically screwed. Prison wasn't supposed to be a high school soap opera. I wasn't supposed to be worrying about men's feelings; I was supposed to be planning an escape so I could get far, far away from this place and find Tully, then go home and never leave my apartment again.

Just as he did with me, Deimos swept over to the fae and walked him out of his cell. I swallowed hard, the memory of the demon's hot breath on my neck making my stomach churn. That first day, he had taken such liberties with me—taken advantage of my fear, using a very *long* moment of weakness to touch me, to wrap his arm around me and whisper in my ear. Back then, he had tried to sweet-talk me, to coo and purr, to make it seem like his crew was the safe port in this hellish storm.

What tactic would he use on the fae?

A fae who didn't exactly seem fazed to be here, despite the bruises peppering his skin, the dried maroon blood under his nose, a streak of it cutting from his mouth to his chin. The guards had beaten the crap out of him—that much was clear—and yet he strolled alongside Deimos with such a confident stride that it made me wonder…

Had he been in prison before?

Was this old news?

Did he play the political game behind bars?

The thought of Deimos acquiring a fae underling didn't sit well with me, and from the way both Elijah and Rafe watched the situation unfold, their smiles gone, the feeling was mutual.

Deimos and the fae stopped at his usual table, his tattooed hand sliding seductively down the fae's arm, lingering over his fingers. Right. Apparently seduction was his *only* angle. Rafe and I exchanged a quick glance before I fully turned around on my stool to shamelessly stare, the cellblock silent save for the ever-present tick, tick, tick of a wall clock over the door. The air thickened, even with our collars muting magic and shifting, and I all but held my breath when the fae moved in and murmured something in Deimos's ear. Over the demon's shoulder, he caught my eye, shamrock-green eyes twinkling with mischief and mirth.

When he stepped back, the fae did so with an apologetic smile and a hapless shrug. Deimos's entire demeanor suddenly tightened, his hands in fists, his shoulders rigid. Even the guards seemed to sense the impending fallout, loitering by the door with an eye on the scene, just Cooper and some new warlock who picked his nose and ate the findings when he thought no one was watching. Thompson had disappeared at some point, the one glimmer of sanity amongst our captors gone. Not good. Not good at all. Not the oppressive quiet. Not the fury twisting across Deimos's face. Not the way his gang were all rising off their stools, hackles up and teeth bared.

The storm broke when Deimos threw the first punch. His fist cracked hard and furious across the fae's jaw, and the entire crew pounced. Avery and Blake ripped the fae off his feet and dragged him onto the table, all of them closing in like a pack of wild dogs tearing into a carcass.

No, not a carcass. A very much *alive* animal, one who felt every bite, still kicking and bleating and *begging*—

Only he didn't beg. In fact, as I shot up, heart in my throat and ears ringing, panicked like I'd never been for another prisoner before, I swore I heard the fae laughing. High, clear, melodious belly-aching *laughter*. No. That couldn't be right. It was just a trick of the acoustics, another lie in Xargi Penitentiary.

Six on one was hardly a fair fight, especially after the disorienting experience of check-in—the strip search, squatting and coughing, shoved in a jumpsuit by strangers who had just examined you naked. It wasn't fair, and it *definitely* wasn't right. I staggered forward, eyes wide as I searched the pile for the fae, but there were so many bodies in one place, and Constance wouldn't stop *shrieking* with absolute delight, dark fae blood under her talons...

"They're going to kill him!"

"No, they'll be stopped just shy of that," Elijah insisted when I whipped around to my guys, who, while standing, didn't seem keen on making a move to stop anything. Not that I blamed them: getting involved only made things worse. But… But…

The fae didn't deserve to die—or end up in the infirmary just for pissing off a jerk like Deimos. In fact, he should get a medal for whatever he had said that sent the demon into a rage. None of us had been able to really trigger him yet.

"Yeah, well, it shouldn't come to *that* either," I snapped, marching around the circular cellblock and searching out the guards. Cooper and the other warlock lingered at the door, arms crossed, mouths stretched in cruel smiles. They chatted amongst themselves like they were watching a damn basketball game—probably taking bets on the fae's odds of surviving the attack. Pathetic. All of them. Absolutely *pathetic*.

Even though I had spent my life on the sidelines, always taking a back seat, never involving myself in anyone's business even outside of prison, something about this place made me want to *fight*. I'd seen brawls between inmates. I'd witnessed guards slam supers against the walls, scream in their faces, make them wriggle and squirm in agony with hexes that ought to be abolished. I'd met others torn away from their lives, their families, their homes—all to fill the cells of Xargi Penitentiary. It had happened to me: kidnapping, abuse, violations of my body and my mind and my magic.

And…

Enough.

Just—*enough*.

I clicked with Elijah and Rafe's way of doing things because we were so similar. Don't make waves. Don't draw attention. Just sit back and survive. I understood that—lived it, breathed it. Heck, it was practically my family's motto, the dwindling Fox coven's code of conduct. Keep to yourself, take care of each other, and everything will be fine.

Only it wasn't fine. I was the last Fox witch left, alone in the world and shouldering my dad's paranoia to this day.

Elijah had broken the rules. He had made waves, drawn attention to himself—fought for me. Protected me from Deimos. Kept the demon off my back and beat a guard bloody for leering at me. Shorter and weaker, I couldn't defend him like he did me, just a witch nobody saw as a serious physical threat, but I could pay his actions forward. I could step in for someone else.

I could make waves, just like my dragon.

"Stop!" My shout fell on deaf ears, and I waved furiously at the guards, pointing to the dogpile, incredulous—but not surprised—that they were just letting it happen. "What are you doing? *Stop* this!"

The pair chuckled and nudged each other in a *look at this hysterical woman* kind of way, and the moment quickly spiraled into just another incident where I felt helpless and lost and so very small.

"Keep your panties on, Fox," Cooper ordered, his tone harsh—like *I* was the one out of line.

"A little hazing never hurt nobody," the second warlock told me, his wolfish smile making my stomach turn. *Ugh.* I shoved down the desire to flip them both off and marched toward the writhing pile of fists and fury and feet, the fight in full swing.

Fight. As if *this* was a fight. It was a mob attack and nothing more.

I stuttered to a halt just on the cusp of it, fire in my belly that sparked and hissed like it never had before. Only for all the fight brewing in me, I had no idea where to put it—what to do, when to dive in, who to set my hands on first. I'd never been in a fight before. It never even crossed my mind.

Not on a rare drunken night out at the club when someone cut in front of me for the bathroom or spilled their drink down my back on the dance floor. Not when customers at the café belittled my staff right in front of me. Not when some neighborhood kids threw rocks at Tully for kicks. Using my fists *or* my wand to settle things had never been my style.

And I'd like to think it wasn't because I lacked courage, but because I could solve problems with words instead...

Words didn't matter in here.

I lunged for Helen, smallest and meekest of the bunch, the little sparrow shifter loitering on the outskirts and smacking at the fae's legs whenever she had the chance. However, before I could latch onto her arm, Deimos's head snapped in my direction, his eyes completely black. He snarled and flashed a set of perfectly white, unnervingly sharp teeth—a predator guarding its kill.

Screw him.

I refused to be bullied by this tattooed freak a second longer. Trembling, I swallowed hard, braced myself, and—

Elijah beat me to it. Just as Deimos started to extract himself from the dogpile, black gaze glued to me, a huge body shoved between us, this massive wall of *man* blocking my view. The fire in my gut exploded, coursing through my every cell, fueled by Elijah's proximity. It melted the fear, made me stop shaking. In his shadow, I found strength: I was ready to *fight*.

He was just much better at it. Swift as a striking viper, Elijah dug into the gang and ripped the two shifters in identical blue jumpsuits out. He tossed Helen and Faustus away from their usual table, and when the bird shifters righted themselves, they both appeared to *try* to get back in—only to lose themselves in Elijah's gaze. I knew the feeling well, but rather than eliciting desire, the dragon's unflinching stare seemed to scare the absolute shit out of them. Both shifters folded, eyes plummeting to the ground and shoulders rounded as they scampered back.

Gods, alpha energy was so stupidly *hot*.

"Stay out of it, Greystone," Deimos ordered, his voice gruff and foul, nowhere near his usual seductive purr. Elijah squared off with him as the assault slowed on the table, the demon's lackeys stilling and glaring us down, fae blood on their knuckles and splattered across their cheeks.

"Stop being a twat, Deimos," Elijah fired back. "*This—*" He dipped his head toward the fight, to the fae on his back with his head lolled to the side, his gorgeous mouth stretched wide with soundless laughter. "—is petty, and you know it."

Deimos rose from his place in the middle of the table, one foot on either side of the fae, lording over his carnage like a lion guarding a fallen gazelle.

Which made *us* the circling hyenas?

Right. That was just laughable.

"Whipped by a female, eh?" the demon snarled, wiping the blood from his mouth, his black jumpsuit splotchy with dark wet spots.

"Just sick of your shit, honestly." I flinched when Rafe materialized at my side out of nowhere. Elijah fell back, the three of us standing in line, and I noticed both men had crossed their arms, their elbows *just* in my personal bubble enough to make a point. *She's with us.* Sleeves rolled up, Rafe seemed ready to get his hands dirty for the first time since we'd met.

Now, the million-dollar question: Was it because Elijah had thrown himself into the fray, his best friend stepping into the minefield that was Cellblock C's political landscape? Or was he standing beside me because I'd asked—without really asking—for them to have my back? Or… Or was he actually sick of Deimos being a bully?

Impossible to tell—and that was starting to really bug me.

But no more than all the spilled blood must be bothering him. As Deimos stomped off the table, using one of the stools as a step, his lieutenant Constance had taken it upon herself to lick the fae's bloody hand clean. She knelt at his side, eyes shut, ecstasy written across what would be a beautiful face on someone less batshit insane. Her tongue swept over his bloody knuckles, lapping up the dark, glittery red smears.

Was this killing Rafe? Did vampires crave *all* blood, or just a specific type? Were some human-only?

Whatever the case may be, the prison was starving their vampire population—and this couldn't be easy for him. Pale-faced and glowering at Constance, Rafe had started to shake, and this time, as Deimos stalked up to us, got *right* in Elijah's face, I shouldered in front of *him*, ready to hold the vampire back as needed.

Not that I… physically could. Collar or not, I was no match for a ravenous vampire.

"Think carefully, boys," Deimos whispered in that unsettling demonic rasp. "This, right here, is a line in the sand. Are you ready to cross it?"

Still sprawled on his back, the fae suddenly cackled, then shoved Constance away, his hand covering her entire face as he tossed her off the table like she weighed nothing.

"My, my," he rumbled, chuckling, all bloody and beaten and bruised. He tipped his head to the side, wriggling his eyebrows at Deimos, Elijah, and Rafe, then winking at me. "Isn't this a *fun* group?"

I inched closer to Rafe with a gulp. Great. Just what we needed. Another psycho who got off on violence.

Still hot though—just infinitely less appealing.

The main door creaked open partially, drawing all our eyes to it, and seconds later Thompson stepped in with his usual air: casual, quiet, not braggy like all the other warlocks. As soon as he saw *this*, the blood, the inmates on top of each other, he hurled the door the rest of the way so that the handle clanged off the stone wall.

"What the *fuck* is this?" he demanded, stalking into the room with his wand drawn. Cooper and the other asshole hopped to, quickly falling in line behind him. "Everybody back up!"

And then the magic really flew. It was what I'd wanted all along—for the guards to just do their jobs—but it should have happened long before that fae ever wound up on the table. Thompson and the others handled us roughly, dragging and shoving and sparking inmates back to their cells when they didn't move fast enough, barking orders, issuing a lockdown until dinner.

"Not you," the least awful of the three growled. Thompson snagged my wrist just before I zipped into my cell. He then hauled me out so fast that I tripped over my own feet, crashing into him with a yelp, heart in my throat.

"What's this?" Rafe demanded, loitering in his cell's doorway, paler than usual, the tips of his fangs exposed with every word. Whether he drank fae blood or not, it had awoken something in him, something animalistic and demanding; I saw it in his eyes, the way they had darkened.

His voice had deepened.

His fangs—just *there*. A shiver cut down my spine, the fear fleeting but visceral.

"Come on," Thompson muttered, ignoring the vamp completely as he marched me across the cellblock toward the main door. I scrambled to keep pace with his much longer strides, shooting a panicked look back to Rafe—who was being ordered into his cell by the nose-picker—and then to Elijah, who had Cooper's wand in his face.

Not that that seemed to matter.

The dragon shifter tracked me with his relentless golden stare—and for once I was grateful for his intensity.

"Where are you taking her?" he snarled, but just as he tried to bulldoze his way through Cooper, a bolt of amber light exploded from the warlock's wand and struck him square in the gut, visibly knocking the wind out of him as Deimos sniggered from his cell. The last thing I saw before Thompson hauled me through the door was Elijah's knees buckling, his hand slamming into the hard ground just fast enough to ensure it wasn't his face, and the last thing I heard...

"Simmer down, boys. Your bitch has an appointment with the warden."

And then the door clunked shut, instantly muffling the chaos of Cellblock C. The usual cacophony of locks shifting into place cut through the dense quiet of the stone corridor, and as I stumbled along behind Thompson, a high-pitched whine stretched between my ears. What the hell had happened to this day? One minute we were playing yet another round of cards, and then...

And then...

Adrenaline had made me forget how wrecked I was after my bakery shift, but as it slowly faded now, the aches and pains and weariness trickled in.

"Is that true?" I asked, every word an effort, my feet desperate for me to sit down and put them up somewhere. Oblivious, Thompson kept his pace even, and I had no choice but to follow. "Am I seeing the warden?"

We darted left where we usually went right, the air cooling, the hallway brightening.

"Yeah," Thompson said, quickly glancing over his shoulder at me. "Don't forget your manners—and don't piss him off."

Great advice. I might have been ready to defend the

helpless new guy against a dick like Deimos, but the warden was another beast entirely. He was king of this place, and whatever fight I'd had in me died at the thought of sitting across from him. Maybe, just maybe, *something* had happened in the outside world that brokered my freedom. Maybe he would issue an apology and send me on my way.

A snort snagged in my throat, choking me. Right. *That* would be the day.

Without another word, Thompson hauled me into a wing of the prison that was totally foreign to me—that my fellow inmates wouldn't believe existed unless they saw it for themselves. After crossing through a set of double doors, we left the dusty stonework and narrow corridors behind for a grand foyer with marble columns and glittering checkered tile. Sunlight spilled in through tasteful windows in the domed ceiling. Paintings in ornate frames adorned the walls. Ivy spiraled around the railing of the staircase Thompson marched me up, its dotted purple blooms giving off a sweet and soothing scent.

This was a whole different world, but at Thompson's breakneck pace, I hadn't the time to properly digest it all. From my hurried glances around the sprawling space, silent except for our footsteps, it was open and airy and *clean*. Rich, splashed with marble and gold and ivory and—

Gone.

Thompson and I blitzed through another set of double doors, which opened into an arched corridor made of black wood paneling. Thin carpet stretched all the way down the dark hallway to the one door in sight, which was partially ajar, sunlight slanting through the opening. There it was—the final destination. Adrenaline spiked again when I spotted a black placard on the door, *WARDEN* embossed across it in stark gold lettering.

Much to my surprise, Thompson didn't knock. He

waltzed right into an office that was so expected, so cliché, that I couldn't help wondering if this was a dream—or if we really *were* on a TV show, this room more like a polished set than a room where someone worked every day. Mahogany desk. A huge empty high-backed chair behind it made of quilted black leather. Desk overflowing with paper stacks and folders. One metal tray that said *Inbox*, the *Outbox* on the opposite corner. A feathery quill and an iron inkpot. Two wooden chairs in front of said desk, one of which Thompson shoved me into. Bookshelves full of thick tomes lined all four walls, so neatly organized and vast that they could give Café Crowley's collection a run for its money.

The room smelled like leather and sandalwood and sea salt. A hearth nestled between two bookshelves directly behind the desk, the fire inside burning low, almost nonexistent save a few flaring embers.

Three evenly spaced windows dominated most of the wall to my right, their pine-green curtains tied to the sides, thin bookshelves arranged between them.

Was that a *human* skull—

"Don't touch anything, Fox."

I nodded, but by the time I looked back, Thompson was gone, the door open, the hallway beyond dark.

Cool. Cool, cool, cool. This felt great. Totally safe.

Adrenaline at an all-time high, I rubbed my sweaty, shaky hands on my thighs and continued my slow scan of the room, trying to keep busy—to not let my mind wander to the worst possible scenario. Eventually, I settled on the black nameplate in the middle of this huge desk, situated right in front of me. It had been staring at me since I'd walked in, but after weeks in either a cell, the block, or the bakery, the warden's office was sensory overload.

Warden Lloyd Guthrie

I stared at the bright white letters, reading but not comprehending.

Warden—Lloyd—Guthrie.

I blinked down at the rectangle, everything inside going cold, and then tried and failed to reach out for it. I mean, I got my hand up, even moved it toward the name that had haunted my entire life, but it fell to my lap just before I could brush the cool obsidian.

Warden Lloyd *Guthrie*—

The door clicked shut behind me, and I sucked in a panicked breath, stiff as a statue, every internal alarm bell shrieking for me to *run*.

"Hello, kitten..."

10

KATJA

This had to be a dream.

I'm dreaming. That was why the room looked like a TV set, like the stereotypical head honcho's office. I must have seen it before on a show, a movie, hell, maybe even a *play*, and now my mind was messing with me. Yeah. That was it. As if Xargi didn't screw with me enough during the daytime, now I needed a new nightmare thrown into the mix.

Only a dream.

Wake up, Katja. Just wake up.

Footsteps on hardwood—prim and precise, nothing like the heavy clunk of guard boots or the shuffling of soft-soled inmate attire. Still as stone, I stared at the overladen bookshelf on the other side of the desk, catching a faint whiff of leather that wasn't from the high-backed chair. Leather shoes. Expensive. Paired with... peppermint. An even more delicate scent, it tickled my nostrils, begged me to turn around and face the nightmare head-on.

But I couldn't.

I couldn't *move*.

As soon as a tall, dark figure loomed in my periphery, my

mind went blank. Like an overloaded computer shorting out, it all went black inside. No high-pitched whine. No racing images. No whispers in my dad's death croak urging me to *run*. Just—silence, except for the drumbeat of my heart, my pulse reverberating through my entire body.

He settled into that huge, imposing chair without a word. Warden—Lloyd—Guthrie.

A handsome silver fox, but I'd known that from perusing the odd society tabloid photo after Dad died—back when I thought I should finally look into what he'd been going on and on about for years. Only the photos hadn't done crime lord Lloyd Guthrie justice. They didn't relay the absolute *power* he carried in his broad shoulders, in his large hands, in the crisp suit and the steely grey eyes that seemed to look right through me, right down to the guts.

And from the way he settled into his chair, hands folded on the mahogany desktop, eyes pinned squarely on me... It was like he'd found my very soul.

Black hair tinged with grey, white at the sideburns. Neat. Swept back. Scottish heritage with a splash of Italian thrown in, if I remembered my research—what little public information had been available, anyway. He wore a pristine black suit far too good for the warden of some crap prison, and I swore the buttons on his shirt, from the glimpses I caught beneath a shiny black tie, were pearls.

Attractive man. Tall. Strong. Lean. Hawkish.

Terrifying warlock.

My shoulders rounded, and try as I might to match his quiet ferocity, I just wanted to slink down to the hardwood and disappear through the floorboards.

"Kitten... Sweet nickname," he mused, his voice a deep, richly aged baritone. A New Yorker, distinctly *not* West Coast. "What your father used to call you, isn't it?"

My cheeks burned harder than they had since I'd arrived,

no doubt a telling beet red from the way the warden's thin mouth twisted up. I said nothing. Did nothing. Refused to even give him a nod. Lloyd Guthrie—if that obsidian plate was to be believed, if this *wasn't* a dream—tapped his threaded hands on the desk once, twice, then leaned forward, his chair softly groaning.

"Do you know who I am?"

I swallowed thickly, gulping a mouthful of knives down a too-dry throat, and then nodded to his nameplate. "Warden Lloyd Guthrie."

Pride bloomed in my chest: I didn't stutter his name. I didn't whisper it or choke it out. No matter how I felt on the inside, despite the cold sweat on the nape of my neck, the blaze in my cheeks, the numb tingling that had engulfed my fingertips, I sounded *strong*. Good. At least I could pretend. Xargi was starting to teach me how to fake it.

Lloyd smirked, amusement glittering in his stony greys. "But do *you* know who I am?"

"I just said who you are," I offered without thinking. It had just tumbled out, punctuated by a silent *Duh* that was probably akin to signing a death warrant under different circumstances. In all my research, I had never stumbled upon anything concrete—just rumors and hearsay, Lloyd Guthrie, warlock mobster, defined solely by his reputation.

But as we stared off now, his smirk blossoming but the mirth dying in his unflinching gaze, I had a feeling his reputation was all he needed. That smile made my blood run cold. *Frigid*. Elijah had set me on fire every day for the last month; a smile from Lloyd Guthrie extinguished the flames I had come to crave and chilled my blood to ice.

Elijah's fire made me feel alive. It made me feel strong and capable, in control in a place where I had absolutely none from the time I woke up to when I crawled back into my cot after the lights-out siren.

Lloyd's ice made me want to give in to the fear—

"You..." I tightened my trembling hands to fists, hoping he couldn't see and knowing he did anyway. The warlock oozed predator before he'd even said a word; he probably missed nothing. "You're a criminal... running a prison."

"A criminal?" His curt chuckle made the hairs on my neck stand up, and he eased back into his chair, the delight shimmering in his eyes again. "Am I?"

I faltered, second-guessing myself, my dad, the cursory searches I'd done on this man over the years. Clearing my throat, I dropped my gaze to my hands, to my white knuckles. "Unless I'm mistaken, you're the Lloyd Guthrie associated with the Guthrie crime syndicate that runs out of New York City... A crime family of warlocks who partake in, er, illegal activities, and..."

"Go on."

I stared up at him, knowing that I should stand my ground even when I would rather look anywhere else right now—*anywhere*. Or, even better, jump up and take a running leap at one of those windows to my right. Crash through. Plummet to the gravel grounds outside—meet some of the wolves I heard howling come nightfall.

"And now you're a warden," I told him. "That's it."

My breath snagged there for the first time. Lloyd's smile sharpened, and he stabbed at the desk's top with his pointer finger as if to drive the point home.

"No, you know there's more."

My stomach twisted and knotted, the measly breakfast I'd had hours ago and the bit of bread I had munched on in the proofing pantry this afternoon suddenly a little *too* present. The churn brought with it a rush of acid creeping up my throat, the sensation infuriatingly familiar, but I pushed through and hoped the nausea didn't read on my face.

"Shall I say it, then?" Lloyd offered in a tone beyond patronizing. I just shook my head.

"I think I'd like to go back to my cell now—"

"Do you know why you're here, Katja Isabella Fox?"

Oh *gross*. Hearing my name coming from his mouth kicked the nausea up a few notches, and I bit at my cheeks, willing my insides to settle.

"Because someone lied," I gritted out, "and said I sold love potions."

"False."

I frowned, waiting for more, hating to have finally heard the truth from *him*. No one but the other inmates believed me. Processing staff, the guards... I was just an ingrate to them, another criminal who had been found guilty. And now this? Just like that—*false*.

Lloyd dragged it out like he enjoyed making me wait, edging me for knowledge—staring at me with eyes like slate, like steel, just the shade to match his metal heart.

You know... If all the stories were true. If Dad really was telling the truth.

And from the look of him, this smirking man, my *warden*, it was impossible to say otherwise now.

"You're here because I ordered it," he said at long last, his voice even and calm, as if we were having the most casual of conversations. "Because..." After fidgeting with his diamond cuffs, Lloyd leaned over the desk again, swooping closer to me and bringing with him a rush of sharp peppermint that almost made me gag. "Because you were mine before you were even *born*."

Smug, ever so pleased with himself, Lloyd Guthrie settled back in his chair again like he was doing me some kindness—like he had decided to allow me a few precious moments to process that monumental bombshell. Only I couldn't think. Couldn't *feel*. Hearing his words had triggered a wall inside me, a mental block that I couldn't get around, couldn't climb over. Just *there*, oppressive and towering, my heartbeat like a pounding fist against it.

"What i-is this place?" I managed, all the smoothness from earlier dead and buried. Gone. My voice broke in a hoarse whisper. In fact, I was barely aware of what came out, only that I was speaking, my sense of self-preservation trying desperately to change the subject. "Supers don't have... prisons."

"Ah, yes." Lloyd pressed his steepled fingers to his lips, considering me, before snatching up an ivory pen from his desk and twirling it effortlessly. "It's a creation of my own design. Xargi is the prototype for penitentiaries I intend to launch all over the world... Proof to the elders of our communities that troublemakers can be *dealt* with at no cost to them. Proof to the few human governments in the know that we can discipline our own." He pressed the end of his pen into his chin dimple, some of his coarse blackish-grey facial scruff making a scratchy sound at the contact—like nails on a chalkboard. "And it's a chance to earn an honest living."

The next stretch of silence implied he was waiting for a response—maybe for me to sing his praises. *Delusional.* I just stared at him instead, horror solidifying in my chest like an anchor.

"Do you like that?" he crooned, dragging his pen over his lower lip. Somehow he managed to read as both rakishly handsome *and* disgustingly lewd. "An honest man?"

Sidestep that land mine, girl. "Are you selling the bread we bake every day?"

He tossed his pen on his desk. "I am."

"And what's forged in the metal—"

"Let me stop you there." Lloyd folded his arms, staring at me like I was a child, a pupil, a little girl for him to mentor and mold to his liking. Patronizing piece of shit. "Every work detail makes a product. We sell that product and put the funds back into the prison. It's all very legitimate."

"It's *not* legitimate," I fired back, the embers flaring inside me, a whisper of warmth coiling up my spine. "Most of us aren't criminals... We shouldn't *be* prisoners. This is a fucking labor camp!"

Lloyd surged forward with a flash of teeth. "Oh, what a *mouth* on you. I like that. I like that much more than I'd have thought..."

His wide eyes, that maniacal cackle, extinguished whatever fire had started up again. I shoved back in my chair as far as I could, suddenly realizing that like almost every other chair in here, it was bolted to the ground. Not going anywhere. *No escape.*

"Xargi is a proof of concept, kitten," the warlock remarked, either oblivious to the fact that I was stretching to get away from him, hands snapped tight around the armrests, or he just didn't care. I bit the insides of my cheeks again, the flash of pain centering, and scowled back at him.

"Stop saying that." He had no right to call me kitten. He wasn't my dad. He hadn't *earned* that privilege. This asshole had no idea who I was. No clue. And he didn't get to talk at me like he did.

"And if I don't?" He fished his wand out of his suit jacket's interior, placing it delicately, almost reverently on the desk. Ivory handle—shocker. Grey eyes flicked to mine, locked on, and the world blurred around us, the slate goading me to react. "Will you show me your claws, Katja? Come on, then... Take a swipe."

My fingers twitched toward the wand, and a stupid part of my brain posed a theory that if I just moved fast enough, I could snatch it up and use it on its master. Never mind the collar. Never mind that wands had hearts and souls of their own, that they were major divas who sometimes freaked out *hard* if someone new used them without permission.

It would be worth the risk if I could wipe that smarmy smile off his face.

If I could never hear *kitten* coming out of his mouth ever again.

But that, like so many other half-baked plans of escape, was just a fantasy. Useless to dwell on. Depressing to consider. So, I sat there, stiff and silent, trembling, seething—seconds away from crying. Because I still wasn't the badass heroine. I was a witch who missed her dad, set off by a nickname that didn't belong to Lloyd Guthrie.

He ghosted his middle finger up and down his wand, the shaft a polished black wenge wood, and then let out a long, drawn-out sigh.

"Do you want to leave this place?"

My heart skipped a beat. Leave... Xargi? I had been waiting for those words, waiting for that offer, from the second I woke up cuffed to a chair. The penitentiary's warden ran the show, and I had no doubt that he could snap his fingers and I'd be free.

But making a deal with Lloyd Guthrie was suicide. It had to be.

"I—"

"You're mine, kitten," he insisted, stroking his wand's handle, gliding over the twin serpents etched into the ivory. I had to watch his hand, his fingers—because the *you're mine* thing tickled my gag reflex, and if I met his eyes, I'd probably hurl all over his ridiculous desk. But his fingers stilled, and a sharp snap made me flinch and look up just as Lloyd flashed a thin smile. "Say the word and you can come home."

I pressed onto the balls of my feet, seconds away from attempting the whole crashing-through-the-window thing.

I'd take a broken ankle and prowling wolves over this conversation. "What the hell are you talking about?"

"Nobody ever told you?" His dark brows shot up, and he sat in suspended laughter, waiting for me to deny it—to spill the truth. Dad had told me a lot in his final hours, but it had all sounded so... so... implausible. The rantings of a sick, paranoid man. Guilt knotted in my gut, and I busied myself with my nails, my refusal to meet his eye answer enough. Lloyd's face screwed victoriously, barking cackles bouncing around the office, and he slapped at the desk hard enough to make me jump again. "*Ridiculous*—but expected. An effort to protect you, most likely, but your father's silence only left you unprepared, kitten. A fool to the end, Augustus Fox..."

Fury nudged aside the guilt, just for a moment, and I glowered up at him, at this mobster pretending to be a warden—pretending he had some moral superiority over all the inmates in here.

Pretending that he... *owned* me. That I belonged to him.

No.

Never.

"You see—" Lloyd wiped under his eyes as his obnoxious chuckles settled. "—your mother was a filthy junkie—"

"That's a lie," I snapped. This asshole had no right to tarnish her memory—none.

"How would you know? You never met her." He sniffed as he snatched up his wand, twirling it between his fingers, those hawkish grey eyes never once leaving my face. "She died in childbirth."

I sucked in a sharp breath, like I always did, to alleviate the stab of loss and longing. Growing up without my mom had left a huge hole in my heart, in my whole life. Irrational as it was, I had always feared Jackson and Ewan hated me for stealing her away from them, my brothers who had had five and three years with her respectively before I came around.

Never once did they so much as hint at that. They died loving me just as fiercely as I loved them, missing her just as much as I missed a woman I'd never met but adored all the same.

Fuck him. I gripped the chair's armrests, nails gritting into the wood. Fuck Lloyd Guthrie for spewing such *lies*.

"She was addicted to wolfsbane—*deeply*," he told me, his tone bored now, like he was going through the motions. "She ran up debts she couldn't pay, and in the end, she came to me. She was from the neighborhood—only sixteen at the time. Getting her out of that hole would have cost me almost all I had, but she was the loveliest witch I'd ever seen... You know, once you looked past the ravages of wolfsbane."

Wolfsbane addict—impossible. She couldn't be... The woman I'd always imagined, who I had heard stories about all my life, was *good*. Strong. She wouldn't succumb to something so *petty*. Cheeks hollow, I shot up, unable to listen to a second more of this, about to call Thompson back into the room when—

"*Sit* down, Katja."

My knees buckled at the weight of his words, at the harsh rasp that would make grown men cry. He didn't shout. Didn't raise his voice. Didn't curse or threaten. Didn't level his wand at me. Just—ordered it. Issued a command that sent frost whispering across my skin, made the blood drain from my face. Numb, I slowly slouched back into the chair.

"Good girl," Lloyd murmured, the threat lingering in his eyes, in the dangerous twist of his lips. "Now, to pay your mother's arrears, to save her life from addiction and the debt hounds on her heels, I struck a bargain: my assistance for her thirdborn child."

I blinked back at him, brain struggling to process *all* of it, never mind *that*. "W-what? Who are you—Rumpelstiltskin?"

Fae made deals like that, bartering tricks for children, but I'd never heard of a warlock doing it. And I...

I was the thirdborn.

She…

She wouldn't.

She *couldn't* have made that deal.

"Her debt necessitated the ultimate price, I'm afraid," Lloyd mused, peering down his nose at me and tapping his wand against his palm. "She agreed. I *saved* her. Paid her debts, got her healthy. *Wooed* her. And then she ran off with your father… Went west and made a little family of her own." His cheek twitched, and he glared down at his wand, wringing it like he was throttling someone's throat instead. "Had two brats, then accidentally fell pregnant with you. And you *were* an accident, kitten." His eyes snapped to mine, cruel and cold. "She had always dreamed of a large family, but she swore to me that she planned to sterilize herself when I came calling."

"You're a liar," I hissed, ignoring the burn of unshed tears, unable to get anything out louder than a whisper. Lloyd pursed his thin lips, then tsked, tsked, tsked, like I was that little girl again.

"Oh, darling, *no*." He then offered what he must have thought was a kind smile, but it only made the churn of my stomach more violent. I pressed against my belly, swallowing down a rush of bile, and Lloyd's eyes glittered like he enjoyed the show. "Unfortunately for Mellony, she loved you before you were born. Refused to give you up… Rather a nasty way to perish, in childbirth. So *rare* for a witch to die of such a *human* cause, no?"

He settled back in his chair, his throne, and looked down on me like he had just won something. Meanwhile, my mind still couldn't put two and two together, couldn't process the information overload—couldn't accept a damn thing.

But my heart knew.

My heart sensed a cruel honesty from the man before me,

and accepting that sent another rush of bile flooding up my throat, my mouth breaking out in the pre-vomit sweats.

This can't be happening. This isn't real. *It's just a dream.*

It wasn't.

Dreams never hurt like this. Dreams were temporary. I always woke up. Always.

No waking from this nightmare.

"Your father refused to give you up," Lloyd mused with a sneer and a shake of his head. "He wouldn't honor the deal. So… I had to, uh, *collect* accordingly."

I should have taken Dad at his word, but I wrote most of it off. Visceral as a jagged knife, the guilt stabbed into my heart now, *twisting* so I really knew it was there. I should have believed him. Everything. I should have—

"But that's a story for another day." Lloyd set his wand on the desk, then wove his hands together and leaned forward, all business again. "Now, kitten, back to my original question. Do you want to leave this place?"

I sucked in my cheeks, fighting the spike of adrenaline, the pinch of excitement, at the thought of walking out of Xargi Penitentiary. Of course I wanted out. I wasn't a criminal. I didn't belong here and I never would.

"Not with you," I choked, tears battering at me with a vengeance. It hurt to say—hurt to deny freedom. But it wasn't freedom. What Lloyd Guthrie intended to offer me, even if he hadn't spelled it out in the exact terms, was still a prison, still a cage.

A gilded cage.

Never.

Xargi's warden chuckled coolly, that incredulous expression suggesting he couldn't believe his ears. "Are you sure? *Prison* is worse than my company? You barely know me."

"I know enough." Even if I hadn't been able to dig up

much dirt on a warlock who probably paid people to keep his skeletons buried deep, this little chat was enough to send me sprinting in the opposite direction.

"Your mother and I made a blood deal," he stated, enunciating each word like he was trying to rein in his temper. "Contractually, you're *mine*." Another surge of sick, this time leaving a vomit-stamp at the back of my throat. Lloyd just sniffed again and fidgeted with his cuffs, the vision of a man unaccustomed to *anyone* denying him. "So, fine, put up a fight. Play the martyr. Suffer a little longer… You know, for *perspective*."

I held up a hand, nausea making me hot, the room oppressive, Lloyd's presence suffocating. "Stop—"

"We'll have more of these little meetings," he sneered, voice overpowering mine. "And I think you'll find them very enlightening. After all, we've got four unspeakable tragedies to cover in your family. Augustus, Mellony, Jackson, and little Ewan… Not a banner couple of decades for the Fox coven, hey? And I've got all the gory details. So much to *share*, kitten. So many opportunities for you to learn what happens when you *cross* me."

A storm of emotion cut through me like a riptide, anger and grief and heart-stopping fear threatening to drag me under for good. Couldn't listen anymore. Couldn't sit here—

I had anxiety-induced vomiting as a kid, but I thought I'd gotten over it, that dry-heaving in the processing cell on the first day was a one-time thing.

Apparently this hellhole drudged up *all* your baggage.

"But, come with me now," Lloyd urged, finally standing, pressing his palms to his desk, searching out my eyes as they darted everywhere *but* him. "Come with me and I'll spare you the specifics."

Oh shit. I shook my head fiercely and gagged. No stopping it. Past the point of no return. *Oh gods no, no, no, not now—*

"You're my property, Katja," he carried on, once again either totally oblivious to the impact this had on me—or not caring in the slightest that I was about to spew half-digested bread all over his pristine hardwood. "I'm giving you the choice as a *courtesy*, but deep down you know… I'm sure you've known all your life, same as your pathetic father, that in your heart of hearts… you've always belonged to me."

The levies broke.

And with a strangled sob, I flopped over the armrest and emptied my guts onto the floor.

11
FINTAN

Well then, this was… new.

After centuries of rule-breaking and mischief, I'd finally received my comeuppance—Mother would be thrilled. Father, on the other hand, was very likely furious that a band of insignificant supernatural bounty hunters had kidnapped the last in line to his throne, Prince Fintan of the Midnight Court, Duke of Vega and Earl of the Lyra Constellation.

How they'd done it was beyond me.

Probably while I was out cold, drunk on bourbon and sex with that wily little nymph minx who had been, of course, nowhere to be found in the harsh light of day. Honestly, this hangover was more of a bitch than usual. *Obviously* they had dosed me when they'd slapped the cuffs on, then the collar. Seated at the center table in the middle of an empty cellblock, all by my lonesome, not a squabbling inmate or faux-macho guard in sight, I rubbed at the leather strap around my aching neck with a wince. It wasn't the first time a collar had found its way around my throat, and it most certainly wouldn't be the last, but this was different. This wasn't for a night of scandalous kink—this was for *real*.

I seldom faced anything real these days. Given my lot in life, nothing really mattered—unless you were the heir apparent, aka my pompous older brother Rollo, who was probably shitting himself right now because Father *must* have sent him into the mortal realm to fetch me. Hundreds of years had crawled by doing as I pleased, when I pleased, and to whomever I pleased.

And now this.

Honestly—found guilty of making fae deals with mortals. If those fuckwits were stupid enough to deal with me, then that was *their* fault. I mean, surely, they listened to the legends: never hand over your name to one of the fair folk. Ever. It was so very simple. Yet six belligerent idiots at that Manhattan club had done so, brazenly, without a care for their futures, all because I'd asked. I hadn't even been clever about it; my courtly entourage might have been sniggering over my shoulder the whole time, but acquiring those names hadn't been my finest work—nowhere close. It had been... simple. Too simple. *Boring*.

Everything was so boring these days.

Except for that nymph. My, *my*, could she suck a cock—

The realization hit me like a mace to the temple.

Oh, for the love of all the stars in the galaxy...

That sneaky wench had *been* the bounty hunter. And I'd just let her into my suite. Shooed the royal guards away, my posse of sniveling courtiers liquored up and dead to the world in the adjoining room.

Well, served me right for being so fucking stupid, I suppose.

But, at the very least, my foolishness had finally—*finally*—livened things up a little. Sure, the walls were dreary in Xargi Penitentiary, the bed hard and the jumpsuit starchy. No one to serve me here, to wait on me, to cater to my every need, but hadn't I secretly longed for the chance to stand on my own two feet?

Well. Thought about it, dismissed it, never shared that pathetic, whiny, childish desire with a soul. Not with my bedmates. Not my kin. *Certainly* not my parents. For my role, my life, had been set in stone from the second I popped out of my mother, and, tedious as that life had become, nothing could ever change it. It was *written in the stars*, or whatever nonsense they told the lesser fae of our court. We royals were *destined* for...

For...

Oh, fuck, I hadn't a clue what I was destined for. Not the throne. Not an arranged marriage like my sisters, their station cementing political unity with allied kingdoms. Nothing.

Just... Prince Fintan, duke of some bullshit star and earl of a constellation no one gave two fucks about.

Huzzah.

I drummed my fingers on the metal tabletop, lips pursed, gaze jumping from one vacant cell to the next. The little rooms circled the common area of the block, smelling faintly of body odor and whatever cleaning chemicals the servants used on the toilets. Some had stronger scents. The dragon stood out, most impressive shifter of the lot, all brimstone and flame, and the demon's cell smelled vaguely of death and rot and Hell's ash.

Then that *witch*. Fiery red hair and sapphire marbles for eyes, so passionate in her defense of me, so valiant as she hurled herself into the fray—

I would bed her tonight. Guards or not, I would *have* her, bless her with all my sexual prowess. She deserved it, of course, for leaping to the aid of a prince.

And from the way she had studied me upon my arrival,

unable to tear those marbles away, blushing whenever our eyes met, she would so thoroughly enjoy herself.

Mind you, this first time she would have to do most of the work. Possibly spend the entire time on top, riding me to her heart's content. Pain dripped from my every pore, the unstylish collar severely diminishing my healing capacity. I'd never been in a fight before. I had started *many* in my time, but someone had always stepped in before my rival dealt the first blow: a palace guard, my private security, one of my siblings—even my courtiers were primed to interject, noble fae of prestigious birth getting their asses kicked, savagely in some cases, all for my smart mouth.

Today was one of many firsts. The most I had suffered in the past was a set of bruised knuckles from getting a few licks of my own in before someone dragged me away, like a royal was made of glass rather than stardust. My eldest brother had always been the true warrior. Rollo had legions under his command, thousands of warrior fae relentlessly devoted to him, ready to ascend to the kingdom's elite fighters once he took my father's throne. The brothers between us had some garrisons to their names too, but they had other specialties that made them valuable.

I had titles.

Names gifted to me by my father as if I truly were a war hero, when really, they were but a formality. I knew it. He knew it. The entire fucking court knew it; some even giggled when the court crier warbled them out. Father pursed his lips. Mother looked away. Rollo rolled his eyes. I drank.

But now I had *real* bruises. A busted lip. A bloody nose. A black eye.

Thrilling, really.

Next time, I might actually fight back—remind them of what I was, where we fae ranked in the supernatural order. Today, I'd sat back and let it all play out to get a read on my fellow detainees, to assess the hierarchy, to learn where loyalties lay within Cellblock C. Very telling, that fight.

My stomach roared suddenly, painfully empty and cawing for something greasy after drowning in bourbon last night. The rest of the jumpsuits had been escorted out for supper a good half hour ago; unless someone was coming back for me, my gut would have to go on bleating until breakfast. Apparently, starvation was penance for starting the fight—never mind that the demon had thrown the first punch.

I mean.

I *had* spurred him on.

Deimos—boring, just like all the others. So predictable. Insult their dick size and they were gone, so desperate to prove to their fallen angel overlord that they were worthy of the darkness he bestowed upon them. So determined to out-alpha the shifters all around them, the only true alpha in this place that dragon who had come to the witch's aid.

Female demons were a little more difficult. No dick to insult, but I had a bag of tricks for them too.

Hopefully I'd get to use them in here—how *fun*.

A series of locks clinked and clanged, and seconds later the block's main door swung open. In marched the guard who had broken up the fight, and I squinted at the patch sewn onto his black uniform: Thompson. *Noted*. By his side, however, was a far more interesting subject, and I straightened at the sight of the petite redheaded witch, that purple jumpsuit *perfect* for her creamy complexion.

A familiar giddy tingle stretched from my head right on down to my tippy toes—the same little prickle I felt whenever I was about to have my way. Which was often. So beautiful, even with her slumped shoulders, her steps heavy and dragging. *Don't fret, pet. I've just the lap for you to rest your weary bones upon.*

Only it wasn't just exhaustion that tainted her lovely

features. Her cheeks had lost their delectable rosy glow, now sickeningly white and hollow. Those glittering sapphires sparkled less than before, dulled by the bloodshot whites surrounding them. Disappointing and annoyingly cliché that a trip to the warden's office produced *this*, but never mind. A few choice words from a fae prince could fix *everything*.

And if that failed, a glorious tumble in the sack really was the finest distraction in all the realms.

"Hello, little witch," I purred. My attempt to gracefully stand and sweep toward her was sullied by one of the fucking nailed-down stools, which I smacked my knee against in passing. With a wince, I limped toward her, fully aware that being both handsome *and* wounded really stoked a woman's fire. She stopped her slow shuffle into the cellblock, the guard now with his back to us as he sealed the door, locks clinking, and I scooped up her hand, ignoring the dazed look on her lovely features. And the—oh, yuck, the frigid sweat on her palms. Well, no matter. Beggars certainly couldn't be choosers, and for her, I might consider begging.

Might.

I bowed low and pressed a chivalrous kiss to the top of her pale, clammy hand. "Thank you, sweet girl, for your bravery."

She just stared down at me, full mouth slightly parted, her other hand limp at her side. Not exactly the reaction I'd expected, but it certainly wouldn't be the first time the attentions of a prince stupefied a commoner into silence. Naturally, I took it as a compliment.

"I have a reward in mind," I whispered roguishly, smirking as I straightened and pinched her delicate hand between us. "Something I think you'll *most* enjoy. Perhaps you could accompany me to my cell so I can ardently express my gratitude—"

Without a word, the witch ripped her hand from mine,

scowling, and turned on her heel. The flutter of her red mane unleashed a cloud of her scent—faintly floral, patchouli and jasmine and rose, and my *word* I needed more. But she stalked away from me—the first of the feminine species to ever do so—outright rejecting my offer and headed instead for the dragon's empty cell.

"Fox," the guard called, loitering by the main door, hands on his hips. "No."

The witch stopped again, seeming to crumble on the spot, and slowly faced him. "Thompson, please, can I just—"

"You're all on lockdown for the fight," the warlock insisted, addressing her with a gentler tone than he had anyone else. Clearly he possessed a soft spot for her, but from the way he spoke, the way he looked at her face and not her curves, it wasn't sexual. Huh. Strange. I crossed my arms with a huff, knowing I had a gorgeous pout, but neither paid me any mind. They looked to each other, the witch—Fox—begging with teary eyes and the guard refusing her with a shake of his head. "Once the rest are back, I'll bring you dinner, but until tomorrow, you're all in your *own* cells."

Did she make it a habit of visiting cells that were not her own? Excellent for me. Clearing my throat, I sidled into their eyeline, flashing her a handsome smile before shining it on the warlock. Even men fought for my attentions—it seemed cruel to deny him.

"Surely, good sir, you could allow her a visit to *my* cell..." I fiddled with my nails, then shrugged a shoulder innocently. "Perhaps for a price—"

"Shut your fucking mouth, inmate," Thompson snapped, his words whip-sharp and promising today's third beating if I wasn't careful. In an instant, my expression soured, and I glared back at him, hands in fists. No one *dared* address a prince like that. Never in my life had some lowly warlock raised his voice to me. I ought to whip him for his—oh, wait, she was coming back.

My whole being brightened the nearer the witch drew, but as soon as she realized I was watching her—something that had made her blush beautifully only an hour prior—she changed course and beelined as far from me as the cellblock would allow. She stalked along the outer walls of the circular room, determined to ignore me, and her cheeks remained a deathly white even when our eyes met.

As soon as she disappeared inside her cell, I returned to the table in a huff.

Curious. This had never happened before. Women never refused me, be they fae or human or any other sort of creature. Another first.

I… wasn't all that sure what to do with myself now.

Rejection—for other things, never a bedmate—always put me in a mood.

Tonight, it only made me want her more. Not because she was a lovely specimen, a pretty witch with plump lips that would look exceptional around my cock, but because she had refused me. Because she had been unmoved by my smile, my words, my presence.

And, shockingly, I rather liked that.

A challenge. For the first time in my long life, a true and honest *challenge*.

At last, someone who didn't immediately bore me to tears.

Perhaps Xargi Penitentiary would be a great deal more interesting than I initially thought…

12
RAFE

"Something's wrong."

I slapped down the next card in my pile—six of clubs—and swept that and Elijah's two of spades back to me. "Just because I'm winning doesn't mean something is wrong—"

The dragon chuckled halfheartedly, tossing his next card on the table. Jack of hearts. "Right, let's get one thing straight. You can't *win* at War. There's no skill. It's all luck."

"You only say that because you're losing." I pursed my lips when I flipped over my card and discovered a three of clubs. Damn it.

Elijah drew the two cards back to him. "Rafe, you know that's not what I'm talking about."

Of course I did. Almost everything in our world revolved around *her* lately, and it wasn't one-sided either. One short month had passed since Elijah coaxed Katja into our little clique, turning our duo into a trio, a move that came with unnerving ease—like she had been the missing piece all along, like we'd been waiting for her to show up and make the puzzle whole. Unfortunately, that came with a lot of other nonsense, drama from the supernatural world that both

Elijah and I made a point in our real lives to avoid. We had bonded all those years back because we preferred humanity to our own kind. No games with humans. No innate struggles, no primal clashes. Humans were so simple.

Katja made things complicated.

For the *both* of us—though I refused to admit that, barely even to myself.

Elijah, meanwhile, still struggled with the fated mate bond. At this point, I had no clue if the witch understood why they were connected—because the stubborn git across the table from me, shuffling his cards and staring at her open cell door, refused to explain it—but she had to have an inkling. The tether between them was obvious. They lit up around each other.

And it infuriated me that I… I was jealous of that. Not intensely or anything. I just…

She was a lovely witch.

Beautiful. Sarcastic. Relatively drama free—except when she decided to involve herself in Deimos's nonsense, taking a page out of Elijah's book to rescue that new fae. She smelled like primroses and sunshine. Occasionally, should our hands brush in passing, she felt like *fire*, though her skin was nowhere near the inferno of her dragon mate. Intriguing, that one. Slowly, we had gone from the occasional midnight chat to consistent nightly conversations, sometimes for hours, both of us lying on the dusty floor and whispering through the mousehole before bed.

Last night, after her visit with the warden, was the first time in weeks she hadn't answered me.

"I… know that," I remarked slowly. My fingers moved with a mind of their own, shuffling my portion of the deck, tricks and all, just to keep busy. "Perhaps she's just in a mood."

"She's been in a mood before."

"Haven't we all?" I slid the top card off my pile, then tossed it to the middle of the table. Queen of spades. Another easy victory.

Elijah added his opposing card without looking. Four of hearts. Tongue flicking over my fangs, I studied his profile with a sigh, slowly sweeping the cards back to me.

"Elijah..." Nothing. I booted him hard under the table, and he flinched, shooting me a scowl that quickly morphed into a smirk when I fluttered my lashes. Most didn't dare poke the metaphorical bear; after all these years, I just seemed immune to his ire—a gift more precious than gold, to be forever on an alpha's good side. "Leave her be. If she wants to talk about it, she will."

"What the fuck did Guthrie say to her?" he growled, shaking his head ever so slightly, brows knitted as he threw his next card into the arena. Ten of clubs—beat my six of spades. "Sick bastard probably—"

"Drop it. You're just going to get yourself worked up, and then if she *does* come out..." I finally glanced toward her cell, despite trying my damnedest all afternoon not to. The prison rotated inmates through work assignments, which meant all my cellmates had staggered shifts throughout the week. By some miracle, Elijah and Katja had the day off, same as that new fae, Avery, and Deimos. Strangely full house today. The demon and his lackey hadn't left their usual table, both reading the best books from the library cart in a merciful silence, and the fae had been asleep since we'd returned from breakfast. Katja wasn't asleep. She'd been in her cell alone for hours, but I just *knew* she wasn't asleep. "You'll be all intense and off-putting, and then you two will bicker as soon as she sits down, and I'll have to break the tension with a—"

"With a poem?"

I fumbled over my next card, swallowing hard when I found him staring *through* me—not *at* me, right into my skull and out the other side. So. She had told him, had she? My pathetic attempt to stop her weeping the first night had become a crutch whenever I sensed her on the verge of tears. Thus far, we had worked through six of my collective works; Katja liked the one about the fae princess and the willow tree the best.

"Well, I... I..." *Fuck* me, I needed to feed. Seven months in this hellhole and I needed more than a few goddamn tablespoons of blood a day. Usually I was much quicker on my feet. Clearing my parched throat, I motioned to my lone card in the middle of the table—nine of diamonds—and arched an expectant eyebrow.

"She must be special," Elijah mused, eerily calm as he placed his card beside mine. Four of diamonds. I took the two back as the dragon shifter tapped his deck on the tabletop, voice hushed as he added, "Even *I* haven't heard your poems."

I offered a dismissive sniff and rolled my shoulders back. "You've never asked, you unsupportive prick."

That wasn't fair, of course. Elijah proofread my articles every now and again, and he had never once refused to be my sounding board during a pinch of writer's block. I just... It had been centuries since I recited my human work to anyone. Poetry was from another time, a different life, and I seldom wished to go back to it—to memories of a starving deckhand, working odd jobs to survive, taking the most dangerous Dublin had to offer to keep a roof over my head every few weeks.

Being attacked in an alley after a rare night on the town with the boys.

My maker leaving me to bleed out...

Leaving me orphaned.

Orphaned vampires seldom survived. We weren't trained like those newly turned in covens, human companions of established vampires who had gone through the official channels, received the proper permits and permissions, to become immortal. No one wanted us. My existence six hundred years on was a rarity.

A damn *miracle,* honestly.

Elijah and I played two more silent rounds in the game of War, the unspoken conversation simmering between us, until—

"Rafe, tell me how you feel about her."

I slapped my next card down harder than necessary, gut bottoming out at the request. "What?"

Elijah's lips thinned, and he withheld his card, leaving mine out there waiting for its opponent with an irritable sigh. "Can we drop the pretense? My inner dragon senses it and he hasn't been out of the cage in *months.*" He worked his jaw, cracking it noisily, and then flicked his card onto the table. "Neither of us want to rip your skull open, so... just tell me."

My king of spades beat his three of hearts. I snatched the cards and added them to my deck, shuffling it absentmindedly. Anxiety was so strange as a vampire: an unwelcome prickle in the middle of our chests where our dead heart lay dormant, like a set of slow fingers with clawed tips stroked at our bones. Odd—unsettling. Difficult to focus on anything without a proper meal in months.

"I..." The prickling intensified as if one of the claws had chipped away at a rib, and I dug my knuckles into my breastbone with a scowl. "It's nothing. She's good company, that's all, and I suppose is becoming a good friend... A *prison* friend, of course. I mean, she's your... your... *fated.*" Why was that such a struggle to say, my throat locking around the word? "I would never dream of coming between—"

"I can't say I like it," Elijah growled, setting his deck aside —as if that would pause the game. Stubbornly I refused him, tossing a card toward the middle of the table, flipping it over when it turned midair and landed face-side down. Two of clubs. *Damn* it. The dragon shifter just stared at me again, *through* me, his eyes more gold than brown, sharpening, burning. "But she looks at you differently than she does anyone else."

I scoffed. "Please. The way she looks at me pales in comparison to how she looks at you—"

"We're complicated."

It was the first time I'd heard him admit it, that his connection with his fated mate was more tangled and messy than clear-cut and clandestine. Shifters grew up on stories of fated mates, soulmates bound together by fate, destined for a life in the stars. They never heard the other side, the tales of fated sweethearts who loathed each other from first glance, who despised the way some divine source had woven their lives together, free will a thing of the past.

Katja and Elijah certainly didn't loathe each other. They meshed well, emboldened in each other's presence, a strong team in the bakery, him protective of her and her nurturing of him—she always gave him her leftovers. Always. Even if her stomach roared an hour after dinner, she did it, seemingly without thinking. But Elijah had never wanted a supernatural mate. He wanted a human: a simple, uncomplicated, beautiful human girl, preferably one from the village back home, who would give him an easy life free of otherworldly nonsense. Instead, he got a witch.

A witch who clearly didn't understand what was going on between them—possibly even resented the fact that he made her *feel* without her consent.

"Anyway, that's not what I'm talking about," he pressed. "I'm not talking about her and me right now, and you know that."

"Elijah, don't think for a second I would do that to you."

No surprise I couldn't look him in the eye as I said it; I just... She made me—*feel*. Not love or anything quite so over-the-top. But comfort. Affection. Attraction. The beginnings of something that I didn't want in the slightest.

"Anyone out there looking for you, Rafe?" Katja had asked a few nights back through the mousehole, whispering it after a stretch of silence so long that I'd worried she had drifted off to sleep on the floor. *"Your coven, maybe?"*

"No coven. I'm... an orphaned vampire. It's just me and Elijah now."

I'd heard her rustling about, shifting onto her side to peek through the hole at me. *"I'm sorry."*

"Don't be. It's old news."

"Still though."

"What about you? Anyone looking for a prison that shouldn't exist? That, you know, doesn't *exist in our world?"*

Her quiet had been answer enough, but in a soft, sad voice she'd murmured, *"Humans."*

That night, we were both orphans, two supers without a coven, without anyone out there looking for us in the right places. I'd felt close to her, even if only for a moment, as if the rest of this shithole didn't exist. We had ended up just lying there, both of us *right* next to the hole, so close yet so painfully far apart, until eventually she wandered to bed and I did the same.

I still couldn't explain it, the bond percolating between us, but it wasn't welcome. Nothing more than friendship was welcome, but it bloomed all the same.

Supernatural drama. *Honestly*. What a mess.

"All I'm saying is that while I might not like it, it's not unheard of," Elijah carried on, tensed as he tossed another card on the table. Our eyes met fleetingly, and I flinched when I noticed his narrowed pupils, thin black slits in a sea of fire, the dragon inside trying to claw its way out, fighting the collar that bound him in his human flesh. When he next spoke, his voice had deepened an octave. "It's not uncommon for a female to take… other mates. We might not be a pack or a clan or whatever, but we're bonded, you and I. You're the brother I *chose*. In a sense, you *are* my clan, and fated mates can sometimes bond with the entire—"

"This is nonsense," I muttered, rolling my eyes and slapping another card down. Elijah swept them back to him with a snarl.

"Can you stop being a fucking cock for two seconds and listen to what I'm trying to say?"

Out of the corner of my eye, I caught Avery glancing our way, and Elijah took a moment to compose himself. When his gaze finally snapped back to mine, his pupils had rounded out, the inner dragon contained.

"Do you think this is easy for me?" he demanded, posture easing for the sake of our audience, his voice gravelly and low. I shook my head, knowing for a fact that it *wasn't* easy for him. He had no control over fate, same as the rest of us. Elijah didn't get to decide if his mate was a one-dragon girl or not, and I imagined that was devastating. But he'd concede to her, no doubt, because of their bond—and that certainly wasn't fair either.

"I appreciate that, my friend," I said with a sigh. "Really, I do. I appreciate the difficulties in all this, but my loyalties are to us. I would never compromise that."

Elijah scrubbed at his cheek, looking more exhausted than he had in months. "*Us* includes her now. I've accepted it… You should too."

The weight of his statement hit like a freight train—so much so that I hadn't even noticed we had company.

"Room for one more?" the fae trilled, a wall of green materializing almost out of nowhere at my side and easing onto an empty stool like he belonged here. Even Elijah flinched, his shifter senses so entrenched in our conversation that the newcomer had gotten the jump on him as well. Not good. In a place like this, no one should *ever* be able to sneak up on you.

I had met more than my fair share of fae over the centuries, especially living in Ireland where the portals between our worlds were so frequent and rooted. Ancient passages stretched from the emerald isle to the Otherworld, and in my experience, most fae were uptight bastards who deserved a good beating just to bring them back to reality. Unfortunately, pummeling a fae had its own set of difficulties. Fast as a vampire. Durable as a shifter. Powerful as a mage and cunning as a trickster. The fair folk were the predator of predators—but at least these collars balanced things out.

After all, never in my long life had I seen a fae speckled with bruises and scabs like a Jackson Pollock painting. Their healing abilities were a mystery to me, but I had always assumed that like shifters and vampires, they regenerated a healthy form almost instantaneously. This one had seen more action in his one day than I had in my seven months. All angles and handsome fairy charm, the bruises did nothing to detract from his natural allure, his messy light brown hair and his impish green gaze. The only positive he had going for him at the moment in my books was that he'd said *something* to really piss Deimos off, a feat neither of us had accomplished—had to give credit where credit was due.

In fact, whatever this smirking fae had whispered in the demon's ear must have still stung, because there was Deimos glaring at us from his table. Miserable, pathetic little shit... Knowing someone outside of his posse had royally pissed him off gave me a special little thrill, but we certainly didn't need the extra attention. This fae brought *heat* with him, first from the staff and now our fellow inmates.

As he glanced between Elijah and me, we offered a stony silence by way of greeting—unwelcome and frosty, usually what we gave everyone who tried to weasel into our duo.

Everyone except Katja.

"No?" The fae clapped his hands and rubbed them together, eyes glinting with the cruel mirth commonly associated with his kind. "Playing War, are we? Deal me in. Half your decks each, just to keep it fair."

"Who the fuck are you, fae?" I demanded, and he seemed to brighten at my accent—no doubt recognizing a Dubliner, finding familiarity in my lilt. Spearing a hand through his rakish hair, the fae's mouth stretched into a smile that predicated a humble-brag. Across the table, Elijah rolled his eyes, both of us bracing for bullshit.

"Prince Fintan of the Midnight Court." Yup, bullshit. "A pleasure to make your acquaintances… Elijah, dragon shifter. Rafe, *vampire*. It's been an eon since I've found myself in such company." He spoke with a lofty high fae accent, a blend between posh English and old-money New York, and then had the nerve to snap his fingers. "Come on, come on, deal me in."

Elijah caught my eye, and I shook my head. *Prince* Fintan, eh? Highly doubtful this one was a prince. There were so many courts in the fae world, so many royal bloodlines and bastards, so many nobles fighting tooth and nail for a piece of the action; it wouldn't be the first time a lesser fae came to the mortal realm declaring they had a claim to the throne. No one could prove otherwise, and fae arrogance carried an annoying sense of entitlement that was easily mistaken for a royal temperament.

Besides, believing a fae at their word, especially in the beginning, was foolhardy at best. Until you could read them, decipher their physical tells, map the rhythms of their slow-beating hearts, it was best to take *everything* they said with a grain of salt.

Elijah straightened to his full height, larger than me and Fintan when he sat up and rolled his shoulders back, then tapped his half of the deck on the table. "What did you say to Deimos?"

"Oh, that little parasite?" In a unison that would have been laughable anywhere else, we three turned toward the demon, who had been staring unabashedly our way since the fae sat down. However, without his full horde as backup, he yielded fast, going back to his book with flushed cheeks and a snarl. Fintan chuckled, drumming his fingers hurriedly on the metal tabletop, a ball of energy despite having had the shit kicked out of him—twice—in less than twenty-four hours. "I told him that while I appreciated his offer to become an underling and lick his boots at every sunrise, I had no interest in sucking micro-dick for the short time that I'm here."

Much to my surprise, Elijah snorted, which had me grinning incredulously—both of which seemed to delight the fae.

"Now, can I play or not?" Those bright green eyes darted between us. "Or are *you* two the true schoolyard bullies of Cellblock C?"

My dragon counterpart conceded first, handing over a chunk of his cards, and I did the same, neither of us offering the suggested half. Let him start at a disadvantage—he hadn't earned anything more yet.

"Talking about Miss Fox, are we?" Fintan glanced up expectantly in the silence that followed, shuffling his cards with a skill that could give mine a run for its money. The deck practically flew between his hands, just a blur of white and black, his fingers dancing. When neither of us answered, the fae chuckled again and set his deck on the table, carefully straightening it out so it was a perfectly uniform rectangle. "Oh, it's just so *obvious*. She returned from her meeting with the warden rather upset last night. Shame it's still bothering her... She's a breath of fresh air in here."

Elijah's jaw clenched, muscles rippling, and he glared daggers at me, pupils in slits again. For Christ's sake. Shifters and their mates—*so* tedious.

"She isn't a conquest, fairy," he rumbled, his snarl a warning that would have made lesser men flee. Instead, Fintan merely plucked the top card from his stack and eyed it curiously.

"No, the good ones never are," he mused, turning the card to reveal the ace of hearts. "Are aces high or low?"

"High," Elijah and I growled in unison. Once more, Fintan ignored the warning signs, grinning like a fool.

"Right. Might as well just give me your cards now, gentlemen."

We did, begrudgingly, neither of us in possession of anything to either beat or match his ace.

"Why are you here?" Elijah rasped, tossing his next card into the middle of the table. I did the same—eight of clubs—and Fintan followed shortly after.

"At this table?"

"In this prison," I hissed, sweeping the three cards back to me. Fintan shrugged with the nonchalance of a man who had never had to care about anything in his life, that smirk implying this was one big game.

Maybe he *was* a prince.

"Got caught taking names from humans at a bar," he admitted with a sigh and a slight roll of his eyes. "I wasn't going to *keep* them... I'm just so fucking bored most days, and I get extra trickstery when I drink. Bounty hunters picked me up, brought me here, told me I was *guilty*... Which I suppose I am, but hardly by fae law." He sniffed, elegantly stroking another card from the top of his deck. "But at least this is a bit of excitement… for as long as it lasts, anyway. I'm sure the rescue party is on the way."

Elijah might have dubbed me a member of his clan, but we lacked the telepathic bond shifters shared with their kin—blood or otherwise. Still, when our eyes met, as usual I knew precisely what he was thinking. *This guy is fucking delusional…*

Maybe. Hard to say with some of the characters in here. He could just be a spoiled fae fuck, or he could be completely off his rocker. Only time would tell, but at least we outnumbered him.

"You here to play games?" Elijah took the next round.

"Only with those who deserve it," Fintan remarked, pouting handsomely when I took the one after.

"You plan to join a gang?" I had to know—had to at least feel him out. The fae glanced between us, wiggling his eyebrows.

"Is there an opening here?" he purred, everything about him—his posture, his tone, his expression—suggesting this was a man accustomed to getting his way. When neither of us gave him that, Fintan cleared his throat and reshuffled his deck, those skilled hands struggling to stay still. "Everyone else just seems so petty. I've done the gang thing—been where that demon is with clout-chasers ready to lick my taint and gargle my balls if I asked." What the ever-loving *fuck*? "It's played out. It's cliché, and cliché is *boring*."

I exchanged another quick glance with Elijah, and once again his reaction surprised me. Exuding a calm alpha aura, he set his cards aside, threaded his huge hands together, and placed them on the table. Pupils narrowed, he spoke with a rich, gravelly dragon rasp that I so rarely heard—and never in a conversation like this.

"We don't play games," he stated, catching Fintan's gaze and holding it. "We don't pull rank. We don't draw unnecessary attention to ourselves. We just want to do our time and get the fuck out of here." He leaned closer to the fae, head cocked. "Now, is that *boring* for you?"

"Hello, dragon," Fintan whispered, swooping close and staring directly into Elijah's eyes. He seemed about two seconds away from grabbing the shifter's face so he could really get in there, scrutinize to his heart's content, but he withdrew just as a snarl rumbled in Elijah's chest. He flashed us both a grin, then tossed his card onto the table. "Maybe in time this whole sit on the sidelines shtick will lose its appeal, but for now, honestly, it's probably what I need."

He gestured to his bruised face as if that was reason enough. Elijah might have nodded and set the four of clubs next to the six of diamonds, but he didn't believe him—a sentiment we shared. *Miss Fox*. If anything, Fintan had weaseled his way into our trio with the intention of getting closer to Katja. Obviously he hadn't realized what a minefield he'd stumbled into, but if he was as observant as he implied, he would eventually see it—the complications, the tension, the tense air that surrounded all three of us.

Perhaps in time he would regret wandering into the fray, moving on to simpler games and easier targets. In the end, that was probably best for a fae who reeked of self-indulgence and wanton extravagance. Katja navigated her prison sentence just as we did, and while from the outside our little group *was* quite dull, we had our fair share of drama brewing, and at no point would the spotlight ever rest solely on Fintan. A man who only cared about himself would eventually gravitate toward a more eager audience.

And, in the meantime, if he didn't keep his hands to himself, Elijah and I would just rip them off.

13
KATJA

"I know something's bothering you."

"For goodness' sake, Elijah."

"It's been bothering you all week, ever since you—"

"Can you just drop it?"

"I wish I could, but you know I can't—"

"*Stop.*" I slammed my recently packed plastic bag down and glowered at him from across the table. Sweat glistened on his brow, his handsome features flushed, his golden-brown waves extra fluffy in the bakery's humidity today. He was so damn gorgeous, every girl's type, but it seriously pissed me off that he was using our weird, unspoken, steadily growing bond against me. Maybe he *could* sense that I had been off since my meeting with Lloyd Guthrie—and rightly so—or maybe he just saw it on my face, had learned to read my expressions because we spent almost every free second together if we weren't forced apart...

Whatever the case may be, whether he actually felt my distress over learning that my dad's lifelong paranoia had been justified and that a psycho now thought he *literally* owned me, or if he was just adept at reading torment on the face of a fellow inmate—I hated it. No matter the source, no matter his reasoning, I *hated* that he was capitalizing on our connection to wheedle me for information.

Did I think he planned to use the information against me? No.

Did I think he was doing this to hurt me? No.

Elijah was a good guy. Sweet, sometimes stoic, annoyingly protective, and seriously good at every card game we played, he and Rafe were two of the best men I'd ever met, and that was saying a lot. Prison offered perspective, I guess. Fintan, on the other hand, was still a wild card, but besides the fact that I couldn't look him in the eye without blushing bright crimson *still*, a week after his arrival, the fae didn't factor into this.

Rafe and his melancholy poems didn't either, his velvety baritone that whispered into my cell every night, smooth as liquid gold, rich as dark chocolate. It also wasn't about him. This was about me and Elijah and the fact that he was driving me up the *fucking* wall this afternoon.

It was my first bakery shift with Elijah in three days courtesy of the rotating schedule, and whoever had been in here before had left the place a mess. Jensen, the guard who constantly Snapchatted and played games on his phone, didn't seem to notice or care that dough hadn't been proofed, that a few buns from a recent batch were burnt on the bottom, that no one had bagged any of the loafs—that no one had even precut the loafs to begin with. Instead, Elijah and I had arrived to a buttload of work—seriously, what had those jerks even *done* for nine hours?—and I so wasn't in the mood.

For any of this.

For bakery duty with double the work.

For Xargi Penitentiary and its rigid routine.

For Williams—nose-picker guard—who openly leered at me in the shower this morning.

For the looming threat of Lloyd Guthrie.

And for Elijah—who wouldn't stop pushing.

"I'm not trying to be nosy," the dragon shifter huffed, spinning a full plastic bag of perfectly sliced rye and tacking a plastic clip on the end. Why was he so good at this? I ran a café; my baked goods should dominate his. Instead, I had a pile of slightly smooshed bread loaves to my left from when I'd manhandled them into their plastic bags and the beginnings of a headache that would probably split into a migraine by the end of our shift.

"Yeah, well, I really don't want to discuss it."

"I know. I'm not a fucking idiot, Katja." Elijah set his packaged loaf aside, handling it so carefully with those huge hands—delicately, same as he treated me most days, even more so since my mood nosedived after meeting with Guthrie. "I can just… *feel* something is upsetting you, and my inner dragon—"

"Can mind his own business," I snapped. Seriously. Just because he had an inner beast who could, I don't know, *smell* misery didn't give him the right to pry like this. Fuming, I piled all the loaves I'd packaged onto a metal tray, then stalked away from our worktable.

What bothered me the most wasn't his poking and coaxing. In fact, most inmates would probably *kill* to have someone like Elijah on their side, innately connected to them, concerned about their well-being enough to fight for an answer, to not be deterred by a grumpy attitude and a few withering glares. I slowed, closing my eyes and sucking down a deep breath. Sometimes I was too harsh on him; he was just trying to be a good guy. If he knew what was wrong, maybe he thought he could fix it.

But he couldn't fix it.

And despite being a good guy, despite our bond, it felt like he was taking advantage of something that I still didn't understand. Rafe had stopped pushing *days* ago. Fintan didn't seem to notice something was off despite following us around like a lost, pampered puppy. Elijah wouldn't let it go, and I'd made my feelings about that clear.

And...

I just wanted to go home.

I missed the café. I missed my job, my people, my neighborhood.

I missed Tully. So, so, *so* much. One day in this place was too long—almost two months illegally detained in a prison run by a sociopath was torture.

Tears made themselves known with a painful sting when I opened my eyes, and I meandered toward the shipment crates a little slower. Unfortunately, the telltale sounds of Elijah's heavy footfalls lit a fire under my ass, and I sniffled back the sadness, then blitzed around the corner, headed to the rear of the bakery to unload my prepped loaves into the shipping containers. Of course none of this gorgeous bread went to the inmates. We sometimes tried to guess where the prison shipped it off to; the writing on the label suggested somewhere English-predominant, and the artisan stamp told me they charged a fortune for it.

Teeth gritted, I balanced the tray on the corner of the wooden crate, then started unloading my haul, neatly arranging the loaves on top of what was already in there. Beyond everything else I missed, I deeply craved the use of my own magic again. It was all there, swirling inside me, flickering in my fingertips and shivering in my chest, but I couldn't access any of it. In time, it would sour from lack of use. All this work, the full nine hours of it, could have been knocked out in one or two with a few simple phrases and a flick of my hands. Sure, my magic had always been a bit unstable without a wand, but it would get the job done.

"Can you just stop for a second?" Elijah growled as soon

as he entered my personal bubble, looming over me, statuesque and broad and imposing. As if it wasn't hot as balls in here already, his presence sent a wildfire ripping through me, starting in my chest, in my fluttering heart, and flooding out to every limb. I had recently managed to put my pathetic earnings toward a pair of underwear and a hair tie now that I had access to the prison shop. No bra yet, but that was a work in progress; at least the black stretchy elastic kept my hair away from my neck during bakery shifts.

Elijah set me ablaze regardless. Which was also just... great.

"Can *you*?" I fired back, glaring up at him and distractedly swiping a hand over the back of my neck. Yup, sweaty. My jumpsuit collar absorbed a lot of it, but that didn't make me any more comfortable. So, as per usual, not only did Elijah fluster me mentally, emotionally, my mind *struggling* to understand the pull between us, but he affected me physically too. And right now, that definitely didn't help his case.

He clenched his strong jaw, muscles briefly rippling beneath the coarse brownish scruff, and, narrowed gaze still fixed on me, he dumped his entire tray into the crate. Just. Plopped it all in, no organization, no regard for the rows of neatly stacked loaves I'd started.

This was the first time he wasn't careful with his work.

Again—not doing himself any favors.

"For gods' *sake*, Elijah," I muttered, immediately diving in and straightening everything out. The dim overhead lighting flickered, and in any other scenario, I might have blamed it on my magic, on the tempestuous storm brewing inside me, the air crackling between us. But there was no magic in Xargi—not for us, anyway. Shitty lights.

Shitty *everything*.

Panic lanced through the flames dancing inside me,

vicious and sudden. I'd outright refused Lloyd's offer, preferring incarceration to whatever that psycho had in mind for me, and at no point did I want word to reach him that I was bad at my job. The guy would probably use any excuse to kick me off a work assignment that so many other inmates considered *cake*; a guard who barely paid any attention, free rein of a sprawling underground space—even if it was hot as hell most days—and all the freshly baked bread you could scarf down when no one was looking. Bakery duty was a dream, same as the kitchens, the library, and the new greenhouse. I didn't care if they stuck me somewhere else, but if I got a reputation as a slacker, I just *knew* Lloyd would use it against me.

He seemed like the type.

Just as I reached in to fix the next row of loaves, Elijah snagged my wrist and hauled me upright. I went with him, unable to muscle my way out of his hold even if I tried, and then glared, *hard*, conjuring up the sternest expression I could muster.

"I'm worried about you," he admitted gruffly as his thumb stroked the underside of my wrist, gently brushing over my racing pulse. The physical contact seemed to grab us both, gazes plummeting to where we touched. Exhaling shakily, I shifted my glare back up to Elijah's face where it belonged, only to find him steely-eyed as well, a mildly annoyed look plastered across his rugged features.

What the—I so didn't understand this shifter.

But his hand felt like fire, a cuff fresh from the hearth, branding my skin the longer and tighter it held on.

"You're hurting me," I croaked. Elijah's eyes flicked to mine, more gold than brown, his gaze that of the dragon. My belly suddenly looped—with fear or interest, I still couldn't tell.

"No, I'm not." He wasn't. "You can take it."

I could. His grip might have been firm, might have seared my flesh and sizzled down to the bone, but in my heart of hearts, I didn't want him to let go. It wasn't pain driving us apart… Not in the slightest.

"Let go," I muttered, the order catching in my throat. Elijah shook his head.

"I can help, Katja, if you just let me in."

"Maybe I don't *want* to let you in," I told him, the fight flaring inside me, briefly shouldering all the other muddled emotions aside. I yanked my arm away from him, twisted it, but he wouldn't let go—wouldn't stop looking at me with the eyes of the beast. "Maybe I don't *need* you poking around my head in here… Have you ever considered that?"

"Of course I have." He followed along with slow, lazy steps when I backpedaled, like he was just humoring my escape attempt. "But you can't help it, and neither can I, so… stop being stubborn and just tell me."

You can't help it, and neither can I. What the hell was that supposed to mean? I stomped my foot, my prison-issued shoes useless at absorbing the brunt of the stonework below, about two seconds away from stomping on *him*.

"Piss off, Elijah."

"No," the dragon rumbled without hesitation, just following me around the back of the bakery beneath the flickering lights. Shadows danced across his features, but they did nothing to cloud his expression, the resolute determination that made me both hate and respect him in that moment.

"Yes."

"No." His voice echoed off the walls, and we both stilled, heads snapping in the general direction of the bakery's main door. Nothing. Jensen probably hadn't even noticed we weren't within sight anymore, but we still waited a few beats longer. Xargi had a way of screwing you over if you let your

guard down; I knew that from experience now. When we seemed to be alone, we faced off again, me glaring up at him, Elijah scowling down at me through a hooded golden gaze. He huffed, breath striking me like dragonfire.

"Katja—"

"*Oh*, for…" I closed the distance between us in a single stride, pushed up onto my toes, grabbed his collar, and yanked his mouth to mine. Kissing him was a last resort, the only thing shocking enough to finally just shut him up. But it was supposed to be a quick, hard peck.

It wasn't supposed to feel like fireworks.

It wasn't supposed to linger.

And most of all, my lips weren't supposed to soften, to fit so perfectly against a mouth that had been driving me nuts for the last hour. His free hand slithered down my body, rough and wandering over my curves, until it splayed possessively across my lower back. The other held my wrist tighter, both working together to drive me into his chest. Elijah exhaled a hot breath against my cheek, not a flicker of shock in his eyes—only desire. Carnal and raging. Explosive need that knocked the wind out of me. Flames hot as the sun ready to burn me alive.

All that in a *look*—in his eyes and nowhere else. Because he might have gripped me tight, yanked me flush against him, soft lines colliding furiously with a wall of unyielding muscle—but he did all that with restraint, his body stiff…

Like he was fighting me.

The fireworks suddenly sparked lower, pinwheeling in my belly, exploding between my thighs, and my eyes fluttered shut to block out the gold, to stop staring directly at the beast, challenging the dragon—

"Hey, idiots."

We sprang apart just as Jensen rounded the corner, stalking into the bakery's depths for what seemed like the first time based on his darting, curious gaze. Phone in one hand, his free one fidgeted with his belt, the warlock's mouth twisted in a grimace. Did he suspect anything? I mean, Elijah just stood there like a giant tree, stiff and glaring at the floor, fists at his side. Meanwhile, there was me, cheeks on fire, breath feathering in and out, struggling to keep it normal, to quiet my thundering heart.

"I need to, uh, use the facilities," Jensen announced. Right—classic oblivious warlock moment. Thank the *gods* for small mercies. He picked at his belt again, almost dancing in place, and then under his breath muttered, "Fucking potluck breakfast..." As if realizing he'd said that out loud, he straightened and stopped fussing, shoulders back like he was a guard we ought to take seriously. "Can you hold down the fort for like twenty minutes?"

I just stared back at him, mind full of static.

At least Elijah managed to nod—to look somewhat present, if a little furious.

"Great." Jensen tucked his phone into his uniform's breast pocket, then tapped his wand like we'd forgotten all the guards carried one. "Don't fuck this up, or you're both in solitary for a week, *comprendo*?"

Yeesh. That was the most atrocious butchery of the Spanish language I'd ever heard, that Alabama drawl wrapping around the word in a way that was almost offensive. When neither of us responded, Jensen gave us a look like we were slow in the head, then tapped his ear, expecting a response.

"Yes," Elijah rasped. Our phone-obsessed guard might not have realized it from the way he stalked—waddled—off, but I caught it, every damn decibel. The depth. The subtle roar. Gravel and woodsmoke and whiskey and oh *no*. Elijah sounded different—darker, more dangerous—and it made my body *sing*. Thrown by the reaction, by the sudden and intense desire throbbing through me, flooding my veins and demanding *action,* I pivoted on the spot and beelined toward our workstation. Just put the bread in the bags. Just get through the next six—*ughhh*—hours and use the humdrum, repetitive tasks like a cold shower.

Only I didn't make it back to the table.

Relief sparked when Elijah caught me by the elbow. Need flared when he dragged me hard to the left. Resistance reared its ugly head, almost because it *had* to, when he hauled me toward the walk-in proofing pantry.

"Elijah," I hissed, feet stuttering over stone. "Stop—"

"Shut up, Katja," he growled in that *voice,* so unlike him—vaguely threatening and utterly wild. Why the *hell* did I find that so hot?

The shifter wrenched open the pantry door as he had a hundred times before over the last month, but this time it bounced off the wall, hurled with such force that I swore I heard something crack and splinter. He shoved me inside, forceful and infuriating in the way he manhandled me like a guard.

Only I didn't want to cower like I did with the black-suited warlocks skulking around Xargi's corridors. As I rounded in place, immediately assaulted by the pantry's chill compared to the bakery inferno, I wanted to *fight*. Hit back. Shove him. Rake my nails up his chest—down his back. Nip at that tempting lower lip like it was *mine.*

A whoosh of hot air washed over me as Elijah dragged the pantry door shut, slamming it into place hard enough that the hinges whined. For a beat, he just stood there, back to me, shoulders rising and falling like he was chasing his breath, but when he turned, he stared me down with the eyes of the dragon. I swallowed hard, taking this brief pause for what it was: a chance to back out. To shatter this moment with a much-needed dose of reality. But my feet had grown roots, my knees had locked, and neither would budge.

Not until he grabbed me again, snapped that strong hand around my forearm and yanked me forward, spinning us, and shoved me up against the door. The brief flash of pain in the back of my head felt oddly welcome, and I grabbed at his jumpsuit just as he descended on me, mouth crashing to mine. He caught me with my lips slightly parted, and he took full advantage of that, parting them further with his brutality, claiming me with his tongue, marking me with his teeth.

Elijah struck me as a nice guy. Stoic and quiet and contemplative most times, preferring to observe a situation before reacting—any situation that didn't involve me, at least. Yet compared to everyone in here, he was so *good*. Earnest. Thoughtful and protective and selfless—

But he didn't kiss like he was good.

He kissed like a villain, forceful and rough, *taking* what he wanted, thrusting me against the door with a soaring figure of pure muscle. He kissed me like he was guilty, like he had sinned and deserved penance.

And I *loved* it.

This side of him just *did* it for me.

And it shouldn't. I didn't need more reasons to be drawn to him, for my traitorous body to crave him, but I'd never be able to shake this feeling—the feeling of being dominated. Of *wanting* to be dominated, taken, ravished.

Highly aware that we had twenty minutes, maybe less, maybe a few more, my hands flew up his chest and reclaimed a bit of the control. My fingers seized the first button on his jumpsuit, frantic and shaky, fumbling to undo it like I hadn't been buttoning my own for the last fifty miserable days. As soon as the first fell, the next came easier, and then the next, the next, until suddenly I'd parted the seas, the blue fabric falling open to reveal a sculpted torso. At least, I assumed as much from the feel, my eyes shut, my mouth occupied —*plundered*—by his. But when my knuckles brushed the searing skin of his navel, nudging at what felt like a sharply defined V headed southward, I tore my mouth away with a gasp.

The faintest touch of skin to skin and I panicked.

Elijah conceded, slamming a hand to the door above me, bracing—almost holding himself back as our bodies eased apart. Sure enough, there was that magnificent chest, defined pectorals and cut abdominals and—yup—mouthwatering V-definition that seemed to come so naturally to shifters, that human men slaved in the gym for months to achieve. And there it was. Right there. All for me.

My eyes flicked to his, and while it should have terrified me to stare down the beast, there was something so beautiful about the gold, something so intriguing about his thin pupils. Calculating, almost. Gone was the warm chocolate brown, replaced by a golden sunrise that felt both ancient and cunning, primal and desperately wanting. I nibbled my lower lip, still chasing my breath, fingers toying with the open flaps of his navy blue jumpsuit...

I could say no.

I wasn't here for this—for him. Could still walk away. *Should* walk away. Elijah was just a distraction—

No. It wasn't my mind that screamed it, but my heart, my body. *Stay*.

My trembling fingers abandoned his jumpsuit for mine, hastily wrenching open my own buttons, careful not to rip any out. The unflattering white cotton panties I currently wore had cost a fortune; no telling how much I would have to sacrifice to replace a busted jumpsuit.

The pop of that first button was almost like his go-word. Elijah snapped into motion, just as frantic as me, following my lead by yanking his jumpsuit down his arms, inch by inch unveiling the definition of masculine perfection. Rugged, broad shoulders. Abs to die for. Thighs like tree trunks. Even his prison-issued briefs looked great on him, but the guy could wear a paper bag and still be mistaken for a born-again Adonis.

As I shimmied my jumpsuit down, every inch of me aflame, fire collecting in my cheeks and between my thighs, I pointedly avoided glancing at the huge bulge beneath that thin slip of white cotton, not wanting to read as *too* forward. Not that it mattered: Elijah lacked modesty, shirking the slow reveal by hooking a thumb under the worn-out elastic waistband and yanking it down those sculpted thighs and toned calves. Fabric pooled at his feet, and try as I might to avoid gawking, I couldn't help it—not when his cock fell like a lead weight, its silky tip nudging my stomach.

He seemed just as taken with me as I was with him, that golden gaze raking across my body, lingering on the dip of my throat and the valley of my breasts. If we had the time, I would have liked to just look at him—maybe even desensitize myself to such a gorgeous creature so that I'd stop flushing bright red at the thought of what was hidden under his jumpsuit. But we *didn't* have time. Someone was always watching in Xargi, always waiting to screw you over.

And no one was going to take this away from me.

From *us*.

I shoved my jumpsuit the rest of the way down, clumsily stepping out of the purple material and kicking it aside, not caring that it would be dusty and floury when I put it back on. Elijah went for my panties like they had their own gravitational pull, his expression hard and unfamiliar, everything taut—like he was fighting himself, pushing for restraint—his arm like steel when I grabbed it.

"Do *not* rip them," I whispered hoarsely, shooting him a warning look that finally broke the tightness around his mouth, that shattered the dangerous glint in his eyes. He grinned down at me, all predatory and daring, like he saw my words as a challenge, and I huffed, pushing his arm away ever so slightly. "You know how much they cost."

"Does that mean I can't keep them?" Elijah rumbled silkily, his head cocked. I bit the insides of my cheeks to stop my smile; this wasn't a train of thought I wanted to encourage, even if there was something so wickedly sexy about him carrying my panties around in his pocket as we went on with the rest of our day.

"*No,*" I hissed, "you definitely can't keep—"

He swallowed my words with another kiss, fierce and brutal, more punishing than those that came before, and I wilted against the door with a whimper. I'd never been one for rough stuff in the bedroom, but as I wriggled the cotton down my thighs, let it fall to the floor, I couldn't imagine any other way with Elijah. Outside this room, he *was* sweet and thoughtful, protective and inclusive, patient to a fault about my struggle of coming to terms with being wrongfully incarcerated—kidnapped, actually, by a madman.

But right here, right now, Elijah was a dragon—*the* dragon, alpha to the core.

As soon as I was bare before him, his hands went wandering, roughly perusing my figure, mapping every curve, delving between my thighs and snarling when he found me wet. I whimpered as he stroked me, swept his thumb over my clit, wondering how his punishing mouth would feel against my folds.

But—no time.

My hands found his shoulders when he hoisted me up, and I wrapped my legs around him, locked my ankles behind his back and dug in, the pair of us driven by instinct, moving and rearranging and jostling each other like this wasn't our first time. His cock nudged my slick entrance, and I speared my hands into his shaggy hair, into surprisingly soft waves I'd wanted to stroke and finger-comb and nudge out of his eyes for *weeks*. Today I twisted. I tugged. Just as my teeth and tongue and lips reminded him that I wasn't passive, that I could give as good as I got, my fingers were cruel, using his hair like reins, driving him onward—

Elijah shoved me hard against the door, then filled me with a single, gloriously brutal thrust. I cried out into his mouth, eyes wide, pleasure and pain deliciously twining into one. Foreplay had always been my favorite part of sex, but having been single for years, most of my gratification came from one-night stands—and guys who didn't plan to stay the night weren't super keen on wasting time *before* the deed.

But this wasn't that; Elijah wasn't like them. This was frantic and hurried out of necessity, not only because of the time constraints, the threat of being caught by *anyone*, but also because in that moment, as he stilled and buried his face into my neck, as I adjusted to the sheer size of him, to the way he stretched me, it felt like we had been dancing around *this* all along. Like every conversation, every lingering glance, every heated argument, had led up to him and me coming together just like *this*, fitting so perfectly that it ought to be a crime.

"Are you a-all right?" he murmured, hands trailing up my body, rough at first, then gentle as he cupped my face. I swallowed hard, noting the way his eyes shimmered between brown and gold, like he was struggling against his inner beast. Fighting for control—for me, for my comfort.

"*Hell* yes," I whispered back. I stroked his hands as they held me, then his cheek, the coarse stubble along his jaw, my smile blooming into something tender. There he was—a glimmer of the good guy I knew Elijah to be. Concerned. Thoughtful. Patient. Checking on me, making sure I was okay. The fact that he could be both, that he possessed such an exquisite duality, only made me want him more. Knowing he was still in there beneath the rugged, harsh exterior, beneath the glittering gold, the animalistic snarls, had me craving both sides of him.

In different circumstances, somewhere far away from here, he could ravish me all night long, fuck me within an inch of my life while I screamed for more, and then after, Elijah could be tender. He could cuddle me, hold me until dawn. He was my silver lining in Xargi. Him and Rafe, two men who intrigued me, two men who I'd quickly and unwillingly become infatuated with, were the only things keeping me from falling apart and giving up. This should have felt like a mistake, like I was ruining what we had and sullying the status quo. Instead, I swept his hair back, then rocked my hips. "Don't stop."

Elijah ducked his head with a groan, then nipped at my palm, my lower lip, and kissed me like he wanted to claim me. The first harsh thrust had me seeing stars, the sweetest ache burning bright between my thighs. Nibbling a blazing path down my throat, Elijah gripped me by the thighs again, almost like he was determined to bruise me, mark me, then pumped hard and fast, furiously driving me into the door.

Hopefully Jensen hadn't meandered back in, because there was no subtlety in the way the door creaked and groaned, in the rapid-fire thump of my hips against the wood. If I could walk after this without limping, it would be a miracle—but in that moment, I preferred the limp.

Needed the brutality.

Craved this dragon's fire.

Time fell away around us, and what could have easily been minutes or hours later, I imploded in his arms. My climax came out of nowhere, bright as the north star, savage as Elijah's snarls, ripping through me like raging floodwaters hellbent on destruction. It soaked me from head to toe, *fire* in my blood, pleasure blooming like fireworks again—like a whole display of them, one explosion after another. I slapped a hand over my mouth to muffle a sob, but Elijah soon yanked it aside, replacing mine with his, driving into me harder, faster, prolonging the ecstasy until I thought I'd just *die*.

But… what a way to go.

Elijah's pace stuttered for the first time since he'd started, faltering from a savage pounding to a breathtaking grind, milking another ounce of bliss out of me. His hand clamped down harder over my mouth to silence my cries, and my heart leapt into my throat at the first true brush of teeth over my shoulder. I blinked hurriedly, the dim pantry coming back into focus, his teeth so sharp and *present*.

I'd heard shifters bit their lovers.

Sometimes they marked them, the scarring permanent.

But that only happened when the pair were—

"*Fuck*, Katja—*fuck*," Elijah gritted out, his teeth replaced by his lips, dragging an openmouthed kiss along my shoulder and up my neck. He nipped at my ear when he finally stilled, hips jerking ever so slightly, spilling himself inside me. That little nibble wasn't what I imagined a shifter's bite to feel like. It… It wasn't. He hadn't marked me.

I let it go, ignoring the thought as best I could, hating the bitter stab of loss in my chest. Because I hadn't lost anything. The sex had been spectacular—best I'd ever had, despite the circumstances.

So…

Why did I feel like something was missing?

We untangled slowly, neither of us ready to stop touching the other just yet, all lingering caresses and brushing hands and bodies hovering in personal bubbles. A heavy, tangible silence hung over the pantry, one that surprisingly didn't make me nervous. Sure, I wasn't smiling like an idiot after a phenomenal orgasm or anything, and neither was Elijah, but it wasn't guilt thickening the air. *That* didn't slow my movements or make my mind sluggish.

As soon as I straightened, panties on, something oozed out of me—something hot and sticky. Elijah glanced my way, eyes dipping down to my thighs, and then offered an apologetic look that I just nodded at. Thankfully, I was beyond diligent about taking my potion at the start of each year. The brew to both prevent pregnancy and protect against sexually transmitted diseases was the most annoyingly complicated in my arsenal. The ingredients cost thousands to acquire, and I had spent the entire month of December, *every* December, babying a temperamental, constantly simmering cauldron since I had turned sixteen. I always took it on the second of January, without fail, and then had to weather the unpleasant side effects—a wave of sickness similar to the human flu—for a full two weeks after. But then I was safe for the rest of the year, protected and secure and never needing to worry about having a baby when I wasn't ready.

So, we were covered, Elijah and me, but…

What if I was still in Xargi come next January? What then?

The thought brought a fresh batch of tears to my eyes, but I blinked them back as fast as I could. Without knowing the details, Elijah was bound to misread the situation—take my upset for regret and self-loathing and guilt and all the other crap that came with spur-of-the-moment sex. I didn't feel any of that, and as I buttoned up my jumpsuit, fingers trembling again, I hoped he didn't either.

But… I felt something.

When I looked up at him scrubbing his face, dressed and ready to go back to work like this had never happened, I felt…

Longing.

Need.

Not for another round. Not for his mouth on mine or his hand between my thighs. Not for teeth or fire or punishing caresses that would leave me bruised in all the right places.

I couldn't explain it, but the flood of feeling struck hard, pounding into me with all the savagery that Elijah had, and I slapped a hand to my mouth to muffle a sudden and very unwelcome sob.

The dragon shifter stilled, eyes snapping to me and shimmering with panic. I shook my head, hoping to dispel the fears, and then sucked in a heaving breath, throat thick as I said, "I don't understand it..."

Elijah exhaled softly, reaching out for my arm even as I retreated into the door. He gently cupped my elbow, steadying me, supporting me as hot, cruel tears streaked down my cheeks. Great. Just what every guy wanted after a quickie in a prison pantry.

"I'm sorry," I whispered, shuddering through the apology and wiping at my face. "I'm sorry. I just don't get it. I don't get us—*this*... It doesn't make sense to me, and I'm so sick of wondering—"

"Katja, we're fated."

Three little words, and my brain short-circuited. Arms falling limply to my side, I gawked up at him as the static between my ears reached a deafening roar. We... *Fated*?

"I don't get it either," Elijah admitted with a nervous chuckle, scratching at the back of his neck, that good-guy persona shining through those warm eyes, those full pupils, the faint rose flush in his cheeks. No more animal. No more brutality, all carnal need and pleasure and base instincts... Back to the man, back to two people forced into a life-altering conversation that made my head spin. Elijah shrugged as I continued to stare blankly up at him, my mouth seconds away from just falling open, and he cleared his throat awkwardly. "But, you know, here we are, so... yeah."

Anger raged when my brain finally rebooted—anger and hurt and shock and *outrage* that he had kept me in the dark for the last month and a half. Because he would have sensed it right away, wouldn't he? I had felt it from the second we first made eye contact, but I didn't *get* it. I just floundered around in a mess of feelings, confused and alone and upset, *needing* him and not understanding why. Wrongful incarceration was bad enough, but throw in the fact that my body was responding without my consent, drawn to this *stranger*, and he had just let me go on feeling like that for *weeks*...

Teeth gritted, I reared back and smacked him as hard as I could, slashing across his broad chest and nearly taking a button with me.

"If you knew, why didn't you say something?" I demanded —yelled, almost, voice rising well above an acceptable level for where we were. No telling if Jensen had come back yet, but if he had, he *definitely* would have heard that.

Elijah and I glanced at the door together, holding our collective breaths, and when no guard came trundling through to investigate, he let his out in an exasperated hiss.

I'd... never heard him exasperated before. Annoyed. Frustrated.

Not with me, anyway.

But there it was, plain as day, etched so deep into every feature that there was no missing it.

"Maybe I'm trying to process it all too." He took a step back deeper into the pantry's narrow corridor, walls lined with shelves of proofing buns and loaves. "Maybe *I* don't understand it. Maybe *I* didn't expect to be fated to a witch... Did you ever consider that?" He shook his head with a wince, then pressed his knuckles to the middle of his chest like he was fighting a rush of heartburn. "Did you ever consider that I don't have all the answers? That I can't fix every fucking problem that comes up?"

I honestly hadn't, and that was ridiculous of me. Childish. Selfish. Ever since I agreed to join a prison clique, I had looked to Elijah and Rafe for everything: comfort, security, and support. They had been here longer than me and both had centuries of life lived on my twenty-nine years. Instinctively, I deferred to them both, hid behind them and stayed resolute in my decision to not make waves. To *survive.*

I should have been giving back.

Fated mates was *huge* in the shifter community. While I wasn't an expert on the subject, I knew from gossip and general supernatural lore that shifters were raised on stories of finding their soulmates, the ones destined to walk forever by their side. Some never did, but those who found their fated were *whole.* Fate had selected me for him, apparently, and him for me.

And instead of smacking him, I should have...

Shoving all my feelings aside, I padded after him and pressed a hand to his chest. It then slid up to his shoulder, and even as he turned away, expression terse, jaw hard, mouth in a thin line, I moved closer.

Eventually, I hugged him. Just a hug—nothing more salacious than that. Nothing that would lead us anywhere. I stood up on my tippiest tiptoes and wrapped my arms around his neck, holding him as a tremor ripped through his body. Elijah took it almost as if he *had* to, standing there with his hulking arms at his sides, his huge hands in fists again. His heart thundered, the beat drumming from his chest to mine, and I just held tighter.

I'm so sorry, Elijah.

Here I was, thinking I was the only one struggling.

But to him, he had just found his soulmate. In prison.

And she wasn't who he had always pictured. She was surly and withdrawn and broken, *terrified*, prone to lashing out when things got hard or tense or confusing.

She was damaged goods with baggage a mile long.

"Thank you for telling me," I murmured, threading one hand into his hair, the other stroking the back of his neck. He radiated heat, my body sweltering against him, but I didn't back down. "I'm sorry I… Now I understand."

Finally, *finally*, he hugged me back. Bundled me up in his arms and embraced me like it was the first time, maybe even the last time, he would ever hold me. His grip threatened to crush all the air out of my lungs, but I said nothing, did nothing, just let him take what he needed for once. All this time, he had been protecting the woman he perceived as his mate. He couldn't help it. He hadn't been trying to draw attention to me…

He had been doing what he was programmed to do, same as me. I was drawn to him, if I really *was* his fated mate, because that was how destiny arranged it.

But if that was the case, why was I still confused?

Why was I infatuated with Rafe? Why did I lust after Fintan—physically, of course, his impish man-boy shtick *so* not my thing. If I was fated to a dragon shifter, a good man who had been thoughtful and patient and protective of me from the beginning, shouldn't other men fall to the wayside? Shouldn't they not even enter my radar?

I mean, even as I hugged Elijah, a little part of my mind remembered that tonight, I'd lie on the floor and whisper through a mousehole with Rafe. That sometimes those conversations were the highlight of my day.

And that wasn't fair.

I exhaled softly and closed my eyes, trying desperately to block it all out.

One question answered, a thousand more to go.

But at least I knew a few things for certain.

One: I owed Elijah a ton of patience and a lot more leeway.

Two: I needed to figure out what it meant to be a shifter's fated mate—and thankfully had a rabbit shifter friend in Cellblock B who could lend a hand with that.

Lastly, three: sex with Elijah made me feel alive. Yes, my back and hips were *destroyed*. My toes ached the longer I stood on them in this hug. My pussy had taken a beating and would be feeling it for days. But I felt like a person again, not just a number, not just an inmate, not just a purple jumpsuit with a godsdamn collar around my neck.

And I intended to chase that feeling.

No matter where it might lead me.

14
FINTAN

"You know I'm one of the *fae*, right? Not a fucking wood elf?"

Honestly—assigning me to the greenhouse for work duty… Like I had any real experience with plants beyond smoking them. Inmates might have been clamoring for the position, desperate to work something cushy outside the main building, but I was a motherfucking *prince* of the Midnight Court. You'd never find me clamoring for any paid position that didn't involve judging scantily clad ladies or taste-testing fae wine.

Mind you, I currently had zero access to my vast wealth given it was still my first month, and I *was* getting sick of begging off Elijah, Rafe, and Katja for goods. They had pennies to spare, which I appreciated whenever they tossed a few my way, but pennies barely bought me a single cigarette from the prison storefront. So, perhaps a job would be temporarily beneficial, but for how long I could endure some uppity warlock *fuck* telling me to water and fertilize shit was anyone's guess.

A little over two and a half weeks in this pit and still no rescue. The wards likely put a dampener on my brother's efforts, but *really*. Surely someone in our kingdom was adept at breaking them. They were only witch's wards of *this* realm, after all. How difficult could it be to crack them? Fae magic was far stronger; the cavalry ought to be charging through by now.

"Did you hear me? I said—"

"Oh my *gods*, just shut the fuck up, Fintan," Williams barked, groaning out my name as his grip tightened on my arm. Gravel crunched underfoot as he hauled me across the outer yards of the penitentiary, the sky a hazy blue overhead, the air thick and still inside the confines of the ward, a sea of grasslands stretching out to the horizon beyond it, dotted occasionally by a mountain or six.

Ahead, the greenhouse spanned long and narrow along a bit of unnecessary chain-link fencing—pure aesthetic, the dramatic fucks—its panels opaque glass, two unfamiliar guards stationed in front of the lone door. Xargi Penitentiary soared over my shoulder, looking oddly ancient for its recent construction, an imposing stone structure two levels tall with sentry towers in all the corners, warlocks positioned there to take out any runners.

You know, if the wolves didn't get them first.

I'd spotted four since Williams had marched me out the doors, the process of stepping foot outside *beyond* tedious. So many checks, as if I'd had time to shove contraband up my arse from the moment this fucker had dragged me out of the cellblock and shoved me through winding corridors. And now here we were, on a brisk, forced walk to my new work duty.

A grey shadow whizzed along the base of the greenhouse, bypassing the guards and disappearing around the far corner. Five wolves, then. Shifters, most likely, given the militaristic precision with which they patrolled the grounds. A few wore identical leather collars to the inmates, and although

Williams wouldn't even entertain the conversation, *I* for one suspected that the security pack had a few prisoners of their own, only the collars kept them in their huge wolf forms. Meanwhile, poor bastards like Elijah were in a constant state of blue balls, desperate to shift but unable to let the beast free.

Really. I felt for him. Of all the creatures in this realm, a dragon shifter came closest to my kind in terms of raw, unhinged *power*.

Cruel, to keep him caged.

"Surely we can come up with *something*," I drawled as we neared the greenhouse door, one of the guards unbolting it from the outside. "I mean, if you find a way for me to access my fortune, I'll pay *you* what I'd earn here—"

Williams cracked me upside the head with his elbow, the first display of physical violence in weeks, and then shoved me forward. Right. Fair enough. None of the guards had fallen for my charms yet, but once I had real money to barter with, their tune would change; it always did.

Pain throbbed in my temple as one of the greenhouse guards lurched forward and grabbed my arm.

"Take him before I fucking kill him," Williams growled. I flashed him a flirtatious smile, lips come-hither but eyes murderous. The warlock had the nerve to gulp, his hand flitting for the wand on his belt, but he beelined back to the main building before either of us could get another word in. Coward. Rolling my shoulders back, I massaged the ache away as a new set of steely-eyed, hard-as-stone, boring as *fuck* guards led me into the greenhouse—which turned out to be even larger on the inside than the outside let on.

Magically enhanced, the air thick with enchantments that gave off a slight fruity odor, the interior stretched on for miles. Met with rows upon rows of greenery, I let out a huff. Maybe this wasn't the cushy gig everyone had expected.

Inmates peppered the long metal tables, fussing over herbs and perennial blooms and periwinkle-blue hydrangeas and for fuck's sake, not a hint of either wolfsbane—a killer to wolf shifters, but it gave a hell of a high to the rest of us—or marijuana in sight. *Boring.*

Fans whirred softly overhead, the humidity making the spell-tainted air even more pungent, and an alarm suddenly *buzzzzzed* throughout the entire greenhouses. Inmates leapt back from their leafy charges as sprinklers misted the lot, then got back to work as soon as it was over. Purple, grey, green, orange—a vast array of supernatural folk littered the rows, but it was one purple jumpsuit in particular that caught my eye.

Wily little minx. My grin sharpened. She hadn't told any of us she'd gotten a new work assignment, but it positively tickled me that I finally had some alone time with the witch Elijah and Rafe guarded like the realm's most precious stone.

The dragon had become even *more* intense about her since they'd wandered back into the cellblock last week positively stinking of sex. Rather a tense supper with the vampire after, but I had found a way to keep it light, as always.

Honestly, what would this bunch of misfits do without me?

"On second thought, I would be *thrilled* to devote my time to, er, shrubs and whatnot," I announced, gesturing to the expansive greenhouse with a flourish, and as soon as the guard loosened his hold, I was off like a shot.

"Wait," he called, footsteps trailing after me over a dirt floor. "You need your shift assignment—"

"Oh, I've found it." I lobbed him an easy grin, hands up innocently. "Not to worry!"

Six rows over, fifteen feet down the table, Katja stood harvesting roses. Gloves hiding her delicate hands, luscious red hair braided and tossed over her shoulder, she attacked the task with a furrowed brow, so careful, so precise with each *clip* of her pruning scissors, until—

"Well, hello, darling girl," I purred, sidling right up beside her, swift and silent enough in my approach that she jumped and mangled the stem of the stalk in hand. She stilled with a curt breath, glowering at me out of the corner of her eye, and I leaned a hip on the metal table, the air thick with rose-scented blooms.

How fitting: Katja's scent reminded me of primroses.

"I thought you were a bakery mouse," I mused as she got to work trimming the thorns from her recent acquisition, bushes upon bushes stretching down this row, roses of all colors and sizes awaiting her tender touch. No other inmate assigned to roses; clearly she needed an assistant.

"They're putting anyone with any floral skills in here. I just found out this morning they wanted me," she muttered, shooting me another narrowed look before plopping her de-thorned rose into a white plastic bucket of water alongside six other red blooms, this one slightly shorter than the rest.

"Ah." I spied a cart a little ways away with jars of fertilizer and spray bottles of lavender liquid, none of which called my name. Alongside them, however, sat a pair of gloves far larger than the ones Katja wore—although even they were too big for her—and another set of pruners. After jogging over and grabbing the tools of the trade, I returned to her side and cocked a hip back against the table. "I'd be delighted to work under your tutelage, Miss Fox."

"Any experience with gardening?" she asked as I slipped on the gloves—perfect fit—and then twirled the pruning scissors.

"Not even a little."

"Potions?"

I shrugged. "Drinking them, sure."

"And you're here because?" She peeled through the

rosebush in front of her, on the hunt for the next perfect specimen.

"I dunno—the prison is racist?" Something bright and hot flickered in my chest when she bit back a smile. Amusing the one witch in this whole fucking realm who *wasn't* swayed by my charms was a win I'd take any day. "But I no longer care now that I have a beautiful horticulturalist to study under."

Or on top of. I kept that little bit to myself; overt flirting got me nowhere with Katja Fox. She required a more subtle hand, and sussing out her limits was one of the more enjoyable parts of my day. That and riling up her dragon and vampire bodyguards. They had been so *aggressive* about asserting their claim on her, stating outright that she wasn't fair game, that if I intended to sniff around her, I ought to find a new gang. Well, here we were, two weeks into my Xargi sentence, and I sniffed around her whenever I damn well pleased.

Only it was Katja to put me in my place most of the time, not her hulking protectors.

In fact, from the way she exhaled briskly and slammed her clippers down on the table, I suspected I was about to get another tongue-lashing.

"Does this persona usually work on women?" she demanded, facing me with a scowl and an exquisite pink blush. I smirked down at her, then held up my own pair of scissors between us, examining them slowly, dramatically, all for show.

"You know, with the correct amount of force, I could probably drive these through a guard's eye and into his brain."

Katja blinked those lovely sapphires up at me, her stern expression flatlining to shock. I got a secret thrill out of surprising her, throwing her off. Unlike all the ladies who had entered my orbit in the past, women who flocked to me in court and in the human realm, it wasn't physical gratification that drew me to Katja. It wasn't the opportunity to show her precisely what I could do with my fingers, my tongue, my cock. For once, my words *mattered*.

They rarely mattered to anyone.

Besides the way my heart did a giddy little jig whenever I stunned the disapproval out of her, I liked providing a distraction from this place. She struggled, this fiery witch, with imprisonment; we all did, in our own ways, and if I could break the monotony even for a *moment*, it was yet another victory.

My mouth lifted into a handsome smile, the one that wooed and charmed and coaxed women into my bed—not my words, just the smile… and the crown and the money.

"And yes," I said pleasantly, gripping my clippers' blades in one gloved hand, "this persona *always* works, but I think the title usually wins them over before my dashing personality."

The shock splintered, and her disbelief, that familiar look of incredulity that only made me want to work *harder* to make it go away, returned full force.

"Right," she muttered as she grabbed her scissors and dove back into the bush. "*Prince* Fintan of the Midnight Court… Sure."

I bit my cheek when she rolled her eyes. Rather annoying that no one believed me; lesser nobles and peasant fae had fucked up my credibility for centuries now. Still, surely I exuded the *air* of a royal.

"So, how do you think that's working here?"

I fiddled with a rose's petals. "What?"

"Your attitude," she clarified, finally spotting a rose that fit her unknown criteria and snipping its stem with a noisy *click*. Katja straightened, bloom in hand, and got to work on pruning the thorns. "How do you think it's working?"

I smirked, tapping my clippers against my gloved palm. "On you, you mean?"

"Duh." She shot me a look, then hissed when a thorn stabbed at her thumb. Whether it pierced the glove or not remained to be seen; with the quality of goods around this place, it wouldn't surprise me if these bland, heavy mitts were useless. Usually, I'd scoop up her hand and investigate, brows knit, eyes riddled with false concern. Then I would kiss the wound better, my lips slowly drifting toward whatever I most desired from the woman in question. Her mouth. The underside of her wrist. Her breasts. Down to the cleft of her thighs…

With Katja, I just watched her shake her hand out and get back to work.

"I think it's going *swimmingly,*" I told her, the giddy pitter-patter fluttering in my chest again when she snorted. "You're positively smitten with me."

The witch arched an eyebrow, scoffing, and dropped her latest sheared stem into the water bucket without looking back, those big blue marbles fixed squarely on me. I let the staring match drag on a few beats, then chuckled.

"Don't worry… I tend to grow on people. You'll see."

"Yeah, I bet I will," Katja said under her breath, mouth twitching like once more she was struggling against a smile. I watched the battle out of the corner of my eye, a little deflated when the grin never surfaced, and then halfheartedly picked through the rosebush in front of me. How did she know what to cut? They all looked the fucking same.

Unbeknownst to my many tutors, possibly even my parents, I was a fast learner. Feigning dimwitted frustration in the face of new tasks had been a coping mechanism I leaned on for years, craving the opportunity to prove myself yet also terrified of failure. So, if I came off as *just* stupid enough, they'd still respect me without dumping anything too important on my shoulders. Hardly the most chivalrous way for a prince to sail through life, but I had an army of older brothers and sisters to fill the roles required of them. As the youngest, nobody had expectations. I had always done as I pleased...

And now I was here.

Locked up and wearing a collar, a shame to my court, to my father, to my title.

Pathetic.

Teeth gritted, I rolled my shoulders back and shoved my father's insidious whisper deep down, focusing instead on the roses. Studying Katja's gloved hands rather than her beautiful profile, I noted which roses she ignored and which she selected—those that *just* bloomed were her preference. I followed suit. Hardly a difficult thing, clipping roses, but a teeny, tiny smidgen of pride flourished inside when I held up my first snipped and de-thorned rose for her discerning eye. Katja plucked it from me, scrutinizing it, and then plopped it alongside all the rest in the bucket with a barely-there smile.

"Why don't you like me, Katja Fox?"

Her eyebrows shot up, as did mine. I'd never outright asked anyone before, but none of my sycophants dared let on should they find my antics distasteful. Still, I knew the rumors racing through the court grapevine. I was nobody's favorite prince—unless they needed a prince to host a party, to get pissed off their face with, or to fuck them within an inch of their life. *That* was all I was good for: my money and my cock.

"Insecure much?" the witch said with a chuckle, those sapphires shimmering with genuine mirth that dimmed when I didn't smile back. Perhaps she thought I wasn't serious; I seldom ever was, not even with myself. Clearing her throat, Katja paused her perusal through the bush to her left, then licked her lips, the flicker of her tongue a delectable distraction. "Fintan, I never said I don't *like* you. I just don't like being aggressively hit on all the time."

"I'm afraid that's my default setting." I flashed a crooked grin, but Katja merely blinked back at me, unimpressed.

"Well... Stop."

"But you enjoy it," I insisted, refusing to believe that all her blushes stemmed from discomfort. Some, sure. But I affected her. My charm touched her at least a *little*, and at the moment, that was enough for me.

Not that she would ever admit it. Sucking in her cheeks, eyes narrowed, Katja fixed me with the business end of her clippers. "Look, I'm not here for you to toy with while you pass the time on your sentence. Unlike you, I *don't* belong here. I didn't commit any crimes."

"Neither did I." I scratched at the back of my neck with my shears, enjoying their sharp bite. "I mean, not by fae law, anyway."

She rolled her eyes, back to her rosebush. "Whatever."

"Perhaps it's a defense mechanism," I pondered aloud, all singsongy and obnoxious—because I had never been strong enough to just blurt out the truth. "Perhaps I fear my *truest* self will be rejected immediately and therefore put up a wall—"

"*Gods,* Fintan." Katja shoved me hard with a giggle, and I staggered to the side, chuckling right along with her. Yet again, a moment of honesty spoiled by bravado, by putting on a show for the sake of the audience. Still, I rather liked that I'd made her laugh, that her smile lingered as she picked through roses. No telling what it was about this woman that so infatuated me. Sure, I'd never had a witch before; she was a conquest in that regard.

Some sick part of me liked when she was *mean*. Rollo's wife—future queen of the Midnight Court with three impressive heirs birthed already—was mean. Only to him, of course, and he seemed rather taken with her attitude. Always teasing and pushing one another, the act private and personal, glaringly intimate. Noblewomen in the court were charming and worldly. Intelligent and skilled in many talents.

But they all would have fallen into my bed by now.

Most of them *had* fallen into my bed with minimal effort on my part. No wooing. No courting. They bowed and thanked me when it was done.

None of them were mean.

Katja had a ward around her, one that effortlessly repelled my usual tricks, one that made me *work*.

And that delighted me.

Intrigued me.

For the first time in centuries, the object of my desire *challenged* me, possibly without even realizing it.

I cast her a sidelong glance, fiddling with a wilted rose, pretending to be busy while I studied her. What a gift, this witch.

"Tell me about Café Crowley."

She snipped too hard, fumbling over the request, then shot me a frown. "What?"

"I've heard you mention it in conversation," I remarked casually. Eight days ago, at breakfast, with Rafe—discussion topic: coffee. Lately, I had taken it upon myself to note, catalogue, and file interesting tidbits about her—about all of them, actually—for later use. But just those three, only Katja, Elijah, and Rafe. No one else necessitated that level of detail. Everyone else was an open fucking book: no layers. "Tell me about it."

Setting her scissors aside, Katja laid into the newly clipped rose, ridding it of its thorns. "Why?"

"Because you interest me." Ah, *yes*, there it was—the delectable plume of pink in her cheeks. A dewy carnation, just like those on the table across from the roses. "Therefore, your life interests me. Ergo, Café Crowley interests me—"

"*Gods*, I get it." She shot me another wry grin. "What do you want to know?"

Tossing my shears and my gloves aside, I popped a fist under my chin, then swooped in and fluttered my lashes. "*Everything*, Miss Fox. Everything."

Her flush sharpened in color, which positively tickled me, but I laid off the dramatics when she started to pull away. Begrudgingly, I shoved my hands back in the gloves and pretended to work, my efforts coaxing her to spill a few details about her profession.

And it was oddly fascinating to hear her share her passion. She loved the work. Loved her employees. Loved the books and the drinks and the kitschy aesthetic. Katja's eyes lit up when she spoke of it, so animate and wild, and I did my best to swallow every crude thing that came to mind as I watched and really *listened*, utterly enraptured. No sense in pushing her away—not when she was unfurling her petals like so many of these thorny flowers.

When she eventually tapered off, her smile different, faltering, I let her. Only a fool would push for more than she was willing to give, especially when everything about this place was a painful reminder that she was so very far from home.

That *I* was…

I tossed the one rose I'd clipped and cleaned into the bucket, a measly contribution compared to her nine.

"Katja?"

"Hmm?"

I hesitated, scanning our surroundings for any eager ears. The nearest inmate was one row over and a good fifty feet down the way—another purple jumpsuit with his head stuck deep in the greenery. Above, the fans whirred, the greenhouse humidity suddenly stifling, the glare through the brushed glass too bright.

"Never mind."

"What? No..." She nudged me with her elbow, and a bead of sweat dribbled down the side of her face. "Say it."

Ignoring the urge to brush the droplet away, to *lick* it away, I tightened my gloved hands to fists as she got to work on the bush that I'd been poking at for the last... however long we'd been standing here.

"I... want to go home."

The witch stilled, then straightened, tossing her thick, messy braid over her shoulder and unleashing a waft of primrose that almost made my eyes flutter—like I'd never smelled fucking primrose before. When she frowned up at me, face etched with concern, I almost backpedaled and whispered something lewd. But she had shared a piece of herself with me. She had been open and honest, gifting details of Café Crowley to one of the fair folk, to the sort of creature who hoarded information and used it to their advantage, who trapped unsuspecting mortals and supers alike in their web all because their prey had been foolish enough to *talk*.

She had shared—and trust was a two-way street, especially in here.

"I'm afraid prison isn't as *fun* as I'd originally hoped," I muttered, picking at a frayed string on my left glove, coiling it around my finger and yanking it free. "It's really menial and boring, and most of the creatures here are fucking prats who—"

"Wow, imagine that..." Katja smirked up at me, equally patronizing and breathtaking, then patted my arm. Her touch lingered, annoyingly firm, painfully present, even when she withdrew. "Welcome to the club, Fintan. We all hate it here. We *all* want to go home. Prison isn't supposed to be *fun*."

"Hmm. Yes, well..." Well, what the *fuck* had I been thinking, sharing something so unbelievably naïve and ridiculous with her. *I want to go home*. Hardly sexy, that comment. Not brooding and masculine, so far from alpha male territory that I was practically on a different planet. Heat tingled in my cheeks, shame ripening and rearing its ugly, uncomfortably familiar head—

Until she touched me again. Featherlight at first, she pressed her hand to my arm just above my elbow. My eyes flashed to hers, but she didn't meet them, staring at the middle of my chest instead. And then her touch turned firm. She held me as few ever had, empathetic and comforting and soothing—nothing I'd ever experienced from my father, rarely from my mother, and only occasionally from my sisters. It wasn't pity either. Just a squeeze to tell me that she understood, there one moment and gone the next. She then turned and grabbed the bucket of clipped roses, heading for the rear of the greenhouse, and I trailed after her like a good little dog, smitten, utterly in need of her attention.

Both when she was mean *and* when she was kind.

We must have walked at least a half mile inside the magically enhanced greenhouse, headed for a section with cement floors and a flurry of activity. Produce and flowers and dried, ground herbs were counted, stocked, and loaded into shipment crates, all this hard work headed elsewhere. An elvish inmate in green mused that the funds acquired from the sales *must* go back into the prison, which made me snort cruelly. Back into the prison? *Really*? Nothing about this shithole suggested any real funding went into its upkeep, the main building just some basic stone fort with warlock muscle keeping the workforce in check.

Right then and there, the penitentiary's purpose became so glaringly obvious. It wasn't a stronghold for supernatural criminals, but a forced labor institute thinly disguised as a, what, a rehabilitation center?

Katja refused to join in the hushed conversations, the speculation about where the flowers were headed, which country we were feeding with the produce grown by magic rather than pesticides or genetic modifications. She just loitered at my side, silent, arms crossed and expression distant. I much preferred her being mean to me, but before I could poke the bear, stir her up with my back to the others, a shrill alarm blared throughout the greenhouse, so sharp and screeching that every super present, with or without my exceptional hearing ability, clapped their hands over their ears and cowered.

As soon as the siren ceased, guards rushed in, wand-happy and probably sporting hard-ons now that they finally had the chance to *do* something. Really, greenhouse duty must have been as mind-numbingly boring for them as it was for us. Barking orders and shoving inmates, the few guards assigned to monitor the sprawling space herded all of us to the front, where two more stood waiting alongside a pack of men in smart suits and leather shoes. All but one radiated a supernatural aura, though beyond the obvious human in our midst, a rare one in the know about the supernatural world, the rest were more difficult to discern who was what without the jumpsuit colors. The fellow on the far left, however, had the chaotic shimmer of a demon, handsome and beaming as he surveyed us with bright blue eyes that twinkled like starlight and thin lips stretched into a great white's smile.

Maybe one of the fallen? He had an air of loveliness to him that not all demons possessed.

In the center of it all, a warlock who radiated authority, salt-and-pepper hair and slate-grey eyes. One of the guards addressed him as the warden, then snapped for all of us to smarten up. Eyebrow arched, I glanced left, then right.

Glistening with perspiration, this lot couldn't look smart right now if we tried, with dirt under our nails, smeared across a few cheeks, spattered on jumpsuits.

But the warden was untouched and no doubt untouchable. Sporting a crisp navy suit, a painfully clean white dress shirt beneath and a checkered blue-and-silver tie, he commanded the room with just a look.

He was my ticket out of here.

The gold on his fingers, the cruel twist of his mouth, the wand with its ivory handle hanging loosely in one hand, and the *control* exuding from his every pore meant absolutely nothing to me. In *my* world, this creature wouldn't even ascend to the rank of the lowliest courtier.

Tall, wiry, birdlike in the way he surveyed his captives, Warden Guthrie could still be bought. Every man had a price, and as soon as I had the means, he could name it and I'd be gone.

Along with Katja, if I could swing it.

Maybe her brooding guards too, but I wasn't about to push my luck for them.

Without bothering to address us, Guthrie launched into a big speech about the innovation of the greenhouse—the prison's newest and brightest program, apparently inspired by one of its inmates. He sang its praises, about the rehabilitative properties of working with plants, about the benefits it could offer all us lowly criminals, and the profit it would bring the prison from trade agreements—marked-up prices and all.

Prick. The bastard was a businessman through and through, a warlock I could crush under my boot without this collar. Swallowing a chuckle, I leaned back to whisper the sentiment to Katja, my arms crossed and my mouth sporting the shit-eater grin that had already gotten me punched in here.

Only my words died on the tip of my tongue.

Katja was sheet-white and trembling, her arms folded over her chest like they were snared in an invisible straight jacket. Eyes on the floor, she seemed to be concentrating on her breathing, and a strange, unfamiliar panic skittered down my spine.

What...?

I poked her with my elbow, but she only withdrew further, not daring to lift her gaze from the dirt floor. Confusion ripened in my gut, but when I faced the warden droning on and on again, it vanished. Poof—gone, the reality of the situation painfully clear. Guthrie might have been addressing the suits, gesturing with his arms, his wand, rambling in an aged rasp that probably did it for those lusting after a daddy —but his eyes never left Katja.

Not once.

Master of the ceremony, he conducted this show confidently, yet he couldn't tear his gaze from *her*. The other inmates around me shuffled, picked their nails, wiped at their sweaty faces. Most refused to look at Guthrie, but no one shook. No one quivered in their prison-issued flats. No one looked like they wanted to disappear into the earth and never come back.

Without thinking—and without hesitation—I moved. Ever so slightly, I adjusted my stance so that I was *right* in his line of sight, blocking Katja entirely. Guthrie's next word might have hitched, but he carried on smoothly, chortling about the price markups of our *perfect* succulents. Those searching greys tried to dart around me, peer *through* me, but I made a better door than a fucking window.

At no point did I glare. Fleeting images of my first afternoon came to mind, ones of Katja returning from her meeting with the warden so distraught that she had hid in her cell for an entire day after. Something had happened between them, and obviously the predator wasn't ready to discard his prey just yet. He wanted to toy with her a little longer before the kill, truly relish the fear.

But he couldn't have her. Not here. Not on my watch.

And that made me grin. Bold as sin, I stared back, tuning out his bullshit and peering straight into the slate. No fear. No intimidation. I lacked power in this place, but old Warden Guthrie was more breakable than any of the fair folk—and no slip of leather could ever make either of us forget it.

When the show ended, the caged animals were sent back to work. The suits filed out, Guthrie lingering, searching for her in the crowd, but I made it my mission to block his view from every angle. Eventually, he turned away with a scowl; I'd pay for that, one way or another. Negotiating my freedom would be more difficult because of what I'd done, but that hardly mattered.

And as I strolled along after Katja, back to the roses and the clippers and the cheap gardening gloves, I realized that would have mattered before. With anyone else, I would have weighed my options more carefully—not dove into a fight that wasn't my own without meticulously assessing the pros and cons.

Without determining my gain.

We stopped in front of the same handful of rosebushes we had spent the better part of an hour picking through already, only as I suited up, Katja just stared at the blooms. A pinprick of color warmed her cheeks, but overall, still deathly pale, white enough to give Rafe a run for his money.

"Thank you," she whispered, fidgeting with her gloves. I shrugged, unaccustomed to thanks that I had actually earned.

"I didn't do anything."

"Right." She swallowed hard, the collar bobbing at the midway point of her throat. The base of her braid had started to loosen, and her fingers jumped there next, as if in need of something to fiddle with. "And I don't want to talk about it."

I plucked a leaf from a stem, folding it over and over again before tossing it on the floor. Ordinarily I'd pry, pick and poke and prod for information that might be useful to me in the future. Instead, I yanked on my gloves with a sigh, then rolled my eyes.

"About what? About what a disaster the warden's tie was?" I wiggled my brows when Katja's head snapped my way, her eyes round, her full lips parted with a sharp inhale. Good. She needed the distraction, and I was more than happy to provide one. After all, that tie might have been the finest silk, but it was *horribly* knotted, all bulbous and uncouth. "I mean, *really*... You call that a fucking Windsor knot? Pathetic—"

She snatched my hand almost desperately, clawing at the flimsy glove that I wished wasn't there. Cheeks hollow, the little witch clung to me, gripped my fingers with bone-crushing intensity, as her breath hitched and then fell faster, faster, faster—

Until our eyes met. Until her sapphire blues found my garnet greens. I gawked down at her like a simpleton, like a man who had never felt the touch of a woman before, transfixed, enraptured... caught in a spell. *Her* spell.

In time, her breathing evened out, chest rising and falling more steadily beneath the purple fabric. When she finally let go of my fingers, the blood came prickling back into each digit, and I ignored the burn, still lost in her.

Katja's lips twitched in a grateful smile, fleeting but *there*, beautiful enough that any smile I'd seen before paled in comparison. And then, as the storm clouds crept back in, she returned to the roses.

Strange—to be enchanted by a witch without magic.

I had never protected anyone before. Never stepped up, never stepped in. Never rushed to the defense of another.

But pride flared in my chest, bright as the sun and ten times more powerful.

It felt… *good*.

It felt right to throw myself in front of the fire.

And I felt like I… maybe wanted to do it again.

For her.

Only for her.

…

Wait—*what*?

15

KATJA

Everything hurt.

My back, my feet, my hips, my thighs, my arms, my neck, my head—*every*-damn-*thing*.

The new work regime at Xargi Penitentiary had kicked off right around the start of my second month inside. Non-shifters had a schedule of one week on, one day off, whereas shifters had work assignments each and every day. Apparently, the higher-ups thought shifters could withstand the daily grind, but I knew the higher-ups a little too intimately; Lloyd did it because he was a bastard, a sadist who lived for the suffering of others.

Wincing, I rolled onto my back, my shoulder and hip unable to take my body's weight a second longer. Sixty-six days in prison and at no point was there even a whiff of an offer to replace the paper-thin mattress that covered my wire cot. After a week of work either in the bakery with Elijah—or totally alone for nine hours, like yesterday—or out in the greenhouse with Fintan, all I wanted was a *real* bed. Nothing fancy. No foam topper three inches thick. Just a plain old box spring mattress—just *something* to support my aching body with a little more structural integrity than this.

But even if the prison did somehow find it in their budget to shell out for cot replacements every six months or so, I wouldn't get one. Lloyd Guthrie had made that perfectly clear when we met for coffee last week. He drank his—three cups' worth, actually, like they were fueling his mania. I had let mine go cold, then "accidentally" spilled it across his desk when I got up to leave. How I'd managed that was beyond me, especially after being forced to sit there and listen to him rant about how brilliantly he had orchestrated my mom's death.

How he had ensured a *witch* died in childbirth.

Witches didn't die in childbirth. Not only were we physically stronger than humans, our bones denser, our bodies *tougher*, but we had magic at our disposal. We had midwives with a good century or so of experience behind them, all our lives prolonged with a touch of ancient power.

Some stretched theirs on even longer with potions *way* too complicated for me to consider.

But Lloyd had found a way. Furious at her betrayal, he had made his own fetish doll, complete with a chunk of her hair that he ripped out during their last meeting and the necklace he had torn from her neck. Then, as she gave birth to me, he had stuck pins in the doll. One by one, starting with the least vital spots and working his way inward. Unaware that an effigy was in place, Mom's midwives had set charms and fed her potions to ease the pain—but they couldn't save her.

The last pin had pierced her heart.

And then it was done.

He had stolen her from me seconds after I drew my first breath, as I wailed in my sobbing dad's arms.

The sole victory I could claim from that session was that I hadn't anxiety-vomited—not in front of him, at least. Had I sprinted to my cell as soon as Thompson delivered me back to the block to empty my guts into the pathetic metal toilet? Yup. Was said toilet so small that I missed during one heave, splashing the floor and myself? *Yup.*

We had three more scheduled meetings—with no set date, all at random so that I was always at peak anxiety if a guard called my name—where Lloyd Guthrie would share in excruciating detail how he orchestrated the death of my entire family. Up next was Ewan, the middle child and my best friend until he drowned at our lake cottage when I was eight. Then Jackson, my oldest brother, my protector, who had died instantly when his wand somehow backfired at school. Lloyd had promised to save my dad for last, the freshest tragedy in my mind.

Or I could accept his offer.

Leave Xargi with him. Acknowledge the contract. Recognize that he *owned* me.

Screw him.

I could take it—all his talk. Pigs would grow wings and dive-bomb this prison like kamikaze pilots before I went anywhere with him.

Eyes shut, I wriggled around on the half inch of bedding at my back, trying to find the comfy groove I'd worn into it over the weeks. Everyone else would get a replacement before me; Lloyd seemed determined to make my experience here both horrendously uncomfortable—cue the mattress—and backbreakingly exhausting. He had, however, insisted that he assigned me to the greenhouse *personally*, that he figured I would find joy in the flowers, like he had done me a favor.

I hated that I liked greenhouse duty. Absolutely despised the fact that I *did* find peace in the natural world, but I was a witch… I couldn't help that.

What the bastard probably hadn't anticipated was that

putting Fintan in there with me meant Lloyd Guthrie and his disgusting history lessons were the furthest things from my mind. Not only was the fae eye candy beyond belief, but he occasionally made me laugh.

In a hellhole like this, that counted for a lot.

And then there was Elijah. Lloyd had insisted he put me in the bakery to appease my love of baking, as if running a café involved spending a lot of time in the kitchen slaving away over proofed dough. I enjoyed potions, which could equate to cooking in some respects, so the bakery wasn't the worst work option out there, but it was Elijah who got me through those shifts—when he was there, of course. Lately our overlords had been shoving him in the metal shop most of the week, which meant I was on my own more often than not.

But we had plenty of time to ourselves. Two weeks after the discovery that I was supposedly fated to a dragon shifter and the world felt a whole lot clearer. Things had become *much* easier between us now that I understood why my body responded as it did—why my heart yearned to be near him. In a sense, it was biological, just a quirk of the supernatural world. That didn't mean I liked that an unseen deity had chosen someone for me, prearranged my love story in the stars, took away my right to choose—*our* right to choose. Fortunately, Elijah was a gem, and now that we were both on the same page, it was just easier to breathe around him. We were less combative with each other, the group dynamic noticeably calmer now that our mounting sexual tension had finally exploded, and the fallout was *good*.

Because it could have been bad. Sex could have ruined everything, but it only made us stronger—more in sync. Not that that made the guilt inside me any less prickly. I mean, if I was fated to one man, why was I still interested—to varying degrees—in two others? Elijah hadn't once commented on the fact that I blushed around Fintan, or that Rafe and I connected in a way I hadn't with him. Still, I was desperate for another round with the dragon, starving for the best sex I'd *ever* had, but finding time alone in a prison was next to impossible with a legion of warlocks eyeing your every move.

Under the table, we struggled to *not* touch—feet, thighs, hands. Now that we'd had a taste, physical distance was torture.

Speaking of torture... Poor Rafe. Even though work kicked the absolute crap out of me for seven days straight, it was better than waiting around in the cellblock, twiddling your thumbs, because you couldn't risk going out in the sunlight. While the rest of us left most days, able to stretch our legs and breathe some fresh air, Rafe and the other vampires were trapped in the cellblocks, hiding in shadows, only taking the risk to venture out to the cafeteria for meals. At the very least, our cellblock guards marched us down windowless corridors, but not every hallway was without. No telling if they did it for Rafe's sake, or if that was just the established route for Cellblock C.

Besides my ever-present physical attraction, I just felt bad for the guy, which explained why, despite the ever-present exhaustion, I made myself to stay awake as late as I could for our nightly chats.

They were a staple now, our usual routine excluding the day Elijah and I had first, er, *mated*. Rafe had been silent that night, distant, but he'd whispered an apology as we lined up for breakfast the following morning, and I had let it slide. I refused to admit that I *got* it, his mood, his refusal to talk, but I maybe, sort of, almost did.

Thankfully, there hadn't been any further nights of silence. As soon as lockdown started, we waited ten minutes before meeting on opposite ends of the mousehole to chat about anything and everything *not* prison related. Even though I had been absolutely wiped after yesterday's bakery shift, the last in my seven-day stint, I stayed up discussing the merits of each Star Wars movie with him until I couldn't keep my eyes open anymore. Two hours of space opera dissection with no awkward pauses; people paid for that sort of companionship in Xargi.

I craved our conversations.

With Elijah and Fintan, I had the opportunity to leave the group dynamic. We hung out for the entirety of our work shifts. Rafe didn't get that chance, and while lying on the floor hurt at the end of a long day, it was *our* alone time, and I coveted it, protected it, like it was precious.

Because… it *was* precious.

"Try the other side," my favorite vampire called from his cell. My eyes peeled open just long enough to glare at the wall, and I wiggled in place again, searching for the comfy spot that I *knew* was there if I just worked hard enough to find it. A brief bout of silence followed, and then: "Your left shoulder is shit, witch."

"Stop eavesdropping on my naps," I fired back, mouth stretched in a smile that, surprise surprise, also hurt. He was right though; I *had* screwed up my left shoulder sometime in the last week doing one of many physically demanding tasks required of me throughout the day, but at no point did I request a visit to the infirmary.

If I did, I just knew a certain warden would come trailing along after me, and it wasn't worth the risk.

Even though Rafe and I had the entire day to ourselves when I was off, usually accompanied by one of Deimos's assholes whose schedule lined up with mine, we both usually spent this time catching up on sleep. Only as we crept closer to the end of the workday, dinner about an hour and a half out, I felt more exhausted now than I had when I woke up this morning.

Ugh.

Something soft tickled my cheek, and I swiped at it, grimacing at the thought of some Xargi creepy-crawly skittering over my skin. It came back a few seconds later, followed by an oddly familiar *sniff, sniff, sniff* sound, then the ever so faint whoosh of a cat's exhale.

My eyes snapped open this time, no longer weighed down by the fatigue of the day. Heart in my throat, I stared up at the ceiling, refusing to believe it—Xargi played tricks on you when you were at your weakest. But then a mass of black swooped into my periphery, followed by a few more tentative sniffs and the graze of whiskers I'd known since I was thirteen—

I shot up and scrambled across my bed, adrenaline spiking, breath coming out in panicked gasps.

All prim and proper, Tully blinked back at me with eyes identical to mine, my big black floof of a familiar seated at the edge of the cot, the end of his tail flicking left and right.

No.

No, it couldn't be—

"T-Tully?"

He responded to my croaky whisper with a pur*rrrrrr*, one that started low and then ramped up like a revving motorcycle engine. A sob snagged in my throat, and I lashed out expecting my arms to sail right through him—expecting to meet the cold air of an astral projection. What I got was a solid cat body, fur that I nuzzled into every morning back home when I woke up and every night as I was falling asleep.

"Gods, *Tully*!" I scooped him up and hauled the thirty-pound furball to my chest with a strangled cry. Fear and relief mingled inside me, familiar bedfellows in Xargi, and I held as tight as I dared. While Tully's bushy black tail swished harder and faster now, he rubbed whatever part of me he could reach with his cheeks, purring up a storm, those huge paws frantically kneading my bicep.

"What are you *doing* here?" Tears spilled down my face and dribbled into his fur. Ordinarily the wet offended him, but my familiar took my emotions in stride, pulsing with a magical warmth that I felt in my bones. "I've missed you so much..."

He chattered back at me in his stupid, high-pitched baby voice, the one that everyone at the café laughed at—he was such a huge cat and had such a dainty, squeaky meow. Here, the sound felt like *home*. Witch and familiar, together again, and while I could sense him emboldening my magic, giving selflessly from his own supply to fuel mine, it was a futile attempt. The collar clamped down on the well within, sealing it shut even as Tully tried to top it up. If I ever got rid of this thing, all the raw, simmering magic inside me would go off like a bomb.

"The collar," I whispered. "I can't... I can't take what you give me anymore."

He could use his magic on me, but he couldn't *give* it to me—just another part of my life Xargi had destroyed.

Tully nosed at the leather strap, then hissed, tail darting about furiously. Still, even if *I* couldn't take all that he had to offer, he had the power to heal, magic of his own that he seldom ever tapped into. So I clutched him to me, basking in his healing aura, relishing the warmth of his fur, the scent of...

Well, I'd never been able to put words to what Tully smelled like. But it was good. Always had been. Tully smelled like freedom and security and *life*. Tully's scent was paradise, and I stuffed my face deep into his side, breathing him in as he fixed me up, made me stronger. By the time I finally let my head thump back against the wall, suddenly painfully aware that my cell door was open, the aches and pains of intense labor had vanished. I felt refreshed for the first—and possibly *only*—time in months, and as I turned my back on the doorway, massaging his ears and smoothing my fingers across his scent-gland-riddled cheeks, I vowed to spoil him even *more* when we eventually got out of here.

My familiar was a tubby, lazy, pampered prince, but when we finally escaped, he would ascend to king status. I owed him my life ten times over, even if what he had done—finding me in an uncharted supernatural prison—was what familiars were *supposed* to do for their witches. To some, familiars were servants, underlings, there to do as the witch or warlock ordered, to make them stronger and complement their magic. Tully had been my partner from the moment we locked eyes, him a malnourished kitten and me a depressed teenager.

He had saved me more than once, helped me cope with loss, with soul-crushing grief, and now this?

Tully Fox deserved to be knighted.

"Okay, okay, okay..." Begrudgingly, I loosened my hold on him—not all the way, an unwelcome fear flaring that if I let go, he might vanish. "You need to tell me *everything*."

But I had to release him—had to trust that he was well and truly *here*, that I wasn't losing my mind. Sniffling, I busied my hands with my tearstained face, wiping away the damp and dragging my nose across my forearm. Tully, meanwhile, positioned himself on my lap, nestling in the dip of my crossed legs, prim and proper again, tail swishing. With my back still to the open door, I hoped—*prayed* to anyone who might be listening in this forsaken place—that the guard monitoring the cellblock this afternoon wouldn't suddenly have an interest in doing his job.

Taking a deep breath, I locked eyes with Tully. Blue to blue, I peered into the depths, picking through the fine flecks and streaks, until slowly, the world around us went hazy.

First it blurred, then it darkened—then it was all gone. Black. While witch and familiar had an unspoken bond deeper than any she would have in all her life—although the arrival of a fated mate certainly threw that theory for a loop—we couldn't communicate telepathically. No words shared between minds; magic bound us, and it was Tully's magic that wove the tale.

Pictures flashed by my mind's eye, snippets of memory, the figures shadowy but their faces clear, tinted by a sepia filter. After the bounty hunters—two men and one woman—had crashed Café Crowley and hurled Tully into an unused oven—

Wait.

Those *fuckers* tossed my familiar into an *oven*?

My hands balled to such tight fists that my nails bit furiously into my palms. But the images didn't stop, moving fluidly like some artsy indie flick, flashes and flares, the figures almost dancing.

Screaming for someone to call the police, a horrified Annalise had freed Tully from the oven, which must have locked when the hunter slammed the door shut. He'd then shot out of the café, hot on their trail, scenting their footsteps through Seattle. Found them at a bar, the trio wasting away my bounty on liquor. Detected my location from their conversations—Siberia—and snuck aboard a plane.

My familiar couldn't teleport, but he excelled at shadow magic. Tully could blend with a shadow no matter the intensity or size, and in the darkness, he disappeared.

The images came faster now, time passing, Tully hitching rides around the globe, catching snippets of chatter from other supers about Lloyd Guthrie's new criminal empire at the top of the world. He eventually found the prison, but it stayed hidden behind the ward. From his perspective, the vast grassland was empty except for the faint rainbow shimmer, but he sat for days in the shadows of the nearby mountains, watching trucks and cars rumble down a dirt road and then vanish into oblivion. Warlocks came and went to a nearby village, and although he didn't take the time to show landmarks or much of the scenery, it was obvious Guthrie had stationed his mob henchmen—now guards at his prison—there with their families.

Tully had found a family.

The Thompson family.

He had chosen the least threatening of the Xargi warlocks as they climbed off the transport bus and rubbed up on his leg. Purred. Really put on a show. Exhausted but receptive, Thompson had brought my familiar home to his three kids and a wife *pissed* to be living in the middle of nowhere instead of their Manhattan brownstone.

But the young Thompsonites seemed to *adore* Tully, bits of their arguments over which bed he'd sleep in that night making me grin. At least they had taken care of him, this huge, bushy stray who slept by the fire and on their laps, who watched Thompson's wife cry after he left for work and the kids disappeared for lessons at the village's pop-up academy.

This morning, my darling boy had followed Thompson into the prison. Slunk in the shadows. Hid on the bus. Crossed through the ward when it opened for the guards.

Searched cellblock after cellblock, darting between the shadows, sniffing doors, searching, searching, searching so frantically…

Until he found me.

The last thing he showed me was a misty image of myself stretched out on this shitty cot, hair frizzy and cheeks sunken, eyes stamped with faint black circles that were probably permanent at this point.

And then I was back in the cell, color and light trickling

into my field of vision, stronger and sharper with every hard blink.

"Oh, Tully," I whispered shakily as I wove my fingers into his fur, tears swelling again, "you're my hero."

He returned the sentiment with two deliciously slow blinks and then let me clutch him to my chest again, purring up a storm. I eased onto my side, curling around my familiar and basking in his feel-good aura. With Tully in my arms again, I forgot about Lloyd Guthrie, about my guilt over lusting after other men when a gorgeous dragon shifter had claimed to be my fated mate. I forgot about the awful cafeteria food and the backbreaking labor of solo bakery duty. For just a little while, it was me and Tully, together again, and nothing else mattered. *Nothing*.

But the silence shattered—it always did. My belly looped at the arrival of familiar voices, locks clinking open and inmates returning from their work assignments. The fact that Deimos worked in the library was *beyond* my understanding; of all the possible positions, that had to be the cushiest. And then there was crazy Constance at the other end of the spectrum on janitorial duty, so, in the grand scheme of job titles, mine could have been a hell of a lot worse.

Lips wobbling, I stroked Tully's velvety soft ears, his face, holding back tears and wishing we could have just a little while longer—to suspend my miserable reality for an hour or two so I could well and truly forget this place.

For now, I'd take what I could get. Tully wasn't going anywhere, and neither was I, and that had to be good enough.

I felt Elijah before I heard him, his hulking presence looming in my doorway. If we didn't spend the day in the bakery together, we were each other's first visit once we returned to the cellblock, as if driven by instinct, like birds headed south at the first breath of winter, drawn to the other's cell.

"Katja, are you..." I peeked over my shoulder when he trailed off and found him blocking the entire doorway with that magnificent mountain of a body. Sweat glistened on his forehead, his cheeks, his scruff so fucking gorgeous—just one glance at it and I swore I felt its bite along my inner thighs. He frowned down at me for a moment, then cocked his head to the side, pointing at Tully. "Is that... a cat?"

"Say it louder," I hissed, tucking Tully closer to my body. "He's my familiar."

Rafe's head popped over Elijah's shoulder, the vampire squinting against the sunlight, *just* out of its golden reach, and his dark brows furrowed even deeper when those beautiful aquamarines landed on Tully. His mouth opened and closed a few times, confusion obvious, but before he could get a word out, there was Fintan's olive-skinned magnificence peering over Elijah's other shoulder, a dusting of black soil on his forehead.

"You guys *have* to see this," the fae purred, eyes alight with dangerous mirth. "The fuckwit brigade has officially..." He stopped suddenly, expression shifting to genuine befuddlement and then unabashed delight as he struggled to shoulder his way around Elijah. "Is that a *cat*?"

Rafe rolled his eyes, and I bit back a grin, pleased to have a wall of hotness hiding Tully from the influx of guards. "Gentlemen..." Knowing Tully would *hate* me for it and doing it anyway, I hoisted him up Lion King style to show off the one man in my life who would never, ever disappoint me. "This is my familiar. His name is Tully, he's brilliant at shadow magic, and he's my very best friend."

Elijah's lips lifted affectionately, and he studied Tully with the eyes of the dragon, all molten gold and primal. What I wouldn't give to know what his inner dragon thought about all this—prison, captivity, the collar, *me*. Fintan, meanwhile, offered a tentative nod, eyeing Tully warily, and Rafe managed an awkward wave, boxed out of my cell by the other two. From the slight arch of his brow, I knew precisely what tonight's chat would be about.

And I couldn't wait.

Just as I was about to beckon them in—we occasionally hung out in each other's cells if Deimos's crew was being especially obnoxious, so it wouldn't be *too* suspicious—an alarm screamed through the cellblock. Light strobed around the common area, and the footsteps of additional guards implied a bunk raid.

Oh no.

Not now.

No.

Damn it.

I clutched a puffed-up Tully to me, hurriedly scanning the cell for a shadow to stuff him into—and finding nothing. Darkness was limited with late-afternoon sunlight beaming into the space and illuminating every corner, and the guards tended to obliterate your cell when they came through on these random inspections, tossing cots and using their wands like flashlights.

Tully couldn't—

He…

"Give him to me," Rafe ordered from just outside my cell, motioning for me to hand Tully over with a wave of his hand—his pinky catching the sunlight and sparking, then smoking. He yanked his hand out with a hiss, but I still managed to *barely* hear him add, "There are always shadows in my cell. *Hurry.*"

With a permanently blocked window, he wasn't wrong. Those assholes would need to blast a floodlight or two in the vampire's domain to shoo away every speck of darkness.

Frantic, the alarm screeching and guards shouting for us to take our positions, I leapt off the cot and stuffed Tully into Elijah's huge hands, who then passed him over to Rafe—who shoved the cat into his jumpsuit without an ounce of his dignity intact. My familiar went in yowling, and, from Rafe's wince, claws out. But the vampire said nothing, holding his jumpsuit shut as he zipped into his cell.

Without a word shared between them, Elijah blocked Rafe's retreat and Fintan conjured a distraction, roughly bodychecking Blake on the way over to his cell. True to form, the rat shifter retaliated, all bared teeth and crazy eyes, forcing the guards to intervene.

Shaking, I padded to the spot just outside of my cell, loitering between mine and Rafe's, feet glued in place. As soon as the rest of the block did the same, someone finally—mercifully—cut the alarm, and the raid began, half the guards on Fintan and Elijah's side of the block, half on mine and Rafe's. I risked a glance in the vampire's direction at my left and found his jumpsuit misbuttoned, but otherwise flat and Tully-less.

A trio of guards blitzed by into my cell, Thompson among them, and I listened, fighting to keep my breath even, as they tore everything apart. My metal cot clanged when someone flipped it over, and my pathetic excuse for a pillow landed in the doorway when someone else flung it aside. The toiletries I'd spent my hard-earned wages on clattered to the ground. Book spines split noisily as some dick cracked them open, searching for contraband.

Less than sixty seconds later, they were gone, filing by me and into Rafe's cell, leaving the usual chaos in their wake, but none of that mattered today. I caught Rafe's eye as they tore his cell apart, papers rustling and shredded, a few balled-up notes bouncing across the floor and out his door. Artificial light danced around inside from wands capable of inflicting unspeakable cruelty. The vampire shook his head ever so slightly, a reminder not to react. I managed a subtle nod, then quirked my eyebrow, shooting the unspoken words right back to him. Fury contorted his dark, brooding features, his cheeks sunken and his gaze murderous; Rafe absolutely *despised* cell raids.

Suddenly, the madness stilled. Silence exploded inside, and once again my nails sliced into my palms—

Out they came a few painful beats of my heart later, leaving Rafe's living quarters just as destroyed as mine. I slumped against the wall and exhaled a stuttering breath, my knees weak and my stomach in vicious knots. Grateful tears blurred the cellblock, and I sniffled softly as I glanced at Rafe, another bob of my head communicating all I couldn't say.

Thank you.

He blinked back, purposeful and reassuring, and then busied himself with his jumpsuit, correcting the buttons casually like he hadn't been hiding a fugitive.

My fugitive.

I owed Rafe so much.

I owed *all* of them so much.

I had no idea how to repay them, but it would come to me eventually. If Xargi Penitentiary gave its prisoners one thing, it was ample time to think.

Time to think of a way to pay off this debt of kindness.

Time to think about how to get the hell out of here. If Tully could get in, *we* could get out.

And I would.

One way or another, Tully and I would escape this hellhole—and we were taking my guys with us.

16

RAFE

Brilliant sapphires glittered down at me as I lay flat as a board on my cot. Eyes I had studied for months now, the blue so expressive, so deep, so full of mystery and wonder and the promise of a brighter future—

I had imagined meeting these eyes in the shadowy recess of my cell for ages, pictured them heavy-lidded and blazing with desire. Sometimes I saw them in my dreams, haunting me until morning when an obnoxious siren would rouse me —and I'd suddenly remember that I was *here*, in prison, not out in the free world where I could see those eyes sparkle with genuine wonder…

But they were here now, so big and blue.

Only they belonged to a fucking cat.

"So…" I winced as Tully adjusted himself on my chest, shifting from the seated position where he'd been lording over me since I'd returned from breakfast to standing, all four paws digging into my bones. He then blinked slowly, those sapphires flashing, and started to pulse his claws in and out of me, massive front paws kneading my jumpsuit, my body, like I was a bit of raw dough. "Oh… Okay. So… Yes, ouch." I grimaced when the familiar *really* sunk in on the next knead. "That's… Okay. Right. Whatever you need to… do."

Was this a good thing? My only experience with cats were the feral ones who roamed the property back home, mousers who hissed if you got too close and snarled if you dared reach out to touch. Tully, meanwhile, had broken every preconception I possessed about the standoffish feline, and had spent half of last night pressed up against the mousehole, chittering softly for Katja, and then the rest on my cot, curled up in the most awkward of places.

Behind my crooked knees.

Nestled against my lower back.

Across my neck like a damn lead scarf.

I'd woken up this morning to the fat fuck on my face, snoozing away. Had I needed to breathe, he probably would have smothered me in my sleep.

Unfortunately for my favorite witch, Cellblock F had decided to have a riot on the way to the dining hall during yesterday's supper. The entire prison went into immediate lockdown, leaving the rest of us to scarf down whatever food we could—wasn't exactly difficult to chug a test tube of cold blood on my end—before being hauled back to the cellblock and thrown into our cells. No one in or out. No post-meal socializing in the common area before bed. The rioting idiots had assured the rest of us a security-heavy night, all the lights kept on, patrols marching in and out of the block for *hours*. My fellow inmates had emerged from their cells this morning bleary-eyed and cranky.

Tully, however, must have thought it best to continue hiding in my cell. After all, the infinite shadows offered the best hiding spots. Unfortunately for him and his witch, there simply hadn't been the chance for him to slink back into her cell.

So, he had spent the night here.

And was now clawing up my chest while purring and slow-blinking down at me.

Fucking sadist.

Actually... It sort of felt good. Like a prickly massage from a huge black cloud that in another life could have easily passed for a sidhe, although Tully lacked the telltale white mark on his chest. So. Definitely *not* a witch or a tricky fairy in hiding, pretending to be Katja's familiar all these years. Just a standard, run-of-the-mill familiar—who loved his mistress so ardently that he'd scoured the globe to find her.

"You're a good lad, Tully," I muttered, risking a quick stroke of his sides, then a tentative scratch behind his ears. The feline perked up, arching into my cautious fingers, and closed his eyes. An unfamiliar calm settled over us, and I sank into the strangely soothing act of petting a cat, of listening to his constant purr and enduring the rhythmic clenching of his paws, claws poking through the jumpsuit and into my cold flesh in even beats.

But of course, peace never lasted in Xargi Penitentiary.

My cell door whizzed open, bolting in place along the wall with the usual *clang*, and Tully leapt off me with a hiss, fluffed up and furious, the force of his jump landing like a fucking crowbar to the chest. Knuckling at the dull ache, I sat up and exhaled softly at the same old sights and sounds of guards dragging Cellblock C's inmates away for work duty. They had a blessed half hour after breakfast to collect themselves before the workday began, and what I wouldn't do for a fucking job in here.

Everyone moaned about it, but little did any of them realize that sitting around in a vacant cellblock—occasionally with a friend, usually a foe—for nine grueling hours with very little to occupy oneself with was far worse than the aches and pains of labor. Boring as *fuck*, it felt akin to solitary if I didn't have Katja or Elijah to keep me company. Hell, for all his posturing and absurdity, even Fintan sufficed to pass the time.

With my literary background, I should have been an obvious candidate for library duty, but no one would block out the windows for me. I'd excel amongst our underwhelming collection of books, and yet Deimos had been granted the opportunity to sit in a cool room surrounded by tomes and do absolutely nothing while the other inmates assigned to the same shift kept the catalogue organized.

Really, he didn't *deserve* the library.

"*Please...*" Katja's pleading tone rose above the standard hubbub, and I frowned as I crept to the end of my cot, on high alert should she need assistance. "It's really bad this morning."

Really bad? She hadn't mentioned anything at breakfast about—

"Look, if it's *that* bad, go to the infirmary." Fucking Williams. Cellblock C's dimmest guard came with an extreme prejudice of vampires not uncommon in the supernatural community; the other night he'd had the *nerve* to ram his elbow into me at just the right moment in the cafeteria. So engrossed in my evening fix of glorious type O, I'd actually stumbled, then fumbled, and my test tube crashed to the ground before I could catch it. Blood had splashed everywhere—and then the cunt stepped in it while lecturing me about clumsiness. Elijah had nearly ripped his massive caterpillar eyebrows off, but Katja kept the peace, urging us on to our usual table while I went without for a night.

Fucker.

"You're assigned to the greenhouse today," he carried on, and while I couldn't see him, I could *hear* his smarmy expression. "So you can't just—"

"I'll take over her shift." Ah, Fintan to the rescue. The fae had continued to sniff around Katja like he had every right to, despite referencing mine and Elijah's interest in her anytime the urge struck. Quite shocking now that he had suddenly offered to do a lick of work; usually he spent his time in the greenhouse haunting Katja's shadow—from what I'd heard, anyway—and only did the bare minimum to get through the day. "It seems like cruel and unusual punishment to force a female to work under such conditions."

A beat of silence followed as other inmates were escorted out the main door, and I rolled my eyes. Another classic Fintan move: annoying his audience into an uncomfortable quiet.

He seemed to take great pleasure in doing so. Typical fae.

"Uh, yeah," Katja said slowly. "Thanks, Fintan. It's just really bad cramps, but I'm having a hard time standing upright. I'll be fine by tomorrow, I'm sure of it, but today it's coming out in chunks—like you should have *seen* my toilet. And then now that I've eaten, the period shits are coming—"

"Ugh, *gods*." Williams groaned and I stifled a chuckle of my own, turning it into a cough. "Fine, fine. So long as Fintan picks up the slack, whatever. Just... go sit in your cell and never say period shits to me ever again."

"Deal." She sounded like she was smiling. They were few and far between, but Katja's smiles were some of the most beautiful I'd ever seen. If these bastards would ever give me a proper writing utensil, even something as basic as a quill and inkpot, I could write whole sonnets about her mouth. About the shape of her lips, their color and fullness...

I blinked hard and shook my head, burying the thoughts deep down where they belonged, then readjusted my jumpsuit as my cock stirred with interest. *Not now, you horny bastard.* Pathetic that just the thought of her mouth got me going when I tried so damn hard to make everyone believe, myself included, that Katja and I were just *friends*.

Let's chalk it up to nearly ten months of forced celibacy, shall we?

Sure. That was it. Any man would salivate over a stunning woman if they were in my shoes. It wasn't… I wasn't…

My thoughts were *not* a betrayal of my bond with Elijah.

They were natural and normal and completely expected from a male's reptilian brain—

I glared up at my forehead, mentally warning the snide little voice at the back of my mind that if it whispered anything even remotely close to *doth protest too much*, I'd find something wooden and shove it through my eye.

End it all.

Yeah.

That would show you, conscience and self-doubt.

Pathetic, the voice sneered, and I rolled my eyes, then straightened at the sound of frantic footsteps shuffling toward my cell. They fell silent as the last of the workday migration drifted through the main door, which clanked shut a few moments later, locks snapping into place, barring Katja, myself, and a snoring Avery inside. We only had a precious forty minutes while the trio of cellblock guards dropped everyone off at their designated workspaces. Occasionally I had a blissful *hour* without anyone watching me if the idiots on duty opted for a smoke break.

I smelled her before I saw her, her natural odor dampened by the prison-issued deodorant. Baby powder—nowhere near as appealing as the faint floral that clung to her skin, but whatever made her most comfortable was all that mattered. She materialized in my doorway with a hitched breath, cheeks flushed, eyes slightly panicked.

"Is he okay?"

"He's fine," I assured her as Tully poked his head out from under my cot. Before I could get another word in, the feline issued an earth-shattering *meow* that made Katja launch herself into my cell. The witch collapsed to her knees and crawled the rest of the way, hauling her familiar into her arms the second he was *barely* within reach. Cooing softly like he was a spoiled baby and not the magical accessory he should be, Katja slowly drifted up and settled on the edge of my cot, a purring black bundle on her lap and tears in her eyes. Relief. It billowed off her in waves, her every limb relaxing, the anxious flush in her cheeks melting away.

We sat like that for some time, side by side with about two painful feet of distance between us. She fussed over her familiar as the temporary silence of an empty cellblock set in. *Grating,* all that nothingness. Quiet was a precious commodity in the penitentiary, yet I despised it during the day. It symbolized my weakness, my failing, my inability to contribute while Elijah worked my assigned duty—the bakery technically should have been mine—and his own in the smithy. Thanks to their pop culture, humans considered us apex predators, the pinnacle of evolution with our speed and dexterity, durable and fierce and powerful.

Among the supernatural, vampire shortcomings were obvious, shoved under a magnifying glass anytime magic came into play. Seated next to the witch who lingered in my dreams far more than she should, the two of us locked in a rare moment of solitude, truly *alone,* it struck me like a fucking freight train. Weakness. Failure. Flaws. The undeniable deficiencies of my kind—

"Thank you, Rafe," Katja whispered, stroking Tully's cheeks with her finger, one side and then the other. Her tongue flicked out to wet her lips, and she cast me a shy sidelong glance. "I owe you everything."

Oh. Those words stirred something dark within me, something dangerous and ancient—something that insisted if she *owed* me, then I ought to collect. Swallowing a mouthful of knives, my throat perpetually sandpapery these days, I bit the insides of my cheeks and shook my head.

"It's, uh, fine." My fingers longed to map her curves, to walk the swell of her hip, the dip of her lower back, the delicate hollow of her throat. I clenched my eyes shut for a moment, hoping she wouldn't notice in the cell's shadows, and then forced myself to focus on being *normal* and *not* some lusting, bloodthirsty fiend who wanted to ravish and devour her in equal measures. We had been at great odds lately, poet and monster, and I suddenly realized these precious moments alone only made things worse. "We were fine." I choked it out, pointedly scanning the walls, the ceiling, like it was the first time—like I hadn't memorized every damn brick months ago. "I didn't really do anything."

At this proximity, Katja's natural scent had a slight upper hand over the deodorant, and I gritted my teeth, battling back the surge of displeasure and the rush of exhilaration at the fact that my linens now smelled like her. For Elijah's sake, for hers —hell, maybe even for my own—I had battled my attraction to her for *months*. The last time the dragon shifter had brought it up, he seemed marginally accepting of my interest in her, but I couldn't do that to him. Couldn't… covet his fated mate.

Even if she was lovely—Aphrodite reincarnate.

Even if I *was* a sucker for good conversation, and every single night we had that in spades.

Now here she was, sullying all my hard work, my resistance to her lure, her unwitting siren song, by shuffling down the cot and closing in on me as Tully meandered off her lap and sat his asshole down on my pillow.

While I longed to gaze into her eyes, I focused on my hands instead, fidgeting with the red fabric stretched over my thighs. *No.* I staunchly *refused* to be in a fucking love triangle with my best friend and a witch. I couldn't. I had to—

Her hand suddenly found mine, her flesh an inferno only surpassed by her mate, and before I could stop it, her fingers wove us together. Desire surged, cock swelling with interest again, and my mouth watered as a delicious image danced through my mind…

Of her—naked, sprawled over a luxurious bed so vastly different from the one we found ourselves on.

Her creamy soft skin, her eyes burning with starlight, her crooked finger beckoning me home.

And me, ravenous, a monster, sinking my fangs into her inner thigh.

Fuck. I tugged my hand away, my attempt to be gentle —*kind*, even—failing miserably.

"Katja, maybe you should…" *Go*. Get the fuck out of my cell while I still clung to the tenuous strands of self-control. Everyone always talked about how shifters fought the beast within, the man trying desperately to quell the animal snarling in his chest. But they never mentioned how *we* struggled, how vampires faced temptation each and every night. How we were bound by laws, punishable by stake or sunlight should we break them, that forced us to keep our basic instincts in check.

To swallow the bloodlust.

The *lust* in general.

"No, please just…" Katja fiddled with her nails, cheeks flushed again at my rejection. "I need to… I… Thank you, Rafe." She shuffled about on the cot, one leg bent and tucked under her, the other dangling over the side as she faced me. "Thank you so much for everything."

"Er, like I said…" I scratched at the back of my neck, falling back on all the fake nonchalant gestures I had studied and perfected over the centuries. Tully's eyes locked on mine for a beat, his tail swishing back and forth, my pillow officially his, and I cleared my throat. "It's really nothing. He's a good cat—"

"I'm not just talking about Tully," she insisted. "I haven't had the chance to say it, and I should have sooner, but thank you for… talking to me that first night. And every night since then."

Except the night she returned from the bakery reeking of sweat and sex, of Elijah and sweet briar rose petals and so much more that it suffocated me. The memory hung between us, as unacknowledged now as it had been back then. Loath as I was to admit it, I'd sulked that night. I'd let weakness win and pouted in my cell like a child.

All was right the following night, but weeks later, I despised myself for reacting that way—for punishing her when she wasn't at fault. Neither was Elijah. And, frankly, neither was I. The storm brewing between we three, featuring a lightning bolt of Fintan every now and again, was nobody's fault.

But my responses were *mine*, and I owned the guilt of ignoring her that night.

Jaw briefly clenched, I glanced her way, hating how lovely she looked in the darkness, how the light trickling in from the common area really highlighted her beauty. "Katja—"

"No, let me say this." The witch rolled her shoulders back, as if steeling herself—bracing herself, *preparing* herself, and I feared where this might be headed. "I need to… I wouldn't have made it a week without you being there at night. You've been so good to me, and I feel like I've been taking and taking—"

"We're all just trying to survive in here," I muttered, my one-shouldered shrug halfhearted. She tucked her loose red waves behind her ears with a sigh, her breath the pungent spearmint of the prison toothpaste.

"You make it a lot easier." She paused, only to gnaw at her

lip—wholly unaware what that *did* to me, the flash of teeth a reminder that I longed to claim her with my own, to mark her up, to tear flesh with my fangs. I clenched my hands to fists, shoving those thoughts aside only for them to come back swinging, stronger than ever, when she tentatively touched my thigh. "Sometimes I feel like I'm taking advantage of your good nature... and your friendship with Elijah."

"That's ridiculous, Katja," I said tightly, unable to tear my gaze away from her fingertips on my leg, her touch somehow both featherlight and bruising.

"Is it?"

The wobble of uncertainty had my head snapping up, and I found her studying me with such doubt, such disbelief, that it was like a stake to the fucking heart. "Maybe at first I-I volunteered because Elijah and you... He knew from the very beginning..." *Fated mates*. Why did the stars favor shifters? Why did *they* get soulmates while the rest of us were left to flounder about for eternity? "But now I..."

Now what?

What was I supposed to say?

Pour my heart out—not a chance in hell.

My body responded with a will of its own, ignoring my sluggish thoughts, my scattered mind, and reached out for her. I smoothed a few fallen bits of coppery-red back behind her ear, tending to the shorter layers that always refused to stay with the herd. Surprisingly soft, despite the frizzy ends. Her breath caught as my fingers slid down the curve of her mane, tracing it, then up the column of her neck, along her jaw. My thumb found her lower lip before I'd clued into its intention, plucking at it, tracing the fullness, the rosebud pucker. Victory sharpened in my chest when her lips parted for me, when the pink beneath my thumb trembled ever so slightly...

I reared back with a hiss like she had burned me—for she had. The lightest touch, torturously fleeting, and Katja Fox set me aflame.

And the fire reminded me that she belonged to another.

Their heat was meant for each other; my frost, my dead porcelain, had no role to play in this game.

I can't.

"And now?" Katja whispered, hope twinkling in her sapphires, tenuous and paper-thin but *there*.

Christ. I stabbed my thumb into the would-be mattress beneath us, as if feeling the cot's cruel springs would extinguish the fire. "What?"

"You said at first you—"

"Now we're..." I swallowed hard again—only the knives were gone. My mouth watered for her as it never had before, and that should have been my cue to run. Take a walk around the cellblock. Pester Avery—*something*. "We're friends."

The witch brushed her lower lip with a frown. "Just friends?"

"What the fuck are you doing, Katja?" I demanded roughly. My growl had her cheeks igniting and my cock shooting to attention. *Damn it.* I covered the traitorous bastard as best I could while I shuffled away, seconds from bolting... or I'd pounce. "You belong to—"

"I don't belong to *anyone*," she said fiercely, eyes glistening as she prowled after me. "I belong to *me*, and I decide my fate and my future and..."

We stilled at the end of the cot, me a breath away from toppling over and onto the floor, her on her knees—and her hands fisted in my jumpsuit, buttons straining under her grasp. The physical contact came so easily. After months of whispering through the wall, keeping our distance around the others, it felt so *natural*.

Felt like I never wanted her to *stop* touching me.

Vision slowly clouding over with a bloodlust haze, I snapped and slammed my mouth to hers in a brutal kiss that had her gasping. Before, Katja had been the aggressor, initiating every touch, every caress, stalking me across the cot, but in that moment, she tasted a true predator in all his violent glory. I kissed to claim, to conquer, hands in her hair and tongue between her lips. Her heart roared, her pulse a war drum pounding, pounding, *pounding* in my ears.

And then clarity struck.

My eyes shot open and I reared back, incensed at myself for indulging the beast within. For that was what this had been—just another weakness, another failing on my part.

On her knees, Katja sat trembling in my wake, her cheeks a brilliant rosy pink and her lips swollen…

Bleeding.

My fangs must have nicked that luscious lower lip at some point; a ruby dot plumed without the pressure holding it back, and Katja tentatively wiped it away, blinking down at her fingertip like she didn't understand what had happened.

Me.

I'd happened.

"Katja, I'm…" I trailed off when she licked her lips, hurriedly at first, then slowly for the next rush of blood, locking eyes with me.

Oh.

Fuuuuuuuuuuuuuuuck.

"Don't say you're sorry, Rafe," she murmured. "I… I'm not."

Those two words were my undoing. I lunged just as she pounced, and we collided with the force of two charging armies meeting in battle, this kiss more furious than the first. All raw, undying passion, months of pent-up *need* exploding between us. I raked my hands through her hair, fingers tangling, twining, yanking as they had yearned to do from the very first week. Her delectable little squeak of shock, perhaps even pain, at one of my harder tugs had me grinning savagely against her mouth, and I swallowed every sound greedily, hungrily, her surprise the perfect seasoning to her blood.

B-negative.

A rare and exquisite elixir.

Dangerous—for I had been starved in here. While I allowed my restraint to falter, my hands everywhere, fingers bruising her hips as I steered her onto my lap, I had to keep the true bloodlust in check. Tamed.

Or I might drain her dry.

Elijah would never forgive me.

I would never forgive myself.

She fit so perfectly, straddling my thighs, looming over me with her hands planted firmly on my shoulders. For such a little thing, quiet and pensive to the rest of the prison, an outright delight during our nightly conversations, Katja Fox proved she could be brutal. She was a predator in her own right, a hunter in the highest regard, snapping at my lips, my tongue, marking me even as her life force trickled down my throat. Her nails raked up my neck and over the collar, the slight nudging of the leather paired with a jolt of panic; I had seen what happened when inmates tried to remove their collars.

Snarling, I snared her wrists and wrenched them away, bringing those cruel hands to my cheeks, desperate to feel the sting of her claws. Katja allowed some manipulation, our kiss deep and binding, but she dropped her hands to my chest an instant later, fingers fumbling over the buttons. I bucked up, cock rigid and needy, and she shivered in my arms. As soon as she'd conquered half my buttons, she hastily attacked her own, parting the purple fabric and revealing herself to me—creamy skin and gorgeous cleavage, the perfect palmful of breast hidden away beneath an unflattering prison-issued brassiere.

When I tore my mouth from hers, the witch sucked down a few gasping breaths, her chest rising and falling in hard beats. Heavy-lidded sapphires gazed down at me, and I paused, allowing a moment of tenderness as I brushed the staticky hair from her face, mapped the lines of her nose, her cheekbones, her chin. Still trembling, still chasing her breath, Katja did the same, dragging a finger over the harsh black stubble along my jaw, the hard edges of my features of particular interest. Silence reigned outside my cell door, and behind her, Tully had melted into the shadows.

Did that mean he approved of this?

Eyes locked, an upspoken question stretched between us. *Do we want to stop?*

We should.

Logically, yes, I ought to lift her off my thighs, my raging hard-on, and call it a day. Go back to whispering through a mousehole and savoring every second as I had all these long months.

I kissed her instead. Katja kissed me back, falling easily into the softness that was like a balm for her bruised mouth, for my tormented mind. It was fleeting, the gentle brush of lips, turning harder by the moment, fiercer, and then the firestorm was back, her hips rocking over my erection, grinding down in search of her own pleasure. Her little moans spurred me, damned me, but even as I succumbed to vice and sin, one succinct, coherent thought stood out.

It felt right to hold her.

Not sexually—although that was exceptional too. Images of driving her squealing into the cot, over and over again, the springs screaming as she came undone beneath me, tempted my inner monster, made my cock even harder.

But beyond that, it felt right to just *hold* her, touch her. Even a chaste embrace would satisfy me.

Of course, this was anything but.

Her fingers twined in my hair, wrenching hard when I dragged a harsh, openmouthed kiss along her jaw and down her neck.

That was my undoing.

The hammer of her heart thump-thumping in her throat. The rush of blood through her veins, charging faster and brighter, so fucking tempting. Hadn't fed in months. In too long. Hadn't properly consumed what I *needed* to survive—

The bloodlust won out.

I lost control in a second—and drove my fangs into her neck.

"*Rafe...*" Blood oozed over my lips, my tongue, coating my throat and soothing away all the prison's cruelty. B-negative was my *favorite*, and she was the sweetest I'd ever tasted. Like guzzling a mouthful of rubies, Katja was exquisite in every sense. I gripped the back of her neck hard, plunging deeper, drinking greedily as her hips bucked and rolled, rocking faster over my sheathed cock.

The bite of a vampire was nirvana. Six hundred years since I'd been turned, I *vaguely* recalled the sting—but I wholly remembered the pleasure. A toxin in our bite dulled our victim's senses once it entered the bloodstream, flooded them with pleasure beyond measure. Akin to an earth-shattering orgasm, it stupefied them just long enough for the monster to feed.

Even if I hadn't the time to properly fuck her, at least I could give her this—a flicker of light and ecstasy in this hellscape. Since she'd arrived, Katja hadn't done it herself—slipped her hand between her thighs in the dead of night—or I would have heard.

And how could I forget such music? A symphony of

hitched breath and shudders and my name moaned so soft and sweet. I was an instant addict—to her blood, to her sounds.

Unfortunately, nothing ever lasted in Xargi.

But just for a moment, I could give *and* take.

We both clumsily shoved a hand over her gasping mouth. She giggled against my palm, her hand clapped over mine, and rode me through a sensation that left her limp in my arms. Writhing and mewling, Katja relished my bite as none had before. I drank, feasted, every gulp fueling my fading body, all the while mindful not to take too much.

I had never accidentally drained anyone, not even in my orphaned days, alone in the world and trying to learn how to survive as the beast I'd become. But something about Katja called to me, *begged* me to swallow every last drop.

She'll enjoy it, the little voice murmured, suddenly on my side—yet not. I couldn't do that to her, but I also couldn't peel my mouth from her throat, couldn't withdraw fangs that now craved her above all others. My gut looped and bottomed out, desire clouding my judgment, the pull toward her stronger than ever...

Locks clinked and clanked from the common area; some piece of *shit* had returned early.

Katja flailed back, and had I not guided her, she would have fallen clear off the side of the cot and crashed to an unforgiving stone floor. Shaking, noticeably woozy, she scrambled backward and tried to stand, but I seized her forearms and held firm.

"Wait a moment," I urged softly. "Catch your breath. Let the dizziness pass."

She nodded as Tully hopped back on the cot, and I grimaced at all that beautiful B-negative smeared across her neck and shoulder. Some of it even flecked onto her jumpsuit

—and that bra strap had gone from white to bright red. *Fuckfuckfuckfuck*. Not good. Not good at all.

At least the wound had sealed over. Even on a creature without extraordinary healing abilities, the toxin from our bite encouraged the punctures to clot, while their body would do the rest. Couldn't have casual feeding partners bleed out, after all.

With a purring familiar on her lap, Katja went for her jumpsuit, but her fingers lacked the dexterity to button anything up. I steered her hands down to Tully, silently encouraging her to just enjoy the softness of his fur while I grabbed my pillow, ripped off its grimy case, and then wiped her down. It wasn't ideal—and I would have *much* preferred to lick her clean—but anything else would set off the monster again. Now, how to explain all the blood to the laundry staff…

Never mind. It didn't matter. One disaster at a time.

Once I had tidied her up as best I could, I buttoned Katja's jumpsuit and fixed her hair. If she strolled out of my cell *looking* like she had just been fucked, someone was bound to notice—even if technically that wasn't the case.

Sure, she had climaxed on my lap. I could smell her heady arousal from here, her slickness almost as distracting as her blood.

"I'm so sorry, Katja," I whispered, self-loathing soaring to an all-time high. "I shouldn't have—"

"Do you regret it?" She gathered Tully to her chest, her eyes more focused now, her movements steadier. Nibbling that split lower lip, she waited patiently for me to sort through my own bullshit, even as the thunder of guard boots sounded from the cellblock's common area. B-negative on my tongue, in my veins, coursing through my heart, I knew I had to answer honestly; Katja deserved that much.

"No," I whispered back, chest tightening when a relieved smile blossomed across her face.

"Me neither." Both feet planted flat on the floor, she tried to stand by herself again—tried and failed, plopping back on the cot. On the next attempt, I held her elbow until I was sure she wouldn't immediately topple over. It took a good two minutes before I trusted her body enough to let go, and when I did, she faced me slowly with a long, luxurious sigh, eyes heavy, limbs relaxed…

As if we *had* fucked, the sex perfect and satisfying and just what she needed.

Bloodlust satiated for the time being, I now had a raging case of blue balls.

"I'm not sure why I don't regret it," she admitted, soft enough for a human to miss, speaking more to herself than me. "But I don't."

"I understand." It was an automatic response, one that garnered another warm smile and a kiss on the cheek—and a face full of Tully's massive fluffy tail—before she crept to the door of my shadowy cell. Confident on her own two feet again, Katja waited a few long moments, then darted out and into her cell when the guards resumed their loud, never-ending conversation about tits and beer and the wolfsbane trade.

I ached without her.

Felt parched in seconds.

My words had been a lie: I *didn't* understand shit—about her, about us. No one, supernatural or human, had ever made me want to feast before, stirred me to keep going and going, *taking*, becoming a demon of gluttony and lust. She sparked something in me, her blood like fire pumping through my veins.

I could chalk it up to the near constant state of starvation the prison kept their vampire population in, but that wasn't the whole story.

Barely even a chapter, honestly.

Bloody pillowcase in one hand, I slumped back against the wall, legs dangling over the cot, and closed my eyes. While I longed to slowly let the mystery unfold, to follow the threads one at a time to understanding, to the culmination of *us*, that was but a pipe dream. I had until Elijah returned from his shift in the metal shop to figure it out.

Because he was my friend. My *best* friend. And I had just fed from his fated mate.

As soon as he returned, I vowed to tell him everything…

And accept the consequences, even if they broke us.

I deserved no less.

❧ 17 ❧

ELIJAH

I should have marked her when I'd had the chance.

That day in the bakery—I couldn't have asked for a better opportunity. There we were, fated, on the verge of mated, basking in a rare moment of privacy inside this shithole. Katja had exposed herself to me, offered her body, her heart, and my inner dragon had been desperate to mark her. He had clawed up my chest in his eagerness, seconds away from unifying with *his* mate, our chosen, and I had just… stopped. Ended it right then and there, like I was satisfied with a mind-blowing orgasm, and then it was over.

In the aftermath, she had watched me dress with wide, wanting eyes, like she just *knew* we'd both missed out on something, and I did my best to stuff down the guilt and the shame, ignoring the fact that I was a dragon, an alpha, a shifter in the presence of his soulmate—and I hadn't marked her. Hadn't claimed her for my own.

Instant regret. My inner dragon had exploded, his fury turning my insides to a raging inferno that haunted me for days. Aggressive heartburn. Aches and stabbing pains in my chest. The headache to end all headaches. Usually we operated as one, and even though Katja's presence had roused the sleepy bastard, he and I were centuries old and he was more than capable of keeping his shit together.

But this?

This had been unforgivable to him, and he'd been punishing me ever since.

Sure, it dissipated—I wouldn't survive otherwise, not the first shifter to fall apart because the inner beast rebelled violently enough—but he was right back at it after last night's conversation with Rafe.

He had marked her.

Two tiny puncture marks at the base of her throat, hidden now by her hair. If my theory was correct, they would never fully heal. No balm or salve would shrink them. Katja and I were fated, but the fact that my inner dragon was pissed at *me* and not my vampire companion spoke volumes. It highlighted that Rafe could be a part of our fated connection, that he was *supposed* to mark her, claim her, bind himself to me and her for the rest of all our very long lives.

It was just a working theory. Seated in the prison cafeteria, the inmate population way too noisy at this hour in the morning, I glanced across the table at him. Nope. No burning rage. No intense throb of jealousy. No passionate desire to rip him into little undead vampire chunks and toss him to the wolves. Wrath in all its ugly fury reared whenever strange males so much as glanced Katja's way, yet Rafe had kissed her, touched her, bit her, and my feelings about him hadn't changed one bit.

Did I like that he had tasted her? No.

Did I want to envision them entwined on his cot, all gasping breaths and wandering hands and kisses fierce enough to leave her lips all swollen and bruised this morning? *Fuck* no.

But I didn't want to kill him—and for an alpha with a fated mate, that had to mean something.

Something profound.

Still nursing his vial of cold blood, Rafe appeared too distracted to worry about my lingering stares. Jaw clenched, he glared at Fintan; the fae by my side had been drumming his goddamn spork and finger on the table for the last two minutes, biding his time—like all of us—until Katja left the feeding line and joined us.

"Fintan," Rafe growled at long last, his test tube about to splinter in his white-knuckle grasp. "Would you shut the fuck up already?"

"Oh, sourpuss," the fae trilled back, all bright-eyed and singsongy, his food untouched. "Shouldn't you be in the *best* of moods this morning? You look so... refreshed, like you finally got your full five liters."

Rafe cast a hurried look my way, then shook his head and twisted back to search for Katja in the line. My inner dragon snarled at the reminder, and I stabbed my knuckles to the center of my chest, massaging away the burn, then poked my spork at my grey-tinged scrambled eggs.

I know, I know, you fuck. I get it.

I should have marked her.

At the time, I'd let the man win. Although I had accepted she was my fated and that we'd just had exceptional sex, that we were finally *talking,* confusion had won the day, and great sex and conversation and fate wasn't enough to cull it back. In that moment, I had become so fucking human that it still sickened me. Surrendering to the uncertainty, I had held back. I told myself it was because I hadn't wanted to frighten her, but seeing Rafe's marks on her throat this morning had drop-kicked that theory straight to hell.

Katja wasn't afraid of us.

She feared a lot of the stupid shit in the penitentiary, but *we* weren't on her list.

I'd been a coward—and that was that. No getting around it anymore. No one to blame but myself.

"Ah..." Fintan finally stopped his incessant drumming and tossed his spork aside. "There she is."

Trust the fae to be on the lookout for my—possibly *our*—mate. Sure enough, there was that shock of brilliant red hair weaving through the cafeteria. Her jumpsuit had the splattered remnants of her encounter with Rafe along the shoulder, but so far no guard had called her out on it. Deimos, meanwhile, zeroed in on the new stains immediately during breakfast lineup, and as she passed his table now, he whistled and winked when she glared in his direction.

Rage detonated inside me like a fucking bomb.

Good to know it was still there, the insane jealousy and possessiveness I'd never experienced in my entire goddamn life—this surge of fire, the snarling of my inner dragon, certainly said a lot about Rafe, anyway.

My mouth watered, and as Katja hurried along, head down and tray clutched in front of her like a shield, I was suddenly *very* aware of my teeth. The urge to mark her returned with a vengeance, my inner dragon roaring at the thought of throwing her down on a table and claiming her for all to see. I shoved a forkful of shitty scrambled eggs in my mouth instead, twitching at the obnoxious crackle of Fintan's apple juice bottle to my left.

Shifters spent their whole lives fighting the beast within, quelling their instincts, silencing that literal inner voice, to blend into human society. We differed from the rest of the supernatural community for that reason alone. Always outcasts. Always separate. This fight was nothing new to me, and I bore down as hard as I could, overchewing every tasteless morsel as a distraction.

Marking her, going out of my way to announce my claim, to piss a circle around her, was a huge risk. With the shower incident still fresh in all the guards' minds, if I showed too much interest in my mate, they might separate us for good—move one of us to a new cellblock and ensure we never saw each other again, just to be extra cruel. I wouldn't put it past any of them.

For now, I had to keep my shit together.

Not that my inner dragon understood or cared about any of that. Impulsive fucker raked his claws up and down my insides as Katja settled on the stool between mine and Rafe's, then huffed a lock of hair out of her face. Pain seared up my throat, but I swallowed it down with a gulp of too-sweet apple juice and a wince.

"You know," the witch started, poking at her own mountain of expired scrambled eggs, "they've really outdone themselves this morning."

I grunted in agreement as Fintan guzzled his own juice, slurping noisily at my side. No better way to start the day than some fucking gross eggs, a slice of an orange with what looked like it somehow had *extra* seeds shoved in there, apple juice that was so artificial I could feel the grains of sugar on my teeth, and then a rock-hard chunk of bread.

Magnificent. No wonder most inmates looked like the walking dead.

I snatched up the bread and clunked it on the table. "I find this particularly insulting."

After all, Katja and I had access to the fresh stuff several days a week. The bread we made was *perfect*—and obviously in high demand from the external suppliers, as there was talk of extending the bakery shifts and adding a few more inmates to the crews to up production. The likelihood of another tumble in the pantry looked dimmer with each passing day.

"Oh, yeah, a giant screw-you for sure," she muttered,

picking up her bread and squeezing it in a fist. A few bits of stale crust fluttered to the table, and she glanced at Rafe for his input—only for the pair to lock eyes a little too long, then look away, my mate's cheeks a delicious rosy red.

My inner dragon sneered, then stabbed hard enough to make me cough. Of course the dramatic shit was punishing *me* for that interaction. I held a fist in front of my mouth, and when the subdued wheezing settled, I found my skin speckled with bright bloody droplets. Perfect. The bastard was literally tearing me apart from the inside out, and he wouldn't be satisfied until I marked her.

Do you see where we are? Can you cut me some fucking slack?

A begrudging grumble rattled around my brain as I wiped the blood on my leg, preferring not to look like a human suffering from tuberculosis on top of everything else.

Fintan had gone from drumming on the table to rolling his bread ball back and forth between his cupped hands. I scowled his way, only to find him sporting the standard shit-eater grin as he watched the three of us like we were the best entertainment around.

And we probably were—like a fucking soap opera, me, Katja, and Rafe.

Most days I wanted to punch the fae right in the nose, if only to shut him up, maybe even have a few blessed moments of silence while he was out cold. He still operated under the delusion that he was fae royalty—as did just about every fae I'd ever met—and he flirted shamelessly with my mate right out in the open. The thought of her and him spending hours together in the greenhouse made my blood boil…

But I didn't want to skin him alive.

Didn't want to tear his heart out and eat it as I watched the life drain from his eyes.

So…

Again, perplexing. Fintan and I didn't share Rafe's and my bond, the connection fostered over eight years and deeply fortified in the last ten months. The fae had just appeared one day, and unlike every other male at Xargi, from the lowliest inmate right up to Warden Guthrie, my inner dragon didn't want to slit him from stem to stern.

I didn't relish the implication. Fintan was a stranger—and kind of a pompous ass. The thought of fate aligning us just seemed ridiculous. We couldn't be more different.

The clattering of a plastic tray on the floor had all of us rubbernecking to the far right of the cafeteria, where a new inmate in purple shot up. Male—a small, thin wispy-haired warlock who was white as a ghost and panicking.

"Take it off!" he screeched, grabbing at the leather collar around his neck and yanking. "Take it off, take it off, take it *off*!"

It all happened so fast: inmates shouting for him to sit down and shut up, guards charging toward him—then the inevitable tragedy. He snapped the leather band open with a cry, fueled by adrenaline and fear, and the collar reacted just like the rumors said. A storm of bright blue electricity erupted from the sigils and lashed at every inch of him, frying the warlock to a crisp. Katja yelped, hands at her face, eyes wide. Over in seconds, the blackened corpse crumbled to the ground, the cafeteria reeking of burnt hair and sizzled flesh.

Guards from all cellblocks swarmed the dining area, zipping around tables, bellowing for the rest of us to stay seated. An uneasy quiet descended over the entire hall, and just for a moment, unity had its day. Inmates glanced between themselves, to other tables, the threads of understanding and outrage strengthening, twining, binding us all together. Of course, it would fade. Supers had too much internal bullshit to wade through to ever act as one united force—or we would have overrun this place and burned it to the ground by now. As much as we loathed the guards, we despised each other almost equally.

Out of the corner of my eye, Katja shot to her feet and scuttled some five tables over to Willow. She was still on friendly terms with the rabbit shifter, who sat at her table alone now, tears cutting down her cheeks, and folded over as soon as Katja dropped down beside her. My mate rubbed her shuddering shoulders, flinching when one of the guards snarled for us all to stay *seated*. Fucker. If one of them made a move toward her—to chastise her, to haul her back to our table like it fucking mattered, I'd be back in solitary within the hour.

Much to my surprise, it was Fintan who reacted first, rising from his stool and gliding over to the pair as muted chaos rumbled through the cafeteria. While Katja comforted her friend, Fintan settled beside her and sat up straight, tall, *strong*, meeting the eyes of a pair of prowling guards on their way over. He tipped his head to the side, then flashed that smile that grated every guard here—the one that dared you *not* to beat him bloody.

Muttering to themselves and rolling their eyes, the pair in black fucked off to deal with bigger fish.

My inner dragon merely stalked about inside me, snarling at the situation but not at Fintan, not at the closeness nor the way he reached around Katja to pat Willow's rounded back. In fact, we both acknowledged and appreciated his protective instincts; I'd yet to see him step up for anyone else in here. If keeping him around meant we had another set of eyes to watch out for Katja, to keep my mate safe, then fine—he could be as irritating as he wanted so long as he served a purpose.

Exhaling sharply, I faced Rafe again, all our earlier tension gone.

"We need to get out of here," the vampire growled, bright

eyes tracking the trio of guards who levitated the charred warlock for all to see, then slowly maneuvered him toward one of the staff doors. I gritted my jaw for a moment, then nodded.

"Agreed."

"For real this time." Rafe shot his cold blood breakfast back, then tapped the empty vial on the table. "Not just talk."

We had entertained the idea of an escape countless times since the first day. Unfortunately, sunlight kept Rafe trapped and I would never leave this place without him. Then there was the squadron of armed crooks masquerading as guards, the wolf shifters patrolling the grounds, a warden hell-bent on making his prison baby the first, best, and most productive of its kind. If, somehow, we got past all that, there was still the impenetrable ward to deal with, and then the vast tundra wasteland of Siberia.

All this with our collars intact.

Because neither of us planned to leave this place a scorched corpse.

Not exactly a cakewalk, but it wasn't just me and my friend anymore. I had a mate to think of, a prison family—a clan of misfits. Witch, vampire, fae, dragon. Hardly the most conventional clan, but they were mine. All the petty shit about Rafe marking Katja first—gone. Fintan's antics—white noise. There was a bigger picture to consider, and as the scent of death and char and ash thickened in the air, vile black magic polluting our lungs, I decided it was time to act…

Or risk losing my new clan, the only clan I had ever valued or wanted, for good.

Growling, I shoved my tray away, the prison's breakfast even more grotesque in the aftermath of everything. "Agreed."

18

FINTAN

"Gentlemen..." Towel slung low around my hips, I bowed and gestured toward the shower-room door. "I'll take it from here."

Williams and Katz shot each other a look, then meandered toward the doorway—and clear through it, shutting the door soundly behind. I straightened with a smirk, then crossed my arms and ambled around the wall that separated—barely—the male and female shower quarters.

"And where are they going?" Katja looked beautiful in anything, but wrapped in just a thin strip of cloth that barely passed as a towel, she was exquisite. The shower shoes were a bit of an eyesore, but I wasn't exactly interested in her feet, was I? While I yearned to drop my gaze, to explore the barely concealed curves ordinarily hidden behind that purple jumpsuit, I kept my focus on her face.

For which I should get a fucking medal of honor, really.

"They're standing guard," I told her, about to lean on the edge of the wall, all casual and nonchalant, before opting to stand tall and firm instead. I mean, *yes*, I intended to woo her in this place, but no inmate willingly set their bare skin on the grungy bathroom tile, myself included. Would I rather have seduced her in the greenhouse? A supply closet? *Literally* anywhere else in this entire building? Absolutely. But beggars couldn't be choosers in Xargi—and this was the first time in my extraordinarily long and banal life that I was a beggar. For now, I'd take what I could get.

The witch's fiery brows crept up, and she glanced toward the closed door. "Uh… Why?"

"So no one bothers us."

My shrug had her eyebrows inching ever higher. "*What*? And why would they do that?"

"I've access to my accounts now." Despite my pathetic earnings from backbreaking labor in the greenhouse—labor I only occasionally indulged in, usually when my little jewel was watching—I had been in this shithole a month now. When permitted, I could check my finances, where I'd learned that "charity" donations had been transferred straight from my accounts and into the warden's bottomless pockets. No matter. Unlike many inmates, I now had hundreds of thousands of dollars at my disposal. No amount of slow and steady siphoning by the pricks in charge could change that.

I mean… Based on the assumption that Rollo had acquired a grand hunting party and spent the last month scouring the entire realm for his most impish of little brothers, *theoretically* I wouldn't be here much longer. Neither would Katja. And, I *suppose*, neither would Elijah and Rafe. I couldn't fathom any scenario where she would willingly leave them behind, not after the fucking and the biting and all that nonsense.

Katja stared back at me in an expectant silence, like my statement wasn't obvious explanation enough, and I cleared my throat, then threaded my hands behind my back.

"Well, for ten grand a piece, they'll do as I say... for today, anyway." Her eyes rounded, lips slightly parted, and I beamed as I rocked back and forth on the balls of my feet, beyond pleased with the response. "And I told them I wanted to worship at your altar—"

The witch exhaled a sharp, barking sort of laugh, then threw her hands up, arms still stiff enough to keep her towel in place. "You are the most *ridiculous* man I've ever met."

I tipped my head to the side, smile barbed, and then closed the distance between us in two long strides while she was busy rolling her eyes. Katja started at my sudden nearness, at my swift and silent approach, then stiffened when I caught her by the chin and steered her back to me. Gone was the incredulous grin, replaced with another flicker of genuine surprise, perhaps even a pinch of fear and a dash of uncertainty.

"I'm not a *man*," I whispered, dropping the smug, dashing pretense for a touch of the brooding fire she seemed so drawn to with her dragon and vampire. When she tried to twist away, I gripped harder, fingertips bruising into her jaw like a snare, forcing her lips into a delectable pucker. "I'm a prince, Katja, and I know quality when I see it."

Her throat bobbed with a gulp, the motion making the pink dots on her flesh just beneath the collar twitch. "Why?"

"Why?" Hardly a question of why I saw quality in her—Katja had never struck me as a woman who required a man to sing her praises so that she realized her value—but rather why *her*. I loosened my grasp on her jaw, ghosting a finger along it instead. "Why *not*?" When she didn't immediately swoon, I released her and grabbed my towel, dramatically wrenching it from my hips and tossing it onto the ground, baring myself—regretting it only *slightly*, given the state of the floor. "Am I not beautiful to you, witch?" Cock slowly swelling, heat percolating in my loins, I smirked when she stared as pointedly at my face as I had at hers, refusing to even sneak a peek downward. "Tell me honestly."

"You're very attractive, Fintan," she remarked, still quiet, still slightly unsure of the situation. I could work with that. She then wet her lips and sighed. "You know that, I know that, and the millions of women you've—"

"Don't forget the odd man."

Her eyes narrowed. "Right. Men and women in all the courts and all the worlds know that you're hot. It's a fact."

"And all those others..." I shifted closer, gaze falling to her mouth, then the collar around her throat. What I wouldn't do to remove it, to let loose the magic festering inside. "They pale in comparison to you."

"I bet you said that to all the others too."

Her scoff suggested doubt—not that I could blame her. "Never."

"I..." She leaned in closer, scrutinizing the furrow of my brow, the slight downturn of my mouth. "I don't know why I believe that."

"Because I don't enjoy telling you tall tales," I admitted, flashing a little grin despite my best efforts to remain as stoic and brooding as her other suitors. "No lies, Katja."

"I thought fae can't lie."

My chuckle had her blushing. "Ah, well, that's the biggest lie of them all."

Those lovely sapphires dropped to the ground—not to my magnificent form, but to the filthy flooring underfoot. She toed at the tile, frowning, then pinned me with another searching look that had my cock on its knees. Why did I lust after her when she was serious? When she was mean and teasing and standoffish? Fucking *why* indeed.

As if reading my mind, she forced out another whisper. "Why, Fintan?"

"Because you make me *feel*," I told her. Naturally, I could have played around with the words, made her guess, possibly even kept the truth to myself and fed her the same nonsense I did everyone else. Embarrassing as it was to admit, I had practiced this little speech in my cell. For weeks now, I had searched my depths for honesty, forced myself to say it aloud. I shirked the easy path and hurdled down the one less trod—even when it scared the absolute shit out of me. "For the first time, I feel..."

Feel what, precisely, was still up for debate. I hadn't quite gotten that far yet, but from the way she softened, this seemed like a good start. The heart palpitations and cold sweat on my palms, all hidden beneath a confident exterior, certainly suggested this was what I needed—what I had spent most of my life hiding from.

"I *feel* when I'm with you," I muttered, pleased that I didn't trip over the confession, "and I rather like it."

The shy drop of her eyes and the subtle lift of her lips sent relief pounding through me. Rejection had been a fear of mine ever since I first suffered its brutal sting, and in time, I had learned how to act out to avoid it. Make jokes. Leer and sneer and chuckle my way through life, using what material advantages I possessed to cement bonds. The entire court might have thought me a joke—but I let them. None of them mattered, all those noble fae chasing our coattails, just *hoping* one of their sons or daughters might catch the eye of true royalty...

But to be rejected by someone who mattered...

I couldn't stand it.

And from her first dismissal of my usual charade, her blushes when our gazes first tangled, Katja mattered.

"Listen, little witch..." I caught her by the chin again, tilting her head up as I eased even closer. One deep breath and it was all over. "We can fuck right here, or I can lick your pretty cunt until our time is up." I gripped tighter when her eyes widened and heat exploded across her entire face. "*Or*, we can just talk. Or shower—in separate stalls if you so desire. But I've bought us an hour in which we can pretend we're not in a fucking prison. Pretend it's a bathhouse, darling, and we can be whoever you want."

No one had ever received such an offer before.

And no one ever would again.

Tentatively, Katja reached up and brushed the brown curls away from my forehead. She smoothed my hair back, taking her time to ensure it stayed, clutched in my grasp yet utterly at ease.

"I want to be *us*," she murmured, voice low and certain, like she was whispering a secret for my ears alone, "but I don't want to touch a single tile in this bathroom."

I grinned down at her, relief mingling with need and, for the first time with a potential lover, earnest affection. "I will fall on that sword for you, my beauty."

I had never taken a sword for anyone before—they always took them for me. *Always*.

"Chivalrous *and* rich," Katja mused as she gently coiled her hand around my wrist, then coaxed my fingers from her chin, slowly steering them down to her chest. Nothing too scandalous, of course, just to the broad, flat plane beneath the hollow of her throat, and still my cock responded as if she had steered me between her thighs. Instead, it nudged insistently at her toweled belly, aching for attention. Katja, meanwhile, lost herself in my eyes, and I in hers, her little dubious breath like the sigh of the heavens. "How are you still single?"

I needn't think of a clever response—truth came free and easy for once. "Because none of the rest ever made me feel *anything*."

Her heartbeat quickened beneath my palm before I slowly smoothed it up her neck and over that miserable collar.

Utterly bewitched, I lost myself in those sapphire pools, in the depth they promised, the acceptance they offered, until finally I cupped her cheek, cradling her head in my hand. What a precarious position: one sharp jerk and I could snap her neck. Funny how intimacy and brutality shared so many common threads.

But there was no brutality when I kissed her. No selfish taking, no indulgent tongue-thrusting on my part. Our lips met softly, tentatively. *Romantically*. After centuries of fucking with no one of real importance, I had long since given up on romance. Yet heat flared in my chest, my gut somersaulting in the most pleasurable way, my cock hard against her belly. Easy to confuse a twinge of romance for outright lust, but as our mouths opened to one another, slowly and surely, I finally felt the difference.

Lust was all frantic fire and greedy caresses.

Romance was sugar and spice, taking one's time because you savored the *moment*, every minute detail of the act itself.

The idea for this morning's little fling came about when I considered all the times I'd seen Katja after her *interactions* with Elijah and Rafe. Sex seemed to make her feel better—and who could blame her? She had been hauled off to the warden's office twice since my prison stint began, and each one battered her spirit, ground it into the dirt. As I lay in my pathetic cot, trying to think of ways to brighten her mood, sex had seemed obvious. It always made *me* feel good, after all, but as she sidled closer now, I realized that feel-good from past lovers came from the physical release alone.

Not from… this. Not from the closeness or the intimacy.

Her tongue was a tease, a natural flirt, darting into my mouth and coaxing mine to play. I tasted her smile, saw it stretched all the way to her eyes even with her lids closed and relaxed, and I seized the opportunity to catch her by surprise again. Spiderwalking my fingers up her side, I found the top of her towel and *yanked,* ripping the final material barrier between us from her body and tossing it away. She gasped into my mouth, the hand in my hair tightening and twisting with admonishment, and my dark chuckle had little telltale bumps exploding across her exposed flesh.

Katja arched against me, pebbled nipples brushing my chest, and I jerked her closer with a growl. The sugar gave way to spice, our kiss quickening, deepening, like we were in a race: Who could consume the other first?

Me. I was more motivated.

Unfortunately, she had a leg up on me—not literally… not yet. But with my steely shaft caught between our bodies, even the slightest movement was fucking *agony*. It took everything in my power not to grind against her creamy skin and spill myself all over her tits. Ordinarily I wouldn't have cared. Usually, I went straight for the gold, especially if I was *this* hard and wanting. But with Katja, I took my time, stroking her, mapping her curves with hungry hands. She had a mole on her right hip—raised and a little sensitive when I brushed over it. A dimple on her left ass cheek. Some cellulite on the backs of her thighs. An adorable little pouch above her cunt…

Womanly perfection.

Need more.

Exploring her with my eyes closed was one thing, lost in the kiss, never wanting to part, but *seeing* her was another. Innocently, my left hand climbed her body, smoothing over her heated flesh, cupping her breast in passing, wandering up, up, up—until it cuffed her throat. Hard. Just below the magicked leather, I collared her and thrust her back. Greedy eyes roved her figure, from her tits that trembled with every ragged breath to the delectable flush that stretched from her cheeks to her navel, to the dip between her thighs, the abstract watercolor tattoo—black and blue clouds swirling around her left calf, unexpected and artsy and somehow rather fitting—and then up again to the patch of fiery red hiding my prize.

Exquisite.

Mine.

The declaration appeared out of nowhere, and I clenched my jaw, slightly unnerved by the possessive flames unfurling inside me. Her hands went to my wrist, especially when I squeezed just a *little* harder, panic flashing in her eyes at my predatory grin. I let it drag on a little longer, grasping her like she was a catfish wriggling on the end of my line, before closing in and kicking apart her lovely legs. Katja's breath hitched, but she steadied herself, knees slightly bent and feet flat...

Until I lifted her onto her toes.

Her eyes rounded a touch more, only to flutter shut as my free hand delved down her belly and between her thighs. I stroked her entirety at first, massaging her slickness, smearing her arousal over her nether lips. A caress light as air across her clit had her eyes snapping open, and I made her watch as I licked her desire from three of my fingers, slowly, one at a time. When those fingers returned to her sex, I found her wetter, her pale thighs trembling as I held her up.

I could have had this alone and been satisfied. Sure, my cock jutted out between us, desperate for closeness, starving to plunge into her inferno, but I would take a savage case of blue balls just to keep her on her toes and finger-fuck her through as many orgasms as we could fit in the next hour.

A heady, albeit strained, moan tumbled from her lips when I thrust a finger into her—then another, eventually working her cunt with three while the base of my palm smothered her clit. My little witch was so responsive to me, her hips bucking, her legs shaking with every torturous thrust. She fought to stay up on her toes, digging her claws into my forearm as she used me for balance. While hooded, she kept her eyes on me—on *my* gaze, and as tempted as I was to take mental pictures of her flushed, quivering body, of her toes all pink at the ends from the exertion and her tightened nipples dancing for me, I couldn't look away either.

Especially when she came.

Katja's knees buckled as she writhed and clenched around my fingers. I tracked the pleasure ripping through her, from the blush exploding across her skin to the sagging of her limbs, the climax milking what strength she had and leaving her limp.

Leaving her entirely at *my* mercy.

Fuck.

Jaw clenched, I dragged us across the space, not stopping until my back collided with the cold—grungy—tile beneath the shower head. Katja collapsed against my chest, her arms folded between us, her elbows driving into my torso and my cock stabbing at her belly.

"Ugh, sorry," she whispered shakily, taking in our backdrop. "I can—"

"Shut your beautiful mouth," I hissed, then plucked at her lower lip for good measure. "It's worth it... I can take it."

"My hero." She wiggled her eyebrows and smirked, her sarcasm positively dripping—just like her cunt. Taking her firmly by the hips, I spun her around so swiftly, with such ease, that she gasped.

"Tell me to stop, darling," I urged, planting a hand between her shoulder blades and slowly bending her over, "and I will."

"Noted," Katja fired back. She folded at the waist, following my lead, offering herself to me, and braced on her knees. No, no, that wouldn't do. An idea sparked—somehow, because literally every drop of blood in my body was currently in my cock—and using the grimy wall for support, I lunged and grabbed her arms. Yanked them behind her back. Trapped her wrists in one hand while the other darted around to pluck at her nipples.

"*Fintan.*"

"You know the words," I growled, bending her further. She adjusted with a whimper, widening her stance, preparing, arching her lower back so that I had access to *everything*. The corners of my mouth kicked up. *One hole a day, I think.* While my thumb brushed her puckered little asshole, a caress that made her stiffen with a sharp breath, I had my sights set elsewhere.

And I claimed my treasure—vehemently. Steering my cock with my free hand, I teased her pussy with a few insufficient pumps, just the silken tip delving in, until she tried to push back with a frustrated whine. I tsked down at her, then gave her ass a pair of light—sharp—love taps.

"Patience is a virtue, Katja."

"Not in prison, Fintan."

I snorted. "Trollop."

"*Fuck* you—"

I bucked hard, filling her to the hilt and forcing a long, aching moan from her. My eyes all but rolled back in my head as she clamped down around me, sweet relief on the horizon, but then took a deep breath to steady myself—to come back to the moment and remember that this wasn't about me.

It had *always* been about me before.

And the change felt oddly powerful.

Threading my fingers into her hair, I wrapped her red mane around my fist and wrenched her head back, absolutely *obsessed* with every little noise she made. Katja whined, her sex rippling around my cock, and pushed back into my hips the longer I stayed still. *In time, darling*. Just to be cruel, I waited as long as I could, holding her in place by her wrists and hair, snapshotting her lovely figure bent over and contorted in front of me, utterly at my mercy. She tried to seek her own satisfaction, writhing against me, trying to *move*, but I kept her still, tormented her a little while longer.

Only when I couldn't take it anymore, every cell in my body on the verge of imploding, did I move.

Hard.

Fast.

Punishing.

Yet somehow this pace, this pounding into her and watching her jiggle, had the same romantic air to it as our first kiss. Strange. Rough sex had never struck me as romantic before, but somehow, I couldn't fathom any other way with Katja.

And from the way she squeaked and groaned and whimpered, from the stomping of her little feet and the flailing of her fingers, she loved every damn second of it.

In fact, she spurred *me* on. For the first time, I let my lover set the pace, call the shots, using the pitch of her cries and the clench of her body to drive me onward. The second I abandoned her hair, her head lolled forward, bobbing with every buck of my hips, cock pistoning in and out of her. As soon as I found her clit, tough as it was to maneuver, she was gone again. She scream-whispered my name, her hands in rigid fists, and I offered no mercy, no quarter, pummeling her through another climax that turned her words to babbling nonsense.

Waiting had never felt so exquisite. If we had the luxury, I would have kept her in this room all fucking day and spent at least a few hours edging her. Katja would hate it, hate *me*, but it would only make her downfall all the sweeter.

Unfortunately, we had a limit. One hour alone and the guards' silence—assured in blood, their word unbreakable—for twenty thousand dollars, and the thought of being hauled out of here immediately post-coitus set my teeth on edge. So,

I adjusted my angle, grabbed her hair again, and pounded through to my own nirvana. Muscles tensed, pleasure sharpened in my core, igniting, spreading like wildfire until it consumed every part of me. I came with a hiss and a groan, spilling myself inside her as fireworks exploded behind my lids.

Fuck. It was like I'd never orgasmed before her. Like all previous climaxes were a trial run leading up to the real thing. Panting, I folded forward and dragged an openmouthed kiss over her rounded back. Knees weak, fingertips tingling, vision spotted with black dots, I could have easily collapsed onto her, both of us crashing to the floor—and in a cleaner setting, I might have. Instead, I forced myself upright and released her wrists, both bruised from my hold, then her hair. Gently as I could, I helped her straighten with a shaky arm around her waist, then let her lean on me, head tucked under my chin as she caught her breath. Behind me, I groped around for the shower nozzle, then turned it and shielded her from the meager assault of a barely lukewarm spray.

Katja yelped, sheltering in my chest, until it warmed just a fraction more to her liking. Only then did I feel secure in letting her stand on her own two feet, leaving her for a few moments to shuffle over to my toiletries hamper—which was the envy of the cellblock and one of the most expensive items at the store. Still struggling through the sluggishness of my climax, I dug around inside for what we needed, then sauntered back to her.

Bruised and flushed, Katja was a vision. Standing beneath the shower's halfway decent water pressure, she watched my approach while nibbling on her lower lip, looking neither guilty nor ashamed—but relaxed. Possibly even... content?

"Right." I held up a tiny travel-sized bottle of shampoo. "I will trade you one deep-throating blowjob for this *full* bottle. Note the seal is unbroken—"

She smacked my chest with a carefree laugh, shoving at me while I chuckled, both of us halfhearted in our play fighting. As I fended off her attack, I steered us back under the water—then kissed her, all sugar and very little spice. With my eyes closed, I could pretend we were kissing in the rain somewhere far, far away from Xargi Penitentiary.

Katja had taken my mind off this shithole, and as I kissed her, as I cracked open my shampoo and washed her hair, then let her wash mine, I hoped *this* had distracted her too.

That I hadn't failed now that I'd actually tried at something.

Because if I could make her happy, even for a short while, then...

Well, then that made *me* happy.

And all things considered, that was a victory worth savoring.

19
KATJA

"It must have been terrifying," Lloyd mused, finger slowly circling the rim of his coffee mug, that hawkish grey gaze never once leaving my face, "to be hunted within a lake he knew so well… To feel the predator nipping at his heels with the shoreline so very far away." He leaned over his obviously-compensating-for-something mahogany desk, fighting to catch my eye. "Did you hear him screaming that fateful day?"

Even though I was almost *too* aware of him, I focused on the huge windows across his office. Lightning skittered through a black sky, a storm sweeping across the terrain and pounding into Xargi like a battering ram. I'd only just walked back into Cellblock C, trailing along behind a forever grinning Fintan, both of us soaked to the bone, when Cooper grabbed me by the arm and hauled me back out. At the time, I hadn't bothered to ask where we were going. I knew, dread mounting with each step deeper into corridors stamped with upscale décor and tiled floors.

Today was the story of Ewan's death. Practically giddy, Lloyd had been waiting for me by his ostentatious hearth as Cooper shoved me into the same chair as last time, even dried me off with a lazy flick of his wand, the rush of hot air wicking away rainwater making my stomach turn.

He had offered the same out: accept the blood contract signed by my mom, acknowledge him as my lord and master, and leave Xargi with him this evening. Biting down hard on my cheeks, bones weary from a full day of harvesting sunflowers, I had planted my elbow on the armrest, my chin on my fist, and tried to lose myself in the storm. Tried to track the fattest rain droplets as they parachuted down the windowpanes, all the while wishing the thunder would drown out his smoker's rasp, his husky baritone.

Hating that his cologne was so *strong*, like he had put on more just for me.

Sure, he smelled great—all masculine and spicy and rich—but Lloyd Guthrie was rotten to the core, and no amount of paint on his shiny exterior could change that.

Surprise, surprise: *he* had orchestrated Ewan's death. Only a year older than me, the middle child, the second Fox son, my brother had drowned on a hot July afternoon at our family's cottage. Back then, Jackson had been all about kayaking. Dad had been obsessed with chopping wood and making the *best* bonfires after sunset. I used to enjoy flitting around between all of them, going wherever the wind would blow me.

And Ewan was usually in the lake from morning until dusk, swimming and leaping off the tire swing and cannonballing from the edge of the dock.

Lloyd had hired a shifter assassin—a seal shifter, different from a selkie in that they could shift from man to beast and back again at will. The assassin chased my brother around the lake, herding him away from the shoreline, exhausting him, then grabbed his ankle, dragged him to the murky, mushy bottom... and drowned him. Just like that, this piece of shit with all his money and his grudge and his bruised ego stole my best friend from me.

I'd been eight at the time.

While I remembered the aftermath, Dad finding Ewan's pale, limp body washed up on the shore, the hours before were a haze. At some point, I'd been in the lake with him—then climbed on Jackson's kayak and took a tour of the smaller inlets. Back to the cabin for lunch. Watermelon slices in the hot afternoon. A book in my hands, bathed in sunlight, my hair drying into tight red ringlets that I'd since outgrown.

But beyond that—

"Kitten." Lloyd snapped his fingers as another bolt of lightning cut over the black, a gust of wind splattering the windows with rain. Seriously, could he have chosen a more ominous day? The warden—gangster, kingpin, villain, *bastard*—cleared his throat and tapped the mahogany top of his desk. "I asked you a *question*. It's rude to ignore a superior."

My teeth sank into my cheeks, but I unclenched when the pain became too sharp, on the verge of flooding my mouth with a metallic tang. Was he my *superior*? As far as I was concerned, Lloyd Guthrie was no better than the dirt—a step below the sludge on the shower walls. Slowly, I forced my gaze in his direction, and I let him know *precisely* what I thought about him with a glare…

Which only seemed to delight him.

"Well?"

Still angled away from him, body language reading loud and clear that if I wasn't trapped in this chair with thinly veiled threats, I'd be all the way across the room plastered against the windows. Grey light spilled in through the huge panes, the room lit only by Lloyd's twin desk lamps and the odd blast of lightning. He cocked a greying eyebrow, then fished out a pack of cigarettes from the inside of his jacket.

"No," I croaked tersely. The first time I sat in this chair,

I'd ended our little meeting by vomiting all over the hardwood. Today, I had a better grasp on my anxiety, months of prison time bolstering my confidence—but not enough to quell the churn of my gut and the pounding of my heart. Being in the same *room* as him, even if Lloyd and I didn't exchange a single word, made me wish the ground would just open up and swallow me whole. Palms slick with a nervous sweat, adrenaline had been stabbing through me for the last half hour, my body primed to bolt. It left me light-headed and nauseous, all that fight or flight wasted while I was stuck in this damn chair. "I don't remember hearing his screams."

Lloyd clucked his tongue at me, then lit his cigarette with the end of his wand. A flicker of flame preceded the pungent waft of burning herbs that only made my queasiness worse.

"Pity," he murmured after his first puff, easing back in his huge, intimidating chair in that pristine suit, sporting the same perfectly side-swept salt-and-pepper hair, clean-shaven and leering. I attempted to gulp down the lump in my throat again to no avail; while not a single tear had fallen since Cooper marched me into the warden's den, the floodwaters had been rising ever since he dragged me out of the cellblock and away from the three men who made me brave in Xargi. Frightened as I was of the gangster seated across from me, I refused to let him see me cry this time. Refused to allow him *any* power over me—refused to give him something that said he had chipped another chink in my armor.

"Now, kitten," he rasped, the pet name reserved for Dad and Dad alone followed by a cloud of smoke that had me coughing, "I have the same proposition for you—"

"No." Thunder cracked outside immediately after the last flash of white light, rattling the windows and the bookshelves. The storm had drifted right over us, and what I wouldn't give to be out there, with the wolves and the tempest, if it meant being far, far away from *him*. "Same answer."

Lloyd chuckled, elegant and pompous in the way he tapped his cigarette over an ivory ash tray. "Are you sure?"

My belly roared—*traitor*—and Lloyd grinned like that was the answer he'd wanted. Rolling my shoulders back, I glanced pointedly at the wall clock.

"You're going to make me miss dinner, warden," I insisted. We had another hour before they made us line up and amble down to the cafeteria, but something told me this asshole could waste away much longer than that just listening to himself talk.

"You'll regret it, little one." The cigarette's tip blazed bright orange with his next inhale, the color dancing in his eyes. A tentative glance into them showed the amusement fading—no more teasing and tormenting. My refusal pissed him off, which both terrified and thrilled me. It would probably be my downfall one day, but not today: he still had two more family members to torture me with. Lloyd flicked the ashy tip over the tray, one grey eye narrowing slightly. "I haven't even *begun* to apply pressure."

"Telling me how you murdered my family isn't pressure?" I demanded, voice cracking despite my best efforts to keep it steady—to sound brave. Lloyd scoffed, his smile cold and cruel.

"Just the tip of the iceberg." He extinguished his cigarette having only consumed half, as if this particular prop in his theatrical arsenal was no longer needed. "Tip of the fucking iceberg, pet."

Bring it. I tried to scream it with my eyes, daring him to divulge *more* horrors from my past. Because Mom and Ewan were out there, floating in the ether, clinging to me like a second skin I would never shed—but I had survived it. With each passing day, Elijah, Rafe, and Fintan made me stronger in their own ways. Knowing they had my back against other inmates was one thing, but our steadily growing bonds, like flowers blooming in the middle of the desert, reminded me that this wasn't the end. Xargi wasn't a wasteland, and I hadn't come here to die. With them, I wasn't completely alone.

I could endure.

I could survive him.

Never would I ever accept his offer.

Never.

Even the nightmares had stopped now that Tully snuggled up to me each night. My familiar provided a deep, dreamless sleep, and I came to refreshed and resilient. While still not quite the heroine of this depressing story, I walked with my head held higher lately.

And Lloyd Guthrie couldn't take that from me no matter how many gory details he shoved down my throat.

"*Fine,*" Lloyd growled with an aggressive nod toward his office door. "Just go. We'll be seeing each other again real soon, kitten."

Even though my knees wobbled as I stood, I forced myself to roll my eyes—big and obvious, just for him. The muscles along his jaw flickered, and his grey gaze cut down my face to my lips, then just low enough so that when my hair spilled back over my shoulder, he—

"What the hell is *that*?"

He saw Rafe's bite. Panicked, I dragged my hair forward and staggered around the armchair that had once felt so claustrophobic, now small and ineffectual as Lloyd leapt out of *his* seat and raced around the desk. The damn puncture wounds still hadn't fully healed—not that I *wanted* them to. In fact, I usually nodded off after our nightly chats stroking the marks, Tully purring by my side, but I couldn't understand why they were still there.

Vampire toxin was said to do all sorts of delicious things to their prey's bodies, and I had experienced that firsthand. Besides the pleasure, the toxin in their saliva was supposed to facilitate healing, especially if their victim's heart was still beating. Only I'd also had little cuts and burns courtesy of both the bakery and the greenhouse after Rafe bit me that were just distant memories, yet those two perfectly round dots looked so fresh they could have been added to my skin yesterday, not weeks ago.

"It's—"

"Is that a *vampire* bite? A filthy *vampire* put his mouth on you?" Lloyd bellowed, catching up to me in no time. He shoved his wand under my chin and snapped his huge hand around my throat, and I squealed when he slammed me up against the door. Since being with Elijah and Fintan, along with experiencing the bloodiest of kisses from Rafe, I realized I had a taste for rough sex and the promise of violence in the bedroom. It should have scared the shit out of me—but it was hot, and with my trio, I felt safe enough to indulge in some dormant fantasies.

But this wasn't a fantasy.

Lloyd wrenched my head to the side, exposing my neck, and then ripped at my jumpsuit collar for a closer look. Wand tip stabbing into the underside of my chin, his breath hit hard and fast, peppering me with the remnants of that herbal cigarette. A good head taller and a shocking amount stronger, he pinned me against the door with his imposing frame and examined me at his leisure—like I was a dog.

And all I felt was fear.

No dark desire, no throb of forbidden arousal.

Just gut-dropping, pulse-pounding, throat-closing *terror*. Ice sluiced through my veins as he touched me, poked me, prodded at me, and I swallowed down a surge of bile when his lips brushed my ear with each heated word.

"You have no right to give your body to another, Katja Fox," he seethed, wand pressing deeper, pushing down on my shoulder, opening me to him, exposing my throat as every muscle protested the strain. I closed my eyes tight to catch the tears before they fell, their prickle sharp and cruel, and then flinched at the first hint of his teeth on my skin. "It belongs to *me*, in its entirety, and I haven't given anyone permission to *taste* you."

I chomped down on my lips to hide their shaking, then focused on taking deep, even breaths as my stomach roiled and my mouth flooded with saliva. *No anxiety pukes.* No *anxiety pukes.* This gross bastard had already witnessed the humiliation of me emptying my guts out in front of him; he knew exactly what he did to me, and he didn't get to go on thinking he had that much control over my body.

Lloyd lingered, really drawing out the indignities, checking the rest of my neck for any additional bites, and when satisfied that there was only the one, he grabbed me by the chin and slammed my head back into the door. Stars exploded behind my tightly clenched eyelids, and I muffled my whimper.

"*Cooper*," he barked, mouth right next to my ear again, voice cracking like a gunshot. I flinched away, slowly and hesitantly opening my eyes, and Lloyd wrenched me off the door when the knob creaked. Sure enough, there was my block's sleaziest guard waiting on the other side of the door, stinking of smoke just like his boss, the corridor behind him scented with a cloud of charred herbs.

"Yeah, chief?"

"Take her on the scenic route," Lloyd growled as he shoved me into Cooper's awaiting grasp. The warlock grabbed my arm harder than he needed to, yanking me forward a few paces so roughly that I tripped—much to the enjoyment of both men present.

"Yes, sir."

The door slammed shut as soon as Cooper hauled me off on yet another forced march, the corridor suddenly bathed in shadows, illuminated only by the odd flickering fluorescent that made my churning belly even angrier.

All I wanted in that moment was Elijah. I wanted his protective, possessive gaze sweeping my body, assessing it for injuries, and I wanted the clench of his jaw when he realized I had been with the warden again. I wanted his arm tight around my shoulders in the common area—the only physical contact we dared risk in front of the guards—and his hand on my thigh under the table at dinner. I wanted his brimstone scent. I wanted his eyes like slits, the inner dragon on guard.

He didn't need to say a word to make me feel safe.

He was my fated mate—and I *needed* him.

We were still working through the particulars, sure, and there was no telling what kind of relationship we would have had outside of Xargi... But this was what we had now. Comfort in the closeness. Security in nothing more than a glance.

Cooper dragged me along at a brutal pace, but I kept up, desperate to get back to my mate—to all of them. To Rafe's furrowed brow, knitted deep with confusion and anger and injustice. To Fintan's sharp tongue and laughing eyes, always capable of breaking the tension even when the rest of us were miserable.

Only we didn't take the usual winding corridors back to the shittier side of the building. As instructed, the warlock with a death grip on my arm led me through unfamiliar hallways, up and down spiral stairwells. I didn't find my bearings until we passed the prison shop, which always reminded me of a shanty liquor store with its huge open doorway and goods locked behind bars, the teller in a caged dome at the back. We blitzed by it so fast that I couldn't pick out the faces of the inmates doing a bit of predinner shopping, but the flash of a red jumpsuit made my heart skip a beat.

Made the marks on my throat tingle like they were fresh and sore.

We finally stopped—seemingly out of nowhere—just around the corner from the commissary, Cooper jerking me back when I stumbled forward with the momentum of our march. He positioned me in front of an ordinary door with *Supplies* scratched into the wood, and everything inside me stilled, a cold fear taking root. Because… Well, not exactly the most professional signage, some crude lettering carved into the panels with, what, a knife?

"Uh, what are we—"

Cooper shook me hard enough to jostle my neck and make my teeth chatter, then grabbed the brass knob and turned it. Flung open the door to reveal…

Deimos.

Constance.

Avery and Blake.

A little Cellblock C reunion.

The four loitered around the tiny closet, a space that really did look like a storage room with cleaning supplies and dingy rags piled on the shelves. I planted my feet, eyes widening, adrenaline soaring, but Cooper still managed to shove me inside.

Then the bastard closed the door behind me, the click of a lock making my heart sink.

Okay. I swallowed hard, battling with the lump in my throat. *Okay*. A high-pitched whine erupted, slicing through my skull and growing louder by the second. *Okay, okay*. None of them had access to their powers—all the collars were still firmly in place. *Okay, okay, okay, don't panic*.

Back to the door, I looked to Deimos in his black

jumpsuit, scenes of grotesque torture tattooed over every bit of exposed flesh, creeping all the way up to his chin. At some point since I'd arrived, someone had carved *666* into his temple—so original.

No, pleasant thoughts only. He knew I despised him—I never tried to hide it—but right now, I was also at his mercy. All by his lonesome, the demon sprawled across one whole wall of shelves directly in front of me. Constance giggled to my left, the air thick, and swung her legs from her shelf-perch midway up the wall. Avery and Blake, meanwhile, stood to my immediate right, arms crossed, silent and waiting.

"Deimos," I started, then staggered back into the door, hitting the wood with a noisy *whump*, when he pushed off the wall and stalked toward me. I held up my hands, defenseless, every synapse firing as I searched for just the right words to defuse this. Only adrenaline made my mind frantic and scattered—made my limbs shake and my extremities numb. "W-wait—"

He swiftly closed the gap between us, then gut-punched me with the force of a charging bull. My diaphragm absorbed the hit, all the air whooshing out of my lungs, and, gasping, I folded over without meaning to—I just couldn't stay upright—and Deimos shoved me the rest of the way down. The tinny whine between my ears rocketed up to deafening when I hit the ground, thrust into the middle of the space on my hands and knees, and a blow to the side from someone's foot knocked me over.

It all happened so fast, so furious, that I didn't have time to lash out or strike back. I'd never been in an actual *fight* before, and as all four closed in, laughing and jeering, whatever words they hurled at me muffled against the screechy whine, I just curled into a ball. Protect the important bits: face and brain. My fingers crunched when someone stomped down on them. My back arched and bowed at the unrelenting blows. Someone—Constance, based on the scratch of talons up my neck—grabbed a fistful of my hair and spun me around in a circle, the maenad's cackles girlish and savage.

To my credit, I didn't make a sound besides the odd whimper and cry. No screams—I refused to give them that. No begging, either, because it wouldn't matter.

"You chose the wrong side, foxy," Deimos told me in a singsong voice, his words followed by a harsh pounding on my rib cage. Something splintered, and I sucked in a ragged breath, pain exploding through my torso. "I could have put in a good word for you—kept this from happening."

Finally, the kicks and stomps stopped, and a hand grabbed me roughly by the shoulder and rolled me onto my back. Deimos loomed over me, grinning, pupils so dilated that his eyes were completely black, full demon mode engaged. Still curled up, locked in this position, I wheezed through the agony of a broken rib, tears falling hot and heavy down my face and into my hair. Everything hurt. *Everything*. Something equally warm dribbled from my nose, and a bit of blood teased the corner of my trembling lips.

"You fucked up, witch," he whispered, sweeping his greasy black hair back with a sneer. Constance crouched beside him, then dipped her finger into the blood oozing from my nose and smeared it over my lips.

"Red's your color," she sneered, and before I could swipe at her, some of the fight weaseling back into my limbs, Deimos grabbed me again and flipped me onto my stomach. This time I screamed, my rib taking a hard hit, snot and blood spattering the stones below, tears making the darkness swim.

Razor-tipped nails grazed my neck again as Constance gathered my hair with a gentleness that felt almost mocking. As I struggled through every sob, sharpness stabbing outward from my busted rib, she swept it all into one hand, then shoved my face into the stone, cheek-down, and wrapped my hair around her fist.

Holding it like a dog leash.

Riiiiip. With Avery and Blake loitering overhead, Deimos must have been the one to tear my jumpsuit clean in two, shredding the back, exposing me.

"Maybe you should just take his offer, eh?" the demon whispered in my ear, and my eyes widened. *Fuck* Lloyd Guthrie. Was this what he meant by applying pressure? Fire blasted through me like a nuclear bomb, and I swung back, gritting through the agony to slash at him, at Constance, at anyone within reach. Ineffectual, but as Deimos snapped my underwear's waistband, then hiked the cotton up between my cheeks, it felt good to *fight*.

His knee found my back and drove in hard, forcing another scream from my ragged throat as bone *crunched* in my chest. He then tore my panties off, elastic groaning, cotton ripping, all my bits squished and twisted in the process.

Just as his hand smoothed over my ass, as someone stomped on my flailing legs and bruised my calves even more, there was a crash against the door. A snarl that I felt in my bones. The room stilled, Deimos's fingers ghosting over my slit. Another crash. Male voices escalating outside.

The third crash sent chunks of wood and dust raining down on us, and Constance shrieked as footsteps thundered into the tiny space. Deimos's filthy fingers were wrenched from my body, the knee on my back vanished, and a red jumpsuit flashed overhead as Rafe—*my* Rafe—tackled Deimos to the ground. Shivering with shock, panic, I dragged my body away from the scuffle as best I could, barely taking in the fact that Rafe had started slamming Deimos's head into the ground and showed no signs of stopping. Fangs bared, the vampire smashed him into the stone over and over again, a plastic bag from the prison shop abandoned at the open doorway.

"*Cooper*... What the *fuck* is this?"

A black figure descended on me, but gentle hands found my body this time. Thompson? I blinked up at a familiar and very welcome face, at the one warlock who had always been decent to me.

"Can you stand, Fox?" he murmured as more uniformed warlocks streamed into the room, several dogpiling on Rafe and Deimos while two others dragged the rest of them out. I gargled some nonsense up at him, throat screamed to ribbons, blood dribbling down and soaking into my jumpsuit, then shook my head. Exhaling softly, he helped me up, then stilled when I wailed, his hand veering too close to my rib cage.

"*Katja*!" Rafe thundered my name, features contorted and savage, the bloodthirsty beast lurking beneath a calm veneer suddenly out for all to see. Deimos was gone, but they needed four guards to haul the raging vampire out of the storage closet, and a flash of bright blue beyond the doorway ended it all. Someone had stunned him, his fury subdued, and Thompson waited until the hoard of footsteps shuffled away before helping me limp out.

"Boss's orders," Cooper drawled when we happened upon him leaning against the opposite wall, a cigarette in hand and a smirk on that smarmy mouth. "And no, you can't take her to the infirmary. He wants her to sit in it and rethink some of her life choices. It's a teaching moment."

"Are you fucking serious?" Thompson demanded, his sturdy frame the only thing keeping me up. The edges of my vision darkened, unconsciousness tickling at me, beckoning me into its arms.

"You want to go ask him?"

"I didn't sign up for this shit."

"Yeah you did." Cooper flicked his cigarette butt at me with a snort. "We all did. So, fall in line or get out."

Scowling, Thompson eased me away, guiding me on the most direct route back to the cellblock. He let me take my time, every step an ordeal, my jumpsuit hanging open, my face and hands bloodied, my cracked rib slicing at my insides.

But I did it.

As soon as I spotted the door to Cellblock C, victory swelled from the well deep inside me, the place that housed all my magic. I fucking *did* it. I made it back to my guys, my bed, my familiar—this hadn't broken me, and it wouldn't. I refused to let it, refused to give in to *him.*

If he thought this would drive me into his arms like they were some bobbing buoy in the stormy seas, Lloyd Guthrie was the dumbest man alive. Bones healed. Bruises faded. Scabs eventually fell off. Scars became memories. I would recover from this, an hour at a time, and come out the other side stronger—just to spite him. It would be a cold day in Hell before I accepted his offer, let him own me, no matter what he did to me.

Give it your best shot.

Thompson unlocked the cellblock door and let me shuffle in ahead of him. Elijah shot up from his spot at our usual table with a roar, his shadow exploding into the silhouette of his inner dragon.

Show me the whole iceberg, Guthrie.

With a panicked Fintan hot on his heels, he sprinted toward me, and I collapsed in his burly arms with a wail, groping behind him for Fintan—for someone else to cling to as a few tenuous threads held my world together, thin enough to snap at any moment but still holding strong for now.

I can take it.

20

RAFE

"I can't believe that piece of filth is still here." Standing sentry alongside Fintan outside Katja's cell, I crossed my arms and scowled at a smirking Deimos. The demon sat on his usual throne in the middle of the block, surrounded by his cronies, untouchable. His lot had been neck-deep in a game of cards for ages—*someone* had stolen the deck from my cell during my trip to the shop and subsequent near-murder of a demonic gnat who deserved to be ground into shark chum—and now their overlord got a big kick out of throwing smug looks our way. If I didn't intentionally plant my feet, I would have flown across the block and ripped him apart as soon as he'd returned from the library. "He should be in solitary. All of them should—"

"I can't believe *you* aren't in solitary," Fintan muttered, shooting me a look that demanded I just drop it already—that he was sick of me going round and round about Deimos. *Hypocritical shit.* I arched an eyebrow at the fae, who still had flour dusted across his green jumpsuit and a burn on his sharp cheekbone.

"What?"

"Well, obviously Cooper and Katja didn't just *happen* upon that cheery bunch yesterday," he remarked with a roll of his eyes. "*Obviously* it was orchestrated, and with the way things run in here, you could have easily been blamed for all of it. They could still very well shove you in one of those holes and throw away the key."

Tully's purring spiked inside his mistress's cell, and I glanced over my shoulder with a clenched jaw, irritated that Fintan, for all his pompous talk, was right. What had happened to our girl had been a planned hit—how else would Deimos and the others all be out of the cellblock at the same time? One by one, they had been pulled out before supper yesterday, around the time I too had requested a trip to the shop to stock up on supplies that I didn't *need* but liked to share with my group if they were lacking. Someone had it out for Katja, and while we three had speculated as she tried desperately to sleep through her injuries before lights-out, none of us were certain.

Well. Save Fintan. He had a working theory that the warden had taken a special interest in *our* witch, tormenting her for reasons unknown.

That remained unproven—and Katja hadn't said more than five words since Elijah gently placed her in her cot yesterday afternoon. She should have been convalescing in the infirmary, but no guard would take her. Thompson disappeared immediately after he returned her to us, and we hadn't seen him since, but the warlock seemed to possess a soft spot for her; if anyone could get her the medical care she needed, it was him.

And Tully.

Thank *God* that black cloud had snuck into the prison. Without him, she would still be wheezing through a broken rib. With him, it had healed, downgraded to a painful bruise that still made her wince and shiver, but at least she could breathe freely. He hadn't left her side once, purring and nuzzling, fueling her body with his familiar magic, healing her one tiny stitch at a time. If she had been placed in hospital like she was *supposed* to, the prison healers could have fixed her in minutes.

Instead, she was left to suffer.

Couldn't even stand long enough to get to the cafeteria for the three meals that had come and gone since her attack.

Fortunately, for all his posturing about being fae royalty, Fintan was an exceptional little thief. He had managed to sneak something back to her every time, bread hunks and overcooked meat hidden in his jumpsuit, then *volunteered* on his day off to work her bakery shift. Her *solo* bakery shift, mind you. Poor bastard was rather grumpy about that. By a sheer stroke of luck, Elijah had the day off as well, and he hadn't left her cot since the cell doors opened. While the guards glared and whispered, no one had tried to remove him.

Perhaps they knew better by now.

Or perhaps they remembered what he had done to Phillips in the shower all those months back.

Add that to what had happened to Deimos yesterday, me slamming his head into the ground again and again until it splintered apart. *So* satisfying, the crack of his skull, the surge of black blood across my fingers—not that I'd been able to enjoy it for long. At the time, pure instinct drove my hand, guided me, turned me into an animal. As Thompson escorted me back from commissary, I had felt Katja's pain, her panic, her terror. A vampire's bite formed a connection between predator and prey. Ordinarily the tether faded with time, but mine and Katja's lingered, her more visceral emotions and physical sensations shuddering through me no matter the distance.

Nothing like feeling the woman you fancied orgasm when she was supposed to be showering.

Yesterday, when I'd felt her, I just... reacted. *Snapped.* Accepted the violent, brutal beast I'd become centuries ago. Hunted down my girl and punished those who dared lay a hand on her.

Naturally, Deimos had been taken to the prison hospital. Fucker looked shiny and new today, haughty as always and seemingly quite proud of himself for the blow he had delivered to a rival gang.

Now the geniuses running the show had us all caged together—and they expected us *not* to fight?

Or maybe they did.

Maybe Fintan had a point—

"Hello?" The fae poked me hard in the arm. "You still with me? I really can't handle both of you flipping your shit today, okay?"

I swatted his hand away when he went in for a second prod. "Fuck off, Fintan. I'm fine."

"I mean, I get it." The fae cocked his head to the side, surveying Deimos with an uncharacteristic calm I'd never seen before from him. "I want to skin him alive, heal him, and then do it again. Scoop out his eyes with one of those human ice cream scooper things... All that. But if you lose it and they chuck you in solitary, I can't hold Elijah back by myself."

"I fucking heard that," the dragon shifter growled from inside Katja's cell. Fintan and I looked back, sunset allowing us both to block the doorway, and the fae snorted.

"Good. Hear it, dragon, and take *heed*."

Elijah stared Fintan down, pupils like slits, everything about him hard as stone. It was the sort of glare that would send lesser men fleeing into the shadows, yet Fintan merely stared back, unfazed, and cocked his head again as if daring him to argue. The standoff lasted until Katja dragged in a deep, nourishing breath and shuffled about beneath the starchy linens. Then Elijah was lost to the both of us, back to his protective stance at the edge of the cot, lording over her fitfully slumbering figure like a gargoyle.

If anyone managed to shoulder by me and Fintan, Elijah would absolutely destroy them. Never in the history of our friendship had I seen him so focused—and he ran a *jeweler's* shop back home. The profession demanded absolute patience, precision, and skill, but Katja was his crown jewel, his prized possession, and every iota of concentration he possessed was dedicated to her.

Same, friend. Same.

Chuckling, Fintan shifted his weight between his legs, then leaned against the stone doorway with a huff. How he managed to get away with telling an alpha shifter what to do was beyond me, but at some point Elijah and I had just accepted him as a part of our group, this snarky, teasing, carefree fae who delighted in poking the bear time and time again, then hiding behind Elijah or me in the fallout. For his obscene age, he sometimes reminded me of a teenager, both in maturity and foresight, but here and there he had proven his worth to this...

Pack.

Clan?

Clique?

We were something, we four, and everyone—*everyone*—seemed to sense our bond stretched beyond that of a found family.

Besides, even if Fintan hadn't proven himself, his comment was fair. In a place of shifting schedules and guards ready to fuck us over at the drop of a hat, Katja needed *all* of us to recover. It did her no good if we ended up in a hole for the next week.

So, we stood guard. No one would touch her under our watch—no one had access to her in this state. Hell, she was still waiting on a new jumpsuit to replace the one splattered with blood that Deimos had torn right down the back.

Just the memory of the fabric cleaved in two ignited a *fury* deep inside. My fangs sunk into my lower lip and my hands coiled to impossibly tight fists. Because with that mental picture came Katja herself—the position I found her in, beaten and bloodied, on her belly, vulnerable and exposed.

Although I envied Elijah's innate connection with the witch, I wasn't jealous of him, per se, and I didn't want him to bow out of our dynamic. Nor had I felt inclined to attack Fintan the moment he and Katja were escorted back into the cellblock after their alone time in the shower, back when I had felt her numerous, pungent climaxes all the way in *my* cell, pleasure ripping through me like a tsunami.

But Deimos?

With his hand between her thighs? Knee on her back? That fucking *smile*?

Then to add insult to injury: Blake and Avery loitering around like they were waiting their fucking turn to have at her.

No.

Fintan and Elijah had never once set me off over their separate and developing connections with Katja, but yesterday…

Yesterday I had been *this* close to painting the walls with blood and guts. Had the guards not literally stunned me into submission, I would have torn all three of those twisted bastards limb from limb and accepted my fate. Simple as that.

"O'Dwyer."

I started at the sound of my name barked by an unfamiliar guard. A trio loitered in the open main door to Cellblock C, and, so unaccustomed to being addressed, I just stared back. Most of the vampires in Xargi were shadows, shells of their former selves, unable to work and barely surviving on the pitiful daily dose of blood. We weren't threats; the guards seldom paid us any attention.

But now here was some beefy warlock beckoning me to him with his wand, and my eyes narrowed when he called for me again.

"Come on," his companion snapped, a second wand raised in my direction. "You've got an appointment."

A *what*? Appointments were coveted by inmates, as there was this secret universal hope that we were about to meet with a lawyer. Rarely were we so fortunate.

If anything, *appointment* was code for solitary.

Still as stone, I glanced at Fintan—which must have been laughable to the newcomers. After all, it wasn't like the fae could *do* anything. Whether I wanted to leave the cellblock or not, I was going.

"Stay on your toes," he muttered under his breath, lips barely moving as he picked crusty bits of dough from his nails. Meanwhile, the rest of the cellblock cunts smirked and whispered to each other, guards and inmates included. *Christ*. None of it made me want to leave Katja, but so long as Elijah was still here, his strength unmatched and his resolution like steel, I could breathe a little easier.

If I needed to breathe, of course.

And Fintan had a few qualities I came to admire with each passing day. Tonight, when I reluctantly abandoned my post in front of her door, the fae shifted his stance so that his body—lean and wiry, made for swift movements, a warrior's frame that delivered the killing blow like a dance—blocked the majority of the opening.

As I marched over to the awaiting trio, *three* unnecessary wands trained on me, I couldn't help but wonder if they had finally found me a work assignment. Sure, solitary seemed more likely given recent events, but Xargi Penitentiary worked its inmates to the bone. With vampires sequestered away from the sun, the small population in red jumpsuits were essentially useless—a drain on resources and manpower. They should have been looking for ways to put our strength, speed, and manual dexterity to work ages ago.

Hands clasped in front of me, I let the warlocks lead me out. Through dim stony corridors, they marched me on a familiar path to the stairwell that brought us to the cafeteria. Intense fluorescents haunted my every step, bright and offensive to eyes so accustomed to the shadows. When we bypassed the dining hall and continued lower underground, my suspicions spiked, my hands gripped each other tighter, and the warlocks suddenly moved faster.

Five floors beneath the earth we descended, going deeper than solitary; each guard had the nerve to point it out, to show me the door and tell me to consider myself *fortunate* that I wasn't headed in there. Please. I spent just about all my time in solitary while the others worked. I was a creature of the night, an orphan vampire without the protection of a coven; I was accustomed to pits and holes and dark, depressing places.

Until Elijah.

Until his cottage and his company.

Until fireside conversations and laughter and trips to the village pub.

Until Katja and her smile, her blood glittering like starlit rubies—

We stepped out of the final stairwell into a completely different world. Shock shivered down my spine at the bright white walls and glossy floors replacing familiar dusty stone blocks. Metal doors that gave off the faint scent and pulse of iron peppered the corridor, and all three warlocks really put their back into shoving me along when my feet dragged and my knees locked. Six doors down, one of the fuckers tapped his wand on the iron panel—which I noticed had no doorknob, accessible only by magic—and it opened soundlessly.

Cold whooshed out just as hurriedly as I was shoved in, met by a sterile operating room with the brightest lights yet. Men in white lab coats puttered around, some with face masks, others preparing equipment with their backs to me. Seized by panic, my chest constricted with *fear* sharp enough to crack every rib. My mouth dried up. My fingertips went numb. My brain turned sluggish on the uptake, slowly digesting my new surroundings.

And my eyes…

My eyes locked on the metal operating table in the middle of it all, outfitted with spiked wooden cuffs *just* for vampires. Like iron incapacitated fae and silver poisoned shifters, shove a bit of wood into a vamp's body and they were screwed.

I shook my head and pushed back, only to have a wand jabbed into either side of my neck just below the collar. A good shove and a jolt of something fiery had me shuffling forward at a snail's pace, driven toward the table by the three unknown guards. Fuck. *Fuck*. Outmanned *and* outgunned—not ideal, but maybe…

As soon as I looked beyond the operating table, my brain short-circuited. Men in white coats clustered around a flat-screen, and seconds later X-rays plastered across it—skulls. Skulls with *fangs*. One of the bastards even circled the fangs with his wand, tapping at the markings for emphasis, and the purpose of this room became abundantly clear. I reared back, fighting with earnest now, fear quashed deep down in favor of *fire*. For a bloodthirsty creature of the night, I rarely gave in to violence. In fact, Katja's assault was the first instance where I had lost my shit and relied on my hands, not my words, to send a message.

Tonight needed to be the same.

And I tried.

Damn it, I tried.

As the panicked whitecoats lumbered toward the walls and out of the way, more warlocks in black uniforms poured in from various doors. Dozens of hands found me, wands shocked me, and inch by precious inch, they hauled me toward the operating table. Teeth gritted, I flailed and fought and snapped my fangs at anyone within reach.

Overhead, mirrored panels slanted over the room—

An observation deck.

My torment was for public consumption, apparently.

Against my best efforts, they forced me onto the table—strapped me down with cuffs spiked with wood on the insides. As soon as the little pinpricks broke skin, their sedative effects kicked in. My muscles relaxed. My head flopped onto cold, merciless metal. Restraints were added at my ankles too, shoes removed, and another wave of weakness washed over me as more teeny, tiny wood stakes pierced my flesh.

Humans had loads of dumb mythos about vampires, but a wooden stake to the heart? Devastating. One of the few natural elements that could well and truly kill us.

"W-what is this?" I forced out, tongue thick and heavy, my words slurred. All around me, the organized chaos resumed, masked men and women in scrubs wheeling trays to my bedside, one even dragging a punishingly bright light directly over my face.

"You should be honored, Rafe O'Dwyer." A face suddenly blocked the piercing whiteness. I blinked hard to shirk the spots dancing through my field of vision, only to wince at the waft of garlic that came with the new arrival's breath. One of the myths that *wasn't* true: garlic had no effect on a vamp, but it was an absolutely pungent odor that fused up your nostrils for weeks. Not detrimental—just a nuisance.

Slate-grey eyes peered down at me, cold and assessing, flitting about my face like they were trying desperately to see the value in it. The voice was familiar, even to my sleepy mind, my fading senses, and soon, each blink became a fight, my lids like lead.

"W-warden Guthrie?"

He offered a barbed grin, looming over me in a fine suit, hair perfectly coifed. His pocket square was silk—a deep maroon patterned with white crosses. Really going for the pop culture jugular, eh? While his mouth twisted in a smile, his steely gaze *raged*.

"You've been selected as the first inmate volunteer in our experimental partnership with—"

"Fuck you," I hissed, clinging to consciousness just enough to remember that I hated him. This piece of shit had put me here. He trapped Elijah's inner dragon. He dragged Katja out for meetings that always made her cry. He bled Fintan's accounts dry, taking more than half already to fund the fae's illegal detainment.

If I could just move my arms, I'd snap his neck.

I knew it. He knew. And the gobshite with all the power just grinned down at me, exhaling that garlicky carbon dioxide all over my face. Slowly, as the clamor around the room picked up, he lowered himself just enough that his breath warmed my ear, leaving me at the mercy of the overhead light's relentless glare.

"You bit her," the warden sneered, his rasp bone-chillingly pleasant, "and I understand. My kitten is so lovely... But after tonight, you'll *never* be able to taste her again—or anyone else for that matter."

He withdrew and patted my chest, the edges of my vision

slowly fading to black, my body paralyzed from the neck down.

"He's all yours, boys."

Then the darkness spread, muffling the clinking surgical tools and the beeping machines, blocking out the white light and the masked men, my facial muscles slack.

And a heartbeat later, I was gone.

21

ELIJAH

Where the *fuck* was Rafe?

A full twenty-four hours had crawled by since they took him, and, having just returned from supper with Fintan and Katja, his cell remained empty. Tully had taken up the head of his cot in our absence, seated on his pillow in the shadows, waiting. Even Katja's reappearance hadn't inspired movement out of him; her familiar seemed infatuated with the vampire—not that I could blame him. This was the longest I had gone without talking to my best friend in months, and it didn't help that they had dragged him out of here for fuck knows what.

Hell, he could have been permanently relocated to solitary—or another cellblock. That was Fintan's working theory, that they had decided to punish us further for reasons unknown by splitting us up. Deimos's group, meanwhile, remained strong, outnumbering us by one extra today. The demon had goaded me from the moment we left our cells for showers and breakfast this morning, all the way to now, some fifteen minutes after supper. He wanted a fight. He wanted a reason to get me chucked out so only Fintan stood in his way.

Not a chance.

My inner dragon had been fuming for days. Just pure, blinding *rage* that we hadn't been there to stop Katja's attack—that it had even happened in the first place. Thankfully, Tully had mended the worst of it, and she hobbled out of her cell today on shaky legs, hunched and quiet but relatively functional.

Tensed and tight, I tossed a card into the middle of our table without even looking at it, my gaze stuck on the cellblock's bolted door. Where was he? Fintan swept the three cards away, his ten of spades beating out mine and Katja's offering. To his credit, the fae had kept his smart mouth in check since they'd dragged Rafe away, as if sensing no one was in the mood for his snark.

The tip of flimsy prison-issued shoes nudged my calf under the table, and my inner dragon uttered an approving rumble when Katja's foot settled on top of mine. Seated in Rafe's usual spot, my mate sought out my gaze, not setting her card down until I met her big blues. The downward arc of her lips, the slight lift of one brow, the shimmer in her eyes—so much was said in the subtleties. She feared for him, but she was here for *me*.

Only I couldn't look at her... Not like this.

Sure, I had stood guard for as long as I could yesterday. I had counted down the hours in the metal shop today, my work halfhearted and incomplete by the end of my shift. With no one to take her hours, she had been forced out to the greenhouse, but at least Fintan had picked up the slack.

Or... I hoped he had.

He'd been getting better lately, coming back with dirt under his nails and the odd leaf in his mussed mop of light brown waves.

But now that Katja was awake and *just* healed enough to putter around, I struggled to meet her eye.

I had failed her.

Failed to protect my mate.

For a shifter, an *alpha*, there was no fouler sin, no greater crime.

While we had continued working out the nuances of our fated bond, slowly getting to know each other, not rushing anything—letting whatever we felt develop as organically as we could in a hellscape like Xargi—she was still my mate. Even if Rafe had marked her first, she was *mine*. Possibly ours, given my dragon's acceptance of the other two males in her orbit. And I had failed her.

Miserably.

Black and blue bruises dotted her face like a fucking abstract painting. Tully's healing purrs had mended her lower lip and taken some of the puffiness out of it, but it still looked ravaged. Shadowy rings rimmed her eyes, heavy from a fitful sleep and trauma that might just haunt her for years to come. Her ribs might not be broken anymore, but certain movements still hurt her, agony and alarm flashing across her battered features if she turned too quickly.

She was a mess—physically. I was a mess emotionally, drowning in messy *feelings*, suffocating through my every waking moment. Guilt and fury and panic over what had happened to her—what could *still* happen in the future. Concern for Rafe, for what they were doing to him behind closed doors, how they might be punishing him for intervening in what was clearly a planned hit. Apprehension for Fintan if he needed to step up in my possible absence—handsome and clearly pampered, born with a silver spoon in his mouth whether he was a fae prince or not, had he the courage to throw himself on the grenade for her?

Without her magic, Katja was just so… small.

And I—*we*—had let her down.

I'd never forgive myself.

Never forget what had happened, how I hadn't been there to protect her.

How I had worn this collar for almost a year…

How I let them cage me without a fight.

Rafe and I planned to just serve our time.

Where had all this fire been then?

Back when we had nothing to lose—

"Elijah…" Fintan swiped at my arm. "*Go*."

Just as I'd plucked another card from the top of my tiny deck, a few rounds away from losing War to either one of them, the cellblock door's locks thunked undone, and I shot to my feet as soon as the metal panel swung open.

My inner dragon sensed the doom before I did, stretching his wings and rousing his flames, heat and rage and adrenaline swelling in my gut and bubbling up my throat. I scented it a second later: dead blood, maroon and viscous—the blood of a vampire. As the block's trio of warlock cronies swept aside, a new cluster swarmed in, hauling a limp Rafe between them, dragging his feet, arms dangling, head hanging and bobbing with each step. Katja struggled to her feet with a gasp.

"What did you do to him?" she demanded, her voice soaring several squeaky pitches above normal as Deimos' gang erupted in fits of chuckles and whispers. Even the shifters who had refused to meet my eye months ago joined in tonight, delighted with my best friend's humiliation.

Red bled across the cellblock, my vision tinted by rage. My inner dragon clawed at my chest, *desperate* to get out, more fired up than ever to rip his enemies apart and burn this shithole to the ground. The collar almost seemed to tighten around my throat the more he fumed, and I tugged at it absently—only to rear back when static crackled across my flesh, a warning of a painful, miserable death should I attempt to break my shackles.

Fintan soon joined me and Katja, on his feet and prowling about in front of the table. His eyes, almost neon green in this light, assessed the situation swiftly, and as soon as Katja took off, limping toward the guards and demanding answers, he jogged after her and hooked her around the waist. Her squeal of pain forced my hand, and I stalked toward the pair with a snarl that had the other shifters in the block cowering again—shrinking, as they should, before a true alpha.

Deimos, on the other hand, only laughed harder, the maenad to his right mimicking Katja's pained wail between her cackles.

At the moment, I wasn't sure which enemy to eviscerate first.

Had I access to my dragonfire, I could have felled them all in one brutal breath.

Something slammed into me when I pivoted toward Deimos's table, and I blinked down, stunned to find Fintan there, his shoulder planted in the middle of my chest. The fae shoved back, and I actually *almost* lost my balance.

Stronger than I thought, this pampered imp.

"Just let it settle," he hissed. "Don't give them a reason, Elijah. Don't give them the satisfaction."

The fucker was right, of course, only we shifters—dragons in particular—weren't known for our cool heads in the face of a fight. But for Katja's sake, for Rafe's, I held back, shaking with white-hot rage, with an anger so foul that when Deimos dared meet my eyes, his expression faltered. Just for a moment, my wrath knocked the wind out of his black sails.

The cellblock guards had their wands trained on me as the strangers hauled Rafe to his cell. Katja trailed after them, wringing her hands, her eyes glittering like diamonds beneath the overhead light—glossy and wet, on the brink of tears. She never let them fall, sniffling and brushing a subtle hand beneath each before glowering at every warlock present.

"Careful," she barked, but her words fell on deaf ears when the bastards tossed Rafe onto the floor of his cell, barely inside the door, and left him there in a heap. As soon as she had the leeway to get by, my mate was off, charging forward despite her injuries and collapsing to her knees at Rafe's side. Fintan followed shortly after, yet I stayed still, glaring at all who had wronged us, hurt us, just *wishing* they would raise a hand to me.

Put the wands away and fight fair, you fucking cowards.

But none of them spared me a backward glance. Now that they'd deposited their cargo, the unfamiliar faces disappeared, and as soon as the cellblock door shut and bolted, our minders were back to nonsense conversations about TV shows and female inmates and possible promotions through the ranks.

My inner dragon flashed his teeth, his pent-up fire threatening to scorch us both to ash. When we had the chance—and maybe one day we would—Deimos would be first, but all the assholes who guarded this block were next on the fucking hit list. Abandoning them, my gaze slid over to Deimos, the world so much sharper now, fine details like dust in the grout between cinder blocks and the shading on the demon's neck tattoos coming into focus as some of my inner dragon leaked through the collar's charms. All for shock value, that ink, inexpensive and haphazard. The wings on my back had taken the better part of a year to get right —*that* was true craftmanship.

Not that Deimos cared about craftsmanship, about honor. Not that he valued hard work.

Some demons did. Some prized it above all else.

This one was an acolyte of chaos—I was sure of it now

more than ever, because the gnat had the balls to *wink* at me when our eyes met.

I lurched forward with a snarl, only to once again be held back. Restrained by fae strength, subtle and unspoken, Fintan cuffed a hand around my forearm, then wrenched me round to face him, totally unfazed by my low warning growl, by my posturing and my size.

"*Patience*," he whispered, eyebrows inching up, his mouth slightly quirked. "Give it time and we'll find a way to gut him when we can't be blamed."

With the inferno raging inside, I could have eviscerated the little shit right here and now.

But Fintan was right.

Again.

Katja's sob from Rafe's cell had me moving, and I set aside the deepening grudges—for now—to attend to my clan of misfits. What I found inside the vampire's little room spurred the anger, but just as swiftly came the need to protect—to help. Alphas weren't all fists and fire. The good ones assessed a situation and took the *right* action. When I discovered Katja trying and failing to haul Rafe's lifeless body onto the cot, all thoughts of Deimos and the guards and Xargi itself fell away. I rushed in, sidestepping my struggling mate, her feline familiar weaving around her ankles, and hoisted my friend onto his cot. Fintan, meanwhile, loitered behind, blocking the cell door from the inside this time. When I glanced back, I noted his hand hovering near Katja's elbow as if to stabilize her; she braced herself on the wall instead, totally unaware of the fae's attentiveness, cheeks flushed, eyes wet, and massaged her battered ribs with a grimace.

"Rafe?" she whispered as I crouched at the head of the bed, trying to free up what little space these cells offered, my massive frame making that all the more difficult. Katja perched on the side, the cot groaning softly under the added weight, and Tully leapt up out of nowhere, light and swift as a shadow. The familiar padded around as Rafe uttered a weak groan, then settled squarely on top of the vampire's chest, purring up a storm just as he'd done with his mistress. Bright blue sapphires blinked once, twice, three times at me, slowly, and then the cat closed his eyes—like he was officially settling in to work. The air thickened with a whisper of magic. Katja, meanwhile, watched it all unfold with a frail smile, and, sniffling, she stroked her familiar's ears, then nudged Rafe's arm. "Rafe?"

Slowly, he peeled his eyes open, struggling, and let out another groan.

"T-took my f-fangs," he croaked, his voice scratchy. Katja sucked in a sharp, strangled breath, and this time the tears fell.

"Oh, *gods*." She crept up the bed and lifted his lip, then looked to me, hopeless and lost and breaking apart right before my eyes. Because sure enough, two massive holes sat in Rafe's pale gumline where his fangs ought to be—and there was no harsher punishment for a vampire than the loss of his fangs. The only thing worse was to be strung up outside just before dawn so the sun could fry him to dust, but at least that was a quick death.

For all his healing capabilities, his immunity to most elements in this world, the two things my old friend *couldn't* regrow were a fine set of canines.

"I'll fucking *kill* them," I snarled, the fire back and raring to go. Only before the flames consumed me, there was Fintan, popping his elbows up and bracing on either side of the cell doorway. Blocking me. Barricading all of us inside. My inner dragon fumed at the insinuation, but with a few calm, centering breaths, the man won out—saw the logic in patience and control. After all, half my clan was broken: Katja and Rafe had finally met the horrors of Xargi Penitentiary head-on, tortured by inmates and guards alike, and I couldn't abandon them. Couldn't even *risk* it.

So I stayed put, painfully still and biding my time—but if some piece of shit tried to wriggle into this tiny cell, all bets were off.

Katja's anguished sob still had me pounding a fist into the wall, if only to release some of the pent-up aggression I hadn't been able to fly off all this time. Dust and rocky shards trickled down the dented brick; Tully's purrs stopped for a beat, then resumed seconds later, louder than ever.

"I'm so sorry," my mate whispered, threading her fingers through Rafe's and clutching his hand with both of hers. "I don't know why they—"

"Because I bit you," he said roughly. His throat bobbed with a harsh gulp, pain flickering over his features, and he pushed up onto his elbows. While Rafe spared me a quick glance over his shoulder, he didn't seem to notice—or even mind—Tully hooking his claws in to stay stuck to his chest. He did, however, retract his hand from Katja, and the rejection read plain as day across her face. Head cocked, the vampire shifted about, searching for comfort on a bed that offered none, and then frowned at her—at a woman we both *felt* for, who he had protected and coveted.

Who he now seemed to question.

"Katja, what's w-with you and the warden?"

I opened and closed my mouth, floundering. *What?* Of course we all knew that she had been pulled into Guthrie's office a few times, but as of this moment, she hadn't—

"There are loads of vamps in Xargi," Rafe remarked, all raspy and hoarse—like he'd been screaming. Fintan's bright greens glittered with interest, the fae suddenly hyperfocused on Katja, me and my rage barely even an afterthought as Rafe struggled for every word. "But he chose m-*me*. Came in all garlicky and wearing crosses. It f-felt personal."

Cheeks sunken and eyes distant, Katja confirmed the rising suspicions with her silence. This was the Katja of *months* ago, the one who kept to herself, who guarded her space as viciously as we dragons hoarded our gold. Quiet, calculating with the information she shared—this wasn't a welcome throwback.

"So, what is it?" Like the weight of holding himself up was too much, Rafe collapsed back onto the bed, and in Katja's continued silence, I caught him cautiously steering his tongue around his mouth, probing the gaping wounds. His jaw suddenly hardened, resolve settling in, and he propped himself up again. "He called you his kitten—"

"It's… I… It's nothing," my mate muttered with a slight shake of her head, refusing to meet his eyes—and mine.

"No, it's not." Fintan popped a knee up on the end of the cot, looming over the scene with crossed arms and a scowl. "It's really not, and we both know it."

My inner dragon huffed, a sentiment I shared. These two seemed privy to something *I* wasn't—something about *my* fated. We might not have been deeply, desperately in love, but Katja and I owed it to ourselves to be honest. Fate had a way of dragging it out of you in the end; may as well beat the bitch to the punch.

"The less you know, the better," Katja managed, flashing a weak smile at all three of us—like we would just *accept* that and call it a day. My brows furrowed. Fintan smirked. Rafe let out the largest, most unnecessarily dramatic scoff I'd ever heard, then pointed at his mouth.

"You sure about that?"

Arms wrapped tight around herself, my mate rose and turned to leave, only to find Fintan there, once again proving to be a better door than a window. A locked door at that, towering over her by a full head, wider too despite being the wiriest of us males. She waited, staring up at him, then slowly faced me, clutching her ribs, the look in her eye suggesting that I was supposed to, what, *move* him? Fuck that.

I held my ground, crouched by Rafe, and met her stare head-on. It dissolved from hopeful and pleading to betrayed in a matter of seconds, and while it pained me to witness, something sharp and cruel stabbing into my heart, I refused to fold. If she couldn't be honest with her mate, who in this world *could* she be honest with?

"No, Katja." I finally stood, lording over the lot of them. "Spill it… Tell us *everything*, before the bastards order an early lights-out."

22

KATJA

They wanted everything?

Fine.

I gave them every little godsforsaken thing.

Every horrific detail. From my mom's supposed wolfsbane addiction to the debt she ran up because of it, to the deal she made with Lloyd Guthrie to get out of that hole. To *live* when creditors had been ready to break every bone in her body. Then her refusal to honor the contract. The effigy doll made to ensure she had the most painful delivery possible—her horrific death in childbirth, the first witch in centuries to do so. My dad's refusal to hand me over to a psychotic mobster. The assassin sent to hunt Ewan in a lake—to drown him after he had exhausted himself on the run.

Two more deaths to go, all the gory, gruesome specifics pending. They swirled around my mind if I let them, the possibilities, the strings Lloyd could have pulled to make sure my family really suffered before the sweet release of death.

His insistence that I belonged to *him*.

If he had taken me as a baby, maybe he would have raised me as a daughter.

But I was all grown up now.

And the way he touched me, the way his gaze raked hungrily over my figure, the way he took so many damn liberties with my body—ordered a demon to beat and possibly even rape me…

Accepting his offer, acknowledging the blood contract, was suicide, plain and simple.

By the end of it, I couldn't stop the tears, couldn't staunch the flow. They spilled down my face freely, dribbled onto Rafe's thin sheets with flat *plop, plop, plops* to punctuate every wretched memory. And I hated it. I *hated* to break down in front of my guys. At this point, I was so sick of feeling weak and pathetic because of men in here—because of my past written by a madman. Elijah, Rafe, and Fintan—for all that I felt for them, the bond strengthening from me to them, around all of us, with each passing day—had a knack for charging in like white knights to rescue the princess. I was grateful in my *bones* for their help; without my magic, I was a sitting duck against larger, stronger, and faster opponents, especially when outnumbered.

And *especially* against the sadist running everything, power and wealth and cruelty at his disposal.

Refusing him had been something just for me—my own fight, my own strength. Magicless, powerless, I still had a mind of my own. Still had a backbone. I could say no.

And it screwed me over in the end anyway. Lloyd had taken Rafe's fangs to prove a point. To show me that I had no power in here, that this collar stole more than just my magic.

Sniffling, *struggling*, I wiped my cheeks with both hands, then dried them on my new jumpsuit. A terse quiet blanketed the cell, and when I finally risked a glance at each of my boys, they were… furious. Elijah's eyes had morphed to serpentine slits, flames sparking around the narrowed pupils, the dragon so close to the surface I actually felt his heat. Rafe's jaw gritted so hard, clenched so firm, that the muscles protruded along his strong jawline and a dribble of blood wept from the corner of his mouth; he had reopened the wounds, the enormous holes in his pale gums that would never fully mend. Fintan loitered in the corner of my eye for the whole story, stiff as a statue and uncharacteristically silent. Hands in fists. Knuckles white. Cheeks sunken like he was biting at them.

The only one oblivious to everything was Tully, but my familiar knew precisely what went on in the warden's office. After all, he chased off the nightmares each night, snuggled close and willing me a heavy, dreamless sleep with his magic. Come dawn, he was exhausted, but no one batted an eye at a cat sleeping all day, gearing up to do it again the following night. Tonight, however, he had a new patient, his rhythmic purrs reserved for the only vampire he had ever taken to.

In fact, Elijah, Fintan, and Rafe were the only *men* Tully had ever tolerated. It wasn't like he had chased off past boyfriends or anything: he would just stare at them, aloof and judgmental, until they left.

Now, I probably couldn't peel him off Rafe's chest if I tried.

"Katja..." The vampire all but choked my name, and I smoothed a hand over his thigh, wishing he would just stop talking. What he needed tonight was rest—and blood, *lots* of it—not to listen to the drama hounding me outside the cellblock. It wasn't his fight. Or Fintan's. Or Elijah's, fated mate or not. It was mine—yet here was the first of my prison clique, my guys, paying the price. Rafe popped up on his elbows again, weaving his fingers into Tully's fur as my familiar sunk his claws deeper into his red jumpsuit for balance. "I didn't know... I shouldn't have pressed you—"

"No. You should." A fresh batch of wet slicked down my cheeks, but each tear fell like a hot little droplet of magma. *Anger*—at Lloyd, but mostly at myself. Anger and disappointment. "It's my fault he did this to you."

I held up a hand when all three spoke over each other—to interject, maybe even rush to my defense. They did that a lot, and it gave me a serious case of the warm and fuzzies that I had three breathtaking, strong, compassionate, *hilarious* dudes who were willing to go to bat for me time and time again. But enough. I didn't deserve their white-knight status. We protected each other, but the scales were exceedingly tipped in my direction after the number of times I'd had to be rescued in here. Even if it felt like I finally had a family again, like I wasn't alone after five years of orphan status, *enough*. I'd fucked up. This was *my* fault, despite Lloyd being the sicko who pulled the strings, and I would have to live with that guilt for the rest of my life.

"I should have hid it better," I insisted, pleased that in spite of the fiery tears, I kept my voice even—determined to make them see that I wasn't flawless, that I was a person fully capable of screwing up. Protective hotties might be my kryptonite, but with Lloyd circling, that had become a detriment for everyone involved. Hesitantly, I brushed the pair of thick round scars on my neck, and a flash of pleasure jolted down my body, pebbling my nipples and buzzing in my clit. Beside me, Rafe cleared his throat, jumpsuit slightly tented. I *loved* his bite. Loved how it felt at the time and how I now carried him with me wherever I went.

But I should have made sure no one else, especially Lloyd Guthrie, could see it.

Because of course he would retaliate. His whole history with my family was one big, bloody, brutal retaliation.

"He doesn't own you," Elijah growled, glowering at a spot

just over my shoulder. Slowly, that dragon gaze slid to mine, and he shook his head. "*Fate* is the decider of our destinies."

Eyes locked, I knew he wanted to add a *mate* in there if he could—insist that I belonged to him, and vice versa, because some mystical force had paired us up long before we were born. Our bond was written in the stars, or whatever, and no one could change that.

But I couldn't hear the words right now—couldn't listen to him say it in front of the others and somehow diminish the kindred spirit bond I shared with Rafe, him and me unified by his bite, or the wildfire connection I felt with Fintan, all hot and heavy and *fun*.

He spared me that. Of course he did. Guilt stabbed another hook into me for doubting him.

"Right." I glanced up at the sound of Fintan's cool chuckle, the fae rolling his eyes. "Well, maybe for *shifters*, but that's hardly the case everywhere else." He then shuffled in front of me, blocking the others with his gorgeous angles, his tousled locks and brilliant green gaze. His hands found my shoulders as he stooped to fill my eyeline, eyebrows slightly arched, his tone a little too serious for my liking. "I need to know everything about the contract. Do you understand? *Everything*. Perhaps I can sniff out a loophole." Then his mouth quirked, brevity shirked, and he wiggled those brows in a way that always made me giggle. "We fae are rather adept—"

"How the fuck would she know anything that's in the contract beyond what that *boil* of a man told her?" Rafe asked dryly, and when Fintan eased aside, I found the vampire sprawled back on the cot again, looking absolutely destroyed —like he could sleep for a century. "D'you think he just has it lying around?"

"If he values it, probably." Fintan settled back against the wall, arms folded, ankles crossed, his gaze so very far away as he studied the cell's dark arched ceiling. "I've never abandoned a deal—especially if it was signed in blood. No fae would, and I'm sure our dear warden is the same. He's probably got it here, just to keep it close. I mean, I bet he's *framed* it if he's that obsessed with Katja."

We all glanced warily in Elijah's direction when he snarled, eyes a brilliant and terrifying gold. Fintàn then sniffed, fidgeting with his jumpsuit; he'd been trying for weeks to make it more stylish, but there was only so much you could do with thick, shapeless cotton. Somehow my replacement jumpsuit hung even baggier than the one Deimos had torn, like Lloyd was hell-bent on making me as unattractive to other inmates as possible.

"Well," Fintan said suddenly, his tone light, the sentiment almost an afterthought, "obsessed with your *mother*, from the sounds of it, but obviously you're a piece of her."

My gut roiled, an anxiety barf surging, and I pressed a hand to my belly as I gulped down the flood of mouth sweats. Everything else still ached despite Tully's constant care, my muscles stiff and sore, the pains sharp if I moved too quickly or twisted the wrong way. At this point, the thought of vomit-convulsions on top of all that just made me want to scream bloody murder and hope someone might eventually sedate me.

"Fintan, enough," Elijah rumbled, eyes locked on me, and once again I was weak and small and pathetic, in need of a man, my mate, to save the day. Still, it made me queasy to consider that Lloyd's unhealthy fascination with my mom had jumped to *me*, and I really didn't need Fintan pointing out the obvious.

"I-I can't go looking in his office," I told them, wishing I sounded brave again. "He makes me sit in a chair… I worry that if I'm up and moving around, I'm a target. I… Maybe he'll touch me again—"

Elijah drove his fist into the wall, taking a huge chunk out this time, and I scooted to the end of the bed—if only to give the beast some room to pace. He stayed seated, glaring, seething, grinding his teeth as he looked right through me.

"Mate, can you stop destroying my cell?" Rafe muttered, swiping back at the dragon shifter with a weak smile. "It might be a shithole, but it's *my* shithole, you know?"

Elijah responded with a distracted grunt, one that had Fintan smirking and Rafe sighing. My fated sank deep into thought for a moment, but just as he opened his mouth, a siren blared through the cellblock.

Lights-out.

Early.

Of course.

None of us moved at first, stuck in place and exchanging tense glances, until finally Fintan helped me up, a hand on my elbow, and Elijah trailed after us out the door. We all went our separate ways without a word, the conversation left open-ended, and as I collapsed onto my cot, Tully whizzed inside *just* before my cell door slammed shut, hidden in the shadows like always. He hopped up on my bed with one of his silly squeaky baby *purr*meows, climbing into my lap and kneading in a circle around my thighs.

Eyes watery *again*, I sniffled and hugged him tight, bracing through my ribs screeching in protest, through my stomach's anxiety churn—and through the guilt mounting higher and higher with each passing minute.

As soon as the flickering overhead light cut out, Rafe whispered my name through the mousehole—same as always, kick-starting one of our nightly conversations that could last hours. But I didn't move. Couldn't speak. I just sat on my bed, back to the wall, and clutched Tully tighter.

What they had done to him—tortured him, scarred him for the rest of eternity—was my fault. Anyone in my orbit would suffer an intense scrutiny from Lloyd going forward, and it was time to make my *own* moves. Be my own white knight with my own fucking sword.

No more putting them in danger.

No more letting them assume the risk of associating with me.

Gossip spread like wildfire in Xargi, and it wouldn't be long before Lloyd knew precisely who I spent my time with—and he would pick them off one by one. Silver for Elijah. Iron for Fintan. He'd try to isolate me, threaten me, make me even more afraid of his supernatural penitentiary than I had been on that first day. Cull my allies, splinter my social connections, destroy my guys—break my heart.

No.

No.

I'd do all that first.

For their own good, I had to bow out of this. Walk away. Let Elijah and Rafe go back to coasting under the radar. Fintan could join them—or maybe he would find a more entertaining clique to hang with. Their protection, their survival, necessitated a big move.

Even if just the *thought* of walking away hurt more than all my injuries combined.

"Katja?" Rafe's voice skittered through the hole more urgently this time. Lips trembling, I turned my back on the wall dividing our cells and settled on my side.

"Go to sleep, Rafe," I croaked back. "You need to sleep."

Sleep and recover and heal as best he could—not stay up all night, exhausting himself, hurting himself, chitchatting with the witch responsible for maiming him.

Curled around Tully, I muffled my sorrow in his fur and let the guilt drown me, let the loss stab me, let the heartache scar me—because I deserved nothing less. I'd planned to navigate Xargi Penitentiary alone from the beginning, and it was time to get back to that.

No matter how it made me feel.

No one else was going to suffer on my behalf.

I'd make damn sure of that.

23
FINTAN

I cocked my head to the side, the sludge on the tray in front of me forgotten, and then let out a little chuckle of disbelief.

"What the fuck is she doing?"

We four were a tribe—me, Katja, Elijah, and Rafe. It was *known*. When we had the chance, we did everything together. Moved everywhere together. My time in Xargi thus far had been a lot of long conversations about nothing and *everything* with these three supernatural creatures—beings I wouldn't have stooped to associate with before I'd been pinched, but now couldn't fathom going the day without. It was why I pushed for patience with Elijah even when the battle lust shone so brilliantly in his dragon gaze. I too longed to tear Deimos apart, behead a guard or two—flip this whole fucking system on its head and then burn it to ash.

Fae were warriors.

Impulsive, reckless, petty warmongers who were never content with peace for long.

Had a moment of impulsive, petty recklessness not guaranteed I would lose the witch, shifter, and vampire I had come to consider my own, I would have lashed out long ago.

For I had already spent *far* longer inside these grim walls than anticipated, and I was getting antsy. Bored. *Annoyed.*

Now they'd gone and beaten my girl.

Deformed my vampire.

Enraged my dragon.

I craved vengeance just as much as the next jumpsuit.

But patience, control, and calculation would carry us so much further in here.

This morning, however, had started different than all the rest: Katja wouldn't look me in the eye—and I knew she so adored my eyes. She lost herself in their sheen frequently, and I let her, smitten with the woman who saw me for *me* and not my wealth, status, or ranking relative to a fucking chair that my father had roosted in for centuries.

Yet today this treasure who saw me for me refused to so much as *glance* at any of us. She put herself at the front of the line, ahead of Deimos's gang, for the dull march to the cafeteria, purposefully separating herself from the tribe, and then plopped down all by her lonesome at a table far, far away.

Not even that little rabbit shifter kept her company...

I did a quick sweep of the dining hall, frowning. The little rabbit shifter was nowhere to be found, actually. Curious. And a bit unsettling, given what had happened to Rafe.

Katja sat with her back to us, hunched over, slowly and methodically shoveling this morning's gruel into her mouth. A few moments later, a scrawny inmate in a green jumpsuit settled across from her—a new elf from the greenhouse, if I wasn't mistaken—and they ate in silence.

Peculiar.

"She's doing what she thinks is right," Elijah muttered. We three sat side by side today, Rafe in the middle—as if Elijah and I had subconsciously decided to protect our disabled vampire while he stared glumly at his test tube of blood, *deep* in a full-blown existential crisis. Ripping open my carton of lukewarm apple juice, I peered around the brooding vampire and arched an eyebrow.

"Yeah? And how do you know that?"

Breakfast completely abandoned, Elijah carried on burning a hole into the back of Katja's skull, jaw clenched, his cheeks tinting a dull dark pink the longer I waited.

"She and I..." He shook his head as he snatched up his spork. "I... It's just a thought."

Right. I'd always thought alphas were better liars when it came to their mates.

It was a percolating theory these last few weeks, born just after I fucked her in the shower and saw nirvana in my climax. Although Elijah struck me as protective by nature, he also seemed to give very few shits about anyone else in here. But Katja? The rage in his eyes, the loss of all logic and self-preservation, suggested he would give his life for her. Possibly even for Rafe too. I'd seen it all play out one too many times, a soapy production of a shifter guarding his mate, and, in turn, roping the rest of us into the drama.

"You're fated," I said casually before slurping down some of the syrupy sweet juice, so sugary I felt it in my molars. Disgraceful. For a prince accustomed to the finest life had to offer, the prison's food alone was torture. Meanwhile, Rafe finally tossed back his vial with a shudder and a scowl, swallowing blood we all assumed was frozen and thawed for each meal.

"What makes you say that?" Elijah rumbled, somehow sounding both gruff *and* nonchalant as he poked at his sunny-side-up eggs. Overcooked, of course, without any semblance of delicious golden yolk to be seen. Always eggs in the morning—always shitty, burnt, expired, *shitty* eggs for breakfast. My pair curled around the edges and somehow managed to look both slimily raw and grossly chewy.

Fantastic. I turned my nose up at them, opting to focus on Elijah instead. Between us, Rafe slowly spun his empty blood vial around on the table, chin on his fist, utterly miserable.

Not that I could blame him.

A vampire losing his fangs was like a man having his dick lobbed off.

Catastrophic.

"Let's skip *this*, shall we?" I motioned between myself and the dragon with a thin smile. "The part where you deny and I lay out all the *obvious*. You and Katja Fox are fated mates. *Fate* brought you together here, of all places, which is quite the fuck-you in my opinion, but I doubt you would have found each other otherwise."

Jaw muscles rippling through a clench, Elijah dropped his spork and turned his full attention on me, those golden eyes —dragon eyes, I had come to realize—just *daring* me to continue prying into his personal business. And I would. With pleasure.

"It's why you protect her without question when there are smaller and more pathetic female inmates in this place—even in our own cellblock." Not that any of us bothered with Constance and Helen; although under different circumstances, the maenad would have been a *blast* on a night out. "And it's why you know her intentions time and time again. You're linked. I mean, I have a pair of fucking eyes…" I plopped my chin into both hands, head tipped and eyelashes fluttering. "Are you two hopelessly in love yet?"

The terse silence that followed was answer enough, both Rafe and Elijah glowering at me out of the corner of their eyes as the dining hall carried on operating at its usual dull roar. Dozens of conversations raged all around us, yet ours flatlined. Perfect. Just as I'd thought too.

"Fair enough." Thank *fuck* they weren't all moony over each other; that would have been most intolerable. "I always thought the instant and overwhelming *love* was bullshit. In my opinion, it's an act—like you lot think you have to be besotted from the word go."

Not that I had encountered many fated mates in my lifetime, but I'd heard the stories, and the few pairs of shifter couples who couldn't keep their hands off each other from the *second* they realized they were fated were just sickening, honestly. Just because you sensed a soulmate hardly meant you knew a damn thing about them. While nowhere near a paragon of wisdom and virtue when it came to matters of the heart, I had a brain. And a sizeable cock. And if my fated mate chewed with their mouth open… there would be *issues*.

"Look, you *care* for her at the very least—"

"Obviously," Elijah growled. Probably more than cared for her. Katja was easy to like—harder to bed—and they seemed to share an unspoken bond that the rest of us could never touch. Nor did I want to. What they had belonged to them, just as what she and Rafe shared was hardly my business. Let him bite her all he wanted—

Oh.

Wait.

Too soon.

"And you care for her as well," I added, nudging Rafe's arm with my elbow, on high alert to quell any fangless vampire puns before they left my lips. The glass tube stopped spinning, and Rafe tossed his head side to side, noisily cracking his neck.

"*Obviously.*"

"Excellent. All our cards on the table, then." I chugged the last of my apple juice with some difficulty, tossing the empty carton aside as a dramatic sugar-induced shiver bolted through me. "My working theory, therefore, is that your *fate* has extended to Rafe and me. You're fated, and now *we* are all fated too."

How else could anyone explain why I, Prince Fintan of the Midnight Court, had been picked up by a bunch of supernatural bounty hunters and tossed in prison? This was hardly my failing—but fate intervening, bringing us all together when the bitch knew we most needed each other.

The rest of my posse didn't exactly jump at the theory. Rafe uttered a curt huff, rolling his eyes, and Elijah just gawked at me like I had sprouted a second head.

"That's ridiculous—"

"But not unheard of," I argued, holding up a finger to silence him. Why did they always question every little thing I said? I had centuries on *both* of them and life experience in realms beyond their own. Surely I had something worthwhile to contribute… occasionally. "I mean, look, Elijah, you're an alpha *dragon*. You could conquer nations and rule as the unquestioned lord and master of all who dwelled within…" Without the collar, of course. Pesky fuckers were such a buzzkill. "Yet you don't want to—or at the very least haven't *tried*—to kill Rafe and me, right? I've fucked your mate, made her come twice, and this one bit her before you… but at the end of the day, we're all the *best* of friends."

Another tense silence stretched between us, this time with Rafe looking at me like I had lost my mind and Elijah like he wanted to skin me alive. Right. Overplayed my hand a bit there.

"Or…" I cleared my throat, drumming my fingers on the metal tabletop. A quick glance in Katja's direction showed the witch peeking over her shoulder at us, only to whip around when she caught me looking right back. Honestly. *Ridiculous* creature. Like pretending we weren't an established Xargi tribe would fool an obsessive like Guthrie. "Or, at the very least, we three find ourselves begrudging allies in a fucked-up situation."

"That sounds about right," Rafe muttered, a faint lisp

curling around any *s* words. He'd have to adjust to speaking without those fangs in the way; the vampire seemed to notice, glowering up at his forehead like he was giving himself a mental pep talk to get his shit together.

"If anything, it explains the ease of our connection," I remarked. Hunger winning out, I finally snatched the standard rock-hard hunk of bread and crushed it between both hands, then picked through the aftermath like I was eating the saddest, stalest pile of chips ever. "We might not be in love with her, and she might not be scribbling our names on notebooks surrounded by hearts…" The pair raised their eyebrows at me, and I forced a one-shouldered shrug. "Or whatever women do in those human films. Such drivel." Also known as the movies I watched—alone—when I was very, very, *very* drunk and lonely. "Anyway, that might not be the case, but we're drawn to one another. I don't *really* want to fuck either of you, despite the pleasing aesthetics, but I've also never desired friendship with a shifter or a vampire before. I'm sure you're swell boys and all, but it's… odd. Uncharacteristic for me, just as it is to crave a witch.

"There seems to be the possibility for more outside of this prison." Love and acceptance and growth as a *man* into someone I had always dreamed of, someone *better* than the spoiled princeling I'd become over the years. "Whatever the fuck fate has in mind for us, I mean. Love or not, we're all entwined. Our survival is linked."

"Pretty speech," Rafe said with a snort, eyes drifting to Katja across the cafeteria, even leaning to the side when another inmate blocked his view as they sidled by her table. Unfortunately, it wasn't Rafe I needed to get on board with this—it was the shifter who likely dictated his life around fate's hand. I allowed Elijah some contemplative silence, then hucked a large breadcrumb at him. He batted it away before it landed, lips twitching in a snarl, but after a few hard blinks, the man was back, those pupil-slits round and ordinary once more.

"I can see the... sense in it. Maybe." Oh, *bitter*. So fucking bitter. Though I could hardly blame him: few shifters could fathom sharing their mates, not unless it was with other shifters with whom they shared a pack bond. Wolves commonly shared mates, from what I'd heard. Dragons, meanwhile, tended to fly solo.

And now here we were, two non-shifters swooping in for a piece of the pie.

The delicious, sumptuous, mouthwatering pie.

"Jealous?" Shockingly, it was Rafe who posed the question, a ghost of a smile crossing his lips when he glanced Elijah's way. The shifter studied him for a moment and then shoved one whole fried egg in his mouth.

Bravery in its finest form.

"A little," he managed with a mouthful of egg, his response making Rafe's grin blossom into something real for the first time all day.

"Good. Now you know how I've felt for ages."

The pair locked eyes and fell into a seemingly private conversation—soundless, too, even though I knew for a *fact* they didn't share a telepathic bond. After shoveling the rest of my dry-as-fuck bread bits into my mouth, I chewed slowly, waiting for their little chat to be over and struggling to swallow everything down without choking. When it didn't seem like they planned to include me anytime soon, I leaned forward and shoved myself into their eyelines.

"Well, we fae commonly take multiple lovers," I insisted, earning me another pair of side-eyes from my fated counterparts. Smirking, I eased off, elbow on the table, chin on my fist, wistful as I said, "It's not unheard of outside the ruling monarch for fae to take many wives or husbands or whatever..." As next in line, Rollo was stuck with just the one wife—who was perfect, of course. Everyone below, so long as we weren't destined to rule a court through marriage, could tack on as many mates as we wanted. I had just never felt inclined... until this bunch of misfits. "So, you know, consider me *tickled* pink to be a part of our warped little family."

Rafe rolled his eyes. "Ugh."

"Really though," Elijah grumbled, finally peeling open his juice and risking a tentative sniff. "Sometimes you need to stop pitching and just shut the fuck up, Fintan. You've closed the sale."

Fair enough. I'd warbled about our warped family with a good dose of sarcasm, but in reality, I rather liked them. All of them. Not just Katja—but Rafe and Elijah too. None of the trio took my princely title seriously; actually, they still seemed to think I was bullshitting them. Which meant they treated me like I was nothing special. At least one of them told me to shut up daily, immune to my silver tongue and wicked words. They called me on my nonsense. Put me in my place. Not once had anyone *let* me win at cards; Xargi had taught me I wasn't as skilled at poker as my courtiers had led me to believe.

Rafe and Elijah were absolutely merciless when I returned from the greenhouse cleaner than Katja, with less dirt under my fingernails and a lack of sweat on my brow. Rolled their eyes frequently. Gave me a nudge or a shove or a shoulder-check when I deserved it. No one tiptoed around me or watched their words.

Each of them spoke *to* me—not at me. Not once had I been addressed like I wasn't even there, discussions of my comings and goings nonexistent. They didn't *want* anything from me. Power, influence, wealth, status, *gossip* for being linked to a prince and all the benefits that wrought—this witch, dragon, and vampire weren't bothered with any of it.

We were… companions.

Equals.

A quartet bundled together by fate.

Rafe, Elijah, and Katja were so far from the sycophants I had purposefully surrounded myself with for centuries that they were practically on the other side of the fucking galaxy. I'd used sniveling fae nobles desperate to climb the court hierarchy as a protective bubble for far too long. They all catered to me because they *had* to. Didn't question me. Did as they were told. Let me get away with bloody murder.

Perhaps I had always been afraid that if others saw the true me, if they were allowed to speak their mind, I'd crumble. Because I was the disappointment of the Midnight Court and everyone knew it…

Everyone but these three.

To them, I was just Fintan.

I guess I needed that.

Had needed it for some time—the chance to stand on my own two feet, to have my ego checked, and to be accepted for the snarky, pampered mess I was.

And now that I had it, I wasn't about to let *anyone* take it away from me—including Guthrie.

"We have to get her out of here," Elijah rumbled, eyes fixed on the back of his mate's head again. Katja seemed to shrink under his scrutiny, no doubt feeling the dragon's interest throughout her entire body.

"Away from Guthrie, at the very least," Rafe added softly. "I worry if he can't *have* her, no one can, you know?"

"Wards, wolves, warlocks, and a psychotic warden…" I flipped one of my eggs over, hoping the back might be more appetizing. Nope. Not even a little. "Yes, getting out of here should be a breeze."

My snort had them both scowling, eyes narrowed and

mouths in dreadfully serious thin lines, and I blew each a kiss before plugging my nose and shoving the fried egg in my mouth. *Wretched.* Tasted worse than it looked, not an ounce of seasoning save for the slightly burnt char of the grill. Yet as Rafe and Elijah fell into *another* hushed discussion, I sank into my own little world, mind whirring through all the possibilities of a daring escape attempt. In my time here, I hadn't considered it all that seriously, as I'd been expecting big brother Rollo to charge the gates with half the Midnight Court's army at his heels.

Apparently I would have to get myself out of trouble this time.

Tedious.

But necessary.

The boys were right: with each day that Katja refused the warden's demand to respect the blood contract—a situation I understood in my bones, my kind accustomed to deals—he grew closer and closer to snapping. And if he couldn't claim her, mind, body, and soul, then he might eventually just kill her.

Couldn't have that.

No. No, no, no, no.

Wouldn't give him the *satisfaction.*

Breaking out of Xargi Penitentiary was the challenge of a lifetime, for it seemed near impossible...

But perhaps it was time to defy the impossible. Perhaps Prince Fintan of the Midnight Court ought to shatter expectations—just this once.

Prove them all wrong.

Be the hero.

Defend my warped little family against our enemies.

And for once, come out on top by my own merit.

Or...

Idea. A flash of brilliance. I grinned, shoving the second egg in my mouth, and then gagged dramatically at the assault on my taste buds.

Or, I suppose I could just *buy* our way out of here.

Everyone had a price, and it was time for the right witless pawn to finally name it.

24
KATJA

Purposefully ignoring my boys, *especially* as Rafe tried to navigate the world without his fangs, was one of the hardest things I'd ever had to do.

And it had only been a day.

And... You know, not counting my entire family dying and then having to *listen* to the grim details from a psychopath who thought he literally owned me. That was harder—on my heart, on my mind. But my body yearned to be near Elijah. Longed to sidle up to the fire and bask in the warmth. I missed whispering with Rafe for hours through that mousehole between our cells, and I was desperate to spend today's greenhouse shift with Fintan—nine hours of laughter and chatter with a dash of actual gardening.

Sad, really, to feel so bereft without them. I mean, they hadn't been in my life for all twenty-nine years, and then, *bam*, there they were—like they had been there all along. Scary to consider the intensity of our bonds, both as individuals and as a group, but for their own sake, I had to stay away. Distance myself. Push back anytime they tried to wriggle closer like it was the most natural thing in the world.

Because it *was* the most natural thing—easy and simple, normal in a place that was anything but.

I didn't realize any of this until I went without.

Didn't realize what I'd had until I lost it.

Sure, I had been aware that they catered to me, forming a protective trio of handsome muscle so that no one could touch me when they were around. It still made me a little uncomfortable, having all these men standing up for me, fighting for me, getting in trouble for me, but going without it today and yesterday had been... shitty.

Terrible.

Not the lack of protection—just the lack of *them*. I had a solo bakery shift yesterday, Elijah stuck in the metal shop, which meant it had been easy enough to pretend they didn't exist. As soon as we all reconvened in the cellblock, however, it became infinitely more difficult. Even Tully seemed a bit judgmental when I just hid out in my cell, interacting with no one. Thompson was gone—he hadn't come back since my attack—and the rest of the guards were obviously in Guthrie's pocket. Hopefully they had already reported to him that suddenly I was a loner, that his plan was working.

I would never give in... but let him think he had won this small battle by isolating me. If it meant keeping my guys safe, I could take *this*—the heartache, the longing, the loneliness.

Unfortunately, Fintan was the most difficult to ignore. Elijah and I had our fated mate connection, which made my body topsy-turvy when I forcefully distanced myself from him, and Rafe and I had our intense conversations that made me feel *alive*, like I wasn't being held captive in a prison, the prickle in my neck a constant reminder that we were tied together...

But Fintan had no issues bulldozing personal boundaries.

He had been my shadow ever since Cooper and Williams marched us out to the greenhouse after breakfast, and even though one of the guards there had ordered him to work in the compost section today, he outright ignored them as soon as they turned their back, hot on my heels and talking *at* me as I harvested carton after carton of plump, juicy raspberries. They were due for the States, set to be shipped tomorrow and enchanted not to spoil.

He had kept pushing, my gorgeous fae, nattering on about everything and nothing. Sometimes I could tune him out—me and the others even joked about Fintan's future success as the world's first fae white noise machine—but not today. My mind, heart, and body didn't *want* to tune him out, so I heard every word, felt his every breath on my neck, the heat flaring between us whenever he hovered too close.

And my treacherous heart desired *all* of that. It wasn't love, not yet, but every so often I realized I was veering in that direction, a dingy adrift in a stormy sea, land ahead and murky depths below. I could drown—or I could carry on to the shores.

Right now, I had purposefully chosen the depths, taking in water and struggling for air, but there really was no other choice. No one else I cared about was getting hurt on my watch.

Fingertips stained red with raspberry juices, I plopped the final few berries in and sealed the plastic carton. Nice as it was to work around greenery, the flora thriving under the care of witches and warlocks, elves and fae, even an earth elemental in her grey jumpsuit, greenhouse duty became monotonous after a while, especially if you were assigned to harvest. Pluck the stock, package it, wheel it to processing before it shipped out. I added this carton with all its organic labels and artisan stickers to the last available spot on my metal cart, then sighed as I looked to the rear of the massive space. Time to drop off another batch, the processing area annoyingly chaotic and the guards with clipboards *beyond* curt.

Bathed in greenhouse heat and humidity, the random bursts of sprinklers adding to the overall smothering damp, I brushed the sweat from my forehead and turned around—only to find myself alone, an empty, seemingly endless track of dirt sandwiched between tables of greenery ahead. Fintan had disappeared at some point, maybe sick of being ignored, and longing stabbed through me. Longing and *hurt*, neither of which I was allowed to feel.

I had chosen this.

I was ignoring *them*.

It shouldn't hurt me if any of the three respected that. This was what I *needed* to happen—to be left alone.

So… Why did it feel so crappy to suddenly *be* alone?

Ugh. As the color drained from my cheeks and my gut bottomed out, I shoved the cart with its unwieldy wheels toward processing. The thing felt like it weighed two tons, but the heat made everything harder and my body still hadn't fully recovered from its beating. Tully's constant snuggles and purrs had mended just about everything, but today I had woken up with a dull ache all over and an overwhelming exhaustion that I hadn't let him fix.

In a way, I almost felt like I… deserved it.

That I *should* feel like garbage.

Which was ridiculous and totally projecting and not rational, but here I was, trudging along with a cart of packaged raspberries, relishing the stiffness in my shoulders, my lower back, and my knees. It was guilt manifested—guilt for Rafe's loss, for abandoning my fated mate, for blocking out the one man who knew how to really make me laugh.

I wished he were here right now, ambling along beside the rickety cart, even if the conversation was one-sided.

It was a sea of green, purple, and grey at processing, other inmates loitering around as their harvest was counted and approved. I nudged my cart to the back of the group, happy for a break while I waited my turn, struggling to get my wheels over the bump between dirt floor and grey tiled stone. Perspiration collected on the nape of my neck, back with a vengeance seconds after I brushed it away, and it dribbled between my shoulder blades, no doubt staining my jumpsuit just like everyone else.

Ahead, two guards fussed over an elf's peach collection, insisting some were too ripe, a pair of twin metal doors behind them that led to the magically enhanced shipping department. On the outside, it was just a garden shed. Inside, I'd been told it was the size of an aircraft carrier, another of Lloyd's "legit" businesses removing product each evening.

Maybe it was cooler in there.

Not exactly a thrill to lug boxes and cartons around, but maybe it—

Fintan's reflection suddenly caught in the glass wall to my left. I stared at it for a moment as he drew nearer, marching into the processing sector without a cart—without a single fruit or vegetable or herb in hand. Belly looping, I forced my head down, like raspberries were way more fascinating than the fae who made my pulse race and my heart happy, and I pointedly ignored him as he stalked right by me.

He marched by everyone, actually. Swallowing hard, I peeked up, feeling safe enough to watch his back as he sauntered to the front of the herd, a pair of chunky shears hanging off a belt around his waist.

Wait. A *belt*?

None of us had a belt, especially not one that looked so eerily similar to those on guard uniforms—

Casual as sin, Fintan strolled right up behind one of the guard's bitching about the peaches, reached around him—and snapped his neck. *Crack*. Just like that, the crunch and pop of breaking bone thundering through processing. Every inmate in line fell silent, and my heart plummeted down and out the other side. What the *hell* was he doing?

As soon as that guard dropped, nothing but a limp pile of black uniform at Fintan's feet, his companion immediately went for his wand—but Fintan was faster. So. Much. Faster. Fae speed was legendary, but I'd always chalked it up to their wings spiriting them along. Fintan whipped the shears off his belt and hurled them in the time it took me to blink, and the blade embedded into the other guard's skull so violently that it knocked him backward. He collapsed to the stone floor with a *thunk,* blood pooling around his head like a renaissance halo.

"Fae are *warriors,*" Fintan announced gruffly in the shocked silence that followed. He then swept a hand through his hair, boyishly charming again in an instant, and shrugged one shoulder. "We're not fucking garden gnomes."

Shock rippled through the group, the hum of the fans and the magic-powered generators barely making a dent in the high-pitched whine that stretched through my skull. Inmates glanced nervously at one another, but one of the elves finally wrenched off his gloves and hurled them toward the crumpled corpse at Fintan's feet.

The fae raised a hand, eyebrows arched. "So… Anyone up for a riot? Prison riot, anyone?"

"What about the ward?" the female mage in grey demanded, her red ringlets doubled in size courtesy of the greenhouse humidity. Sweat glistened on her forehead, her cheeks, and I wiped at mine subconsciously, roasting alive in this jumpsuit even as ice-cold fear slithered through my veins.

"We just need the caster to break it," Fintan remarked as he stepped around the fallen guard. "Rumor has it Guthrie made the wards—so let's have him *break* them." Lashing out, he toppled the peach cart, plastic containers spilling everywhere, perfect peaches tumbling across the ground, and then hopped onto it. “Time to storm the keep and behead the king, ladies and gents. *Enough* is enough.” He tapped at his collar, his grin slightly manic. “These fuckers only fry us if we try to take them off—not if we use a trowel to disembowel a guard.”

Oh *gods*. Was that where he had disappeared to? I coiled my trembling fingers around the metal handles of my own cart, thoughts racing, heart pounding. Escape had been on my mind from the second I woke up in this hellhole, even more so after I’d met Guthrie. But… But this wasn’t it. I hadn’t imagined butchering warlocks before riding off into the sunset; any attempts I’d mulled over—attempts that would probably fail but were satisfying to imagine—had always been much more subtle.

Only subtlety wasn’t Fintan’s forte. Apparently it was this—that brilliant tongue capable of doing such exquisite things to me now spurring a crowd into *action*. He fell back on a few more clichés to inspire the troops, but without much prompting, the greenhouse rebellion was underway. Inmates scattered in pairs and groups, gathering weapons from the vast array of gardening tools at our disposal, arming themselves for war. One witch even snatched the wand off the guard with the shears still stuck in his face—not that she could actually use it, but I understood the need to hold it, to pretend. Maybe it gave her courage to wrap her fingers around a wand again.

Courage that I found faltering inside me…

Until Fintan strode to my side, smirking, casual once more—like he had kick-started some teenage hijinks, not an outright rebellion where people, most likely inmates, were bound to die.

Or fry.

"What are you *doing*?" I hissed, grabbing his arm and hauling him away from the unfolding chaos.

"Me and the boys had a chat," he said as he twisted out of my hold—easily, like he wasn't even *trying*—and caught me by the chin. "Time to get out of here, darling."

I blinked up at him, smitten butterflies flitting to life in my chest, affection and incredulity and outright terror colliding, mashing into something that almost tipped off an anxiety puke.

"And *this* is the plan?"

Fintan chuckled, then booped me on the nose. "Well, no, I've gone a bit rogue. Let's just run with it, shall we? See what happens."

"See what *happens*? Fintan—"

Before I could rip him a new one for starting a prison riot on a whim, he snatched my hand and dragged me away. Our fingers threaded together so naturally, finding strength and support in each other, and I power walked after him, body aching and adrenaline soaring. While a flurry of activity erupted all around us, blurred purple, green, and grey jumpsuits racing by, Fintan led me down one long row without breaking his pace, headed for the main doors of the building without delay. I barely managed to grab a pair of scissors along the way, clutching them in my free hand as I clung to him with my other.

Since the attack, I hadn't moved this much or this fast, overly cautious with my recovering body, but the fight-or-flight instinct kicking into overdrive blocked out the painful reminders of that night. The only time I stumbled was when I spotted the corpses of dead warlocks near the front; not exactly disemboweled with a trowel, but Fintan had been quick and efficient with his takedown. Slit throats for the both of them, one missing his belt—and his wand snapped in half.

Which, honestly, was almost as cruelly intimate as snapping his neck.

"So, we're attacking Guthrie?" I asked breathlessly, mind still scrambled but body oddly calm as we paused at the main doors. No trembling or shivering. No weak knees or sweaty palms. Fintan poked one of the front doors open and peered through the crack, squinting against the afternoon sunshine, then shook his head.

"No, *they're* attacking Guthrie." He tossed a thumb over his shoulder at the coalescing inmates. "We're going to pay one of the guards patrolling the perimeter to sneak us through the front gate."

I sputtered up at him, standing my ground when he tried to tug me forward. "What? But you told everyone else—"

"I'm not *wrong*," the fae insisted with one of his cavalier shrugs, eyes blazing with mirth—with a fire of his own, green flames sparking and snapping like I'd never seen before. "If they overwhelm Guthrie, they can take down the ward and free everyone. Let's be honest—inmates outnumber security. But the ward also opens and closes at the main gates for shift changes… We don't need Guthrie for that, and I have a *lot* of money. Prince, remember?"

I groaned. "Oh my gods, Fintan, now is not the time to pull this—"

"Now is precisely the time to buy our way out," he said, wiggling his eyebrows and then shouldering through the main doors before I had the chance to object. Fingers still entwined, I had no choice but to follow him into the sunshine, met with a blast of cool, dry air as I jogged in his shadow, clutching my scissors like they might actually do something.

Like I had the stones to use them on a guard as Fintan had.

Never gonna happen.

I couldn't... stab them into someone's face.

Or leg. Or shoulder. Or *whatever*. It wasn't me.

I couldn't...

Do you want to die here? a stronger me whispered from the black depths of my mind, the butterflies in my chest pounding their wings, circling as one swirling mass. *Do you want to lose to Lloyd? Toughen up, sweetheart. We're just getting started.*

I rubbed at my ear with my shoulder, unsure of where all that had come from—only that it had a familiar tinge to it, a whisper of my dormant magic, as if all the energy, the power, the ancient wisdom brewing inside me had finally taken on a life of its own. Concerning. Without my wand, casting on a *good* day was a bit of a crapshoot. If I somehow got the collar off without frying, I'd probably explode.

Crouched low, Fintan snuck us along the edge of the greenhouse, then darted down the side and out of sight of the main building. Just as we rounded the corner, I glanced back over my shoulder and spotted one of the wolf shifters on patrol near the heart of Xargi. With a sizeable spiked collar of his own, the enormous white wolf stood watching us, ears up, alert, then resumed sniffing the foundations of the main building.

Not all the wolves out here were volunteers.

Some were prisoners, same as the rest of us.

"Now, I know someone monitors the western exterior fencing—"

"Wait." I planted my feet and ripped my hand away, forcing Fintan to stop and loop back for me.

"Katja, we all know what you're doing," he remarked lightly—almost like he was choosing the best words to spare my feelings. "It's too late to pretend we don't know each other, but it's just the time to make a move."

"No, I just..." Embarrassment warmed in my cheeks and

plumed all the way down my body. By purposefully distancing myself from the guys, I had tried to assert my own agency... Now here was Fintan coming to the rescue, and I was the damsel all over again. Not the heroine. *Never* the heroine. Just a helpless girl the heroes carried on their shoulders all the way to the end.

No. Not happening. I had a say in this, even if it wasn't what any of them wanted to hear.

I had a voice, damn it—and it was time to use it.

"We can't leave without Elijah and Rafe," I said firmly. "And *Tully*... I'm not going anywhere without him. Ever."

Fintan's smile stretched the gauntlet in a matter of seconds, from obnoxiously patronizing to strained acceptance. "We will of course immediately return with the might of the Midnight Court at our backs—"

"No." Whether the offer was real or not, I couldn't risk it. "I'm not leaving them behind."

"Katja, we could be out of here this evening—"

"We don't leave them behind," I stated, rising above a heated whisper to assert my point. "Because if we do, we're leaving them here to die." My eyes stung at just the *thought* of abandoning the others to Xargi's clutches. "This is nonnegotiable, Fintan. You go find a guard to buy off if you want, but I'm going back in there for them."

His eye twitched. The way Fintan loomed over me and then glanced along the chain-link fence that caged in the property, it was like he was gauging whether or not he could just scoop me up and go. If he did, I'd *never* forgive him.

"You know," he started, hesitating briefly before exhaling a sharp breath, "the wolves could pick us off before we even get back to the main building. Two inmates, unescorted... that alone could be suicide."

At the sound of doors crashing into the greenhouse glass, we crept along the side wall and peered around together, almost comical in the way our heads aligned, one over the other. What wasn't comical was the mob of inmates moving at a steady clip toward the main building; with so many green-thumbed supers inside, there were fewer egos to contend with, which made elves and fae, witches and mages, the ideal type to start a rebellion—more willing to work toward a common goal without jockeying for alpha.

For now, anyway.

"I think we've found a distraction," I muttered, which had Fintan chuckling behind me. As soon as an alarm erupted from the main building, however, he fisted the loose fabric at the back of my jumpsuit and hauled me out of sight.

"What I wouldn't do for a bit of your familiar's shadow magic right now," he grumbled, our hands loosely entwined again, gravitating toward each other like they had a mind of their own. Like they belonged together.

"I'd settle for *any* magic, honestly." It was all there, swirling deep inside me, pent-up and frustrated and thrumming with my coven's legacy—just out of reach.

Lips pursed, Fintan leaned back to survey the stretch of gravel between the greenhouse and the main prison building, and then returned to me with a huff. Another pointed glance toward the fence hinted at an internal debate—that for once he wasn't just rushing into something, driven by instinct and personal gain.

"*Fine.*" He steered us deeper into the greenhouse's shadow, our backs to the glass wall. "Let's go find your mate."

My heart soared—because at some point he had figured it out. Elijah didn't strike me as the type to discuss our personal relationship, not even with Rafe, but Fintan had just admitted to it: he knew I was fated to a dragon shifter.

But he still held my hand, still looked at me with that otherworldly gaze like he wanted to devour me whole.

He knew—and it didn't matter.

"Let's get *our* dragon and *our* vampire," I clarified, so many words unsaid suddenly dangling between us. "And my familiar."

"I mean, if we've got the space in the escape pods, I suppose his royal highness can tag along."

I trailed after him to the edge of the building, Xargi Penitentiary soaring before us, and I did my best impression of a nonchalant Fintan-shrug. "If Tully even wants to leave this Shangri-La, of course."

"Of course."

Fintan then grinned, acceptance and affection glinting amongst the mischief in his eyes, and we broke off into a sprint toward Xargi—hand in hand, off to rescue a dragon, a vampire, and a cat.

25
ELIJAH

Although forced labor wasn't my *thing*, there were very few places in this pit where I truly felt my most dragon-y self than the metal shop. The fire and the forge, the crash of metal on metal, welding and shaping weaponry and machines, commenting on Colin the elf's exceptional glass-blowing abilities... I tolerated these shifts better than any other setting. The bakery I put up with for Rafe's sake, and Katja's company was a bonus that not even the forge could top.

Here, sweaty and dirty and surrounded by male inmates who liked to throw their strength around, I felt oddly at home. Artistry thrived in the shop. Talent blossomed. Exceptional goods left these doors, shipped off to vendors who sold custom pieces, to supernatural clans that still relied on ancient weaponry alongside tooth and claw, to the human militaries and militias who loved the intricacy of our firearms.

A very small part of me looked forward to metal shifts.

Today, I had showed up alongside all the rest—and discovered I would be reloading bullets for nine hours straight. Tucked away in a dim, windowless room at the far back of the shop, I was stuck on a stool doing *the* most tedious job imaginable. Most shifts had thirteen inmates assigned to this furnace, and although no one had said as much, usually the dimmest fuckers loaded bullets. There was nothing to it—no skill required, no tact or craft or passion. Put all the pieces in the machine. Pull the lever. *Crunch.* The machine stuffs all the parts and powder together. Out comes a reloaded bullet. Put the bullet in the box. Eventually seal a full box. Put the box on the pile. Repeat.

For nine *fucking* hours.

No swords for me today. No arrow tips or throwing stars or double-sided axes.

Just... *this.*

I wrenched down the lever, grinding my teeth as the machine did all the work for me, then pushed the lever back up. The bullet sat waiting in its slot, slightly warm to the touch when I plucked it out and dropped it in the ammunition box destined for some bullshit gun shop in the States.

Of all the inmates assigned to this place, I had the most skill. I did this *professionally* and could withstand the fire—yet here I was, making bullets in a room with no circulation, a rock-hard stool under me and a wood table in front of me, the reloading machine drilled into its top and bullet parts scattered everywhere by the cunt guard who purposefully spilled the containers before he left me to rot.

This was Guthrie's doing.

Just a little taste of the suffering he had in store for any male who associated with Katja...

So be it.

I could outlast him.

He was just flesh and bones, even with his magic.

I was dragonfire and steel, nearing three centuries in age and capable of surviving unspeakable horrors.

What I *couldn't* stand was not being with Katja. Not speaking to her, touching her, *smelling* her—and it had only been a day. We three had agreed not to push her, to give her the space she needed to sort through her own unspeakable horrors. In the end, it might have been better for *her* if Guthrie had no one to use as leverage, but I fucking hated the thought of my mate going up against that filth alone. My inner dragon and I wanted to incinerate the warden, fry him to a crisp and bathe in his screams.

But this was Xargi—and here, no one ever got what they wanted.

And now the odds were stacked so high against us—

A sharp tap on the shoulder made me fumble as I reloaded the machine, so lost in my thoughts, in the mundanity of my task, that neither I nor my inner dragon had sensed anyone creeping up behind. *Fool.* My inner dragon bristled, missing his mate and desperate to fight, but we both faltered again when I scented... Fintan?

Elderberries and dewdrops on grass and the subtle smokiness of aged bourbon—*Fintan.*

Abandoning the reloader, I whirled around and found my fae counterpart standing there with one of the metal shop's guards—a warlock in his early twenties whose voice still broke when he shouted at us. And... he had a knife to the whelp's throat. My inner dragon unleashed a war cry that rattled in my bones and set off a stress headache between my eyes. I stabbed a thumb at the sharp twinge, scowling, seconds from asking what the *fuck* was going on—had I fallen asleep reloading bullets? No surprise if I had... So mind-numbingly boring—

But I scented her first.

Briar rose and candle smoke and a storm raging across a

tumultuous sea... Over the crackling flame and seared metal of the shop, my mate reigned supreme.

Katja zipped into the room a second later, out of breath and flushed, sweat glistening across her lovely face. Fire sparked in her big blues, hottest in all the realms, and for the first time since I'd known her, she looked exhilarated. *Alive*. Stunned, my gaze dipped to the pair of thick gardening scissors clutched in her one hand, the shears bloodless—for now. Had she the courage to use them, to jam them into a guard's throat just as Fintan tormented the pup in his grasp with the blade's razor-sharp tip?

Where the fuck had he even *found* a knife?

A storm of feeling charged through me, clashing, battling to come out on top. Relief and concern and gut-churning confusion that made the room spin as I shot to my feet. My inner dragon had more clarity, snarling, sensing something stupid had happened without me.

"What...?"

"Uh..." Fintan shrugged as Katja fidgeted with her shears, and the fae cleared his throat. "Escape attempt?"

"*What*?" My temper reached critical mass in a millisecond, and it took every ounce of restraint I had not to throttle Fintan within an inch of his life. *Yes*, we had agreed to get serious about breaking out of here, but we were nowhere near ready.

"I saw an opening and I ran with it," he insisted as voices rose from the rest of the shop beyond my little alcove, metal clanging and footsteps pounding. "The greenhouse shift has already breached the main building, and the three guards out there are dead." Fintan poked the tip of his blade under the warlock's chin; the boy let out a whimper, squeezing his eyes shut. "*This* lovely lad will take us through all the locked doors."

I opened and closed my mouth, fumbling for words. Half

of me wanted to take that dagger and slice him from stem to stern—watch him bleed out at my feet. The rest insisted I clap him on the back and embrace him as a brother, because he had done what I couldn't: he had started a chain of events that *might* get us all out of here.

Or, you know, might result in our grisly demise.

Struggling, I looked to Katja, who was locked on me, her gaze unfocused as she chased her breath. One blink and she was back—and then she was on top of me, shooting onto her toes to throw her arms around my neck and squeeze tight. Ignoring Fintan's smug smirk, I wrapped my arms around her lower back and held her, breathed her in, willed her scent to permanently stain my skin so I could carry her everywhere.

My inner dragon purred in her embrace, craving our mate with every fiber of his temperamental being.

"I'm sorry," she choked out in my ear, fingers toying with the hairs on the nape of my neck. "Elijah, I'm so sorry."

"You..." I cupped the back of her head with a frown, wishing I could fix whatever made her words so heavy. Was it the escape attempt? The distance? Both? Or had she felt it too—the longing, the same treacherous ache in her heart as mine when we were apart, even for a day. Now that we had found each other, two souls crafted by fate, absence did *not* make the heart grow fonder. Shaking my head, I crouched so that she could drop onto flat feet, her body still recovering from Deimos's brutality, her legs trembling. "You don't have to apologize."

Sniffling, she eased back and planted her hands on my chest, looking oddly determined as she said, "Yes, I do, so... just let me."

"All right, star-crossed lovers," Fintan interjected, cutting off what would have been acknowledgement from me—acceptance that if she felt like she needed to say or do something, I as her mate would support her. Sure, I'd argue when I needed to. I'd put my foot down when it came to her safety and well-being. But… I wouldn't control her. Never. Fintan, on the other hand, seemed hell-bent on running the show, and had the audacity to sidle between her and I, guard in tow, looking a little too thrilled with the turn of events. "Let's get Rafe and the cat and then get the *fuck* out of here. This one'll give us no trouble at all, right?"

He flicked the knife just hard enough at the warlock's flesh that it split, bright red oozing from the wound. The boy cried out and shook his head. Honestly, weren't all the prats patrolling this place hardened criminals themselves? I'd assumed those inside Guthrie's organization had a backbone, but maybe the best and brightest—like Thompson—had fled for greener pastures when they realized what a shit gig they found themselves in out here.

Pleased, Fintan tapped the boy under his chin with the flat side of the blade. "Fantastic." He then looked between me and Katja, brows up. "Shall we?"

While Katja hopped to, immediately headed for the door, I couldn't move until I'd said my piece. Grabbing hold of Fintan's green sleeve, I hauled him back when he tried to trail after my mate.

"You are putting her at risk, Fintan," I hissed, hoping he realized what he had started with his trademark impulsivity. If something happened to her in all this, I'd kill him. The fae merely glanced down at my huge fist, then snorted.

"This was *her* bloody idea!"

"Hey…" Katja wheeled around in the doorway, hands on her hips, the end of her scissors nudging at the wall. "The riot was *not* my idea."

"Coming back here was most certainly your idea," Fintan argued, his grin tinted with dark delight—like he relished a fight before a fuck. My inner dragon growled at the thought but seemed more focused on Katja than the other male fate *might* have chosen for us to share her with.

Arms crossed, Katja sidled back into the little room, eyes on me.

"Nobody gets left behind," she murmured. In an instant, I melted, all soft and gooey on the inside, infatuated with her even more now that I saw her loyalty in a crisis. This new side of her set off the protective alpha in me, my inner dragon on high alert for possible threats, but it also made me want to bend her over this table and make her mine in front of everyone. Fuck her until she begged for mercy, then mark her over and over again, my bite forever burned across her flesh.

I just smiled instead, wholly on board with whatever these two had in mind—because from the look in her eyes, the pride, the promise, the confidence in what she was doing, I figured I ought to encourage this. An alpha's mate could withstand our strength, our fury, our darkest side. Yet they also made *us* better. Whatever we needed, we found it in them, and they in us. An alpha wasn't exempt from growth, from personal betterment. Before Katja, I had always assumed I would pluck my fated mate from obscurity and tuck her away in a tower, dazzle her with jewels and keep her *safe*.

But my mate wanted to fight.

Katja longed to stand on her own two feet—to make the difficult call when necessary. I'd suspected it the second she ran to Fintan's defense on his first day, but I saw it now, bright and glaring, her tenacity and her potential. The days of distance and quiet were gone. It was time to make waves.

"Let the record show that I wanted to bribe someone to *quietly* sneak us out the front door, but here we are," Fintan insisted when I started toward her. He stiffened as I passed by, flinching ever so slightly when I raised my hand and clapped him hard on the shoulder. Our eyes met, dragon and fae, and an unspoken understanding passed between us. In no way did I condone him doing this without consulting Rafe or myself, but it was happening. No going back now. No stopping it.

He had *tried* to take the less dangerous of the two paths, but Katja dragged him down the one full of thorns and brambles—all the way back to me. And Rafe. And, of course, Tully.

I could respect that.

But I also wouldn't let *anyone* hurt her either. She ought to be better armed than she was now so that despite our collars, she could still protect herself.

"Come along," I rumbled, snatching her hand as chaos erupted in the metal shop. "Let's find you a more suitable weapon."

"*Yes…*" Katja squeezed my hand as she hurried to my side —the perfect match for me, this little witch. Her eyes all but glittered when they drifted toward the semiautomatic rifles prepped for shipment this weekend, and when they met mine, I realized I was a fucking goner. She nibbled her lower lip and pulled me toward the firearm of her choosing. "Let's find us both a weapon to—"

"Oh, little mate…" I yanked her back and stole a hard, fiery kiss that had her gasping and Fintan chuckling. When we broke apart, I cupped her chin and arched an eyebrow. "I *am* the weapon."

26

RAFE

I awoke to a blitzkrieg.

My eyes snapped open at the distant explosion, the walls of my cell shuddering. Dust sprinkled down on Tully and me, the lone lightbulb overhead swinging back and forth. Another *boom,* followed by the wail of a siren, and as I blinked the fog of my afternoon nap away, I legitimately thought I was in London and the Germans were bombing the absolute shit out of us—again. Back in my flat, unable to enlist—medically disqualified after a checkup by a human physician I had vampirically encouraged to scribble whatever I told him on my chart. The war. The war to end all wars—

Only Tully wasn't there during *the* war.

Another crack-*boom,* more violent than any of our recent thunderstorms, followed by another misting of chalky dust from the walls and ceiling. Then just the siren—and men shouting. Groaning, I sat up, forcing Tully to sink his claws into my chest so he didn't tumble off. We had retired to my cell hours ago if the heat on the window said anything, the sun at a different spot in the sky now, and the silly familiar continued to purr away, steadfast, stubborn enough to think he could regrow my fangs. Unfortunately, their loss was one he couldn't fix, magic or not, but I found comfort in his company, in the constant vibration of his deep, soothing purrs.

Just me and Deimos in Cellblock C today, the bastard off from library duty and the rest of our crews gone.

And now—

Wood splintered outside my cell, then another *boom* sent chunks crashing across the block. Metal warped with a pitchy groan, and Williams gave a lone shout before being silenced by gunfire. Two shots—*bang, bang*—and then nothing but his moans. Tully whipped around, doubled in size and completely rigid. Both of us tracked the warlock guard's wand as it bounced across the floor outside my doorway, away from him, like someone had kicked it.

What… the hell?

Tully clung to me as I tried to stand, growling low, his tail swishing, and I finally had to just peel him off in order to get upright. The familiar toppled to the ground with a yowl, then darted for a nearby shadow. Brushing the dust from my face, my hair, my arms, I staggered for the opening at the end of my cell, still blinking the sleep away, all the while wondering if this was a nightmare.

Until I saw them.

My *people*.

Elijah, Katja, Fintan—and a guard hostage. The main door to Cellblock C had been blown apart, most likely by the wand in the trembling warlock's hand, and just as Katja opened her mouth to greet me, lips stretched in a nervous smile, Deimos blitzed out of his cell and across the block. The demon moved like a great black shadow, faster than I'd ever given him credit for, sprinting by Elijah and straight out the door. Smart. With none of his cronies here and bedlam unfurling outside, we could have *finally* just killed him.

No great loss there.

But what—

Was that a *gun*?

I blinked down at the pistol in Katja's left hand. No one else had a gun. Fintan had the thin blade that most guards carried on their belts a breath away from slitting his hostage's throat, and then Elijah had... himself, nothing but a metal shield at his side.

So. Katja had shot Williams. Bang, bang. One in the leg, the other in the shoulder—if the blood pooling around the fallen, moaning, sniveling guard suggested anything. My mouth watered, but I forced myself to ignore the buffet —for now.

"What the hell are you doing?" was the best I could manage under the circumstances. Elijah, Fintan, and I had discussed whisking Katja away from Xargi, but we hadn't gone beyond a general agreement that it was absolutely critical to get her as far from Guthrie as possible before he went full psycho and killed her.

"Escape attempt," Fintan told me, his eyes brighter than usual, his tone suggesting he rather enjoyed the unfolding carnage. Typical fae. Must have been Unseelie as I'd always suspected. "Get with the program, Rafe."

"What?" I stabbed both hands through my hair, frustration on the rise. "*Now?*"

Looming over the group, Elijah just shook his head when our eyes met, his expression twisting into something that said he understood my feelings—and to just go with it. Let it happen. Right. Sure. Totally logical and not going to fail at *all*.

Another explosion rocked the prison, and I braced on the doorway while Katja did the same on Elijah's arm, more dust shuddering from the ceiling and coating the block's common area in white—like falling ash. Like the blitz. I pinched the bridge of my nose, pushing a lifetime of memories aside, my gums still sore from the extraction. The holes had healed over, but they would never be filled.

"We aren't leaving without you," Katja said when the structure around us stopped shivering through the aftershocks. She studied me with wide, imploring eyes, begging for forgiveness. I'd seen that look many times in my long life, and I'd never been more inclined to accept an unspoken apology before. Only now wasn't the time or place for this—not when the prison was probably *literally* on fire.

Seconds later, Tully shot out of my cell and went straight for his witch, those squeaky kittenish chirps making her whole face light up. While thrilled that we were all back on speaking terms, this wasn't exactly the scenario I had in mind for a reunion. Watching her scoop up Tully and hug him tight, I wanted to do the same, to drag them both into my arms and whisper that I would never let her go.

That I didn't blame her for what Guthrie had done to me.

That I would also forever possess the memory, hazy as it was, of one of my fangs plopped into a vial of acid—just so the researchers could see if it would fizzle away.

It hadn't.

Unfortunately, I wasn't strong enough to say *any* of that. So soon after the extraction, I still battled many unwelcome feelings, struggling to come to terms with the loss. Rather traumatic for a vampire to lose his fangs; we could be a stoic bunch, steeped in tradition and ancient rites, but we had all once been human—and that never *quite* disappeared, even for the vamps who had gone full bloodlust. *Feeling* was a sickness we carried from man to creature, vampirism and emotion two diseases for which there was no cure.

So. Basically I was still traumatized and needed a minute to process.

But I'd rather process *with* her than apart.

After all, I wasn't the only one suffering. Katja carried her own trauma, and the thought of her trudging through all that misery alone made me ache. We needn't *talk*, needn't whisper a word through the mousehole, for us to champion the other's path to recovery.

"Okay, so, right..." I strolled out of my cell, mindful of the sunbeams streaking out of the ones around me, and then folded my arms. "Is there a plan, or...?"

Or were we just making it up as we went along?

"This little darling is going to take us out the front door," Fintan insisted, giving his captive a jostling for good measure. The warlock shut his eyes tight and flinched away from the knife tip poking into the soft underbelly of his chin. "They have charms to open and close the ward issued exclusively for the guards." Hooking an arm around the warlock's neck, Fintan used the other to jerk up his black sleeve from the cuff to the elbow, revealing the ancient symbol for Mercury, the god who walked every road, on his pasty forearm. "Tattooed on their skin—keys to the ward. Clever, no?"

While I could see the logic in that, there was still one giant, obnoxious elephant in the room.

"And when do you intend to do all this?" I motioned to the sun cutting across the block from Katja's cell window, the beam sprinkled with dust. "In case you haven't realized, it's sunny as *hell* today."

"We're going to cover you with our jumpsuits and just go," Katja offered, tugging at her purple lapels. "It'll be temporary, but you'll be fully covered... and then we can figure it out outside the ward."

"Touching." It might have sounded sarcastic, but I had to bite back a genuine smile—because they had considered me and all my failings. They weren't going to leave me behind, even if I slowed them down. Still, this plan was weak at best, and I wasn't about to risk it—wasn't about to risk *her*, my bite looking fresh as ever on her throat, the memory of it both painful and exhilarating. "But I'm not thrilled about the, er, just figure it out part."

"For fuck's *sake,* you dark cloud," Fintan growled. "It's the best we've got, so stop moaning and just get on with it."

Elijah's eyes narrowed. "Fintan."

"He has a right to express his concerns," Katja said tersely, shooting the fae a glare to match her mate's. She then looked to me, her fear spiking within the connection we shared—vampire and victim, those puncture wounds refusing to heal, tethering us together for longer than anyone who came before. Perhaps forever. In a way, we shared what she and Elijah had: a mental, possibly even spiritual link, wherein we could communicate without saying a word.

Her expression faltered when I gritted my teeth, mild annoyance sparking on my end. "How thoughtful of you, allowing me my opinion about the thing that will kill me instantaneously—"

"Come *oooonnnnnnnnn,*" Fintan droned, nodding back to the door with a long, drawn-out groan. "This is a waste of time. Someone just put a bag over his head and be done with it."

"Fuck you, fae."

"It comes from a place of love, vampire," he purred, blowing me a kiss over the sniveling warlock's shoulder. "Just move your *ass* already and we—"

A shrill cry detonated over the cellblock, sirens of varying pitches and intensities exploding from the ceiling speaker. I clapped my hands over my ears, but that didn't stop the horrendous noise from slicing through my skull. Elijah felt it just as severely, the intensity forcing his eyes to roll back into his head before he folded over with a snarl. Doubled in size again, Tully flung himself away from Katja and rocketed into her empty cell like a missile, leaving his mistress to suffer the assault alone. Her knees buckled, and Katja plummeted to the ground, wrists shoved against her ears, hands in her hair, eyes wide with panic.

Xargi had so many sirens—but this was new, something of Guthrie's design, no doubt. Something to subdue *everyone*, so calamitous that I felt the sound vibrations in my marrow. Fintan had even abandoned our ticket out of here, but the warlock couldn't withstand it either, rolling around on the ground, lips moving like he was screaming for someone to make it stop. I dropped to one knee just as a cool, viscous liquid dribbled from my ears—my eardrums had burst. They stitched themselves back together, vampiric healing abilities slow but present even with this damn collar, but then they burst again, another spurt of dead blood splashing against my palms.

When the shrieking stopped, it *felt* like the blitz again, my hearing muffled even with the bells ringing, ringing, *ringing* inside my skull. Shadowy figures darted across the remnants of the cellblock's busted main door, and seconds later someone hurled a dark, round disc into the room. I blinked, stunned, as it clanged and bounced across the floor, wondering if this truly *was* wartime.

"*Grenade—*"

The flash bang exploded in a hail of light and sound, tossing me onto my back and making Katja screech. Her terror reverberated through me, brighter and more focused than anything else, and I fought hard to blink the spotlight out of my eyes. The ringing between my ears intensified, and I rolled onto my stomach and twisted forward just in time to see another grenade tossed inside, detonating before it landed in a cloud of thick, black smoke. Through the swelling darkness, I spotted it: the door repairing itself, splintered wood and jagged metal floating off the ground and zooming back into place, magic thickening in the air as the guards sealed us inside.

The fog would either kill us or render the rest of them unconscious—and I couldn't allow for either. Staggering to my feet, I tugged my jumpsuit over my nose and mouth, but as the black expanded, all-consuming, it sapped the energy from my limbs. I needn't breathe, but it still wormed its way inside me all the same, turning my legs to jelly. The cellblock slid in and out of focus as I stumbled forward a few paces, then collapsed again. Beneath the smoke line, I saw them—my people. Katja on her back, head lolled to the side, eyes open but vacant. Elijah shuffling toward her, pupils like slits, his inner dragon fighting to protect him, to save his mate...

He offered a hand to me, the beast inside recognizing a friend, a brother, and I reached back. Beside them, Fintan pushed up on wobbly arms, only for his face to go slack seconds later, and when his elbows buckled, that regal nose met the ground in a horrendous face-plant. Bone *cracked* noisily on impact. Elijah lilted onto his side, body sprawled over a limp Katja, dragon's eyes on me, hand still stretching, fingers grasping...

No. It wouldn't end like this.

Get them in a cell. Barricade the door. Bash open a window and hide in a shadow. Let the fresh air clear their lungs.

Plan.

Teeth gritted, gums aching, vision tinged red, I summoned every bit of strength left at my disposal and hauled my body forward. Silver lining: the smog had turned so thick, so heavy, that it blotted out the sun. Even as the others faded from view, I crawled in their direction, desperate to take Elijah's hand, to throw Katja over my shoulder, to haul Fintan along after us—

A familiar set of locks clicked and clunked open. The darkness ruffled with the *whoosh* of the cellblock door. A red beam blazed through the black, a dot appearing on my shoulder.

Whump.

Someone fired a wooden projectile, and I hissed—bared my nonexistent fangs—when the stake buried itself into my right shoulder, slicing through flesh and bone and muscle like I was made of butter. Pain exploded through my every cell, followed by a swift and violent sedative lull that knocked the wind out of me.

I was gone before I even hit the ground.

27

KATJA

Everything hurt when I came to, but for once, my wrists were standouts—in a league all their own. The pain there remained sharp and constant, bitter and cruel, even as the rest of the world dripped back into focus on the other side of my heavy eyelids. Sore shoulders—the right had taken the brunt of that fall when the flash-bang grenade went off—and an aching lower back. This wasn't the first time I'd woken up in Xargi strapped to a chair, but as I moaned and shifted about, trying to get the circulation flowing again, I prayed it would be the last.

A cloud of herbal cigarette smoke whooshed across my face. Heart sinking, knowing *exactly* where I was, I clenched my eyes tighter, bracing against the sting of tears.

I didn't want to—couldn't do this. Wanted to fold in on myself and pretend today hadn't happened—pretend I *hadn't* gotten my hopes up about an escape, about using that guard and riding him all the way through the ward with all my guys and Tully in tow.

But we had failed. Miserably. No telling where they were,

but in the darkness, I knew I was in the place I despised most of all.

Mahogany and varnish. Furniture polish. Old books. A rarely used fireplace, all for show. Lloyd's cologne, more pungent than usual, and his rich aftershave. No. No, no, no, *no*.

"I know you're awake."

He sounded so much closer today, and I gritted my teeth, slowly peeling my eyes open and bracing for what I'd find. At least I didn't flinch when I found him sitting on *this* side of his desk, less than a foot away, leaning back with a smoldering cigarette in one hand, the other braced on the mahogany. My heavy gaze dipped down to my shackled wrists, bound to the chair's armrests with the same punishing cuffs from the first day, my original prison accessories. They glowed a faint blue, enchanted this time to do... well, I had no clue, but I lacked the strength to test their limits. The source of all the sharp pain was obvious: the metal had worn my wrists raw, stripped back the outer layer of skin and left red rings in its place all the way around.

Wonderful.

Taking a deep breath, I lifted my head with some difficulty, my neck sore, muscles strained after however many minutes—hours—my head had been hanging like this. A quick glance out the huge windows to my right showed that the sun had only just set, the sky splashed with amber and a rosy pink, darkness closing in.

"Did you feel so very *tough* today, kitten?" Lloyd murmured with a flick of his cigarette, the ashy end sprinkling onto the floor. "Brandishing a *gun* of all things—like a little human. How very brave... and stupid."

"You think any of us want to be here?" I cleared my too-dry throat, wincing at yet another flash of pain. "You're surprised today happened? I'm surprised it didn't happen sooner. You're illegally detaining—"

"Oh, spare me the theatrics," he snapped, clomping one foot onto the leg of my chair. The jostling made my heart skip a beat, then race furiously, adrenaline soaring. "I'm tired, kitten. Tired of waiting for you."

"Maybe we should just cut ties, then," I said, enough steel in my spine to meet those dangerous greys, just for a moment. I arched an eyebrow. "I mean, this is doomed to fail, me and you. We'll never be happy with each other, so—"

"*Enough*." He shoved at my chair and shot to his feet. I muffled a whimper, lips tight together, instinct begging me to *run*. My magic curdled deep inside, overflowing and compounding, promising disaster I didn't let off some of the steam. For the first time since I'd found this damn collar around my neck, my magic turned its wrath on me, scalding up my windpipe like a case of severe heartburn, desperate to get out.

"Please just—"

"No, kitten." Lloyd swooped in and grabbed me by the chin, fingertips biting into my cheeks and forcing my jaw apart. His greying lashes fluttered as his eyes dropped to my lips, and when I let out a stuttering breath, pulse throbbing between my ears, his other hand latched onto my throat and squeezed. "No, now is the time to *listen*."

I sucked down a gulp of air while I still had the chance, my panicked gaze darting around—spurring him on. Lloyd zeroed in on my windpipe, crushing it slowly, and I flailed, chair rustling, but all the restraints held firm. They did their job, cuffs slicing deeper into my wrists, ankle bonds tough as steel.

Even the collar that had slowly become a part of me, an appendage I wanted to cut out and discard, dug into my skin after months of just *existing*, normally uncomfortable but largely ignorable. As Lloyd went from gripping to strangling, electricity suddenly hummed through the leather—like the charms thought I was trying to take it off. A squeal clawed up my crushed windpipe when the next bolt zapped at my skin, sharper this time.

The noise seemed to bring Lloyd back to the moment, the storm clouds lifting in his eyes, and he eased off as I coughed and gasped, breathing a little harder himself. Slowly, he peeled each finger from my face, my throat, and then righted himself, sweeping a hand through his tousled salt-and-pepper waves, then smoothing it down his matching black, grey, and white suit combo. Pristine as always, so put together…

And now sporting a very obvious erection.

Tears burned again, threatening to spill over if I so much as blinked, and I looked up and away, head tipped back just enough to rein them in.

"You're going to be such fun, kitten," he remarked softly, striking out and catching the one traitorous droplet that slipped free. He let it dangle off his fingertip, then flicked it away like he'd done with his cigarette, which now sat in cinders on the floor, abandoned. One vice replaced with another.

"No more terms." Lloyd perched on the edge of his enormous desk and fidgeted with his tie, righting it, tightening it, eyes never once leaving mine. "Here's what's going to happen. If you don't leave with me tonight, I'm going to take those urchins you spend all your time with and destroy them. Elijah Greystone, Fintan of the fucking Midnight Court, and my personal favorite—Rafe O'Dwyer."

While I knew I shouldn't have given him the satisfaction of seeing me panic, I did. Again. I gave him my horror with my slightly parted lips, my eyes wide like saucers, the blood draining from my cheeks.

And I hated myself for it.

Why couldn't I be stronger?

Why couldn't I be the fucking heroine *ever*?

Outside, I was an independent witch who ran a successful business all by myself. In here, I was cuffed and chained and powerless...

Fuck him. Fuck him for putting me in this position, for making me feel so small.

Fuck me for letting him.

"You think all I can do to the vampire is remove his fangs?" Lloyd said casually. A beat later, his tone dropped and darkened. "*Watch me*. I'll rip them all apart, one piece at a time, and you, kitten, can have a front-row seat to the carnage." He sniffed, ticking each of my boys off on his fingers. "I'll peel the flesh from that fucking fae's bones and feed it to the wolves. I'll lob off the vampire's limbs and toss them into the sun so you can watch them fry—have us a *bonfire*. And the dragon..." He cocked his head to the side, staring so hard at me like he could see clear through to my soul, to my heart and all its desires. "I'll pull out the dragon's teeth, rip out his nails, pluck every hair from his head. We'll see how deep we need to dig to find his scales. They go for quite a bit on the black market, dragon scales... Better than any armor out there. They even repel magic—did you know that? His hide is worth a fucking fortune."

Heart racing, I swallowed hard at the churn of an anxiety puke, which was dangerously close to mingling with my pissed-off magic and choking me. This was why I had tried to separate from them, but Fintan had been right: it was too late for that now.

I'd damned them all.

"I..." *Think quick, Katja*. These weren't empty threats; Lloyd would do everything he said and more to my guys if I didn't respond correctly. Tough as it was to wade through the brain fog, I stitched together a slapdash plan that just might work—if I had the leverage over this creepy asshole that I hoped I did. If not, we were all screwed. "I have some conditions."

Amusement flickered across his features. "Oh, is that so?"

With a deep breath, I sat up straighter, businesslike, as if I were dealing with a particularly douchey vendor. Warmth dribbled down my wrists, blood plopping onto the floor from the fresh cuts, but I blocked it out—tried not to count how many seconds stretched between each drop.

Fifteen.

Fifteen seconds and then *plop*.

"The collar comes off," I said evenly. "My magic is turning foul the longer it just sits there. It's making me feel ill, and I..." No need to give him further ammunition. "It has to come off."

Lloyd considered it for a moment—*plop*—and then nodded. "Agreed. Can't have you rotting from the inside, but no wand."

"Sure." Like I even needed a wand at this point. As soon as the leather disappeared, I'd probably go off like a bomb. As a warlock, surely he expected that. Every super and shifter in here was suffering with pent-up magic in one form or another.

"Second..." I licked my lips, unsure if I wanted to play this card just yet but knowing I would hate myself if I didn't. "Tully comes with me."

"What the fuck is a tully?"

Ugh, just hearing Lloyd say his name made the anxiety churn amp up a notch, like he had finally found the heart of me and stomped all over it. "He's my familiar. He... He's a cat. He followed the bounty hunters who took me and snuck in with a guard. He's been living in the shadows of my cell for a while now. He's... my best friend. Please."

Panic reared its ugly head again when Lloyd's face twisted, his teeth gnashed, his fury so sudden and dark that it made me jump. But it was gone just as quick as it appeared, replaced by an unreadable calm—calm that wouldn't last, a maelstrom swirling beneath the surface.

"I can't have some familiar protecting you from me," he growled, and I frantically shook my head.

"No, he won't." Of course he would—Tully would die for me. All familiars would die for their witches and warlocks; the only difference with me and him was that it went both ways. I'd give my life for that spoiled brat ten times over. "I promise—I'll make sure he doesn't interfere. I just want him with me. He... He's good at healing."

Lloyd's lingering erection implied a penchant for violence and a mean sadistic streak; I would probably need Tully's abilities in the very near future.

The warlock considered me for what felt like an eternity, then sniffed and picked a bit of fluff off his suit's charcoal-grey jacket sleeve. "If he fucks with me, I'll skin him and wear his pelt as a hat."

Another surge of anxiety vomit, fire sizzling up my throat. "Okay, and lastly—"

"What makes you think you get any more *conditions*?"

I knew I'd been pushing my luck, and I nudged it just a little further with a flick of my head, tossing my hair over my shoulder to show off the side of my neck Rafe hadn't scarred. Lloyd's gaze plummeted to my throat again, to the pinpoints of pain left by his fingertips, to the bruises forming slowly but surely. *Gods*. He was going to choke me until I passed out regularly, wasn't he? A shiver raced down my spine, eyes burning with a new batch of tears, but I pushed through, needing this last condition approved most of all.

"Lastly," I started again, voice thick, each word a chore, "Elijah, Fintan, and Rafe are taken care of once I'm gone.

They're treated well in here. I'll do whatever you want, go wherever you want, so long as they are looked after... or freed."

Lloyd chuckled coolly. "I'm not releasing them. They have a sentence to serve—which has just been extended for causing a riot and murdering a handful of my guards, I might add."

"Okay, just..." Gods, I couldn't believe I was saying this, *doing* it, throwing away my life and legitimizing this bastard's insanity. But I would. For them, I had to. "None of them get hurt. Or maimed, or tortured, or singled out. They stay together in Cellblock C. Just leave them alone, and don't order any *other* inmates to do the dirty work for you."

"My, my... That's a tall order, kitten." He pinned me with a frighteningly serious look, and just as I started to really sweat, he flipped, mouth twisting into what he must have thought was a sinfully handsome smile. "But you're worth it." Easing off his desk, Lloyd tipped his metaphorical hat to me, bowing slightly as he said, "*Agreed*." His hands then settled on the back of my chair, caging me in on either side, and he dropped down to my eyeline, his breath hot and his eyes wanting. "Now, seal it with a kiss, Katja Fox... like you've made a deal with the Devil."

As much as I wanted to squeeze my eyes shut and turn away, I just sat there and let it happen. Stared at him as he planted his thin, vile mouth on mine in a hard, domineering kiss. Lloyd's eyes fluttered before they closed, and his soft, barely there moan had me fighting my gag reflex. I looked away, out the window and beyond the blurry horizon, then squealed when his hand suddenly fisted in my hair and wrenched my head back. His tongue thrust between my parted lips, and I did everything in my power not to bite it off.

I took it. I took *him* and his mouth that tasted like burnt basil and nicotine and mint. I sealed the deal. I dealt with a man who thought he was the Devil, who saw himself as invincible and all-powerful.

In these walls, Lloyd Guthrie was exactly that.

The harder he kissed, the more I wanted to just vomit into his mouth. Instead, I kissed back—*barely*—so that he wouldn't make me do it again. Nothing too enthusiastic or he would know it was an act.

An eternity later, he retreated, looking all too pleased with himself, still hard as a rock.

"Good girl," he purred, and another shiver of disgust shot down my back. A cold numbness followed, slow and steady as it worked its way down, cutting me off from him, from this place, from *everything*.

Disassociation.

I used to do it a long time ago—processing so many deaths in the family was bound to mess you up a little, but I had taken the steps. Gone to therapy. Processed the grief to the best of my ability. Come out of it a different person, but still whole. No need to disappear inside myself anymore. No need to run from reality.

But maybe that would be the only way to survive what was to come.

Lips wobbling, misery burned behind my eyes, in my nose, and I looked back to the windows again, trying desperately not to cry.

"Tell me, kitten," Lloyd murmured as he ghosted a finger along my jaw, over my swollen lips, mapping me, *touching* me. "Do you love them?"

The dams finally broke, and I twisted my head away with a strangled sob. Humiliation and anger and disgust and heartbreak spilled down my cheeks in hot, wet tracks, and I hated myself for crumbling right before his eyes, but I couldn't stop it anymore. The buildup had been going on for too long, everything stacking higher and higher until it toppled over. Crashed and burned.

Maybe I *did* love them—each one, Elijah and Fintan and Rafe. All to varying degrees, our relationships separate yet heavily intertwined in Xargi. Maybe I had been lying to myself, deluding myself into believing it was *just* sex with Fintan, *just* great conversation with Rafe, *just* a soul bond with Elijah. Just, just, just.

I'd played myself for a fool. We all did, four fools denying what had blossomed between us in the armpit of the world.

It was easier that way—to pretend we weren't in love.

Because I loved them.

I did.

That was so painfully clear now that I folded over and wept at the thought of never seeing them again, of never experiencing our love, of watching it grow and flourish. Right now we were just seedlings barely sprouted above the soil, little wisps of green poking above the black earth, all cozy in the same garden bed, all complementary to each other.

And Lloyd was the boot, trampling each of us to nothing before we had the chance to bloom.

I had to love them.

I wouldn't throw my life away for anything less.

And that made what was about to happen so much worse.

Gasping, fighting for air, struggling against the panic, I sat upright again, and through teary eyes watched Lloyd grit his teeth, grind them, glower down at me—then whip around and swipe everything off his desk. I yelped as it all clattered viciously to the floor, glass shattering and papers flying. He grabbed his desk lamp, the sole survivor of the first attack, and hurled it at a bookshelf. The crash made me jump, and I turned away as stained shards came whizzing back in our direction.

Whatever wasn't nailed down, he threw. Destroyed.

Smashed into itty-bitty pieces under his polished loafers. A pulse of raging magic detonated from him, and the shock wave knocked books off their shelves and splintered the windowpanes. Fueled by his fury, a fire sparked on its own in the hearth. Since meeting Elijah, I had tasted so much fire—in him, in myself. I welcomed its burn, but this one, the flames snapping and hissing and crackling, terrified me. It wasn't the comforting heat I felt with my dragon, not the inferno that bolstered me, made me feel *strong* when I had nothing else, just a witch without her magic.

This was a warning, a message, an omen for the future.

I feared its wrath.

I feared *him*.

This man, this warlock, was going to kill me one day. Maybe tomorrow, maybe next month, maybe ten years from now—he was going to snuff me out in a rage just like this one.

I closed my eyes, chest shuddering as I braced against another breakdown, twitching and flinching as Lloyd continued to obliterate his office.

All in absolute silence.

No yelling or cursing, no snarling or sneering. Just cold, methodical *fury* that seemed to go on forever.

When it finally stopped, when I dared open my eyes again, there was practically nothing left. Curtains torn. Every book on the floor. Huge imposing chair overturned. Firelight engulfed the room and white spiderwebbed cracks covered both windows.

And in the middle of it all, Lloyd Guthrie. He'd barely broken a sweat, not a hair out of place, tie slightly askew again. He fixed that without ever taking his eyes off me, without even blinking.

"So, you love them," he growled, that smoky rasp strained

and dangerous. "That's fine, kitten. I understand… But you'll get over that soon, won't you?"

I nodded frantically, an outright *lie*, my heart shattering and my world ending. Lloyd stabbed a hand through his hair and then grinned as his gaze dropped to my neck again.

"Good girl."

28

ELIJAH

While my last memories of Cellblock C were hazy, a few stood out stronger than the rest. Black smoke filling the air, thick and suffocating. Fintan unconscious at my side. Rafe crawling for us, reaching out, me and my inner dragon desperate to draw him near. Katja's limp body beneath me, her eyes open and glossy.

I am *the weapon.*

Pathetic. What sort of protection had I offered in the outbreak? My snarling presence had kept other rioting inmates away on the way to fetch Rafe, but beyond that, I'd been helpless. Useless. *Again.* No more than a block of muscle—dead weight against the might of magic.

I hadn't expected a blazing triumph, but I had hoped to at least make it to the ward before shit really hit the fan. But it made sense that they came for us so fast; at the first whiff of trouble, Guthrie would have secured his prize.

And he had.

He had stolen my mate right out from under me.

Hands cuffed behind my back, a trio of grim-faced warlocks in black escorted me down the hallway to the door that we had busted through for Rafe and Tully. All the locks back in place. The wood repaired—fortified, even, with thicker metal hinges and additional bolts, some with an iron hum, a few others made of silver.

A warning.

After the dozen locks slid open, an empty cellblock greeted me on the other side. I'd come to in the cafeteria with dozens of lesser shifters and supers, some bloodied and battered, but myself untouched. Honestly, I had expected to wake up in a hole, confined to solitary for the rest of my miserable days, buried and forgotten.

Instead, they brought me here.

Uncuffed me.

Shoved me inside and slammed the door.

Not another inmate in sight. Just... eerie silence. Someone had repaired the place, swept away all the dust and mopped up blood. Williams bled puddles of the stuff after Katja had shot twice as he reached for his wand. Then there had been Fintan with his broken nose, blood oozing, dark and rich. They had probably cleaned some vampire blood too from Rafe—my last true memory of my friend, my vampiric brother, with a wooden stake in his shoulder.

It was like nothing had happened.

Only *everything* had happened. Xargi Penitentiary, from what I'd seen, was in pieces. Inmates across the prison followed those from the greenhouse, arming themselves and rising up. Some did it for the sake of chaos. Others for freedom. I had done it for my clan of misfits on the slim chance that maybe, just maybe, they could get the fuck out of here and taste free air again.

And now I was alone in a stained jumpsuit, patches of dried blood splattered across the navy-blue, dust in my hair and Katja's scent on my skin. Fading. Fading *fast*. My inner dragon bristled at the thought of losing that little piece of her, stalking around inside me, flapping his wings, stretching, *bellowing* such mournful sounds, calling for his mate.

No answer.

The silence stung.

Jaw clenched, hands in fists, I checked each empty cell just to be sure. Even Tully was gone, all the shadows abandoned. I lingered between Katja and Rafe's cells after I'd made a few rounds, unable to stop moving, barely able to breathe. Where were they? What was being *done* to them? Who was I going to flay when all this was over?

Everyone.

I'd kill them all. For Rafe. For Katja. Hell, even for Fintan, who, while impulsive, had only wanted to help us—to save her.

With my inner dragon's song thundering around my head, pounding through my veins, I veered left toward Katja's cell, desperate to run my nose along her cot, bury my face in her pillow. Scent up, keep her with me even in my solitude—

Only the clinking of locks stopped me, and I whipped around, seething, ready to pounce…

On Rafe. Same as me, he lingered in the open doorway, backed by a trio of unfamiliar guards. They uncuffed him. Pushed him inside. Slammed the door behind him. Without hesitation, we marched to one another and embraced as brothers. My inner dragon stopped baying for Katja, just for the length of that hug, then started up again as soon as we broke apart, Rafe rubbing at his shoulder with a wince.

Besides the gaping hole in his jumpsuit where the stake had pierced, he also looked relatively unscathed—disheveled, yeah, but I probably didn't look much better.

"Where were you?" I demanded, studying the slowly healing wound inside that hole, his flesh waxy and pink as his delayed healing abilities kicked in. The vampire assessed me with an equally keen gaze, looking me up and down with a shake of his head.

"They locked me and a few other vamps in the library closet." He hesitated, black brows knit, everything about him hard. "I thought for sure they would have put me in solitary... or just tossed me in the sun. Guthrie had an excuse to take us all out."

I grunted in agreement, stabbing a knuckle between my eyebrows when my inner dragon temporarily lost his shit just hearing that name. Pain thrummed behind my eyes; what I wouldn't do to fucking *shift* already and unleash the hellfire bubbling inside.

"I was in the cafeteria," I managed when Rafe prodded at me, his question unspoken but obvious. "With the general population."

"Anyone said anything to you?"

"Guards?"

"Hmm."

I shook my head. "No."

Which was... odd. With Katja, we all had a target on our backs, and some of the goons had been using that lately to imply a whole load of bullshit. But this evening had been radio silence.

"Me neither," Rafe muttered, taking stock of the cellblock with a quick sweep. "No one's kicked the shit out of me either, which is—"

"Concerning," I said gruffly. This was a change of pace. Even if we hadn't been singled out by the warden, Xargi guards got a twisted thrill harassing inmates. Physically. Verbally. No doubt sexually. The fact that no one had said a word or put a hand on us except to cuff us for transport set me on edge more than anything.

Rafe's eyes met mine, that sea-glass gaze riddled with

worry—with icy suspicion. "Agreed. Where're the others? Any idea?"

"None." *Pathetic*. An alpha who lost his clan, who couldn't do a mental head count in the wake of a disaster, didn't deserve to *be* an alpha. Rafe exhaled sharply, then gritted his thumb into his shoulder, massaging it absently.

"Fuck."

Yeah, that about summed it up.

We whipped around together when the door opened again, my inner dragon silent for a beat, sniffing boisterously, searching for Katja's scent—only deflate and then *rage* when Deimos and Constance stumbled into the cellblock. In an almost violent contrast to us, the demon and the maenad looked like they'd been in the brawl to end all brawls: cuts, bruises, scrapes, shredded knuckles and torn jumpsuits. Pink hair matted, Constance limped along without a sneer or a crazed cackle, and Deimos's left eye was swollen shut, dried blood caked under his nostrils. His lieutenant leaned heavily on him as soon as the guards removed their cuffs, and the pair shuffled straight for their cells, parting without a word and vanishing inside.

Right.

This day was a mess—and the mindfucks just kept on coming. Deimos was a pet favorite amongst the guards, but someone—or someones—had beaten him to a pulp.

"What—"

"Where's Katja?" Rafe growled, grabbing my arm and forcing me back around to him. Deimos and Constance hadn't seemed to penetrate his radar. I shook my head, a snarl rumbling in my chest, my inner dragon bathed in his own fire at the thought of her absence.

"Wish I knew," I muttered, steeling against the next onslaught, then coughing up a bit of smoke. Fantastic. "The guy inside won't stop calling for her. He's losing it."

Rafe pursed his lips for a moment, then patted at my shoulder. "We all are. She probably is too. Her emotions are… a lot. Do you feel them?"

"Barely." We needed to strengthen our bond before I truly felt the ebb and flow of her feelings. When we were in the same room, I could read her like a book. Separated, I struggled to connect to the tether that stretched from her heart to mine—and it pissed me the fuck off that Rafe could sense her, all from something as simple as a bite.

"Well, something's gone wrong on her end," the vampire insisted softly, retracting his hand and sliding both into his jumpsuit pockets. He even leaned back on his heels, putting some subtle distance between us like he realized the minefield he had stumbled into. We seldom discussed *both* our connections with Katja. To his credit, he usually addressed mine, but he *felt* for her. It was so obvious that even a blind man could see it—the look in his eye when he spoke about her. I could hear it in his voice, his tone affectionate, warm, even in the direst of circumstances. Rafe reserved that inflection for me and his work.

And now Katja.

He would give his life for her—of that much I was sure.

No matter how I felt about that, no matter how jealousy flared in the *man*, my inner dragon was at peace sharing his mate with a blood-brother, Rafe's loyalty, sincerity, and integrity mattering above all else. He would protect her. Cherish her. Call her out on nonsense when I was too smitten, too entangled in our fated bond to see clearly.

I needed that.

I needed *him*.

We both did, Katja and me, same as this orphaned vampire needed a family, a clan, a coven.

But this orphaned vampire and my mate had issues of their own to settle at some point, tension still simmering between them since Rafe had lost his fangs. Hopefully they would have the chance to make it right.

The cellblock door opened and closed twice more in the hour that followed, but only to let in Faustus and Helen, both of whom had been in the cafeteria with me. It wasn't in their nature to riot, nor to follow. Fiercely independent, bird shifters seldom grouped together unless their inner birds traveled in flocks. They had gravitated to me tonight, however, sensing my alpha status without ever acknowledging it, hovering nearby in the cafeteria, shuffling closer as more inmates were thrust into the fold. Now, they beelined for their cells, disappearing inside same as Deimos and Constance. Rafe and I continued to loiter in the common area, waiting impatiently for the return of our mate, for the reappearance of our impulsive fae.

And when Fintan finally *did* make an appearance, he was the first of us to look like shit.

Bloodied nose in a splint, eyes black and bruised. As soon as the cuffs left him, he was off in a fury, moving faster than I'd ever seen him, and headed straight for us, his speed a rival for any vampire, murder glinting in his bright green gaze.

"You two all right?" the fae demanded, and the shock on Rafe's face echoed my own. Straight to the point, direct—no dillydallying around. How very unlike Fintan. Strange to not realize how much a person had grown until it clocked you upside the head.

"Fine," I said, motioning halfheartedly to Rafe's shoulder —because that about covered the extent of our injuries. "You?"

Fintan pointed to his nose, scowling. "Did this to myself, apparently... You know, after those fucks gassed us. Woke up in the infirmary to some little chit bandaging me up when she could have just magicked the bone or whatever back to normal, but never mind. Otherwise, yeah, not a hair out of place."

And there he was—the fae who never shut the fuck up.

Still waiting on our witch, we remained in the common area for another hour. Avery and Blake never made an appearance either, but Deimos didn't come looking for his cronies. In fact, no one left their cells, the block quiet, somber, lacking the usual chatter and laughter from the demon's gang, lacking our hushed conversations at one of the side tables. No cards. No games. No books.

No Katja.

My heart soared when the locks finally *did* clink open again, but it was only Cooper and two other guards I didn't recognize. Williams had taken a shot to the shoulder and leg courtesy of my mate, who was *beyond* sexy when she handled a gun; I'd wanted to slam her into the wall and fuck her raw at the sight of her brandishing a weapon, but then everything had gone to hell so fast it made my head spin.

"Lights-out, inmates," Cooper barked, directing us three toward our cells with a flourish of his wand. "We're on lockdown until tomorrow evening while we fix this fucking *mess*."

None of us moved. We stood there, arms crossed, a united front of three on three—at a huge disadvantage, collars firmly intact, but willing to go down swinging.

"What about Katja?" Rafe hissed, glancing at Fintan and me on either side of him. "Where—"

"*Now*, inmates," Cooper bellowed. Sparks snapped and fizzled from the end of his wand, and he *just* missed Fintan's ear with a jet of neon blue—on purpose, hopefully, because fuck *me* no one's aim could be that bad at this distance. The fae didn't even flinch, but his lip curled.

"She gave in," he said suddenly, just as we three disbanded. Rafe and I stilled, his words panging between us, and Fintan's eyes sparked with bloodlust once more. "She gave in to Guthrie... It's why no one's beaten us or tossed us in solitary. Why this fuck didn't hit me."

"I just figured he was a terrible shot," Rafe mused, glowering at the trio of guards watching us, their wands aimed at our chests.

"He's right," I croaked. So painfully right—that explained everything. Her continued absence. Our unusual welfare. Why Deimos and the others had taken a beating and we were standing here smelling like roses.

She couldn't distance herself from us in here.

But she could do it outside of Xargi.

In Guthrie's clutches, just like that fucking *bastard* wanted.

"She made a deal," Fintan said hoarsely, staring right through the guards, seeming whole galaxies away as he added, "for *us*."

"No one's going to ask you again, shit for brains," one of the unfamiliar guards barked, and right on cue, the three moved in to manually separate us. One stabbed his wand into Rafe's neck, the fizzing electrical buzz reminiscent of a taser. Another went for Fintan, shoving his chest, the jerk of his head making him wince through a noticeably broken nose. When Cooper came for me, I stood strong, immoveable, my inner dragon tearing me apart from the inside, furious and heartbroken and *screaming* for his mate.

Our mate.

Our witch.

Our girl.

Gone.

No.

As Fintan and Rafe dragged their feet toward their cells, I imploded. Clocked Cooper right in the face, his cheekbone shattering under my fist. He went down hard, unconscious, and the other two warlocks pounced as an alarm ripped through the block. I fought with everything I had, snarling and shouting, furious and lost, my mate slipping away from me by the second.

More guards poured into Cellblock C, and the fact that none of them stunned me—only dogpiled on top of me and steamrolled me toward my cell—confirmed everything.

She had sold herself for us.

Sold herself so that we could carry on, incarcerated but safe from a madman.

And I'd never forgive myself for putting her in that situation—for not finding a way to save her sooner.

Don't deserve her. Don't deserve the gift fate gave you.

By the time twelve guards wrestled me into my cell—shocking me in the ribs and the neck with their wands, gut-punching me, boxing me in the kidneys, knocking my knees out from under me again and again, one arm snapped around my neck in a chokehold—every breath plumed black. Smoke seethed from my nostrils. Fire scorched up my throat. I saw through my inner dragon's eyes, the collar's control over us precarious but *there*.

I eventually landed on my hands and knees, coughing up a mouthful of hot blood as the guards bolted. Slammed my cell door. Locked it tight. Caged the beast.

Alone and broken, I raged for her, bellowed something guttural and primal at the top of my lungs, some ancient call forcing all Xargi to tremble before me. Dust sprinkled down on me, and the lightbulb over my quivering cot swung like a violent pendulum. The door shuddered and the window rattled.

But the walls held.

In the end, my mate didn't answer my cry.

And I feared she never would.

29

KATJA

Seated in the back of a chauffeured stretch limo, Tully on my lap and Lloyd to my left, I stared out into the darkness speckled with twinkling starlight—barely visible against the hazy outdoor lighting of Xargi Penitentiary. Slowly, the driver steered us around a curve, headed out from the rear of the building and down the side, on the way to the main front gates. On a death march.

One story ends, another long, horrible one begins. Then the sweet release of death.

I swallowed thickly, hugging Tully to me and sinking into my seat, trying desperately to drown out Lloyd's rambling. He hadn't shut up since we left his office after I ditched the jumpsuit, where his hand had snapped around my arm and hadn't let go until we were in the car. Even though he wasn't touching me anymore, unless you counted his thigh jammed up against mine, I could still feel his fingertips on my skin, bruising into my flesh like claws. I didn't dare look, but tomorrow morning, wherever I was, I knew I would find five purple marks, ugly and glaring, a stark reminder of what I was in for now that I... *belonged* to him.

"And the *view*," he all but moaned, basically talking to himself at this point, infatuated with the sound of his own raspy voice. "Oh, kitten, you're going to love it. Panoramic views from the master bedroom, which we will of course be sharing. I already have a new wardrobe on the way for your walk-in closet. The en suite has this spectacular jetted tub that you'll never want to leave... And then, of course, there's the playroom." I caught his wicked leer out of the corner of my eye. "That's still under construction. I'd be happy to incorporate your thoughts on the design..."

I nodded just to show that I was listening—I wasn't really, but screw him. At no point did I want to do anything that might encourage him to grab me, shake me, or repeat any of the crap that had spewed out of his mouth. Tully carried on kneading my arm, but his claws gritted in harder with Lloyd's gaze sweeping over us.

My familiar hated him.

Hated him—like I'd never seen him hate anyone before. I'd had to bear-hug him to my chest to keep the enormous black cat from shredding Lloyd's face to ribbons the first time they met, and Tully's yowl had ricocheted through the lobby when our new master tried to pat his head. We'd had a talk as I got ready to leave: no hurting Lloyd. It was part of the deal to keep my guys safe, and I couldn't put them at risk. Tully might have adored all three—Rafe in particular—but his connection to me, to my emotions and sorrow and pain, might just push him over the edge.

"I thought it might be a bit *obvious* to go red walls for the playroom," Lloyd said with a luxurious sigh before lunging at the champagne bottle chilling in a nearby holder. "And black is even more cliché, so I've got some color swatches for you to go through tomorrow while I'm at work..."

Biting down hard on the insides of my cheeks, I let my head loll to the side so I could look out the window at the gravel grounds, at the shadowy wolves patrolling the outskirts, on high alert after the riot.

Ugh. He made me sick, just being near him igniting the churn to end all gut churns, but it was my simmering magic that threatened to really mess me up. As agreed, I hadn't been allowed a wand after Lloyd removed my collar in his office, taking his time, hamming up the creep factor with his hands around my neck, his fingers brushing through my hair, his lips caressing my ear with every disgusting word. Once it was gone, my inner well threatened to go nuclear—just spill over and erupt so that magic flooded from every pore. Only I wasn't permitted to cast; nothing big, nothing beyond a few cosmetic glamor spells that Lloyd had approved before he sent me off to change out of my jumpsuit with a hard smack on the ass and a guard watching my every move.

If I didn't let some of this out soon, I'd empty my guts onto his lap—and I just might never stop. My simmering magic needed an out, and it needed it *now*.

But I had to play the part—for Elijah, Rafe, and Fintan. I had to be a good girl if they were going to survive Xargi. Maybe they would find their own way out, and maybe they would serve their full sentences, longer today than they had been yesterday.

All for trying to help me escape...

The familiar burn of tears had me blinking hard and sniffling, tearing my gaze from the window to the front of the limo. With the divider down, the warlock driver was just *there* —and our eyes clashed in the rearview mirror, mine blue, his a chocolate brown that instantly had me thinking of Elijah.

The warmth of his touch.

The comfort of his presence.

The fiery rumble coloring every word—

Only the driver's eyes lacked all of Elijah's warmth, and despite the distance, I could practically feel his stare dripping down my body—right to my cleavage. Humiliation scorched in my cheeks, and I eased Tully up higher to shield myself as Lloyd rambled on and on about the new house. Not that Tully could cover *everything*; Lloyd had shoved a tiny red dress at me before he sent me off to change. Short. Tight. Thin. Useless cap sleeves and a plunging neckline. Easy to predict what my impending wardrobe would consist of if he was doing all the choosing: Lloyd Guthrie wasn't exactly the most imaginative psychopath when it came to womenswear.

He had even given me back the enormous black heels I'd come in with and then insisted I straighten my hair. Add some *color* to my cheeks—I'd supposedly looked a bit pale when we met up tonight. Sickly. *Shocker.*

Shuddering over the gravel, the limo eased around the front of the prison, then straightened out, the guardhouse at the main gates dead ahead. Lloyd would lift the ward to let us pass, and once we were through, Xargi would disappear, forever invisible to the outside world behind the magical barrier. Lips pressed together so they wouldn't wobble, I risked a quick look back at the building that held my fated mate captive. My vampire. My fae—prince or not, I still wasn't sure. And it didn't matter. I loved Fintan for who he was, for his humor and his wit, for his bravery and his audacity. The fact that he *might* be a prince never factored into anything; although Rafe's poetry had certainly endeared me to him that very first night, and I craved his depth ever since.

Gods help me. This was it. The great stone building swam the longer I stared at it, tears blurring everything, making it so much *worse*. I'd never see them again. Never touch them, laugh with them, play cards late into the evening and pretend the rest of the world didn't exist—

Why are you accepting this? I faced forward with a frown, that little whisper at the back of my mind sounding more like me than I had felt in months. She was still in there, the confident business witch who had built Café Crowley from the ground up, who had been profitable for years, who loved her staff and spent most of her days smiling. A lonely witch, sure, but that Katja had been braver than the one sitting in the car tonight.

And it wasn't magic that made her—me—brave. It was gumption and guts. It was taking a risk on a business that could have bankrupted me. It was surviving alone in Seattle, just me and Tully, after the only other member of the Fox coven, the last piece of my heart, was torn away and burned to cinders, Dad's ashes scattered around the roots of a newly potted fern that thrived on my apartment balcony.

I… I could be her again.

Gumption and guts.

Risk.

I had so much to lose now, a found family stuck inside those stone walls, precarious, trapped under Lloyd Guthrie's thumb—same as the Fox coven.

No more.

Be brave, kitten. I'd stopped hearing my dad's voice inside Xargi, but I swore I heard him now, his murmur tickling my ears.

Maybe his spirit had *finally* come back from the beyond, if only to inspire me to *fight*, not flee.

And maybe it was just me missing him—missing the woman I had become after his death.

No more letting others decide my destiny.

My fate was my own. Not Elijah's or Fintan's or Rafe's—and it sure as *hell* didn't belong to Lloyd Guthrie.

This was my story—and no one was coming to save me.

Time to step up and be the heroine, for my sake, for Tully's, and for the men I loved.

Even if, in the end, I might not survive it… at least I'd go down swinging.

Refusing to sink into a mental risk-analysis spreadsheet—because that guardhouse was creeping closer and closer with every cycle of the spinning tires below—I hugged Tully tight. Those huge blue eyes blinked at me, bright and annoyed, and I stared into them, hoping he could sense my intention through our bond. His tail stopped swishing. His kneading paws stilled. A flick of my eyebrow had him *purring* in consent—but that stopped when I glanced pointedly at Lloyd.

We need him, buddy.

Two slashes of his tail, back and forth, to express his discontent.

Then a slow blink, just for me, followed by a flood of warmth I seldom ever felt. After all, Tully hadn't ever needed to protect me so overtly—not until a bunch of bounty hunters waltzed into my café and shipped me off to Siberia so I could become the plaything of a madman. His reach engulfed me, and as soon as it touched Lloyd, the warlock stuttered, no doubt sensing the shift in the air, the swell of familiar magic. Brows furrowed, his head snapped in my direction, and, grinning, I met his eyes unflinchingly.

Just as he opened his mouth—I let go.

Every ounce of pent-up magic exploded out of me, blowing a hole in the roof, shattering windows, ripping the limo apart from the inside. Red and blue and purple blasts of light melded together, not a single spell uttered, just wild, unfettered magic pulsing out of my hands. Gravel filled the air. The front of the limo exploded, engine overheated and overrun by raw, untapped *power*. The explosion ripped us from the back seat, flung us through the air, and we landed hard, even inside Tully's protective bubble, some fifty feet from the totaled vehicle.

With Tully still tucked into my chest, my back took the brunt of the fall. Skidding through rough pebbles and dusty dirt, I grimaced at the pain—which my familiar saw to in an instant, bubble deflating, his focus shifted to my well-being.

And then I felt like I was floating, a strange buoyancy washing over me—yet my feet remained firmly on the ground, rooted in the moment. Pushing up on my elbows, I took a quick scan of the accident site. The limo had disintegrated, its parts scattered across the rocky moat surrounding the penitentiary. Fires smoldered in the ruins, blue flames from my magic clashing with the standard orange that sparked and dimmed along the ground. No warlock driver to be found, but I spotted a puddle of what *might* have once been a person—no longer in solid form, just a huge smear of blood and flesh and tufts of hair.

Floodlights erupted from the four guard towers, bathing the prison grounds in a furious white light. I brought up my hand to shield my eyes, adrenaline skyrocketing at the sound of boots on gravel, men's voices rising, wolves howling.

No going back now.

Something told me Fintan would approve, while the other two would watch on with disapproving looks as they rolled up their sleeves, ready to get their hands dirty.

Each handsome face flashed in my mind's eye, but the courage came from within, much of my rotting magic expulsed, the well regenerating, refueling, as I set Tully aside and crawled for a groaning Lloyd. Flat on his back, the warlock clapped a hand to his forehead, dazed—like Tully's protection had been a halfhearted attempt, just enough to keep him alive but not necessarily well.

Ehh. Not that I could blame him.

Rocks bit into my palms and knees as I rushed to Lloyd, the stupid red dress he had forced me into intact but hiked up, exposing the thong that I'd discovered inside the folded garment.

Just as he started to rise, I scrambled up his body,

straddling Lloyd and yanking his wand from the custom-tailored pocket inside his jacket. Teeth bared, a lioness and no longer the lamb, I jammed the end at his neck. Shock flashed in his eyes, and I fisted his stiff shirt collar and twisted.

"My, my, my," he choked out, hissing softly when I stabbed his wand under his chin and forced his head into the dirt. Still, he had the nerve to *smirk*, to ghost his free hands up my calves to my bare ass. I tugged harder on his collar, fury twining with adrenaline as he whispered, "You surprise me, kitten."

"Don't you ever fucking call me that again," I spat, which only made him chuckle. And you know what, I understood the arrogance. Not only was he a narcissistic sociopath, but he had an army of security closing in, wolves a fun little addition to his ranks.

Well. I had his wand.

And—

Something jabbed into my foot when I bore down on him. Frowning, I lashed back and into his pants pocket; my fingers closed around something cold and metallic.

A Swiss Army knife.

How handy.

Multifaceted, even.

Lloyd stiffened when I straightened with a newly acquired weapon in hand, but his face read like he knew just how to play me.

"What are you going to do with *that*, kitten?"

Tipping my head to the side, I popped out the knife portion, hesitated—then slashed at his throat, nicking his skin *just* enough to unleash a thin dribble of blood. It crept down his neck and plumed over his shirt collar. Lloyd flailed as if to roll me off, but I stabbed his wand to his temple, then pressed the knife back to the open wound with a little more pressure. The skin warped and split beneath the blade, another spurt of blood painting the silver red.

"You move, you look at me like you usually do, you cast *anything*, and I'll slit your throat," I growled, ignoring the incoming storm of boots and paws. When Lloyd just stared at me through murderous grey eyes, all the horrible things he planned to do to me after this if I failed playing across them like a black-and-white film, I pressed hard and zapped him with his own wand. Just a simple jolt, a little hex that first years learned at the academy to shock their friends with, like dragging your feet across carpet and poking someone. He flashed his teeth. I arched an eyebrow. "Do you understand? *Answer*, you piece of shit."

Prowling around Lloyd's head, Tully suddenly stopped and hissed. Ten feet away, a charging guard went down, clutching at his throat and writhing on the gravel like he was choking. It was only then that I noticed how close they were.

"*Subsisto*," I murmured, sweeping Lloyd's wand in a circle around us. Even with a conduit, my magic was more unstable than usual, firing from the tip like a hailstorm of bullets. Each guard it hit not only froze in place, but they were hurled back like rag dolls. Tully, meanwhile, had entered a staring contest with the nearest wolf shifter, the imposing figure dark grey and larger than all the rest—the alpha. Collarless, the wolf bared his teeth, same as Lloyd—and my familiar doubled in size, standing his ground and uttering a low warning growl.

One step toward my familiar and I hit the wolf with another stunning spell. Lloyd's wand resisted to a degree, shivering in my hand, intentionally throwing my aim. It preferred its owner to a stranger, but my magic was just a shitstorm of *power* at this point, pent-up and highly aggressive, bullying its way through the conduit whether the wand wanted us or not.

What I wouldn't give for *my* wand, which was hopefully still sitting in my desk drawer, untouched by any of my human employees—or some super who came sniffing around the café in my absence.

"*Heard*, Katja," Lloyd gritted out with a stiff smile. "I hear you. I respect you—"

"Good." As if he actually respected me: his hands were still on my ass. Eyes narrowed, I reached back and zapped each, and he shoved his fists into the gravel as if to make a point. A cool breeze decided then was the opportune time to rip across the prison grounds, ruffling my stick-straight hair and whooshing over my exposed thighs, and I resisted the urge to tug down my dress. "Now that I have your attention… Take down the ward."

Lloyd gawked at me for a beat, then snorted. "You can't be serious."

I pursed my lips, then dug his knife into his throat. Lloyd twitched and kicked out beneath me, hissing as I sliced a few inches of flesh open, a stronger gush of blood pouring down his neck and watering the earth. For once, the anxiety churn was gone, replaced by a very welcome *focus*, anger and intent melding with the adrenaline, steadying my hand and centering my thoughts.

"*Katja Fox*," he hissed, twisting his head like that would even do anything, his tone leaning more toward harsh father figure than the gross *daddy* he had been masquerading as ever since we'd met, "you stop this immediately—"

"You have time to sort out the bleeding," I mused as I flicked the blade under his chin, opening up a line of red there too. "It's not deep enough to do any real damage… yet."

I tapped his cheek with his wand when his hands shot up, then readjusted my thighs so that my knees dug into his arms, pinning them. Then, with Tully circling, guards positioning themselves all around us, half the wolves slinking off and the others sniffing at their stunned alpha, I set his wand tip *right* over his eye. Xargi had taught me so much about myself, about my capabilities without magic—and I didn't need to utter a damn thing to maim him. I just needed to jab his wand into his eye and press until something popped.

"Remove the ward," I repeated. My calm firmness promised that this was the *last* time I would tell him. The way he flinched, the dance of the bulge in his throat with a not so subtle gulp, suggested the message hit home.

But Lloyd had run a criminal empire before this. Threats probably bounced right off him, especially with his cronies lining up to take the shot.

To put me out of my misery.

Not today, boys.

Lloyd called my bluff; he did nothing but stare, goading me to make a move. So, eyeing the small army of warlocks clustering around us, I removed the blade from his neck, wiped it clean on his stubble, blood smeared up his cheekbones like blush, and then placed it on the other side of his throat. Lips pursed, I poked at a few spots, then looked him dead in the eye.

"I'm sure you know the *exact* pressure needed to sever the carotid," I said with a sigh, leaning on the blade while stabbing his wand into his cheek—right between his teeth, just as he'd done to me with his disgusting fingers time and time again, squeezing my jaw and forcing my lips open. "You just let me know if you feel your life slipping away and I'll—"

"Katja," he choked, *kitten* a distant memory as he stared up at me with rounded eyes. I shrugged, breaking the first bit of skin with a cavalier slash.

"I have nothing to lose," I whispered, then leaned in close

enough to brush his ear with every word. "And don't ever speak my name again."

This man had killed my parents, my brothers. He planned to make me some sex slave, just another piece of property, a pretty doll to screw whenever the urge struck. He had already taken everything from me, but still came back for *more*.

And he had threatened my guys.

A part of me wanted to just drive the blade in, consequences be damned, and deal with the ward some other way.

Maybe he saw that, how close I was to the brink, seconds from going nuclear, because Lloyd sucked in a stuttering breath, then flicked his gaze pointedly toward his wand.

"I'll need that to remove the ward."

"*Good boy*," I sneered, easing it away from his face and flipping it between my fingers, offering him the stupid ivory handle. "If you do anything beyond that, you know what happens."

Shifting in place, I allowed his right arm out from under me, then gave him only enough leeway to prop himself up on his elbow. As soon as his hand coiled around his wand, I slashed at his throat again, and right on cue, Tully appeared at our sides, glaring the warlock down, unblinking and huge, his magical aura almost suffocating.

"What do you hope to accomplish here?" Lloyd murmured with a shake of his head, patronizing as hell. "Your lovers are still collared. You would condemn them to a life without magic or access to their inner—"

Rolling my eyes, I drove the Swiss Army knife into his neck—just the tip—and glared down at him as another rush of cold calm fury washed over me. If he thought pinning the blame on *me*, like he hadn't concocted this whole batshit scheme just to make a dollar, would somehow soften my hand, Lloyd Guthrie was delusional.

With a hiss and a scowl, Xargi Penitentiary's warden jabbed his wand straight up. "*Exsolvo tutela.*"

A jet of white shot out of his wand, straight as an arrow and thick as the floodlights sweeping the prison grounds. It collided with the ward's domed top, then flared out, skittering like lightning, cracking the magical barrier just as Lloyd's rage had splintered his office windows only a few hours earlier. As soon as the light touched the ground, it dissolved into a gentle mist, taking with it the ward and the invisibility it projected over the building, over Lloyd's supernatural abomination.

His work camp.

His death camp.

My vision blurred briefly, relief seeping into the inferno raging inside, and my hold on the knife loosened just enough that Lloyd seemed to think he was allowed to sit—

Purple fire suddenly exploded in the ward's place, shooting up from the ground, bright and furious. I shrieked at the onslaught, magenta flames circling Xargi, obliterating the guardhouse as it blazed through, reeking of old magic and wanton destruction.

Seconds later, horns—a whole symphony of baying horns from the other side, blasting through the ten-foot-tall ring of fire and threatening to burst an eardrum. I clapped my hands over my ears, same as Lloyd, and braced against the attack.

"What are you *doing*?" I shouted, replacing my hand with my shoulder so that I could shove the knife back at his neck. Only the threat didn't seem to hold the same weight anymore; Lloyd sat up fully, eyes wide, the firestorm reflecting in his bewildered greys.

"That..." He shook his head, bloodied and panicked, me still straddling his lap and his half-hard cock, not a lewd comment to be heard. "That is *not* me."

30

FINTAN

At the first blast of a fae war horn, I thought I was dreaming.

Only I was awake.

Stretched out on my cot, head pillowed on my folded arms, the last however many hours spent ruminating the failings of today—I could have sworn this was just another rescue dream. But my eyes were open, and I hadn't nodded off and holy *shit* had the cavalry *finally* arrived?

Took them bloody long enough.

"I know those horns," I whispered to no one in particular, staring up at the depressing ceiling, at the extinguished lonely bulb that had kept me company come nightfall all these many months. *The Host of Horns*—heralds of doom and triumph and tragedy. Markers of ceremony and parades. The collective voices of all the court as my father rode into the night with his raiding party, off to pillage lesser kingdoms, conquest in his eyes and savagery in his heart.

I had heard those fucking trumpets all my life—and I'd never been happier for their existence than this very moment.

All the frustration for today's failing ebbed. The fear for

Katja's fate—gone. In their place, exhilaration. I rolled off my cot, light and bouncy on my toes, and practically skipped to my cell's tiny window. Wildfire raged in place of the ward, lavender flames snapping at a black sky, spurred by the horns, by the army undoubtedly waiting on the other side. I grinned. My brother's best friend and lifelong confidant had recently ascended to the Master of Midnight—the court's high priest, the maestro of magic and history. When Rollo became king, this dramatic shit would be his chief advisor.

No one put on a show like the Master of Midnight.

His violet sea struck terror into the hearts of our enemies, burning brighter than the stars and hot as dragonfire.

The horns intensified, varied in pitch and depth, a war song bleating from their mouths…

I snorted. Rollo must have been fucking *fuming* to still be in the mortal realm after all these many months, waiting, searching, charged with bringing his wayward baby brother back to court. The ward could have hidden me away for good, but in its absence…

Invasion.

For my kidnapping was a declaration of *war*.

How fun.

A few cells down, Elijah started up again. He had been bellowing for his mate ever since they locked him away—not that I could blame him. His inner dragon was probably driving him up the wall, raging over the fact that a competitor had stolen her.

Well.

We would see about *that*, wouldn't we? I'd never stuck a foe's head on a spike before, but I would do so with Guthrie. Let Rafe or Elijah cleave it from its perch, then plop it on top of a spear with the Midnight Court's banner fluttering below. Yes—*plan*.

Just as I eased away from the window, bored with the

maestro's same old tricks already, battle lust simmering in my heart, there came a mighty crash from Elijah's direction. Hands threaded behind my back, broken nose on fucking fire, I sauntered toward my sealed door and pressed an ear to the wood, then flinched back when another *thud* reverberated through the walls, the door's rattle drowned out by a cry that teetered between dragon and man. *Thrilling*, really. If only we could remove these collars—I'd give my left nut to see Elijah shift.

Dragons were so rare these days, even in my realm.

More thumps. More roars. Metal splintering and springs groaning.

Then *thunder* ripped through the cellblock, followed by the pitter-patter of wood chips raining down on the floor.

Had he…?

Had he broken through the door?

Such a magnificent battering ram, Elijah Greystone.

How fortunate that he had fated with Katja; I couldn't rescue her all by myself, and there was no one more tenacious than a shifter on a mission to find his mate.

"Back in your cell, inmate!"

Ahh, Cooper, you dumb bastard. Positively giddy, I pressed against my cell door again, listening to the telltale echoes of flying fists and a snarling shifter. Blasts of magic illuminated the doorframe briefly, followed by a mannish squeal that had me snorting again.

Then silence.

I pushed closer, ignoring the throb of pain through my entire damn face, then reared back when the door unbolted and slid open. Same as it did every morning. Only we were far off from dawn; it was nearing midnight—my *favorite* hour.

Tiptoeing out of my cell, I paused at the sight before me: Elijah holding warlock Cooper in a headlock, both panting, their hair askew, cheeks red, the cretin's wand a few feet away on the floor, forgotten. Then—a sharp jerk, and the guard who had gone out of his way to make our lives miserable, who once flicked lit matches at me in the shower, crumpled to a heap on a dragon's feet, neck snapped, eyes vacant.

Yes. Things were about to get *awesome*.

I met Elijah's slitted gaze with a grin and a bow, deference given where deference was due—for I stood before a true alpha whose eyes glowed with a raging wildfire. He had, in fact, busted his cell door clean off its hinges, then, if all the other open doors were any indication, had bullied Cooper into opening the rest before offing him.

Fantastic.

"You know," I mused, sauntering a few paces toward the fallen warlock, "we could have *maybe* used him."

"Are you seriously going to lecture me about hindsight?" Elijah speared a hand through his rumpled golden locks, eyebrows shooting up. "Really? *You*?"

"Just cut his arm off," Rafe insisted, stalking out his cell's doorway without a backward glance—hopefully for the last time if me and Elijah had anything to say about it. The poet vampire didn't exactly strike me as a warrior, but he had beat the snot out of Deimos for attacking Katja, so perhaps the dragonfire that bound us all together sparked in his dead heart too. Time would tell. He slowed on the other side of a table, tapping his fingers on the metal surface with a shrug. "I mean, we only need his arm with that tattoo… Maybe it'll unlock something besides the ward."

"Ward's down," I said absently, totally transfixed on Elijah as he grabbed Cooper's limp arm, shoved the sleeve down, and then stomped on his elbow hard enough to snap the bone like a twig. He then tore the tattooed forearm off at the joint, spraying blood like a tidal wave. Satisfaction rippled between the three of us when Elijah hucked the arm to his friend, who then tipped his head back and opened his mouth, holding the severed arm up and guzzling the free-flowing red like a starving man devoured his first meal.

Fair enough. The poor fuck had been in this cesspit for the better part of a year now; perhaps this truly *was* his first real meal in all that time. The pittance served in the dining hall could hardly sustain a vampire long-term.

"Wait…" Elijah wiped his bloody hands on his jumpsuit with a frown, dragon eyes locked on me. "Did you say the ward is down?"

"I think it's a fair assumption." How else could the Master of Midnight pull off that display? "And I think we have a foxy little witch to thank for that… There's more to our girl than we thought."

Feisty vixen, Katja Fox. She had enjoyed brandishing a weapon during today's revolt a little *too* much to ever go back to the life of a boring café owner. The look exchanged between Rafe and Elijah suggested that her fire was nothing new, that they had *known* she was a warrior all along. I rolled my eyes. Sure. She was a saucy creature in her own right, but no need to diminish her glory in battle *now*.

"And that infernal racket?"

"The Host of Horns," I remarked, my grin sharpening when Rafe winced against the second wave of trumpets. "My brother's here… Most likely with the court's army backing him. I *told* you pricks I was a prince."

"For fuck's sake," Elijah muttered, his eye roll near identical to Rafe's, but at least they had the decency to smirk while they did it. Perhaps they had believed me all along. Perhaps they just liked riling me up.

No one had ever purposefully riled me up before except my sisters.

All the other sniveling courtiers, my various entourages through the centuries, focused on placating me.

More proof that I had found my tribe—my *true* friends.

"Well, just wait until you meet him," I carried on. "Honestly, he's *so* stiff and boring and proper… Rafe, you're going to love him."

The vampire straightened, blood smeared over that strong chin and rugged jaw, down his neck, severed forearm in one hand—and he then hoisted his middle finger with the other, eyes narrowed. I snorted just as the other inmates slowly made their way out of their cells. While the bird shifters lingered in the doorways, meek as ever, assessing the scene before them in silence, Deimos strode right into the common area like he owned it, demonic swagger intact, and his maenad sycophant pranced along after him.

"Gentlemen," he purred, eyeing each one of us intensely, no doubt calculating the risks of what was about to come out of that foul mouth. "We appear to be allies in the end, no matter how temporarily, no matter our history…"

This fuck.

He had the sheer *audacity* to…

Every jovial bone in my body steeled at the memory of Katja's battered face, her shriek of pain as I caught her around the torso when Rafe returned from his… operation. The aftermath of it all, the poking and prodding from Deimos and his cronies. Katja shuffling around the greenhouse, broken, her injuries only tightening Guthrie's noose around her. Rafe's sudden lisp without his fangs—Constance parroting it whenever she had the chance as Deimos cackled at her side.

Ordinarily I let drama and turmoil slide…

But this fucking *fuck*.

No matter our history.

For the first time, history mattered to me. It mattered so deeply that it had already scarred into my marrow, something to haunt me for the rest of my days.

I had never cared enough about anyone before to consider exacting revenge, but in that moment, a burning vengeance drummed inside me. It shrouded the edges of my vision, darkness billowing, tunneling my focus to the demon who I had fantasized about gutting and stringing up by his own entrails.

My eyes slid over to Rafe, then Elijah. None of us said a word—we just *moved*. Rafe and I had speed at our backs, my fae wings hidden in this realm and tapered down by the collar, which resulted in me and the vampire blitzing toward Deimos as one, as equals.

Constance abandoned him immediately, skipping back to her cell in a flourish of bright pink hair, her grey jumpsuit melding with the shadows.

"Now, now, *wait*..." Deimos retreated slowly, as if he didn't take our threat seriously—like he thought he could *talk* his way out of this. That hit close to home. Now I saw it, how fucking annoying it was to listen to someone prattle on when they should really just shut their bloody mouth. The demon held up his hands innocently, fingers splayed wide and weaponless. "Gentlemen, I can make life *very* comfortable for you outside of these walls—"

Rafe and I reached him first, closing in on either side. His charm vanished in a flash, replaced by demonic fury. Eyes wholly black, he bared his teeth and lashed out, taking generous swipes with nails that were *far* too sharp by prison dress code regulations. Ten little blades slashed at us, but I dodged and weaved with ease, snapping one hand around his wrist and the other just below his shoulder joint. Rafe mirrored my hold on the other side, and when our eyes met, the brooding poet finally offered a smile worthy of his predator status.

"Ready, Mr. O'Dwyer?" I crooned, Deimos wriggling and snarling and struggling between us. Rafe wrenched his arm straight, as did I, and the vampire closed his eyes for a moment, as if to really take it all in. When they opened again, bloodlust shone bright.

"*Ready*, my prince."

I cocked an eyebrow. Was the sarcasm *really* necessary? Elijah's chuckle as he strolled toward us suggested so, a little bit of brotherly ribbing before we got down to business. *Fine*. I'd probably never escape my title with this lot, and with them, *prince* wasn't a term of endearment.

But I needed that.

So desperately.

"One," I started.

"Two," Rafe growled.

"Wait, wait, we can make a deal," Deimos cried, jerking harder, black eyes snapping between us. "Please, we—"

"*Three*." Elijah's low snarl spurred us on, and we ripped both arms out of their sockets in tandem, unleashing another wave of blood with which to drown Cellblock C. Only the spray was black this time, spattering across our jumpsuits, our faces, up our arms, hot and sticky and scented faintly of death. Rafe made no move to lick the black splotches away—apparently even starving men had their limits—and Deimos howled loud enough to make the block tremble, his pain a chorus of varying baritone timbres.

Music to my pointy fae ears, honestly.

Deimos folded to his knees, jumpsuit sleeves fluttering around him like useless wings. Slowly, his gaze soared to an approaching Elijah, and for once, he held his tongue.

Dying beasts always sensed the end.

Without a word, Elijah gripped the demon's face, twisted hard left, then right, then left again. He planted a foot on Deimos's chest, pinning him to the wall—and cleaved his fucking head straight off his shoulders. Bone and cartilage came loose with a squishy *pop*, spinal cord snapping, and as soon as Deimos's head left his body, Elijah tossed it aside like the piece of garbage he was. No pomp. No ceremony. No parting words or victorious grins.

Just another day at Xargi—taking out the trash.

Magnificent.

Behind Rafe, I spied the maenad loitering in her cell doorway, caressing herself, eyes wild and manic, full mouth kicked into a seductive pout. No surprise that carnage got her off given her kind's history, and before Katja, before Elijah and Rafe's companionship, that was a mare I would have happily ridden until sunrise.

Now, when Elijah took a menacing step toward her and she scampered into her cell with a crazed giggle, I let her go —happily.

"So…" I clapped my hands together, beaming at the pair, at the brothers I had *chosen*. "Who's ready to meet the family?" The pair swapped wary looks, and I patted Elijah on the chest as I breezed toward the cellblock's main door, soaked in demon blood and ready for more. "Don't be nervous, boys… The future king of the Midnight Court is going to *love* you."

31

KATJA

Shimmering teal arrows cut through magenta flames, humming with magic, shot from unseen archers beyond the wall. Their tail feathers cut through the air with a whistle that reminded me of clear, high bells, razor-sharp tips slicing into warlocks like pins through paper, and imploded as soon as they hit the penitentiary. Stone blasted, spiraling and splintering, little pieces of that hellhole stark against a purple backdrop—the most beautiful firework display I had ever seen.

Seconds later, warriors charged through the fire, untouched by its raging heat, the baying horns at their zenith. Fear solidified me on top of Lloyd, and we both just sat there, helpless, watching as an army invaded the prison grounds, as it washed over all in its path like raging floodwaters. Most of the warlock guards bolted as soon as the invaders appeared, sprinting in all directions, collared wolf shifters at their heels, anarchy unfurling beneath the relentless floodlights.

Dressed in lightweight steel armor, flexible at the joints and stamped with stars, the warriors showed no mercy—they cleaved down anyone who stood against them with swords and axes and arrows forged by magic. Lloyd's warlock cronies took a few out, blasts of color zipping around the once silent grounds, but then a second charge poured in from the left of the prison, then the right, more trumpets erupting from the rear. They had the place surrounded, the fire holding us all in. No escape. Nowhere to run.

Lloyd suddenly shoved me off his lap with a snarl. Gravel bit into my bare arm when I landed, shoulder taking the worst of it, but he had barely twisted around and away before I jabbed the Swiss Army knife into his calf. He went down with a shout, fumbling, blood painting the little grey stones at our feet, and I crawled after him, frantic but focused, to snatch the wand from his hand. Like hell he was just going to slip off into the night while all of us were slaughtered.

Nope. Not today, asshole.

Trembling, I staggered to my feet. Even if my knees were seconds from buckling, I still shoved Lloyd's wand in his furious face and shook my head.

"Don't you fucking *move*."

"I have a panic room underground, kitten," he growled. "We can go there—"

"*Mutus*," I hissed. A burst of soft yellow struck him in the mouth, sealing his lips until I undid the spell. There were less invasive spells to keep someone quiet, but I needed him totally mute until I decided otherwise—not something that might fade at the most inopportune time.

Like when the small band of warriors peeling away from the rest finally made it to us. Drawing in a shaky breath, I kept Lloyd's wand at his throat, ready to knock him out if necessary, then halfheartedly tugged down my dress so I was at least sort of covered by the time the squadron arrived.

The warrior at the helm was the tallest of the bunch, his helmet the most ornate, insanely detailed with the star patterning and a deep indigo mane trailing down his back, threads of dark purple and blue spilling out the top of his helmet, blending together like the midnight sky…

I blinked hurriedly, mouth falling open. *Midnight.*

Had Fintan been honest with us this whole time?

Flanked by two armored guards carrying flagstaffs with fluttering material at their spiked tips, a constellation of stars against a black backdrop, the warrior went for his helmet, which had only left his eyes visible in slits…

And the second he removed it, I saw Fintan. Not *exactly* the fae I loved, but an obvious relative. Older, gruffer, more weathered in the face, he had the same brilliant shamrock-green gaze I had fallen for that first day. Thick, luxurious hair spilled down to his armored shoulders, a shade darker than I'd expected—the espresso to Fintan's warm French roast. Not a stitch of facial stubble, clean-shaven with the same rugged jawline that I loved to rake my nails over during a toe-curling kiss. Handsome. Regal. He carried himself like a king.

Oh, *gods*, Fintan had been honest from the start.

While I held up one shaking hand in surrender, I kept the one with the wand on a seated Lloyd. The bastard at my feet motioned frantically to his mouth like someone might actually help him, while Tully wove protectively around my ankles, which wobbled in these stupidly high heels.

"Be still, mortals," the fae barked, the wind brushing his mane aside just briefly enough to show a pair of delicately pointed ears. "I am Prince Rollo of the—"

"Midnight Court?" I offered, throwing caution to the wind and *hoping*, just this once, things would go our way. Those bright greens zeroed in on me, and I swallowed hard as every ounce of color drained from my face. Terrifying, the intensity of his stare, the weight of it threatening to crush me into the gravel. As if posture created an air of authority, I rolled my shoulders back and lifted my chin. "Are you by any chance here for *Fintan* of the Midnight Court?"

Mercifully, the horns had died down, still bleating but at half the volume, musicians in battle armor flitting around the warriors charging for the main building. Already, someone had planted a black flag on one of the guard towers, a heap of bloody, broken warlocks piled at its base.

"My youngest brother, yes," Rollo growled, taking a menacing step toward us. While Lloyd flinched back, knocking into my legs, I held firm—not like I could move even if I wanted to, fear rooting me in place. Tully hissed at Xargi's former warden, then puffed up when purple fire erupted at the penitentiary's front door. While Rollo's men cast the flames quick glances, the prince refused to look away from me. "You have illegally detained a member of the royal court—"

"He's inside," I insisted, wand stabbing into the back of Lloyd's head. "I can show you."

Rollo's eyes narrowed, his scrutiny falling on me like a ton of bricks, and that deepening frown spoke volumes. Not that I could blame him if he was suspicious: given how I was dressed and the mute, bleeding warlock at my feet… Hardly a crystal-clear situation he'd stumbled into.

"Fintan and I… We…" Oh, gods, how to describe it to his *brother*. "We, uh… I…"

Lloyd's head snapped up, splitting his neck wounds open again just so he could sneer at me—petty bastard. Rollo, meanwhile, seemed to soften, his handsome mouth twitching like he was holding back a smile. With a flick of his hand, the fae warriors at his back sheathed their swords.

"Ah," he murmured with a knowing nod, and just like that, color raced back to my cheeks like a blazing comet. Humiliation burned at what he must have suddenly thought of me in this skimpy red dress—what Fintan's reputation implied about the nature of our connection. Sure, we'd had phenomenal sex in the world's grossest bathroom, but it had only happened once—with all of them. One fleeting moment of intimacy in a hellscape of Lloyd Guthrie's design, yet I loved them from months of conversation and card games and shared work shifts, from countless meals in the dining hall.

I was *not* his brother's prison floozy.

So, I didn't deserve that *look*.

Rollo offered me his hand, armored glove and all. "Come along, then, little witch. Take me to him."

"We..." Oi, was the whole family this hot? Nothing like having *those* looks and a title to boot. If he was single, women must have waged wars just to claim him. While Lloyd huffed and shifted about at my feet, I did my damnedest not to let this prince see just how much his handsomeness and control flustered me. "Fintan and I were cellmates in the penitentiary. We're friends..." Rollo's dark brow cocked like he didn't believe me even a little. "We... Okay, more than friends. Anyway. Doesn't matter." Gods, how embarrassing. "We need to remove his shackles before he leaves. These bastards charmed collars to stifle all our powers. And *this* one..." I poked Lloyd in the back of the head again in lieu of kicking him as hard as I could in the kidney. "He's running the show—and he holds all the keys."

Probably.

Me and the boys had speculated what powered the collars many times over. Sure, the sigils engraved in the leather were what hindered our abilities, but something else charbroiled inmates when they tried to take them off. Just because the ward was down didn't mean any of us were truly free.

If those collars stayed, Xargi Penitentiary would haunt the men I loved to the end of their days.

Lloyd had removed mine personally. Disappeared into a little room behind one of the bookshelves in his office, then emerged less than a minute later to peel my collar off like a fucking perv.

Couldn't be all that complicated a process, then—right?

Before I could share that little tidbit with Rollo, the fae prince swept forward, beyond intimidating in his armor, a massive sword sheathed at his side and a trio of curved blades hanging from his belt, the glint in his eye murderous. His gloved hand found Lloyd's hair, even as the warlock flailed in protest, and hauled him upright like the man who had tormented the Fox coven for decades weighed nothing. He then shoved Lloyd toward Xargi as inmates sprinted from the side doors, falling to the ground before fae warriors, crawling toward salvation. Midnight Court flags topped the main building, Lloyd's disgusting experimental prison utterly overrun.

"*Walk,*" Rollo barked. After another rough shove toward Xargi, the fae pointed a finger at me, not an ounce of warmth in his voice as he added, "You too, witch. And if either of you cast, you die..."

"So, he's actually a prince, huh?"

When I woke up this morning, miserable and alone and fighting to stay away from the three men who made my heart sing, I never would have thought *this* was how the day would have gone. A prison riot. Conceding to Lloyd—then literally and magically kicking his ass. A fae army invasion and meeting Fintan's big brother.

And now here we were, striding through the fancier corridors of Xargi Penitentiary as the prison came apart all around us.

Rollo had sent men out to find his brother already, but freed inmates raced through the halls, blitzing by us and their muzzled, limping warden, desperate to get outside. Guards ran. Some fought, but they paled in comparison to Rollo's garrison. The main man himself, meanwhile, strode alongside me, all armored up, his helmet tucked under one arm and Lloyd at the end of the other. He had maintained his grip on Lloyd's neck all this time, through run-ins with warlock guards and brief interludes with escaped prisoners. At one point, sirens screamed through the halls. Then they stopped—and they hadn't started since.

Situated at the front of the group, elite fae warriors at my back, the future king of the Midnight Court to my left, and Tully in my arms, I could have sworn this was a dream. A fantasy, even, to see Lloyd bleeding and tethered, trapped in Rollo's metal grasp, the sigils on each armored finger suggesting they kept the warlock from teleporting.

Not that he had the chance to really hunker down and focus enough to dematerialize from Xargi and reappear somewhere else. Rollo refused him an inch of leeway, shoving him along, kicking him when he faked a fall. Even now, as we climbed the stairs from the prison's guest foyer, checkered floors and marble columns behind us and Lloyd's office at the end of the shadowy corridor ahead, he rushed Xargi's warden along, not caring—barely even noticing—if he stumbled. Instead, he seemed distracted by me for the first time since we had breached the prison as an invading force, glancing down at me with a frown.

Quite a ways down, at that: I'd abandoned those stupid heels, my feet and calves unable to take the strain after months of flat soles, and someone had snatched Lloyd's wand from me seconds after Rollo threatened to kill us if we cast.

"What do you—"

"I mean, he introduced himself as a prince," I insisted, readjusting my hold on Tully, arms trembling at his substantial heft. It had been *ages* since I carried him around like a baby for this long, and from the swish of his tail, the tenseness of his entire body, and the calculating look in his big blues, he wasn't exactly relishing the special treatment like he used to. "But honestly, we all thought Fintan was full of shit. Because, you know, no offense, but that bird likes to chirp."

Rollo slowed as we neared the top of the stairs, scrutinizing me for a moment before his wary confusion shattered, replaced by a wry grin and a strange twinkle in his green gaze. "I misjudged you, little witch."

I lifted my chin ever so slightly. "Katja."

Prince Rollo offered a nod, his movements regal—almost exaggeratedly so compared to his brother. "Katja."

We paused at the very top of the staircase, the whole garrison halting, a moment of mutual understanding passing between us as our eyes met. When we started up again, I walked a little taller, my footfalls silent compared to the constant thunder of heavy footwear on tile and armor clinking with every step.

Seriously. How weird was this day?

"That's his office," I said, pointing to the closed door at the end of the hall. Once again, Lloyd tried to twist and squirm out of Rollo's hold, but that only earned him a rough thrashing, the fae prince slamming him up against the wall and trapping him in place.

"Why isn't he speaking?"

"I took his voice." I shrugged when Rollo glanced back at me, blooming like a wildflower under the first rays of morning sunshine; after all, I could have *sworn* he was impressed with me—but maybe I was finally impressed with myself. "It just seemed best for everyone not to hear his poison, you know?"

If looks could kill, I'd have just died ten times over from

the glare Lloyd hurled my way. Despite the panic flashing through me, I glared right back, because *fuck* him. Even Tully hissed, swiping his huge paw in Lloyd's direction, claws extended and thirsty for warlock blood. Rollo, meanwhile, watched the whole interaction with a smirk, even chuckling softly when things settled, patting Lloyd on his bloody, grimy cheek before hauling him off the wall and thrusting him down the corridor.

While the office door was locked, Rollo had two of his men shoulder through, splintering the wood and ripping the hinges off the wall. For months this place had tormented me, made me sick with just the smell of the books and leather and mahogany. Now, striding into it ahead of Lloyd and Rollo, it wasn't that scary. Just a room, all the crap righted and back in place after Lloyd's tantrum. Just a boring, nondescript *room*. An office designed by the same decorator who did TV sets, it was *that* pretentious.

"Show him," I ordered, motioning to the bookshelf Lloyd had vanished behind before he removed my collar an hour ago. "Show him what's back there."

Rollo charged across the room, dragging Lloyd along by the neck and shoving him into the shelves next to the hearth behind his desk. Trembling, the rumpled warlock grabbed at the bookshelf's siding—and just *opened* it. He hadn't even bothered to charm it closed, and for some reason, that made me *furious*.

Knowing now how easy it was—that our salvation was behind an unlocked door in a madman's office…

Before any of us could slip into the secret passage that bookworms fantasized about all their lives, Lloyd rounded in place with some difficulty, then tapped at his throat.

"Does he need to speak?" Rollo growled, slamming him into the brick hearth, the back of his head making a solid *whump* on impact. Lloyd, however, just stared at me, full psychopath raging behind the flint, pain his aphrodisiac—or was it only *my* pain that got him hard?

"Doubt it," I muttered, setting Tully down on Lloyd's desk with a scowl, then crossing my arms. "I can give it back if that's what you want."

With a hurried nod, the fae's patience finally started to wane more openly, and I swished my hand in Lloyd's direction. The movement was halfhearted, the *Loquere* incantation flat and emotionless, but my magic struck him like a runaway bus. A burst of bright yellow slammed into his face, busting his lower lip and blackening an eye.

Yikes.

Should probably get that under control. Cheeks hot, I glanced back at the warrior keeping Lloyd's wand captive; the spell would have been neater with a conduit, but I wasn't particularly bothered about the injuries it inflicted—more the implication that Fintan's girl wasn't as skilled a witch as they might have hoped.

"There isn't much space inside," Lloyd croaked, smearing his bloody lip along the top of his hand—addressing Rollo but glowering at me. "Your garrison should wait here."

"My lord," one of the warriors protested, but Rollo's swift dismissal, nothing more than a raised hand, silenced any protests.

"Show me," he ordered, and Lloyd cocked his head to the side, finally looking at the prince with an all-too-familiar smugness that made my skin crawl.

"Wouldn't you rather make a deal?"

As if that was the tipping point, Rollo grabbed him by the front of his perfectly pressed shirt, then *hurled* him through the bookshelf opening, stalking in furiously at his heels. While I hadn't been invited, I sprinted after the pair, morbid curiosity and desperation forcing my hand.

In all the time that I had known Lloyd Guthrie on a

disgustingly personal level, he struck me as honest. He relished the gory details of my family's past. He delighted in sharing all the sick, twisted things he planned to do to me outside of Xargi. He defanged Rafe, and I had zero doubt he would have made good on all the other threats he raised against the dragon and fae I loved if I hadn't given in to him…

So when he had said the space behind the bookshelf was tight, he wasn't lying: the three of us barely fit, the square footage made even smaller when Tully came prowling in. Lit by a single soft orange light hanging somewhere way up high, the room was narrow but exceedingly tall, magicked to fit the narrow shelves creeping up three of the four walls. Free-floating and less than a foot in length, hundreds of little wooden blocks dotted the walls, and on each sat glowing crystals of all colors and sizes, the shelves stamped with a small copper plate.

Etched into the copper: a number.

Identification for each inmate.

A crystal assigned to a number… powering the collars.

Magic vibrated in the air, unseen but present, foul enough to make my stomach turn.

"Oh, *gods,*" I whispered, a hand over my mouth, eyes watering. Every trip to the cafeteria was a reminder of just how many supers and shifters the Guthrie empire had kidnapped since Xargi Penitentiary opened, but seeing it all now, dozens upon dozens of crystals pulsing with power and color in the shadowy room like we were standing in some screwed-up nightclub…

It hurt.

And it put things into a painful perspective. I hadn't seen Willow in almost a month; was she one of these crystals, or had she tried to remove her collar? Did the color dim when an inmate died? Were the unused crystals then tossed outside, just a bit of useless rock, lost in the pebbles that guards and wolves stomped all over without a care in the world?

"What was my number, you bastard?" I demanded, voice wavering for the first time since I climbed on top of him and slashed at his throat. The warlock peered around Rollo with a sneer.

"You were unassigned, kitten," Lloyd purred, totally unfazed when Rollo slammed him into one of the walls, a handful of crystals tumbling to the floor around him. "Never officially an inmate—just a guest of the warden… I kept you safe in my pocket most days."

He patted at his chest, at the hidden pocket my crystal must have sat in.

Close to his heart.

Ugh *gross*.

"Enough," Rollo barked, his voice like a cracking whip. "Give me my brother's crystal—I assume its destruction will remove his shackles?"

"That's the basic premise, yes." Lloyd squirmed in the fae's grasp, his shirt collar stained red as his neck wounds continued to ooze. "Unfortunately, I can't recall Fintan of the Midnight Court's inmate number off the top of my head… If you'd let me peruse the records, then maybe—"

Rollo went off like a bomb, detonating a blast of primal fae magic that knocked me back into the door and shattered every crystal in the room. Like the east wind exhaling across a grassy plain, *power* whooshed through the tiny space, whipping our hair around, the tassels hanging off his helmet dancing. Crystals reduced to powder, the room came alive with color, grains flying up my nose and in my ears. Tully lost his footing, swept up in the mini-tornado, and I threw an arm over my eyes against the raging dust storm.

And as quickly as it started, it stopped. I yelped as all the floating particles poured down, blanketing my shoulders, my hair, piling at my feet. Slowly, I lowered my arm, blinking the bits from my lashes, resisting the urge to dig a knuckle in there and rub away the itch.

"Right," the fae prince muttered, wiping the dust from his armor with a frown, "sorted."

In the storm, there was distraction. Rollo had released Lloyd at some point—and made no move to cuff him again. After all, the warlock's usefulness had run out, the task completed, which left him free to—

"Ah, ah, ah," Lloyd sneered, snatching up a disoriented Tully by the scruff of his neck. My familiar yowled, flailing, claws out, and my heart pitched into my gut as Lloyd wrapped a hand around his head. Wild grey eyes darted to Rollo, and he clutched Tully tighter when I scrambled toward them, my familiar's neck so vulnerable, so easily broken with one sharp jerk. "Move and I snap his neck, kitten."

Fucker. I stilled, the tiny room made even more claustrophobic by the panic clawing up my throat, the mounds of shattered crystals at our feet.

"I have no quarrel with you, fae," Lloyd insisted tersely. "Take your brother and go, but the girl comes with me. By a blood deal, she is my *property*."

Rollo said nothing, did nothing, just looked back to me with a slightly quirked brow. *Shit*. Fae respected contracts; they dealt in them regularly. If I nodded, I was done. The connection I shared with his brother probably wouldn't even *matter*—I belonged to this sadist, and that was that.

The prince exhaled softly, almost disappointed, and I realized my eyes, my wobbling lower lip, had betrayed me.

Tully, however, didn't give two shits about the legalities of a blood contract. A guttural growl rumbled through him, muffled behind Lloyd's hand. His tail suddenly poofed and slashed about, and seconds later Lloyd dropped the enormous black cat, both hands flying to his own throat instead. The warlock collapsed to the ground, colorful dust gusting around him, and scratched at his neck, gasping, red-faced and panicked.

Beyond pleased with himself, my spoiled familiar sauntered away like he was wiping his hands clean of Lloyd Guthrie for good, tail up and hooked at the end as he made his way to me.

Flicking his feet like he'd just taken the world's biggest dump in his litterbox.

Gods did I ever love him.

Elijah, Rafe, and Fintan might have had my heart, but Tully Fox would always and forever be my main man.

Wordlessly, Rollo swiped a blade from his side and offered it to me by the handle. At least nine inches in length and forged of pure silver, the handle mirrored the star constellations patterned on his broad chest plate. I stared at it for a beat, then looked up at him, everything inside gone quiet. My heartbeat steady. My hands still. My knees strong—nowhere near buckling anymore.

Tully eased up on his unseen hold of Lloyd's throat, and the warlock gulped down a strangled gasp as Rollo faced me.

"Free yourself, Katja," the prince said softly, his blade hanging between us. "Take it or not... The choice is yours."

I didn't hesitate.

I took the blade, coiled my fingers around the ornate handle, and gripped hard. My familiar released Lloyd from his magic, allowing the warlock to topple over, gasping and heaving, coughing into the rainbow dust all around him. Barefoot, I marched right up to him, crouched down, and shoved him upright against the wall. Gritted my free hand into his shoulder, nails digging into his expensive suit jacket.

In his hateful eyes, I saw my mom's face, the one I only knew from photos—taken from me too soon. I saw Ewan and

Jackson, my best friends, my brothers, stolen, their lives cut short. I saw Dad, my rock, my protector—heard his death rattle and felt him slipping away from me.

"Kitten," Lloyd rasped, his hand suddenly on my thigh, stroking my bare skin with his thumb. Too intimate. Too familiar. Like he still owned me. "Don't do something you'll always regret—"

I thrust the blade into his left eye and didn't stop until its tip thunked against the wall. Fae-forged, it cut through his eye, his brain, his skull, and right out the other side. While I shook when I let go, falling back on my heels with a stuttering breath and staring at a listless monster, I knew for the first time in my life… I was free.

And I regretted *nothing*.

32

KATJA

By the time we made it back to the visitors' grand foyer, the inmate population of Xargi Penitentiary had finally discovered there was a whole different side to this hellhole. A veritable rainbow of jumpsuits littered the hall, clumps of supers scattered between the marble columns, scuffing up the once pristine floors with blood and dust from the bowels of Xargi. Among them was the odd warlock guard, some who, maybe like Thompson, weren't total dicks to the cellblocks assigned to them. For all I knew, the rest were dead—like their warden.

And it didn't matter.

I didn't *care*. With Tully in my arms, traipsing after Prince Rollo with a battalion of fae warriors flanking us, I felt secure—and not because of the armed guard. I had my familiar and my magic again, and the man who had decimated the Fox coven had met his grisly end by *my* hand.

The only thing that would make this moment better was if—

"Rafe!"

My vampire stood out in the sea of lost inmates, not

only because he was one of the few red jumpsuits, but because of *him*. Ridiculously rugged and handsome, a supermodel with heart and soul. His gorgeous aquamarine gaze soared up the staircase to me, and Tully wriggled out of my arms—smitten little traitor—and blitzed through armored fae legs down the stairs and straight to him, me at his fluffy heels.

Rafe marched away from the crowd, many of whom retreated as Rollo and his posse ambled down the stairs, and he met me with open arms and relieved smile. Sprinting barefoot in the most ridiculously tight red dress imaginable, I'd never been happier. I flew into him with a strangled cry, and even though it was like running face-first into a brick wall, I gritted through the pain and latched on tight. Arms around his neck, I stood up on my tippiest toes as relief coursed through my veins like a salve.

"Are you okay?" I whispered shakily, trembling in his embrace—for once with *happiness*, not horror or fear or agonizing loss. Exhaling sharply, the vampire buried his face in my neck, then made no effort to hide the way he breathed me in, dragging his nose along my shoulder.

"Better than," he rumbled back. "You?"

Over his shoulder, I spotted Fintan in his green jumpsuit weaving through the crowd of gathered supers toward us, and I nodded.

"Getting there," I told him, voice thick, eyes darting about in search of the fourth member of our little prison gang—the one who possessed a third of my heart and had since long before we were born. Bound by fate, my dragon ought to be here right alongside us.

But only Fintan approached, nose in a splint, dark purple rings around his eyes. He was totally fixated on Rafe and me, the intensity of his stare and that ridiculously confident stride making my knees weak—until he looked slightly beyond us. Then he stumbled, all the smoldering sexy melting away, replaced by an endearing boyish affection.

He'd spotted his brother.

And from the expression on his face, from the way Rollo had fought tooth and nail to get into the penitentiary, those two loved each other.

As Rafe loosened his bone-crushing hold on me, Tully circling around our legs and purring up a storm, the fae blitzed by, slowing only to pinch my ass in passing, and when I peered over my shoulder, I found Rollo yanking him into a brotherly bear hug.

A rogue tear slid down my cheek, and Rafe brushed it away, black brows knitted with concern, but I shooed his fears off with a smile and a giggle and a hard, fleeting kiss that turned his concern to dumbstruck affection.

I hadn't meant to cry—but they were tears of joy, something about seeing siblings who loved each other plucking at my heartstrings…

Made me briefly remember the good times of my childhood, the ones spent with Jackson and Ewan, brothers who I adored just as openly as Rollo and Fintan did each other.

They had reunited at the bottom of the staircase, and when the hug finally ended, Rafe and I drifting in their direction, entwined and moving as one, Rollo grabbed Fintan by the shoulder and held him at an arm's length.

"You wear the scars of battle, little brother," Rollo thundered, booming it like he wanted *everyone* to know. Rafe snorted, and I poked him sharply in the side, a warning to let them have their moment. The vampire's brows shot up again as he threw his arm around my shoulders and tucked me against him, that smirk daring me to reprimand him out loud.

Fintan, meanwhile, scratched at the back of his neck with a chuckle. "Ah, yes, well—"

"How did you damage your nose?"

"Naturally, it was defending my lady's honor," the fae crowed, motioning back to me dramatically. The whole garrison glanced my way, some smirking, others whispering. Rollo, meanwhile, folded his arms over his broad chest, lips twitching like he was fighting back another smile.

"Is that so?"

Fintan scoffed. "Don't you believe me? Of *course*. Would you not defend such a fetching creature, brother? Surely in all your time alive, you've experienced that *moment* when you must choose between your life and that of your heart's—"

"They gassed us this afternoon during the riot," Rafe said dryly, loud enough to stop what was shaping up to be a very long, overwrought Fintan monologue. "He fell on his face when he passed out and broke his own nose."

"Ah," Rollo murmured, smirking, his nod implying he had expected as much.

Which rubbed me the wrong way. Fintan had been brave time and time again in here. He *had* stood up for me. He deserved recognition.

My fae just snorted and took a good-natured swipe at Rafe. "Well, we were gassed defending *her*, you fangless fuck."

Much to my surprise, Rafe flipped him off with a grin. No angst. No brooding. No self-conscious covering of his mouth. I hadn't been apart from my guys for all that long, but when had everyone gotten so comfortable chatting about their raging insecurities? Had I missed something big?

Now, however, wasn't the time to pry into it. As Fintan introduced Rafe to the future king of the Midnight Court, Rollo's entourage loitering in the background like they had nothing better to do, I did a quick sweep of the foyer. Former inmates continued to stand around, whispering frantically, all wrapped up in their collars. Uncertainty rippled through the clusters of gathered supers, and I hated to see it—but I wasn't exactly obligated to step up and take charge, was I?

"Took you bloody long enough to storm the keep, brother," Fintan teased. Frowning, I rejoined the group, fingers loosely threaded through Rafe's, some of the relief from before giving way to stress. Where was Elijah? What were all the supers cloistered around us supposed to do now? We were in the middle of Siberia, for goodness' sake.

"We found your relative location months ago," Rollo insisted, passing his helmet over to a nearby warrior and removing his chainmail gloves. "Getting through the ward proved near impossible, unfortunately. We simply had to wait until it was removed—at no point was it open long enough to feed the army through, and the warlocks who came and went had protection of their own. We didn't want to make our presence known—"

"Funny." Fintan sniffed, examining his dirty nails with pursed lips. "Because that cat broke in without an issue." All eyes dropped to Tully, who had situated himself firmly between Rafe and me, slow blinks aplenty, still a purr machine. Fintan offered him a quick little scratch behind each ear, shooting his brother a look over his shoulder. "Perhaps you ought to assign him to the war council. I suspect he'll make a strong siege tactician."

"Where's Elijah?" I blurted, unable to stand here and shoot the shit anymore like we were at the saddest cocktail party ever. Rafe drew me closer with a kiss to my temple, his hand twining around mine, his skin cold but his touch beyond reassuring.

"He's freeing those in solitary," the vampire told me, and before I could demand why they had let him do that alone, Fintan interjected like he could read my mind.

"Holster your weapons, darling... He wanted to do it himself," the fae said, hands up in mock-surrender. "Seemed rather important to him, so we came to find *you*."

"Next step will be to get out of here," Rafe carried on, his tone taking a turn for the serious, ever my brooding vampire as he adjusted the leather strap around his neck. "But the collars—"

"*Excindo*." My softly murmured spell struck him like a charging bull, knocking the vampire a few feet from me. Oops. I really *did* need something to rein my magic in. Fortunately, the spell did its job: as soon as the flash of black charged from my fingertips to his collar, the leather ignited with shadowy flames that sizzled around the band, reducing it to white ash that dusted Rafe's shoulders like freshly fallen snow.

Eyes wide, he smoothed a hand over his throat, then looked to me, mouth opening and closing soundlessly.

"Prince Rollo and I already took care of the collars... I guess I probably should have led with that," I told him with a slight lift of my chin. *Defending her*. Sure, my guys had stood up for me more times than I could count in here, but with my magic back, I had a debt to pay—and this was just the start. Every so often, *they* deserved to be rescued, whether they liked it or not. "The sigils will still bind your abilities, but at least now you can remove it."

Fintan tore clean through his, needing both hands to split the material, and soon enough loitering supers and shifters followed suit. One by one, the collars that had ruled our lives inside these four walls fell away. Former inmates stomped on them, spit at them, set them on fire. Many of the shifters immediately let their inner animals free, tearing through jumpsuits during the transition, and those straps of leather were quickly met with teeth and claws, the foyer filled with growls and howls and cries, the air around us positively *bursting* with magic.

And it was… magnificent.

The scene blurred as another flood of emotion washed over me, leaving me no choice but to just hold on and enjoy the ride, the current raging, the rapids fierce—I'd never felt more *alive*.

"Right, so…" Fintan smacked his brother in the middle of that starry breastplate, then motioned toward the wall of doors that led to the outside world across the foyer, their shattered windows tinted purple with fae fire. "If we don't want to personally experience a cave-in, I suggest we get moving."

"*What?*" Seriously, what had these boys plotted without me? While I hated to abandon the unfolding beauty of shifters and supers finding themselves again, Fintan and Rafe left me no choice. Each locked on to one of my hands, then marched me right out Xargi's front doors. Rollo and his warriors trailed behind us, and once we were in the great outdoors, met by the scent of scorched earth and ancient magic, by the crunch of gravel underfoot that grated on my nerves, by the cries of bird shifters taking flight, those left in the foyer followed. Former inmates from all blocks spilled out through various doors, and as soon as someone saw another had removed their collar, off came the leather, the air thickening with a new punch of power.

Pockets in the purple flames appeared, allowing inmates to pass untouched, and while some took advantage of that, particularly the collared wolf shifters, many just drifted around on the outskirts, lost. Displaced. Searching for *home* and finding the Siberian tundra in the throes of autumn instead.

While Fintan, Rollo, and Rafe discussed the logistics of assisting some of the stranded supers and shifters, I hovered outside the group, staring at Xargi, *waiting*. Studying the faces of every jumpsuit that blitzed out, scrutinizing anyone in blue, desperate to find Elijah's golden curls, his rugged face, his enormous frame in the mix.

Nothing.

Arms crossed, I wandered closer, searching frantically now, a series of horrific thoughts wheedling into what was supposed to be a victory. But there was no real celebration without him. No success if we weren't all together. No—

"Willow!" At least one navy blue jumpsuit came with a familiar face. The petite rabbit shifter staggered out one of the side doors, her collar gone and her face coated in dirt, her loose brown hair an absolute rat's nest. I sprinted toward her, hating how dazed she looked, how she stumbled, how her one good eye had a slash through it that she didn't have the last time we had sat together in the cafeteria. Slowly, she turned in my direction, and by the time recognition flashed across her lovely features, I'd crashed into her and dragged her into a hug.

She stood limp for a moment, arms dangling at her side—no surprise if she questioned all this. In my time behind bars, I'd had so many dreams about this exact moment, about blowing a hole through Xargi's walls and strolling out, free as a bird, the prison in cinders behind me.

"Oh, *gods*, I was so worried about you," I whispered, hugging her harder like that might wake her up.

And it did.

Finally, my Cellblock B dinner companion wrapped her arms around me with a sob. We stood together like that, locked in an embrace that would have gotten us beaten just hours earlier, holding each other, lifting the other up.

She could go home now.

Back to her children, her harem of husbands.

Freedom tasted brilliant, even as fae fire burned the world around us.

"They put me in solitary," she muttered when we slowly eased apart. Tears cut through the brown smudges on her face, and she rubbed at her cheeks with both hands, rolling her eyes. "Apparently refusing to suck off a guard is a *deeply* punishable offense. Been in a hole for three fucking weeks."

A familiar fury lashed at my insides, an inferno sparking for her. "Have you seen the one who put you in there? Is he still alive?"

If he was, I swore to the *gods* I would cut off his—

"Your dragon killed him," Willow admitted softly, purple reflecting off her clouded eye. She rubbed at the red ring around her neck, then shot me a coy look, voice lowering as she added, "But I *did* curb-stomp his disgusting face on the way out… Gave him a good kick in the nads for the afterlife. Pretty satisfying."

"You're really living the Xargi dream." I tried to keep my tone light, not wanting to sidestep her newfound freedom and the delivery of some deserved justice, but just the mention of Elijah with no follow-up was driving me nuts. "And… You saw Elijah, then?" When Willow nodded, scanning the purple flames, fingers drifting to her jumpsuit's buttons like she was seconds from stripping down and shifting, I cleared my throat and stepped into her wandering eyeline. "Not to diminish your accomplishments by talking about a boy, but… do you know where he is now? Is he okay?"

Willow studied me for a beat, unbuttoning her jumpsuit and then shimmying out of the too-big material, letting it pool around her feet like a navy mountain. "Uh, yes, I'd say he's doing pretty good, actually."

I nodded, pretending to *not* be fazed by the totally nude woman standing in front of me all of a sudden. "Oh. Great.

Thank you so much…" Shoving the awkwardness aside, I grabbed her shoulder and squeezed, our eyes briefly locked. "Really, for everything… For your friendship and conversation, thank you."

"Same to you," the rabbit shifter murmured, gripping my forearm tight for a moment, then releasing me just as I did her. She stepped back, flipping off a nearby warlock gawking in his purple jumpsuit without even glancing his way. "If you're ever in Brisbane, you've got a place to stay."

"My place in Seattle always has a bed for you."

"Yeah, but not for the fifteen of us," Willow mused, grinning, "but I appreciate the sentiment. Ciao for now, doll."

In a flash, she vanished, shrinking from delicate woman to tiny rabbit—who could really hoof it over the gravel. She zipped around wandering supers, just a blur of light brown in the darkness, then crossed a gap in the purple flames without looking back or breaking her stride—making her way home to her family, like she had always wanted.

Like she *deserved*.

Now, my family still wasn't quite as whole as I would have liked. Nibbling my lower lip, I glanced back, hands on my hips, to find Rafe still chatting with Fintan and Rollo, Tully in his arms; my spoiled familiar had that vampire wrapped around his massive paw. All we were missing was—

The ground shuddered, gravel jittering around my feet, the cursed walls of Xargi trembling as a low, guttural rumble echoed from its depths. Conversations dimmed around the grounds, the fae flames flickering, shrinking, halved in size by the time the next roar thundered through the prison. Arms falling limp at my sides, I staggered toward the building while jumpsuits fled in every direction, then stilled with a gasp, eyes wide, heart in my throat, when the roof over our old cellblock exploded. Embers and ash and dust spewed everywhere as an enormous figure broke through the stone that had kept us caged, the shape rising like a monster from legend, a primordial being clawing out of the depths—a titan shattering the bars of Tartarus...

Elijah.

In his true form.

Oh.

My heart skipped a beat at the breathtaking dragon that scaled the ruins of the penitentiary, his bellow rattling in my bones as he roared into the night sky.

Backlit by stars and moonlight, he was exquisite—the sunrise against the darkness, illuminated by fae fire, his scales a russet red, coppery orange, and a lush, buttery yellow. Shaking off the dust, the stone bricks that must have weighed a hundred pounds each, he stretched his huge wings, each one tipped with a spike that had to be as tall as me. They carried on down his back, from the nape of his skull along his spine, right to the tip of his tail—protective thorns of pure obsidian, equally intimidating and beautiful. Powerful claws gripped the crumbling structure as he stalked along its rooftop, cracks skittering through the remnants of Xargi Penitentiary. Each huff of dragon's breath carried like the west wind...

I had never been more impressed by anything in my life.

Never been more instantly infatuated with someone.

Never craved danger like I craved *him.*

Wings flared, the dragon reared back and unleashed a firestorm across the penitentiary. The fae fire paled in comparison to the crimson scorching across the building, dissolving thick and suffocating stone walls to ash in seconds. Distant cheers tickled my ears, but the entire world fell away in his presence. Nothing else existed outside of that dragon and his fire, his scales like sunshine and his wings the ultimate freedom.

As flames decimated the penitentiary, I swore I felt his

gaze drift to me. Even in the dancing light, purple and orange colliding, fae flames and dragonfire turning the night to day, I knew those eyes. I had seen them before, desperate to break free, desperate to *see* me, trapped inside the body of a man—the man that I loved. The man fate had chosen for me.

Our bond solidified in that moment, fear of this ancient beast ebbing like the lowering tide. Steel stretched between us, forged in dragonfire—utterly unbreakable.

I needed him.

Now.

Needed to touch him, explore him… Kiss him.

Hold him.

Feel his arms around me and his teeth on my flesh.

As the fae fire perimeter dimmed, dropping from a formidable wall to magenta embers in burnt grass, the dragon took flight. Shot up in the air, bellowing loud enough they must have heard him around the globe, then soared in a sweeping circle over what had once been our prison—our tomb in the making. With a smile so wide my cheeks ached, I watched him stretch his wings and loop through the sky, belly underlit by his own fire, by flames that would erase Xargi from the history books for good.

When I looked back to the others, I realized I wasn't the only one infatuated with the sight. Fintan watched the dragon's dance with his mouth literally hanging open, as if speechless for the first time in all his long life. Rafe raised a fist in solidarity when Elijah swept over the cluster of fae warriors, and Tully's big blues tracked him, tail swishing with interest.

As soon as he touched down in the Siberian grassland, the earth shuddered again, this time hard enough to send me stumbling, and I took off in a sprint, heart pounding, my sights locked on the first and last dragon to ever set my heart on fire.

Silhouetted against a hilly backdrop, against a grassy plateau that stretched for miles and miles all around, Elijah's dragon form stood leaps and bounds ahead of all the natural beauty. Starchy grass tickled my calves as I ran barefoot toward him, slowing only when my brain finally processed the sheer *size* of him, this creature tall as a mountain and broad as the ocean, dominating everything in his presence just by *being*. He folded his wings in as I crept forward, and his next huff of breath had his nostrils flaring and my hair whipping around. I braced against the hot gust but didn't stop until I was within an arm's length of him.

Close enough to touch, I lost myself, just for a moment, in his physical prowess, in this towering creature who could crush me with just one of his massive clawed feet. Golden eyes appraised me, and when he dropped his huge head down, face flared with scales and talons like protective armor, Elijah shone through all of it. His calming presence caressed me, even like this, and I raised a trembling hand, holding it between us for a moment, hesitating…

Until he nudged his snout against my palm. Dwarfed by his massive frame, my little hand was nothing as it ghosted along his fiery muzzle, as it stroked scorching scales and brutal spikes. An ant poking at a shoe—that was how I felt.

But he was beautiful and patient, entertaining my cautious exploration only until I reached his wing joint. Then, in a flash, he was gone, shifting from dragon to man so suddenly that it made my head spin.

Gods, I had missed him.

We hadn't been apart more than a few hours, but the sight of Elijah standing before me, still tall as a mountain and broad as the ocean, naked and panting, glistening with sweat, with the effort of the shift—it made my eyes water. Made my knees weak. Made my heart *sing*.

Without a word, I charged at him like a missile. He met

me halfway, scooping me into his arms, my feet dangling off the ground, and hugged me so tight he crushed the air from my lungs. Something *cracked* sharply in my back—and I didn't care. I could take the alpha's strength. I *craved* it, needed it, loved it. My fingers wove into his thick tousled locks as I exhaled a shaky sob against his neck.

"I love you," I whispered, the confession coming out of nowhere, my brain off and my heart on. "I know we don't really know each other outside of this place... I know it's soon. It's *crazy* to be in love like this, and I know it could just be the bond—"

"I love you too, Katja," Elijah growled against my skin. "I don't care if it's just the bond." Slowly, he lowered me so that I stood flatfoot before him, then forced me out of the hug, wrenching my arms from his neck so that he could hunch down to cup my face. His eyes shimmered, starlight caught in the glossy sheen, and he chuckled. "We have the time now. We have each other. That's all that matters."

I sniffled, brushing the damp away when it dribbled down his cheek. "And Rafe and Fintan?"

His fingers slowly worked into my hair, massaging the base of my skull, tipping my head back. "We have them too."

Just when I thought I couldn't love him more, he said *that*. He accepted what my heart needed—all of them, each one different and imperfect and a piece of me that I couldn't live without.

Smoothing my hands up his sweaty torso, over rippling muscle and the pounding drumbeat of his heart, I eased onto my tiptoes to kiss him—only for Elijah to weave his fingers through my stick-straight hair, combing it out on either side with a scowl.

"What did he do to you?" he grumbled, his warm browns giving way to the dragon's gold, his grip on me tightening. I clutched at his forearms corded with muscle, delicious and *mine,* and smirked.

"You should be asking what *I* did to *him,*" I whispered back, a touch of darkness blossoming in my smile when his eyebrows shot up. "Did you expect anything less of a dragon's mate?"

Or a vampire's partner? Or the lover of an Unseelie fae prince?

"No," Elijah rumbled, looking very much like he wanted to devour me whole. "I didn't."

Ugh. If he wanted to devour me, let him *do* it, right here, right now, right in the grass—

"Get a room, you heathens."

Fintan's shout landed just before our mouths collided, the charge shimmering between us positively electric—and definitely interrupted. As Elijah hooked a possessive arm around my waist, the look in his eyes promising that this lull wouldn't last long, I eased back around just in time for Rafe and Fintan's arrival. And while I would have preferred to be shoved to the ground right now with a dragon's mouth skimming my body, this stupid red dress shredded to pieces and any lingering traces of Lloyd on my skin wiped away, standing with my three guys, my heart whole and Tully immediately back in my arms... well, that was pretty phenomenal too.

"So, uh, what do we do now?" I asked after a painfully long fifteen seconds of awkward silence, the four of us exchanging glances as if acutely aware that this was the first time we were all interacting as free supers off Xargi's grounds. Tully nuzzled under my chin, purring, kneading, and my bed flashed in my mind's eye—my *own* queen-sized bed with all the blankets clumped and pillows stacked high, waiting for me back in my Seattle apartment. "Do we just... go home?"

Did we date internationally? Cross-dimensionally? I loved each man present—Elijah for his protectiveness and his acceptance of me as I was, Fintan for his humor and his impulsiveness, and Rafe for his wit and his comfort. But, really, we had met in prison, trapped inside this fucked-up bubble for *months*, the scope of our budding relationships dictated by others.

And now we were just… here.

Free to do what we wanted.

With… whoever we wanted.

What if they walked away? What if Fintan went back to his courtiers and Rafe buried himself in his next book? What if Elijah thought fate had made a mistake and kept looking elsewhere?

What if I was the only one willing to start from the beginning—to explore who we all were to each other outside of handcuffs and jumpsuits and leather collars?

What if I wasn't enough for these three to—

"I…" Fintan pressed his lips together, almost like he was *considering* his words before he just blurted them out. The air stilled around us, the winds dying down, the rustling of the grasses falling silent. Rafe and Elijah exchanged glances that were way too serious for my liking, and I hugged Tully tighter, this irrational fear in the pit of my stomach like a lead weight dragging me down, down, down…

"I have a suggestion," Fintan admitted at last, shattering the quiet, the corners of his sly mouth quirking. "It involves a lot of booze, a bit of dancing, a palace stocked with all you'll *ever* need, a bath the size of a stadium, and…" He nudged at Rafe with his elbow, then winked at me. "And a sun that never rises."

"As long as it's far away from here, I'm game," Rafe insisted, catching my eye briefly, his gaze promising a long talk somewhere private—later. My subtle nod had him flashing a shy grin, and Elijah squeezed my waist, watching it all unfold.

"Agreed," the dragon said, his voice giving way to a seductive grit that had my toes curling. "So long as I can spread my wings, fae."

Fintan swept a hand through his hair, roguish and alluring in the way he growled, "I swear, dragon, you'll touch the fucking stars."

Nibbling my lower lip for a moment, I eased away from Elijah, needing to stand on my own two feet as I said it—as I surrendered to *us*.

"As long as I'm with you three, I don't care where we go," I told them. "As long as we're together… I'll be there."

Always.

EPILOGUE: KATJA

No drink would ever taste finer than the fae wine of the Midnight Court, nor could any liquor on Earth make me so deliciously tipsy in a single sip.

Unfortunately, I had learned my lesson the hard way two weeks ago: guzzling three glasses of the glittering amber liquid had left me hungover for the first four *days* of my trip to Fintan's court in the Otherworld. The only plus there was that I hadn't struggled alone: Elijah had been just as bad as me, downing several bottles of the stuff the first night and paying for it the following morning, then Fintan came in at a close second to him. Meanwhile, Rafe got off scot-free—the human blood provided by palace servants turned him into an *animal*, but that was hot.

Not embarrassing.

Nothing like vomiting all over a palatial bathroom to really endear yourself to your man's royal parents.

But tonight was different.

Lesson learned.

Only a sip of the sumptuous elixir at the start of the night, lots of bread and water throughout the festivities, and then a half sip toward the end as things wrapped up beneath a firework display that outdid any I had ever seen. Hell, the organizers had even managed to shape one explosion into a dragon in Elijah's honor, who—while pleasantly tipsy—had stripped down for a cheering crowd, then joined his firework doppelganger to make this a night to remember.

After all, the night *was* for us. In the eyes of the Midnight Court, a fae kingdom where the sun never rose but the stars shone bright, we three had rescued their captive prince from Xargi's evil clutches. Fintan came out a hero after he embellished the inmate rebellion he had started on a whim—and for once, we let him say whatever he wanted—while Rollo shared tales of Elijah's dragonfire and my skills with a dagger and Rafe's tenacity at the hands of a madman who had stolen his fangs.

In the Midnight Court, my beloved vampire had found them again, the pair he lost replaced by a set of golden canines that he could swap out with smaller ivory ones when—and if—we ever went home.

As I skipped down a marble corridor illuminated with floating white orbs, dressed in a slinky silk gown that was practically see-through, *home* had barely crossed my mind. Two weeks of fae hospitality was enough to make you forget the human world completely—forget the politics of our supernatural society, forget the horrors of Xargi. Exquisite food and gorgeous grounds, this world so lush and green and speckled with blossoms that flowered even without the sun…

Seattle was a distant memory for the time being.

Even Tully had been spoiled rotten, hailed for his courage and ingenuity after tales were spun by Fintan—exaggerated, again, which we let slide… again—about my familiar's prison break-in.

Here, we wanted for nothing.

Elijah had license to fly anywhere, to crest the tallest peaks of the court's sprawling mountain range—to touch the stars with me on his back, exhilarated and enamored.

Rafe never needed to hide in the shadows, bathed in perpetual night. Vampire prejudice didn't extend to the fae courts; they admired his speed, his strength, and his bloodlust. He also had a raging hard-on for the royal library, where he spent most of his time if he wasn't with us.

My pampered familiar even had his *own* personal attendant, one fae assigned just to him, always brushing him, allowing him to scratch up her skirts, feeding him whole fish as he lounged on a massive pillow like he was a *god*.

And I…

I had all that and more.

I had my boys.

My freedom.

My *life*.

Sure, we were in the hazy honeymoon period. This still wasn't *real*, so much of our time spent drinking and lovemaking and laughing and exploring Fintan's homeland…

But after Xargi Penitentiary, I could do without the pains of reality—just for a little while.

"Katja…"

Rafe's dark whisper tickled the nape of my neck, but when I whirled around, up on my toes and barefoot, I found a relatively empty corridor behind me. The enclosed stone bridge stretched from the main palace to Fintan's wing, which stood tall and proud like the galaxy's most phallic tower *ever*—we still hadn't stopped teasing him about it. Arched open windows lined the walls on either side, allowing the air to flow through—air that was always like that first breath of fall, crisp and cool and perfect for snuggling under the blankets with a man who burned hot as the sun. Or a man as cold as ice.

Or a fae just uniquely skilled with his impish tongue.

While illuminated by the enchanted orbs, charmed to look like floating stars, light as bubbles and warm to the touch, the hallway was filled with shadows—the perfect hunting ground for a vampire.

The alluring air shattered a little when Fintan and Elijah lolled around the corridor's slight bend. Arms thrown over each other's shoulders, drunk and merry, they started up an old fae tune, Elijah's deep baritone the perfect complement to Fintan's rich tenor. My dragon had proven himself quite talented at picking up obscure and useless languages—as Rafe had dubbed them—and, ugh, *gods*, it was hot as hell to have him and Fintan whisper filthy things to me in a dialect as old as time.

Best of all, it made my heart happy to see the pair getting along.

To see them *all* bonding—and not just because of me, but because they enjoyed each other's company.

A clan of misfits.

After a quick scan of the shadows, I turned slowly and continued my amble down the corridor, hands in my luxurious skirts. Every outfit I wore was fit for a queen, my closets filled to the brim by Fintan's sisters—who had showed up that first day to discover their brother's girl severely hungover and in possession of nothing beyond a prison jumpsuit to wear to court. After that, it was one magnificent gown after the other, and once I had stopped puking up fae wine, me and the princesses got along just fine. Some better than others, but he had *nine* sisters—the odds were stacked against me that I would be besties with all of them.

Tonight was no exception to the fancy-dress policy. After all, I had appearances to maintain in court, and I did so in a beautiful silvery-white gown patterned with glittering stars.

The thin straps over my shoulders probably wouldn't last the night, the men behind me prone to destroying my outfits, and the plunging neckline had kept Fintan distracted for most of dinner. And the *skirt,* oh—flouncy and layered, the material fell like petals to the ground and had *pockets.* Practical and breathtaking.

Every arched window I passed opened to the magnificence of the Midnight Court. The kingdom glittered all around the palace, a court made wealthy by the abundance of diamonds in their mountains. Blanketed in midnight, the city reflected the sky, thousands of little white lights sparkling like the unfettered stars above. Surrounded by majesty—but here, in this winding corridor, also totally alone. Fintan's personal guard had left us at the entrance to the prince's domain.

And that was just the way we liked it.

"Come here, little witch..." Rafe's seductive growl made the hairs on the back of my neck stand up and sent a flood of giddy goose bumps down my arms. Lower lip caught between my teeth, I slowed, sensing he was close, maybe even *right* on my heels, then whipped around to find... nothing.

Same old corridor, Elijah and Fintan still a ways down, singing and laughing and teetering side to side.

Sober as ever, Rafe had all the power tonight.

And that was just the way *I* liked it.

I sprinted down the stone corridor with a giggle, skirt trailing behind me like a comet's tail, like I was the heroine of an epic fantasy romance being pursued by her lover. And I was, of course, being pursued—more like *hunted,* not just by a lover, but a predator too.

Hair blazing, wild and free, I threw a glance over my shoulder, expecting to find a shadow in the shape of a man—nothing. Again. Lips pursed, I faced forward—then screeched when I crashed into Rafe's much too solid chest. Clad in a full black suit, right down to the socks and the tie, luxe and rich beneath my fingers as they clawed at him, shoved at him like an escape was even possible. When our eyes met, hunger and desire blazed bright in his, and with a flash of golden fang, he hauled me off to the side and thrust me up against a patch of wall between two arched windows.

"Found you," he growled, one hand fisted into my hair, the other plunging down my skirt and cupping me between my thighs. I gasped when he wrenched my head to the side, then squealed when he pounced. A pinprick of pain always bloomed before the explosion of pleasure, a vampire's venom inducing an orgasm unlike *any* I had ever experienced. No matter how I was feeling, no matter where my mind was, a bite from Rafe made me come like we had been at it for hours, like he had worked me into such a frenzy that I just might *die* if he didn't let me sink into oblivion.

Eyes clenched shut, I halfheartedly pushed at him, twisting at his jacket and squirming against his steely frame, hopelessly pinned as he drank from me. Fae fireworks paled in comparison to the bursts of light and color pinwheeling behind my lids, and my legs drifted apart like they had a mind of their own, allowing Rafe in. Through the blinding haze of pleasure, of ecstasy coursing through my veins and sapping the fight from my limbs, I vaguely felt him massaging me, grinding the base of his hand into my clit so that my cries turned squeaky with every fiery flare in my belly.

He only relented when the others arrived, walking into a scene already underway, chuckling amongst themselves. When Rafe reared back, my blood smeared his mouth, dribbled down his neck—stained my lovely dress—and he dragged me away from the wall, showing me off for Elijah and Fintan with a few clicks of his tongue.

"She's fucking shitfaced," the vampire announced, his eyes bloodshot and his voice rough. I twisted out of his hold, a touch light-headed but perfectly capable of handling myself after his bite. I mean, this wasn't the first time—not even of this trip—and it definitely wouldn't be the last.

"Am *not,*" I protested, adding a childish stomp just to make them grin like the wolfish predators they were in the bedroom—three men who catered to me everywhere else, who spoiled me, kissed me sweetly in the rain, and protected me from outsiders.

Who had their way with me behind closed doors, rough and unrelenting, dominant and brutal and *mine.*

Before I could recite every drop of fae wine I'd had to drink tonight, Elijah swept in, his hulking frame wrapped in maroon; golden hair like a halo, body dressed for sin, my dragon was the best of both worlds. He jerked me to him with a firm hand on my lower back, then dragged his tongue from my bare shoulder all the way up to my ear, his deep rumble making my sex clench and my belly loop with anticipation.

He hummed, deep and dangerous, eyes burning into the side of my face as he nudged me back into the center of the trio. "She tastes like fae wine."

"Gentlemen, if I may?" Fintan interjected, all prim and proper in a dark grey suit almost identical to Elijah and Rafe's, down to the pearl buttons and golden cuffs with slits in the back for his wings, his lofty accent hammed up now that he was back home. He took a prowling step toward me, then another when I scampered back and bumped into Rafe's chest again. The fae prince cocked his head to the side, mouth stretched in a sinful smile, and nodded down to my skirt. "I believe you are missing the most important elixir of all..."

I zipped around Rafe when Fintan lunged for me with a starved look in his eye, my giggle arcing into a squeal when I felt him swipe at my flowing skirts. Unlike my prowling vampire, my fae saw no reason to creep in the shadows, to take advantage of the permanent night offered in his court. He pursued me down the rest of the corridor at a steady clip, jogging compared to my full-tilt bolt, perfectly capable of catching me in a heartbeat if he so chose, his wings an exquisite deep amber and protruding from the back of his suit.

Instead, he *let* me stumble into the double doors that peeled open into his bedroom, the tower soaring overhead, filled with rooms for pleasure and bathrooms like world-class spas and walk-in closets the size of my Seattle apartment. I shoved at the huge wood panels, the constellation Fintan lorded as an earl carved into the oak, and then barreled through when the locks mysteriously gave way.

Mysteriously. Right. All three of my men enjoyed letting me think I had bested them—and then thoroughly proving that I hadn't. Most of all, I enjoyed letting them. As soon as the doors parted, I stumbled clumsily into Prince Fintan's enormous bedroom. Before me stretched a sea of white and gold marble, a round bed in the center big enough for ten. Writing desks and golden maps of all the fae courts suggested his parents had high hopes for a scholar when they'd furnished the space, along with the hundreds of books stacked deep on the towering shelves. Three armchairs sat around a slate hearth, in which roared a plum fire that never extinguished, and behind them was a free-floating bar—literally with no legs—that navigated the room under some enchantment, rattling to your side whenever your drink was getting low.

This place always took my breath away.

And that was when one of them got me—always. This time it was Fintan barreling into his bedroom after me, his breath hot on my neck as he hooked his arm around my waist and yanked me flush against him. After nibbling at my shoulder, hands wandering my body possessively, he retreated just enough to grab the back of my dress and rip it right down the middle. I pouted at the protests of the fabric, the designer's meticulous work ruined by a horny prince.

Silvery-white silk and lace and sequined tulle gathered at my feet, the rest of me totally naked; it drove all three of them *wild* knowing I went to these court events without panties or a bra. Sometimes we left early for that reason alone.

My nipples pebbled at the onslaught of chilly night air, trembling with every ragged breath, and I shot onto my tiptoes with a giggle when Fintan cuffed the back of my neck and hoisted me up just a little. Held me in place. Made me *wait* for the others to arrive. And when they did, Elijah and Rafe sauntered in like they had all the time in the world, eyeing my nudity with fiery interest. While Elijah drifted toward the fireplace, drawn to the magic fae flames like a moth to a—well, you know—Rafe lingered, golden fangs still tinged red as he flashed a grin and let out a delicious chuckle when he tweaked my nipple.

Fintan, meanwhile, let his free hand rove unchecked, smoothing over my hips, my ass, my breasts, before eventually delving between my thighs, a finger thrust through my slick folds. He greeted the wetness with a satisfied huff against my throat.

"She's positively *dripping*," he announced, teasing me with his lips and teeth, that talented tongue sweeping the curve of my earlobe, and Rafe shook his head with a sharper, more biting laugh that made my toes curl.

"When isn't she?"

Fintan's amusement dripped across my skin like lava, hot and all-consuming, and he dragged me back into him, cock rigid and sharply insistent against my bare ass. While Rafe meandered over to his usual armchair—the center piece directly in front of the hearth, throwing caution to the wind as a vampire drifting so close to the flames—Elijah settled in the largest seat of them all, the grand black pleated chair to the left, foreboding and regal and woefully out of place amongst Fintan's light décor. A throne for a king—for an alpha. A conquering dragon.

Tipsy on fae wine and these three, I reached back to stroke Fintan over his pants, smoothing my hand up and down his rigid length, wondering if I focused on the head, then he might abandon whatever he had in mind and just *take* me right here and now. Instead, the fae prince thrust me out at an arm's length, tsking at my efforts, then steered me toward the trio of highbacked chairs. Plum flames warmed my calves as I rounded in front of the seats, the silent audience, thrones upon which my kings sat and watched me touch myself just a few nights back. I stumbled a little over the black bear rug underfoot, but my knees were grateful for it when Fintan pushed me down.

"You know what to do, dearest darling," he rumbled in my ear, his hand creeping down my bare back, tracing my spine, then smacking me hard on the ass to spur me onto all fours. I complied, body on fire with three sets of eyes watching me intently, hungrily, these dominant lovers who always had their way with me—but in the end, were under *my* thrall. There was such power in submission, in surrender. Over the last two weeks, I had explored that for the first time in my life, willingly giving over my control to men who adored me—who would never hurt me.

Not unless I begged for it.

Crawling on my hands and knees, lower back arched to thrust my ass into the air, I crept toward Elijah and freed his swollen cock from his trousers. Even with the wine driving me, making me feel light as air and free as a bird, I tackled the buttons and the zippers and the delicious black briefs that clung to his huge thighs with ease. He stood tall and proud before me, his cock largest of the three and a bit more intimidating, but I dragged my tongue its full length all the same, circling the silken tip before plunging it into my mouth. The dragon inhaled sharply, hands gritting into the armrests, his whole body stiffening ever so slightly—a subtle reaction shared between the two of us, lost on Rafe and Fintan.

A weakness that I adored.

A reminder that even though *I* was naked and they were fully clothed, me on my knees and them seated, I had all the power here.

Intoxicating, that kind of control.

Freeing, too, the surrender I gave to them willingly. Happily.

As I bobbed up and down on his shaft, only able to take about half in my mouth before I gagged and coughed and choked on him, Fintan nudged my knees apart with no more than a fingertip against my skin. At first I thought he had done it for *me*, to help me stabilize, but seconds later his mouth brushed my inner thighs—then his tongue swept through my folds and swirled around my clit. A throb of pleasure had me moaning, even with my mouth full, and both Fintan and Elijah groaned in response. While the dragon's huge hand threaded into my hair, guiding me up and down, setting a hurried pace, Fintan's hands bruised into my ass as he consumed me like a parched man drinking at an oasis.

Of the three, he was the best with his mouth.

Rafe could make me come in seconds.

Elijah consumed me, mind, body, and soul anytime we touched.

Together, they made *the* perfect lover—unmatched by any the world had ever seen.

How had I ended up so lucky?

Maybe it was karma for Xargi—for suffering in a cell, for a psychopath picking off my family. I had endured horrors behind bars, but now? Paradise. Even a normal life with these three, just going about our daily existence in the most banal circumstances, sounded like nirvana.

Elijah watched me with an unrelenting gaze, irises a fiery gold while his pupils turned to slits, his inner dragon just as infatuated with our intimacy as the man. I fluttered my lashes up at him, totally smitten with the way he stared during sex, so possessive and powerful, an alpha who knew exactly what he wanted that it was impossible to resist him when he turned that all-consuming gaze on me. I held it for as long as I could, rising up and down, swirling around the head of his shaft and flicking my tongue in all the ways I had learned made him twitch, only I lost it when Fintan homed in on my clit—when he got *technical* between my thighs.

Because even though I knew how to drive these three men crazy, what to do when we were alone and naked to turn them savage, each one knew how to play me too. In fact, I was convinced they shared *notes* at this point. In their own ways, Rafe, Fintan, and Elijah were slowly becoming experts at tearing me apart and putting me back together again.

And I loved them for it.

Although, my least favorite thing was edging—which Fintan was especially good at and took great pleasure in torturing me with whenever he had the chance. On the cusp of another climax, every muscle tensed, my blowjob technique gone to shit, the fae stopped that *thing* he was doing with his tongue. Just. Disappeared from between my thighs, leaving me hanging on the edge with a patronizing chuckle that echoed between all three of them.

"Such a greedy creature, isn't she?" he mused, slowly reclining back on the bearskin rug, wings splayed wide, and I glowered at him over my shoulder. He shot me a smirk and a wink, then undid his trousers and eased his shaft out, rigid with desire and glistening at the tip. "You want to come? Do it yourself, little witch."

"Fuck you," I fired back, only to let out an indignant squeal-giggle when he lunged forward, spurred by fae speed that I could never match, and snatched me by the hips. He yanked me back and pierced me with a single brutal, *glorious* thrust, filling me to the hilt. Ever the showman, Fintan kept my back to him so that the others could watch me bounce—something they had recently admitted to, each one surprisingly into watching another man screw his girl—and I took a fleeting moment to adjust to the position. Braced on his thighs, I folded my legs so that I could steer the ship, set the pace, rock to my own rhythm.

But then suddenly there was Rafe, materializing in front of me, his speed surpassing anyone in this court. I gasped, heart in my throat, then opened my lips obligingly when he presented his cock—nudged it against my cheek, smeared his arousal along my lower lip before plunging into my mouth. Eyes wide, I sat up straighter to properly take him, completely distracted despite the fact Fintan continued to stretch me, dominate me. The fae dragged a teasing hand along my back, raking his nails softly over my skin. The pair offered me just a few moments to adjust, and then, like they shared some warped telepathic connection that *I* wasn't included in, Fintan bucked his hips up hard just as Rafe grabbed hold of my face and thrust.

I had never been all that adventurous in the bedroom before them. Kink seemed tiring and overwhelming, but now, I couldn't imagine going back to just one man having his way with me. Even if only one of *my* guys had his hands on me, his teeth on me, his body utterly consuming mine, at least one other was watching—or demanded details after, getting all riled up himself before pouncing.

Who knew I had a secret dark streak? That vanilla just wouldn't cut it anymore—not ever, ever again?

Of the three, Rafe was usually the roughest. He fucked the hardest, no matter the hole, and tonight was no different. While Fintan rocked me back and forth, occasionally arching up to hit that *amazing* spot inside me or reaching around to fiddle with my clit, Rafe—my sweet, empathetic, brooding vampire—twined his hands into my hair and used my mouth with wild abandon. Never mind the drool dribbling over my chin, the tears swelling in my eyes. He stared down at me, all serious and masterful, and had his way with me with almost no regard for my comfort.

When I choked or gagged, he grinned.

When Fintan spanked me, he chuckled.

Only when the fae's pace quickened, his breath catching and his grip bruising, did the vampire ease back. He retreated with a sigh, allowing me to draw a full breath for the first time in an eternity, and watched unflinchingly as Fintan pounded into me. Made me bounce. Elijah even shoved him out of the way, probably sick of staring at his friend's back, and both stroked themselves as Fintan claimed me for his own pleasure.

Mine, meanwhile, was on the brink of detonating *again*, wet and swollen between my thighs, my clit aching for someone's mouth, anyone's fingers. But when Fintan stiffened and growled, spilling himself inside me, marking me up with his fingertips—temporary, unlike Elijah's mark on my shoulder and Rafe's bite on my neck—I wasn't allowed to come.

Again.

Ugh.

Just as I slipped my fingers between my folds and gently

pinched at my clit, Rafe grabbed my arm and hauled me off the fae. Dragged me to his usual chair in front of the roaring fire and bent me over the armrest.

Up on my toes, ass in the air, I planted my hands on the rigid cushion and stilled when Rafe's fingers whispered up the backs of my thighs. A moment of gentleness promised a thorough ravishing, and I closed my eyes, savoring the sweet caress before yelping when he took me hard by the hips and shoved into me. Claimed me. Made me his in front of the others. Lashes fluttering, I pushed up so they could watch every part of me—Fintan sprawled on the rug, head pillowed on his folded arms, hazy with post-orgasm bliss; Elijah on his chair, stroking himself faster, his eyes bright and beastly.

A familiar hand wove into my hair. Tugged me back. Added an arch to my neck that always drove the vampire pounding into me nuts. His hips quickened, his pace brutal, the slap of skin to skin ringing out in a bedroom accustomed to the symphony of moans and squeals and wet. No more orgies though—not unless it was the four of us. Fintan had barely even *glanced* at any of the gorgeous fae men and women of the Midnight Court since we arrived. Rarely accepted a drink from them. Ignored all invites for a secluded catch-up somewhere on the grounds.

Briefly, I'd been afraid that I wasn't enough—that *we* weren't enough for a prince accustomed to lavish luxury. But from the way he watched Rafe and me now, eyes shimmering with need, his cock already at half-mast again, we were more than enough.

This was precisely where he wanted to be, same as me and the others.

Taking me from behind, Rafe became the savage lover who wore the mask of a quiet writer everywhere else. In here, he fucked hard and fast, making every bit of me wobble, making my eyes roll back in my head as fiery pleasure seared through me, my muscles tensing, an implosion imminent—

And then he fucking *stopped*. With a strangled snarl, he spilled himself inside of me, same as Fintan, and immediately withdrew. My head drooped forward, and I let out a frustrated moan that had the trio chuckling again—apparently tonight was the night to edge Katja, because usually by now I'd have had at least three climaxes and would be begging for a break before the next one. *Ugh*.

"Oh, darling, are you disappointed?" Rafe teased, his hand finding my hair again before hauling me off the armchair. My sweaty back met his clothed chest, my legs weak and on the verge of collapse as I stumbled into him. He dragged his fangs up the column of my throat just as Elijah stood, and the vampire licked at the blood still smeared from his previous bite. "What happens if *none* of us let you come?"

"Then I'll make myself come," I managed, eyes locked on Elijah as he crossed toward us, towering over everyone, his aura engulfing the massive room.

"Is that so?" Rafe whispered. Then, without warning, he hoisted me up, one arm hooked around my waist as his free hand bared my neck to him again, then buried his golden fangs in my throat. Pleasure exploded with the intensity of the *sun*, and vaguely, I heard my own mottled scream of relief. It vanished immediately when he withdrew, my body buzzing and desperate for more, wet heat slicking down my neck to my chest.

Spurred by the savagery, Elijah didn't take his time. He scooped me up, hands bruising my thighs, and sunk into me with a single thrust. Stretched by him and dangling precariously between two men who I loved with all my heart, I came undone. That alone was enough to tip my tormented body into the black, and I came with a breathy cry, abdominals tensed and eyes clenched shut. The climax sapped any fight from me, tangled my tongue and jumbled my words. Elijah watched it all with a gritted jaw, the muscles dancing just as my pussy tightened around him, then dragged a possessive hand up my body to the mark he had left on my shoulder the very same night we left Xargi.

Here. In this room. The second we were all alone, he snapped—stripped me out of my jumpsuit while the others watched, all of us grimy and stinking of rebellion, and pounded me into Fintan's pristine bedlinens until we imploded together. His teeth found my body ravenously, and beneath the royal canopy, he had marked me—his fated mate—and branded me forever.

Since then, he hadn't been able to *not* touch it. Sometimes he stroked it absently, his arm on the back of my chair at meals and his fingers grazing the mark that would never fade, but others, like now, had more intention. Even with Rafe holding me up, feeding from me, pleasuring me with his vampiric toxin, Elijah planted a hand over the mark and gripped tight as he rocked his hips to mine.

While Rafe had been rough and Fintan an absolute tease, Elijah was all passion. Deep, purposeful movements paired with a lot of soul-consuming eye contact. I lost myself in his golden irises, in the dragon gazing deep inside me, right down to my core. Magic quivered in my belly, spurred by our connection and sparking at my fingertips. No spells cast, of course, but the intensity of our bond usually set off the unstable well inside me—like my magic was just tickled to be so near the man ordained to be *mine* by fate.

Time lost all meaning when Elijah was inside me, and when he finally stilled, head bowed in almost reverence and his mark prickling like fire, I was done for. Light-headed. Weak. Boneless. Pleasure addled and in no place to stand on my own two feet.

As soon as he finally eased out of me, my body slick with

sweat and my thighs painted up by my guys, Rafe scooped me into his arms and perched on the edge of his usual chair. He held me in the afterglow, cuddled me, as his toxin sealed my open wounds. Elijah kissed my temple, stroked my cheek, gently cupped my chin. Fintan fetched something soft and silky and soothing to drape over me as one of them—I was too far gone to be sure of which, my head in the clouds and my body floating into oblivion—carried me up to the enormous bath one floor above.

I came back to them sometime later, surrounded by rose-scented suds and dunked in pleasantly toasty water. Someone had washed my hair, my red mane soaked and tamed, and while I slumped back against Elijah, Rafe floated in front of me massaging my feet.

Then there was Fintan shooing off the servants, a feast of grapes and cheese and more fae wine set out at the rim of this mammoth tub. Inhaling deeply, body totally relaxed except for the pleasant dull ache between my thighs, I pushed off Elijah's chest, then reached back to grab a cube of cheese that tasted an awful lot like brie and a handful of grapes. Needing some space, I settled on the marble bench that ran the perimeter of the pool—alone and content and beyond satisfied.

Golden orbs drifted throughout the room, like candlelight only everlasting and much brighter. One touch and you could change the color; I tapped one that floated by and it bled from gold to light green, identical to the juicy grapes in my hand.

"Wine, anyone?" Fintan held up a recently uncorked bottle, shaking it a little. I crinkled my nose with a grimace.

"*Gods* no," I insisted. "I'm drunk enough on you three."

"Stop trying to see if you can make me vomit again," Elijah growled, his arm stretched along the pool's porcelain edge, fingers toying distractedly with my hair. "I know your schemes, fae."

Fintan rolled his eyes and filled a lone champagne flute with a snort. "Fucking lightweights."

Unable to help myself, I watched, utterly enraptured with the spill of strawberry-pink liquid that sparkled in the orb-light. An explosion of fruity sweetness filled the air around us, but just to be safe, I stuck to my grapes and cheese. Munching away, I settled into the usual post-frolicking chatter in silence, slowly swishing my feet back and forth beneath the bathwater's bubbly surface. The boys, meanwhile, discussed what tomorrow had in store for us: a trip to a royal vineyard.

Another day spent in a drunken haze, likely to end the same as tonight.

Perfect.

Just the holiday I needed after Xargi, but that was all this was—a holiday. A honeymoon period all new relationships fell into, reality and hard work and maintenance waiting on the cusp of a bubble that could pop at any second.

And it was better to be prepared for that pop than for it sneak up on you.

"So," I started, grapes and cheese demolished, my hands free to pat at the rose-scented white bubbles, "what's next?"

"The vineyard," Rafe drawled, smirking at me when my eyes narrowed. "You really need to work on your listening skills, love."

I flicked a bit of sudsy water at him. "No, I mean after all that… After all *this*, what's next?"

"The world, darling," Fintan said without missing a beat. He then let out a long, luxurious sigh as he sunk down to his shoulders, arms outstretched, head tipped back, and eyes closed. "The world."

Out of the corner of my eye, I caught Elijah shaking his

head, my mate operating on a similar wavelength and not always all that impressed with Fintan's devil-may-care attitude.

"And more realistically?" I asked, glancing between the three. Rafe's teasing smirk fell away, replaced with a more serious expression, followed by a shrug when our eyes met.

"I think it'll be time to go home soon," Elijah remarked after a few pensive moments. But, where, exactly, was home now? After all this time out of Seattle, away from Café Crowley, my apartment, did I even have a home to return to?

Almost as if he had read my mind, Rafe cleared his throat and muttered, "And where do *we* four call home?"

I drew a soft breath, about to float the option of traveling between the US, Britain, and the Midnight Court for a little while, just to see what we could make of our unique relationship, when Fintan let out another languid sigh and stretched.

"In each other, of course. We find home in each other," the fae prince announced. When the silence stretched on, he cracked one eye open, then the other, and sat up straighter when I let out a snort-cackle.

"Fintan, I love you, but *gross*," I teased.

"Boo," Rafe added.

"*Stop* trying to make me vomit, I said," Elijah barked playfully, all three of us splashing him—and with more than just a flick of water too. A whole tidal wave washed over the fae, who eventually ducked for cover below the surface and swam a ways away, a vampire hot on his heels, the pair cutting through the bathwater with the speed of a great white on the hunt.

Cheesy as it was, he was right. Home was no longer a place with these three, but a feeling. As Elijah and I laughed, each choosing one to cheer on when Fintan and Rafe tussled in the middle of the huge bath, shoving each other and trying to force the other underwater, I knew for a fact that we could be happy anywhere—in this realm or another.

As long as we had each other, we were home.

None of us would ever be lonely again.

And after a lifetime of death and disappointment, loss and loneliness—that sounded pretty fucking phenomenal to me.

THE END

BONUS CONTENT: KATJA

Ten Years After The End

"Are you sure you don't want me to stick around?"

Annalise glanced up from her desk, blonde brows arching, and then shook her head with a grin.

"Girl, get out of here and take your babies trick-or-treating."

She and I had been in a similar situation almost a decade ago, with my then café manger loitering in my office doorway, offering to help with inventory while I shooed her out the door for the night.

The same night the bounty hunters dragged me to Xargi Penitentiary.

The night everything changed.

While chaotic for any Café Crowley location, tonight would be business as usual; this wasn't our first rodeo wandering the decorated suburbs of Shady Oaks, and Annalise wasn't exactly a stranger to handling the Halloween rush without me.

"I know, I know..." I smoothed a hand down my princess gown—pink, to match Sleeping Beauty's, Aelin's favorite of the bunch, but designed in the Midnight Court so that it was practically couture. "Halloween is just usually a crazy night—"

"And that's why we're fully staffed and paying them double to be here," Annalise insisted, tossing her pen aside, spreadsheets splayed in front of her, a mirror image of my old life before Xargi—before everything. "Seriously, Katja, we are solid. Go and have a great time."

"Do you—"

"Stop heckling Annalise." A hand smoothed up my back, curving ever so slightly around my neck with a familiarity that used to make our human business partner blush. Tonight, after ten years of trying to understand my relationship with Fintan, Rafe, and Elijah, she just smirked and busied herself with paperwork. I, meanwhile, craned my head back and lost myself in a pair of bright shamrock-green eyes, the pair twinkling with mischief for Fintan's favorite night of the year.

Of course he loved it. Besides the fact that our little gremlins turned into sugar-crazed monsters, both the human and the supernatural celebrations for Samhain were all about debauchery and mayhem and partying until dawn. Naturally, as parents none of us had partied until dawn in years, but at least he still dressed up: the Prince Phillip to my Aurora, just as Aelin demanded.

Her twin brother, Áed, had wanted us to go out as the fairies from the film, but Fintan wasn't having it, so he got what he got.

"You look handsome," I mused, fiddling with the red feather tucked in his cap. "Does this mean you're ready to go?"

"We're *all* ready to go," Fintan purred, snatching my hand and yanking me out of the doorway. He then poked his head in and flashed Annalise a winning smile. "Have a magnificent night, you."

Despite being married to her punk partner, Charlie, for nearly six years at this point, her cheeks still flushed a dull pink anytime *any* of my boys looked her directly in the eye and smiled. Drove Charlie absolutely bonkers—and Fintan did it just to rile her up at this point.

Exhaling sharply, I grabbed him by the fluttering red cape and hauled *him* out, offering one last goodbye to my professional rock before turning and struggling down the back stairwell in all this fucking tulle.

In the last ten years, Annalise had not only bought into the Café Crowley business model, but she had helped me launch locations in LA, Portland, Chicago, and Brooklyn. With Fintan backing us as a bottomless investor, the sky was the limit, and the café's kitschy Halloween schtick was a hit wherever we went.

Shady Oaks, a small coastal community in Washington, was the most recent to take on our very specific brand of weirdness. We had chosen it two years ago just as Oliver was about to start his elementary education at its supernatural academy; given his mixed heritage, we had all agreed it was best to let the professionals tackle his witch and dragon side. Not only that, but I couldn't stand the thought of sending my firstborn out of state, possibly even out of the country, for him to get a solid education; here, we could literally drive him to the charmed front gates every morning and pick him up each afternoon. Few parents in our community were that lucky, supernatural academies rare and scattered across the globe, very few taking on a mix of shifters *and* supers in one place, never mind hybrids.

In fact, we hadn't expected the support initially. Shady Oaks was home to a thriving coven of earth-based witches. They lived in their own gated community and practically ran the town, but Shady Oaks Academy had everything Oliver needed to thrive before going on to more intensive programs. Under the age of thirteen, supernatural parents could tutor their children as they saw fit, but we preferred him—and the twins—receiving the support of highly skilled professors who could give him the best start in life.

Fortunately, we'd had luck on our side. Not only did the academy take anyone and everyone who applied—so long as you could afford the sky-high tuition—but the local coven had even offered us a house in their exclusive community. Humans coveted the million-dollar homes in Shady Acres, which were rarely for sale and never sold to anyone outside of the supernatural world who put in private bids.

While we had politely declined the invitation, we maintained a positive relationship with the coven while living downtown, *finally* putting down roots, no longer hopping between the US, Britain, and the Midnight Court with the whole gang in tow as we'd done for eight years after Xargi. As soon as we decided on Shady Oaks, we were fortunate enough to snatch an entire building when it came up for sale, then stuck a Café Crowley at its base and renovated the top four floors for our home. Last year, Elijah had been able to purchase the storefront next door and opened his second jewelry business.

Arm in arm, Fintan and I drifted down the single flight of stairs to the main floor, passed the staff breakroom and out the EMPLOYEES ONLY door into Shady Oaks' Café Crowley in all its strange, gothic, Halloween glory. Even though the sun had *just* set, the place was hopping; we not only offered half off everything on October 31st, but supers and shifters ate free today with their exclusive membership card.

As an early evening darkness blanketed the city, fall creeping toward winter at a steady clip this year, all sorts filled the booths and tables, my collection of books untouched but the Halloween-themed baked goods and hot drinks a raging success. Everyone present was in costume for the extra 10 percent off their total purchase, which had Fintan and I weaving around humans and supers alike in party-store outfits and over-the-top masks.

And it wasn't even six yet. While some Shady Oaks locals were still wrapping up their dinners, we liked to hit the suburbs early with all the little ghosties and ghoulies. Not only was I uncomfortable keeping the kids out late, but Samhain had fallen on Wednesday this year and they had school bright and early tomorrow morning…

Which they would all inevitably attend in a sugar-coma after Fintan let them eat *way* more candy than they should like he always did when the rest of us had our backs turned.

After letting a cluster of costumed human teens barrel by, Fintan and I breezed out into the chilly evening, taking a sharp right to not block the front door, then stumbled upon—

"Holy *fuck*." I smacked Fintan as soon as the words left his mouth, mindful of all the young ears wandering the sidewalks tonight, even in the core, but the fae was too distracted by Elijah to even notice.

Correction: Fintan was distracted by Elijah dressed as an enormous sunflower. Sporting a green Lycra bodysuit and a headpiece of massive yellow petals, the towering dragon shifter was most definitely a *sight*. In the twenty seconds we'd been outside, two cars had honked at him in passing. He rounded in place, glowering at us, and I held a hand over my mouth to stifle my giggles.

"It takes a really secure man to wear that," Fintan mused, gaze sweeping up and down Elijah's magnificent figure. The bodysuit had been distractingly thin when he first tried it on last weekend; thank goodness he had opted to wear a few additional layers beneath, even if they boiled the shifter alive for the next few hours—at least no one would catch a peek of something they shouldn't. Just as Elijah opened his mouth, wildly unimpressed with his outfit, Fintan clapped him on the shoulder. "I applaud you, friend, for your commitment to our brood."

Nudging the fae out of the way, I swooped in, hands delicate over Elijah's chest, and stood up on my toes to kiss his cheek.

"You look *adorable,*" I murmured, which made him grin even as he rolled his eyes skyward. Eyes, I might add, that looked nowhere near the gold-slitted gaze of his inner dragon, who had probably retreated so deep inside that it would take days to coax him back out. For any other alpha, dressing like this would have been humiliation in its highest form—but as soon as the twins asked for one of us to partake in their costume idea this year, my mate had been the first to volunteer.

"What's his issue?" Fintan jerked his thumb toward Elijah's shop when both of us glanced his way. Seated on the stone hedge that ran the length of the front windows, slumped and arms crossed, was my firstborn son with Elijah. Half warlock, half dragon shifter, Oliver sucked in his cheeks, then let out a loud, dramatic huff and kicked a pebble across the sidewalk. Fintan, meanwhile, meandered over to Elijah's side, frowning. "Looks like his costume is having some influence."

Oliver had spent the last two hours locked in his bathroom applying costume makeup to complete his zombie schoolboy ensemble, while I'd taken ages yesterday artfully shredding one of his old academy uniforms, making it weathered and bloody, just to add some authenticity.

And now he looked miserable.

On a night when strangers were obligated to give him candy just for ringing their doorbell.

Seriously.

I planted my hands on my hips and shook my head.

"He's still upset with us," Elijah said before I could, the shifter slipping a pair of green gloves on to really complete the outfit.

"Well, that's just the way it's going to be," I muttered, forcing myself away from the eight-year-old's pout to fix one of Elijah's petals when it drooped into his face. "He can sulk all he wants."

It broke my heart to see *any* of my babies upset, but this was one transparent manipulation I just wasn't falling for.

"What happened?"

Fintan had been stuck in the café all day, which meant he missed the massive eruption between Oliver, me, and Elijah on the ride home from the academy.

"He wants to trick-or-treat with his friends from school this year," I said with a sigh, totally understanding my little guy's position but in no way ready to let my baby bird fly yet. Fintan sniffed and readjusted his cape, then picked a bit of lint from his greyish-blue stockings, princely in every movement.

"And?"

"He wants to go by himself," Elijah clarified gruffly. Neither of us had ever experienced an Oliver blowup like that before, shouting and arguing from the back of the car, perfectly logical but *way* out of line. Fintan glanced between us like he was waiting for more.

"Again… *and?*"

"And…" I huffed, in no mood to fight with *him* about this as well. "And he's eight, Fintan. He's not going trick-or-treating alone."

"Hardly alone when you're with friends," the fae insisted, fluttering his lashes up at Elijah. "And besides, he's a *man.*"

He chuckled, totally immune to the heat of our glares,

then rounded on the spot when the café door jingled open. Slowly, carefully, out walked Rafe with a half-fae-half-witch twin in each hand, my littlest darlings wearing the most adorable, puffy bee costumes I had ever seen, stinger, antenna, black stockings, tiny wings and *everything*. Ugh. Unable to help myself, I dug my phone out of my skirt pocket and snapped a quick photo despite having taken a million at the store when we first found these little numbers.

"Gahd *zooks*," Fintan declared, over-the-top as always and dropping into a sweeping bow that had Áed's chubby cheeks dimpling. "Behold! The two finest bees in town—my heart is whole at last!"

While the spitting image of their father—but with my eyes—the twins really were the finest bees *anywhere* tonight, but maybe I was biased. As per usual, only Áed shared Fintan's enthusiasm. His sister, Aelin, who had been serious from her first breath, stomped forward, dragging Rafe with her, and peered up at all of us.

"Papa, the bees are *dying*," she stressed, six years of age and already an activist. Her nose crinkled when Fintan tucked some wayward cinnamon-brown curls back into her costume's hood, and her massive blues shot from him to me, then Rafe. "This is a political stance!"

"I know, sweetheart," I assured her, trying and failing to match her tone because I was seconds away from losing it. "A very righteous political stance."

"You know, if my stinger was in the front," Áed started, eyes shimmering with his dad's impish mirth as he pointed to his backside, "then it would look just like my—"

"*Áed*," Elijah growled. "None of that. Come here."

As Áed toddled over to the massive flower he had insisted be a part of his and his twin's costume aesthetic this year, Aelin continued to rant up at Fintan about the dwindling bee populations. Meanwhile, dressed in a full black suit with three pillowcases thrown over his shoulder, handsome and debonair and ridiculously stylish compared to his fae and dragon shifter counterpart, Rafe sidled over to me, hands in his pockets, and thrust his chin toward Oliver.

"Still in a mood?"

"Very much so," I replied through a strained smile. He then righted my plastic tiara and threaded his fingers through mine, the whole group migrating over to a pouting Oliver. Only then did I notice that my son's biggest admirer was already on damage control: Tully sat at Oliver's right on the stone ledge, purring and nuzzling against his arm. My familiar absolutely *adored* the family's firstborn, finding the twins a little overwhelming most days, and still slept in his bed, especially on really stormy evenings.

"Chin up, old boy," Fintan cooed as we crowded around Oliver, cars ambling by in the background, the din from Café Crowley rising and falling every time the door opened and whooshed shut. "Life isn't all that bad."

Sullen blue eyes snapped up to him, on the verge of another tantrum. While he had my eyes, he had his father's curls and the beginnings of the same strong chin. One day, he would be a heartbreaker—but the look on his face was breaking *my* heart tonight.

"I don't *want* to trick-or-treat with a bunch of babies," Oliver bemoaned, and there went my breaking heart, stitching itself back together with thick, frustrated threads. My darling Aelin, however, seemed in no mood to let her big brother get away with *anything* tonight. Blunt as brass, she planted herself in front of him, then snapped her fingers twice.

"Tonight is about spreading a message, Ollie," she announced, not an ounce of sympathy for his predicament. "So, stop pouting and get up!"

Oh. Well, my little girl could learn tact another time.

Before she had the chance to lay into him again, I took her by the shoulders and gently steered her back into my skirts. Her other half, meanwhile, was fussing over his antenna, tapping at Rafe's leg and pointing at the bent one in a panic.

"Oh, just let him go," the vampire insisted as he straightened the black wire coming out of Áed's hood. Elijah and I turned on him with identical *Et tu, Brute?* glares that had him smirking.

"Honestly, it's Shady Oaks," Fintan declared for all to hear, "not New York in the seventies. Oliver…" My son shot to his feet a little too fast for my liking, and a part of me wondered if this was a ploy that had been rehearsed once or twice before we got out here—it wouldn't be the first time. Fintan refused to meet my eye—because that would be his undoing—and focused intently on Oliver. "How many of you want to go out together?"

"Six."

"Any parents?"

"Madison's mom said she would check in on us," he admitted with a one-shouldered shrug. Madison Greenaway —daughter of Matilda Greenaway, second-highest witch in the Shady Oaks coven. Right. That wasn't… awful. And he wouldn't be totally alone, or out there with just one other eight-year-old for support. And maybe they were just going to go door to door inside Shady Acres, which wasn't *too* bad—

"Look, I'll take him over and pick him up," Rafe offered before shouldering in front of Fintan and looking Oliver dead in the eye. "You're coming home at *nine*, do you understand? It's nonnegotiable."

"*Rafe,*" I snapped. Was this really happening right now? Here, on the sidewalk? *Minutes* before trick-or-treating kicked off just a few blocks away?

"Darling, we're overruled," Elijah told me as he

distributed the pillowcases between our three. In an instant, *everyone* looked to me: Oliver, the twins, my guys—*Tully*, the little traitor. Mom usually had the final say in just about everything, and while I knew what I wanted to say, that I wasn't ready for my Oliver to stop going door to door with us just yet, that I wished I had known last year was our final Samhain trick-or-treat together while it was happening…

I also knew what would make everyone happy.

"Take Tully with you," I ordered, trying not to smile when Fintan and Oliver subtly bumped fists. Collusion. Honest to goodness *collusion*, happening right under my nose.

"Really? You sure, Mom? I won't be too late—"

"Tully goes *everywhere*," I told him. "You aren't going out with humans—they'll all know why you have a familiar with you, so no making him wait in the bushes."

Before I could share a moment with Tully—an unnecessary one, because my smitten familiar wouldn't let Oliver out of his sight—my little dude who was growing up too fast charged in for a quick hug. At what point was it officially uncool to hug your mom? Were we almost there? When he tried to pull away, I grabbed him and held on just a little longer, then sent him off toward Rafe, who cuffed him by the back of the neck.

"If you *aren't* where we agree at the *exact* right time, you know I can find you," the vampire warned, eyes narrowed, voice a pinch lower than usual—even a smidge threatening. "Remember, the darkness is my ally, little dragon, not yours."

Oliver nodded enthusiastically, pillowcase in a death grip and feet already carrying him away from us. Before following, Rafe kissed the twins on the cheek, then stole a quick peck from me.

"He'll be fine," he murmured, briefly cupping my cheek and stroking my chilled skin with his even chillier thumb. "Be right back. Love you."

"Love you," I muttered distractedly.

Then they were off, just like that, my boy finding and asserting his independence—with Tully slinking around his feet, a constant shadow from now until he was back home with the rest of us.

"Let's goo*oooooooooo*," Áed demanded as we remaining adults watched Oliver disappear down the block and around the corner, headed for Rafe's Benz in the underground parking garage. He stomped his foot, a petulant little bee, then smacked his hand to his forehead. "Or we're going to miss all the good candy!"

And on that long, whiny note, the herd drifted into the suburbs, the twins hitching a ride on Fintan's shoulders. Eventually, we merged with the rest of the costumed masses, little ones of all ages charging from decorated house to decorated house, most of them human with a pinch of a supernatural aura here and there. At the first house, Fintan set the twins down but hung back on the sidewalk while Elijah ushered them up the path to the door.

"You good?" I asked as he dug out his phone from the waistband of his princely leggings. The fae nodded, face underlit with the screen's too-white glow, thumb tapping around.

"Just calling Rafe to make sure Oliver got on okay..."

Uh-huh. *Just as worried as the rest of us*. I nibbled my lower lip, waiting until he had the phone to his ear before easing up on my toes to kiss his cheek. Then, surrounded by kids, nodding to a few other parents in passing, I wandered off to join Elijah and the twins, my little kitten heels click, click, clicking across the huge stone slabs that led from the sidewalk to the porch.

As always, Áed and Aelin held out their pillowcases for their loot, but while Áed wandered back to the sidewalk showing Elijah his haul, Aelin lingered at the open front door, rooted squarely in place before a slightly confused human woman in a laughable witch's hat.

"Uh, is everything all—"

"Ma'am," Aelin interjected, voice crisp and clear, her chin slightly lifted and her antenna bobbing, "do you have a moment to discuss the plight of beekind?"

I bit back a smile.

Oh *gods*. This was going to be such a long—wonderful —night.

ACKNOWLEDGMENTS

Thank you to Amanda, my editorial GODDESS, who is always ready to read my latest first draft word vomit. You make my fears smaller, and that means a lot. Shout out to Sandra, my fantastic proofreader at One Love Editing. You may specialize in contemporary, but I'll bring you over to the dark side yet.

Much love to my friends, my family, and my sun and stars for always supporting my author dream.

Most of all, thank *you*, dear reader, for taking this journey with me. When I released my debut reverse harem novel, I had no idea what an amazing, supportive, open community I was diving into, but reverse harem readers are some of the nicest, most wonderful readers out there. I'm so grateful to be in this community, and I can't wait to share the many, many, *many* reverse harem romances percolating around the ol' brain with you for years to come!!

In the meantime, don't forget to leave a little review, either on Amazon, Goodreads, or your social media. As an indie author, I rely on reader squees to help spread the word about my work, and I appreciate every word you write!

See you in **November 2020** for the first book in my academy reverse harem trilogy, **Root Rot Academy**, which will have a liiiiive release on Amazon and Kindle Unlimited! We all love academy stories, but I personally love to write the sordid romances between professors. And a headmaster. And a surly fae librarian. Wheeeee!!

To make sure you don't miss out, don't forget to either join my mailing list by downloading the Caged Kitten bonus content, or by joining my Facebook reader group. I'm really active there, and we have a blast!

See you next time!

xoxoxo

Rhea

ABOUT THE AUTHOR

Rhea Watson is a Canadian reverse harem author who loves a good paranormal romance. She writes layered alpha heroes with rough exteriors who melt for their strong, independent soulmates.

In her spare time, Rhea babies her herb garden, bows to her cat's every whim, and flies through Netflix shows like it's her day job.

Also by Rhea:

ALL THE QUEEN'S MEN SERIES

(Standalones, Same Universe)

Reaper's Pack

Caged Kitten

ROOT ROT ACADEMY

Term 1 (November 2020 ~ Live release!)

Term 2 (January 2021)

Term 3 (March 2021)

RHEA WATSON WRITING AS EVIE KENT:

To Love a God (Lily of the Valley, #1)

FACEBOOK READER GROUP

WEBSITE

www.ingramcontent.com/pod-product-compliance
Lightning Source LLC
LaVergne TN
LVHW041054080826
845145LV00007B/1568

* 9 7 8 1 9 8 9 2 6 1 0 7 1 *